the
'idiot spy'
(the series)
book nine of ten

the carbon factor unleashed

c. benjamin lattimore

the carbon factor unleashed
Published: September 2022
Printed in the United States of America
ISBN: 978-1-7334945-8-8

a lattidreamer™ publication
© C. Benjamin Lattimore, 2022

to Marisa, my bride
Your allegiance to my work is spiritual!

ACKNOWLEDGEMENTS

my children, Christopher, Monica, and Courtney—my grandchildren, Isaiah, and Desmond. A heartfelt expression of love to my older sister Mary E., and my younger brother, Darryl A., and to all of my nieces and nephew. Yet again, and again, and again, special regards to my true friends, Maurice E. Cheeks and Reginald W. Wilkes, who recognize that I am, who I am—Ben Lattimore, an almost anomaly!

special acknowledgements to Marisa, Jill, and Catherine.

ethereally, lots of love to Mary Alice, Walthro M, Barbara Ann, and Walter Eugene. To my friends, Gordon Gant, Joseph Bongiavanni II, Monique Gorham, Rahsaan Stevens, and my newest guardian angel, Mrs. Marjorie C. Cheeks.

CHAPTER ONE

In the year 2018, the National Basketball Association (NBA) enshrined a number of marque players, coaches, and front office personnel, into the Basketball Hall of Fame (HOF) in Springfield, Massachusetts. The list of inductees was exhaustive and, consisted of some of the best female and male point guards, three-point shooters, centers, superior defensive and offensive players, and the people behind the scenes—the front office crew. As the many fans, former players, inductees, families, and friends enjoyed the experience with exuberance and awe of those being inducted, earlier during the day, a sinister looking clown with balloons and a box, entered the facility and subsequently, placed four small containers in the four corners of the Springfield Symphony Hall where the event was to be held.

#

Later, as player after player made their acceptance speeches, the event became extremely emotional after one of the recipients stumbled into a tearful interlude regarding his mother's sacrifices, in order that he, and his two brothers could survive and avoid the nonsense of the projects, and gang involvement. Yes, basketball became most of those being inducted into the HOF, ticket out of poverty, ideally, but not factually, away from the despair and violence. Yes, Cheekam Brilkes was heralded as a classic point-guard, praised for his leadership that led to a championship in Philadelphia, and was ultimately rewarded for his performance.

At the conclusion of Mr. Cheekam Brilke's passionate acceptance and thank you presentation, a loud voice came over the public address system that had tapped into the main control center. The message preempted the host of the ceremonies, and simply announced in a deep and demonic sounding voice, "Bravo, Bravo, Bravo! That was simply magnificent, expressive, and a wasted speech. Good evening revelers, my name is Victor Cherendolof. I am an ex-Russian patriot, and I am here to begin what will be the first of a series of catastrophic attacks against the imperialist, colonizing, and enslaving American government. No need in trying to run to the nearest exit. My statement is conclusive in all sense of the word!"

As people began to head for the exits, Mr. Cherendolof stridently announced, "There are four small devices placed strategically around this magnificent hall and once detonated, they will hopefully, be the preamble to the first successful test and utilization of the Carbon Factor formula in a live situation. You people should feel special because you are the experimental, control, and comparison groups, and what happens to you will dictate my future deployment of this dastardly weapon. By the way, I love basketball and admire most of you. However, you're mostly legends, and your legacy will bring more attention to this matter than you can imagine. Look at you, Dr. A, Billy D, Alph, Welgin, Sareem, Will, and many others. I salute you and bury you all at the same time."

Within seconds, a thunderous sound was heard in what could be considered, surround sound, and within a quarter of a mile radius, all of the downtown Springfield area was in the process of being consumed. Everything was completely obliterated and turned into ash and smoke. This cataclysmic explosion could be heard and felt from as far away as New Haven.

Between eight and ten thousand people were killed immediately from the ominous blast. Local and national leaders decried this murderous event as the work of people from hell who had no heart or soul. Forty-five hundred people were murdered in and around the Symphony Hall.

At the US Open, three suspicious packages were retrieved from trash bins and a fourth from a parked vehicle that was used to shuttle celebrities around. Appearing to be of the same configuration as the small containers that obliterated most of the downtown area of Springfield, the authorities were perplexed about the nature of the packages. In Gainesville, Florida, at a Georgia State versus University of Florida football game, four devices were discovered prior to kickoff.

In a nationally televised statement, which corrupted and hacked each of the national network stations, the mysterious ex-Russian patriot, affirmatively stated, "I have allowed you to find in separate places on the east coast, similar packages to the one that caused that happy event for me, in Springfield, Massachusetts. Did you guys enjoy my show? Anyway, I will continue to place my retribution devices around your country until the people responsible for the murder of fifty of my colleagues including two of my brothers, have been turned over to me. To demonstrate, my further resolve, it is my intent to set off another devastating bomb on the west coast in the next forty-eight hours or so, unless I am assured that progress is being made to turn the killers of my people over to me in an orderly manner. As you can see from the impact and reach of my detonation in Springfield, my devices spread like the plague—gathering victims along its way! Forty-eight hours or there will be significant loss of life on the west coast or in Middle-America."

Chapter Two

At *The Sanctuary*, in sunny St. Thomas, Ben Beckmire and his group enjoyed the warm blue water, constant fellowship, gourmet food, drinks, and relaxation. When word of that dastardly deed hit the cable stations, it was Ms. Viola who exclaimed, "They be killing people to get to my people."

As she walked out of her room, she yelled, "Someone set a bomb off in Massachusetts and killed thousands of people. I think it's the Carbon Factor." Those in the immediate vicinity stood still and watched Ms. Viola repeat, "Someone has figured out how to use that mess."

# # #

In another room, the Sarge was entertaining his lovely bride and asking her where she ultimately wanted to live after the conclusion of this adventure. Courtney told him, "Not far from my friends, family, and when I say not far, I mean within walking distance."

Jong knocked aggressively on his door. When the Sarge appeared with a frown on his face, Jong announced that he believed that someone had duplicated the formula for the Carbon Factor and conducted a trial run in Springfield, Massachusetts. The Sarge asked, "What makes you think that it's the Carbon Factor?"

"I'm only guessing because I'm no scientist, but the description of the results and how it consumed the environment and individuals, is indicative of how the Carbon Factor is supposed to work, I think. I'm not sure, but some devil has found out how to utilize our nemesis or, there is something else out there that can accomplish things just as bad as what the Carbon Factor was projected to be able to do.

CHAPTER THREE

The group collectively watched the television stations as reporters depicted the on-ground views of the areas and victims. The military, police, Homeland Security, FBI, NSA, and everybody else were trying to figure out how and what weapon was utilized.

When Mr. Utz and his team arrived on the scene two hours after the event occurred, and after viewing the catastrophe from a helicopter, he called the White House and told the president, "Someone has figured out how to use the Carbon Factor. The entire country should be placed on alert. Mr. President, this matter requires you to exercise your executive powers and place the nation under martial law."

"Mr. Utz, those demonic people who had the plans to that device must have sold it to one of the countries on our watch list. I'm no dictator but if you feel this is what's required, then I will speak to the Joint Chiefs of Staff and provide them with an audio of your suggestions. I will get back to you as soon as I can assemble the cabinet and the joint chiefs."

"Mr. President, those people did not sell the Carbon Factor to anyone. We have a new player and I'm sure his or her demands will be forthcoming."

# # #

As the group continued to watch the various news outlets in search of a clue, little Ms. Beatrice who was watching a program for children with the others, said to LaGina, "That is a scary balloon delivery man." She yelled, "Mom, can you come see this scary man?"

When Luana walked into the area where the children were, one of the wall units was showing adult type footage of the devastation. Luana stopped in her tracks and yelled for the Sarge and her husband. Knowing full well that all the TVs were on a record basis, she rewound the one unit and said, "My daughter thinks this person is a scary balloon delivery person."

As the Sarge and Chakes watched, the clown's face was painted but not with a happy face. He was also seen transporting a case of something into the Symphony Hall in Massachusetts. Luana said, "Why would a clown deliver balloons at 0800 hours to a place that is unoccupied? Look at the shape of the box he's carrying, looks like you could fit four half gallon products in it. As they continued to watch the clown enter the premises, it would be exactly twenty-six minutes later before he would exit the predominately empty building."

The Sarge asked Chakes to assemble the entire team. He indicated to him that he wanted all eyes on this one for suggestions. Chakes walked away and the Sarge knew that this event was going to directly implicate his group, one-way or the other. The Sarge walked over to little Ms. Beatrice and asked, "Did that clown scare you when you first saw him?"

"No, he didn't scare me, I just knew he was a bad person with something bad in that box he was carrying. Was I right?"

The Sarge replied, "You were right and I wish you would tell me, your mom, great grand mom, and your dad, every time you see and feel that way about people who do not belong in the puzzle. Will you do that for me?"

"Mr. Sarge, you know I will."

# # #

When the group assembled, the Sarge said, "The person on the screen was picked out by Beatrice as a bad person. I'm not going to try to justify my utilization of her cognitive skills to suggest that we go on alert, but I will. People, you all know that there are strange forces that cover our very existence. When a child calls out that there is a boogeyman in the closet, an adult had better damn well check it out. Here is a look, from my perspective, of tomorrow's headlines—"They lied to the Pope, and to God! They made a deal with the Diablo"!

Asiram stated, "Daddy-in-law, we did not lie, we gave what we thought was the actual product. We all know we were played, but I for one will never think that this group would provide destructive information to people who would kill fellow human beings. No, Sir, I will not accept that headline. We tried to prevent this very thing, but we're going to be blamed for all those deaths. We should get on our plane and head for your homeland. We don't stand a chance of justice here. We need to be airborne in the next hour. I'm so glad our plane has no name!"

The Sarge looked at her, and then around the room, and said, "You heard the lady, I personally want to watch this place disappear from my view. One hour, people. Jong, get on that phone and tell the pilots its up, up, and away in less than an hour."

Montomie, Whitmore, Gladstone, and McArthur felt their hearts sink to their feet. The Sarge noticed their reactions and said, "People, we have more than one plane. If you have a serious notion, set of feelings, or whatever you want to call it, give them a call, and tell them this deal is real. If they love you, they will catch alternative transportation and find their way to the great land of my ancestors."

Montomie looked at Gladstone and said, "I don't think it's wise that we communicate with them until we're actually enroute and/or landing in Australia. Do you agree?"

Gladstone replied, "I do, let's inform the others that we won't reach out to them until we're sure that the group is safe, and on the ground in the outback. This is un-fricken believable—you can't make this shit up. I was planning to propose a more stable union, and now, here we go again. Life is what life is, and it provides you with complex scenarios and dares you to figure out how to get what you want, need, and desire."

# # #

As the group arrived at the airport, Ms. Viola told her associates in customs, we ain't got a lot of time to dilly-dally with protocol. We need to get on our bird and blast towards a friendlier place.

In essence, the group walked through customs, and onto their plane without any hold up. Once Jong had completed a head count, he realized that they were one short. Jong had Mallory count behind him and he too came up one short. The Sarge looked out of the window and saw Whitmore standing near the gate. From where the Sarge was sitting, it appeared as if Whitmore was crying. Without indicating anything to anyone else, the Sarge walked down the steps of the plane and over to Whitmore and said, "So, Whit, I guess, this is it. I'll tell the guys you love them, but your cancer is getting the best of you and you don't want to disappoint the group."

"How do you know about my cancer?"

The Sarge stared at Whit for a moment, and then said, "If you come with us, my family can give you roots to control it, but no one can guarantee longevity. I will say being with us will give you, eyes, ears, and a huge support system. Get on the plane, have your friend coordinate with the other ladies, and flown to the outback. I can get you covered, but I can't and won't promise a miracle. I really need you, and I realize that you love Michael's sister, Azuree. She can accompany the others to my homeland. Please, my brother, I beg you! Get on the plane or we'll all perish. We are strong together, but when splintered, we are vulnerable. Please, Whit, get on the plane. Take a minute and tell her how this can work. I'll have the pilot wait until you come on board. If you stay, I stay. If I stay, they stay. If they stay, we all die in the same place. Your choice my brother."

The Sarge turned to walk away and Whitmore said, "I'll be there in five, my friend, and leader. Give me five!"

#

Once Whit was on the plane, Jong did a head count and gave the Sarge the thumbs up. The Sarge yelled to Carla, "It's show time Captain. Get us to that other place safely."

Courtney asked, "Do you think that situation in Springfield is related to that dreaded Carbon Factor?"

"Honey, I don't have any information on what happened, and until I have a better understanding, I'm not going to spread my uneducated suppositions as to what caused it. I heard that there was a verbal transmission to the people in the Symphony Hall prior to the explosion. I would really like to know who spoke to those people before they were murdered."

"Ben, did you ever hear anything about what the Carbon Factor could do?"

"Baby, in all that we've been through, I never once heard anyone say what the results of an explosion using the Carbon Factor would be like. I just thought it was another dirty bomb. Let's call Zanthius up here for a second and see if he has any intelligence on that matter."

A few minutes later, Zanthius sauntered up the aisle and said, "Guys, I was trying to take a nap. What's up?"

"Son, during all of your travels and exposure to the Carbon Factor, did you ever come across any information that suggested what the impact of a detonation of the Carbon Factor would be like?"

"Dad, I never saw or heard anything about what the product could allegedly do. I mean there was a lot of technical gibberish that was way over my pay grade, but no one ever stated publicly what the aftermath of a detonation would look like. I know we are all thinking that the bombing in Springfield was tied to the Carbon Factor formula, but the jury is still out."

"Son, I don't know, but I'm not ruling it out. When you go back to your bride and boys, ask her if she ever heard of any defining results of an explosion using the Carbon Factor formula."

Courtney cut on the news and put a headset on. She nudged Ben and suggested that he look at the new pictures that were being released on the bombing. As the two watched in horror, Courtney grabbed his arm and squeezed it tightly. The area looked as if someone had dropped a neutron bomb on the area because the devastation was widespread and not limited to the Symphony Hall. The Sarge said, "Oh, my God! That is more than a localized bomb. It almost looks as if it were a nuclear detonation. What sick and deranged individual could have done that?"

#

Captain Carla came over the intercom and stated that they were sixty minutes from Sydney and suggested that people begin to prepare the cabin for arrival. Jong inquired of Mary Alice, "Do you think we need flight attendants on the plane?"

"Why do you ask? I mean we seemingly keep it clean and assist the crew wherever possible. If you feel strongly about it, then present it to the others."

"I think I will. They would have to know, how to babysit, run an ad hoc educational program, provide services to the group such as serving food stuff, etc. I think if we add those other criteria to the picture, then it makes sense."

#

The group deplaned and entered the lobby until the aircraft was refueled. Everyone watched the horrific pictures that were being shown on each television in the terminal. Most concluded that this was no ordinary bomb and that they probably got out of dodge in the nick of time. John Lee asked Jilkes, "Do you think that there is another kind of bomb that did that?"

"I'm not sure, but I'll say one thing, that ain't your typical C-4 kind of explosion. Notice where it started and where it ended. Look how all those structures near the detonation site look, especially the grey coloring of the buildings. Now look at the buildings far away, they have all of their color and are pretty much intact."

"You be one smart cookie, but you overlooked the color of the cars that were close by and then those that were blocks away. This thing looks like it just sucked the color and everything else out of things in the area."

The potential number of dead was listed on the screen and everyone felt sad and wondered what kind of fiend would do such a thing? As the group left the terminal for their plane, an urgent text message came over the Sarge's phone. It was Mr. Utz suggesting that they head to that mystical place and stay there until they heard from him.

The Sarge said to Jong, "We need to get this thing in the air and I mean now."

Jong gave his brethren a look and they proceeded to encourage people to get on the plane post haste.

Thirty minutes later, the beautiful unnamed airplane blasted down the runway and into the night. Once the seat belt sign was turned off, Mallory slid over to the Sarge and inquired, "What was that all about?"

The Sarge pulled out his phone and showed him the text from Mr. Utz.

Mallory said, "You are one well informed son-of-a-bitch. This is why you're our leader and will remain so, until the earth consumes us all."

#

In the Northern Territory, the group's extended family welcomed the group and provided them with a feast for kings and queens. Darryl and Sue Lyn were happy to see their clan, as Sue Lyn wallowed around carrying their baby that would come out any day now. The Sarge kissed her and asked permission to touch her stomach. After receiving permission, the Sarge felt her stomach, and then kissed her forehead. After a few pleasantries, he walked away and found Ms. Viola. He said, "Ms. Viola, I don't know anything about women being pregnant. When I was on the plane, something told me to touch Sue Lyn's stomach, and after doing that, all was not right. Now, I know you believe me when I say things here ain't like anywhere else. I need you to address Sue Lyn and help reshape her baby's head."

"Mr. Sarge, sir. You no be the only one who get visions. I got the same kind of vision, and as soon as I isolate her, I'll help her reformat what's going on inside without a lot of pain and drama. She and I, along with Dr. Beckmire, will take a walk down by the water and when she comes back, she'll be walking straight and not be crooked. Your wife will know what to do."

"Ms. Viola, that scoundrel of a son-in-law be lucky to have you as a mother-in-law. Thank you so very much and you know, if I can make it happen for you, then so be it!"

#

The feast was magnificent and everyone felt at home, warm, and safe. The Sarge said to the group, "I need to make some assignments without people asking me what, and why.

These assignments will be for women only and I'm sure you people have those little popguns. Guys, keep your damn hands down please."

The Sarge watched as Sue Lyn, Courtney, and Ms. Viola headed into the bush. The Sarge sent Rashida, Marisa, and Okema, to the east; Mary Alice, Somara, and Carla, to the west; four village women to the north; and Monica, Asiram, and Yeshida to the south. He stated, "Learn the bush and its neighbors, don't harm the animals, and watch out for each other."

Asiram who is usually vociferous and engaging, said nothing, and bonded with the women like never before. As the groups began to provide unknown protection for one of their own, Asiram said, "We should do this more often. We're not shallow, we know how to shoot, fight, and love, so why not perform security duties and other hazardous chores that our menfolk so often do?"

# # #

The Sarge said to Darryl, "I think Ms. Viola and my wife can help Sue Lyn's problem. Have faith and hopefully, we'll see the outcome when they return. Now, tell me about the business plans, the defenses, the banking, Hutang, and everything else. I left you with a big schedule, but one that a Beckmire could accomplish without any challenges."

# # #

One hour and ten minutes later, Sue Lyn walked into camp without any issues. The Sarge saw Ms. Viola and bowed to her. He walked over to Courtney and kissed her dearly.

Courtney said, "You are one damn clairvoyant, man. You are also my man, and boy, how I love you. You saved that girl and her baby. They were both on a collision course with death. How did you know?"

"Honey, when I'm on my way or here, strange shit keeps happening, and I just react and hope I'm not going crazy because some of the things that I focus on, borders on insanity."

CHAPTER FOUR

The Sarge received another text message from Mr. Utz that stated he would call him within the hour. The Sarge looked for Mallory, and when he came upon him, he said, "Mr. Utz is going to call me within the hour. I need you to stay close and try to figure out how, we've been implicated in perpetuating that horrific catastrophe."

Forty-eight minutes later, the Sarge's phone rang and it was Mr. Utz. He began the conversation by saying, "I'm so happy your group got out of dodge before people started looking at you in connection with the Carbon Factor. I'm sure you've watched the news and saw the devastation and loss of life that occurred from that blast. Listen, all public paintings of this event leads to you and your group. Now, since you're in that very mystical place, I can fight for you without your being here. However, when I say you need to show up and do a deed, don't dilly-dally and waste time about details, get on your fricken plane and meet me where I want you."

Ben Beckmire thought about what had been said, and quickly stated, "Mr. Utz, you really don't understand me or my people, do you? We don't march to any band other than our own. We did not detonate a bomb, we did not sell a bomb, we did not sell the formula for a bomb, we did not design, manufacture, and/or place any devices in the Symphony Hall. Insofar as your demanding that we be at your beck and call, my friend, otherwise duly noted as horseshit, go screw yourself and the donkey you road in on."

The Sarge hung up the phone and Mallory said, "Oh, shit! What just happened?"

"We didn't do anything wrong and we didn't kill any innocent people. Therefore, why should we have to respond to any group, government, or individual for something we had nothing to do with? I don't get it. People have to realize that we're not a machine that you can reprogram. We're a family and we respond to each other, obey all laws, but we're not someone's bitch, to be battered, used, and abused. I am no whore!"

Mallory looked at the Sarge and said, "We will all survive this or die from this, but it will be together." He snapped to attention and saluted the Sarge.

Thirty minutes later, the Sarge's phone rang again and it was Mr. Utz. He answered it and said, "Let me be noticeably clear, you come at me like that and I will never respond to you or assist you in the future. We're not your minions! Get that through your head and if I so feel like it, I'll call you when I find a need. Good day Mate!" He hung up the phone and yelled, "We're not for sale!"

Michael met up with, Montomie, Gladstone, McArthur, and Whitmore, and said, "Guys, I have made arrangements for your associates to meet you here in the outback. Unfortunately, my friend, is unable to make this journey at this time. I will keep you abreast of the arrival times and make sure that you're at the airport with the appropriate reception kind of goodies—flowers jerks! As he turned to walk away,

Gladstone inquired, "If you need to have a conversation about your friend's decision, then let me or any one of us know?"

Michael tried to sculpt words that would sound macho but realized that the group of men he was facing were as real as it gets. In a teary moment, he announced that he was unable to reach his new friend and felt that the worse may have occurred. Michael thanked the guys and reported, "I will make sure your people have the time of their lives."

Each man felt bad for Michael but were more concerned about their own status in relationship to their chosen mates.

Darryl saw Michael and asked, "What troubles you here in this land of plenty?"

"Sorry, boss! I am feeling a bit nostalgic about a certain person. I'll be fine in a few. Thanks for asking."

Darryl said, "Michael, I can introduce you to one hundred beautiful women who would petition you for affection and understanding, but not try to secure your carnal needs."

"Boss! It's not about anything physical, it's about how my heart bleeds for this woman, and how much I love the very sound of her voice. I don't need pleasure; I've been blessed with the notion of love—a thing that can only be measured from within one's own sanctuary."

"How poetic, my friend. I have noticed and the women in our group have noticed that when you're out and about, you're all about business. They say you never flirt, look askance, or make untoward suggestions and, therefore, they respect you. Anyway, if you need me, let me know. You know how I feel about you. Whatever you need to find peace, let me know. If possible, and if I can help, I will."

#

Mr. Utz called back, but this time, he facetimed the Sarge. Once the picture became clear, Mr. Utz could be seen bowing extremely low and saying, "People should be able to make their own decisions. I apologize for my indiscretion."

The Sarge said, "I will call you tomorrow and discuss, if in fact it's in our best interest, how we jointly try to figure out what demon committed that beastly act in Springfield. Thank you for calling back and understanding who we are, and not who you want us to become. G'nite."

Mallory said, "I thought he was going to kiss his own ass. Did you see how low he bowed to you? Wow, your greatness. You make leaders bow to you and your tribe obey you. It's time for a damn coup."

"Well, my brother, good luck with that one. All you have to do is tell me to go home and learn a trade and I'm out of here. However, my sons, well they may present a problem for you, and that nephew of mine clearly is beyond regulating. He's the real deal and not to be trifled with. The guy has visions that scare me. I only get notions. I rarely see things clearly, but this guy gets the date, time, location, and the individuals, in his shit. He's not to be minimized."

#

At dinner, Asiram asked for a huddle with the Sarge, Courtney, Mallory, Monica, and Darryl. At the gathering, Asiram said, "Two things have put me on alert. The first thing is that the women are capable of taking up defensive positions. And secondly, I heard a loud but clear scream from Sue Lyn. Is she okay? In addition, I have, as well as others, a strange feeling that we're being indicted on all sides for the event in Springfield."

Ben Beckmire said, "I was going to address that issue with the group, but I want us to enjoy this place, the people, each other, the children, and our blessings. There is the strong likelihood that complete armies will probably be coming for us soon. We had nothing to do with Springfield. Every indication from the Vatican to our trials and tribulations relative to that demon formula, makes us prime suspects. They probably think we sold the formula to some regime and now they're reaping havoc on our citizenry. Now, about your comment of women taking up the point positions, well, I think it's about time that everyone who can bear arms do so, but in a more aggressive and authoritative manner. I didn't suggest that maneuver to window dress. I need each person in this group to be able to lead, make decisions, and fire their weapon accurately at an opposing force."

"Who do you think the woman to lead this should be, Sarge?"

"I used to think it should be you, but you seemingly have grown into a baby production function."

Asiram punched him on the arm and said, "My question was rhetorical with no answer expected."

"I know, but if it gives you peace of mind, my choice would have been, Okema."

Asiram looked at him and said, "You're going to pay for that one, Mr. Benjamin Sarge Beckmire."

# # #

After the huddle, the group reassembled and were joined by Wajickee, who had a few words for Ms. Viola, and a potion for Whitmore. He told Whitmore to drink it down and let the earth at least ease his burden through the fruits of the land.

Dinner was suspect, but tasteful. The concoctions were different but were earth and water based. After dinner the Sarge said, "My families from here and from over the water, we are facing the most challenging time of our existence. The very thing that we refused to barter, trade, or outright sell, will probably be blamed on us for what happened in Springfield, Massachusetts. We left our place in sunny St. Thomas for our place here in the outback. I have and will remain diligent in placing our families first and foremost in my mind. Having said that, I want to baptize our women with the responsibility of the full security of our group while we are here in the outback. I'm sure some of you will say, what exactly does that mean? Well, I'm going to ask my daughter-in-law, my daughter, and Okema to convene a meeting of the ladies and flush out the requirements of securing us here first, and then back at home when we have to face a new demon. Others of you will ask, what will the men be doing while we're securing them, knitting? Well, let me honestly say, I don't know yet but I need eyes around and on all of us at all times."

The Sarge paused for a significant amount of time and just stared at the group. He eventually said, "On another matter, my nephew and his wife have put in place all of the necessary people, machines, banking industries, loan organizations, training programs, mining engineers, security, and everything else you can imagine to extract and sell the gold and diamonds. It's only a matter of time before someone will try to break into our current bank by attempting to annihilate our friends and my family, in the billabong. I worry about using them as guards because someone will find a way to poison or blow the billabong up. Therefore, tomorrow, I want to extract the goods from the billabong and deposit them into a real bank. Are there any questions?"

"Oh, I forgot one little matter, a birdie told me that a small jet left the east coast for the west coast and after refueling will dead-reckon to Sydney and from there to the Northern Territory. It's carrying some precious cargo for Montomie, Gladstone, Whitmore, and McArthur." There was some screaming and the Sarge saw that Michael was dejected. He said, "Oh, and I forgot to mention the wonderful gift for Michael." Michael smiled and looked to the heavens.

CHAPTER FIVE

In Springfield, Massachusetts, people from all the major security agencies were there sifting through the rubble and trying to identify bodies. The bodies that were recovered, had one distinct characteristic; each corpse was completely void of carbon (C) and water (H_2O). Each corpse resembled what a mummy would look like after hundreds of years in a sarcophagus. Although the agencies tried to keep a lid on their findings, locals began to discover victims who were completely emaciated and posted pictures of them on social media. Many thought the pictures were an advertisement for the 'Strolling Dead' program.

#

In Muncy, Pennsylvania, where the Muncy State Prison for Women is located, four packages were found at each corner of the prison. The materials were immediately seized by the FBI and transported to one of their laboratories.

It was later determined that the packages were filled with sour milk and were of no consequence. In City Hall in Philadelphia, four packages were identified and removed from the four corners of the passageways in the center of City of Hall. Those packages were filled with a nitrate solution. At the Forum in Los Angeles, larger devices were removed that contained suspicious combustible materials.

In one week, twenty-two suspicious devices were removed, and after further testing, were deemed non-threatening. Across the globe, thirty-six such packages were removed from significant places and all were determined to be harmless.

Little had been mentioned about Victor Cherendolof, the alleged mastermind of the disaster at the Springfield Symphony Hall. Every intelligence agency in the world was trying to figure out who this person is and locate him. The one thing that caught everyone's attention was the fact that the placement of the devices were identical and only the architecture was different. Each device, be they harmless or not, were placed approximately the same distance from each other.

Larry asked John Lee, "If you were going to kill entire cities, why would you place dummy packages around the world? Also, since those packages were found in what I consider around the same timeframe, then you must be an organization and not a single individual."

"Well, Mr. Smarty pants that be a good observation and one that I concur with. How he placed all those things at the same time and no one sees his ass? That be impossible. I think you be right up the creek with that one and I support it because he would have to be Superman or some shit!" John Lee professed.

"You're right John Lee, but what perplexes me is why go through all of those macerations to create panic. You just killed thousands of people, so why the ruse? What are you really trying to do, or preparing to do?"

"I be thinking he or her be getting ready to make a big statement and right before our eyes. I think they be giving us clues, but when it happens, it's going to be bigger than that there thing in Springfield. Them there people be getting ready to set the place on fire, and if I be thinking this thing through, it's going to be universal. Why else would you send these things all over the world, filled with all kinds of bull crap? My gut says, they be going for high dollar places. We be needing to talk to the Sarge about this one Larry."

# # #

At the campsite, Jilkes said to John Lee, "So, I see you got yourself a new African American to abuse."

"Now, your black ass knows, ain't nobody going to replace you and nobody had better try to replace me. This here smart man and I figured this thing out and wants to share with you laymen, ain't that right Larry?"

"Ah, yes, John Lee."

Larry looked at his dad, and said, "My new best friend, and I, feel that the placement of those fake devices is the preamble to multiple destructive detonations of the same kind that happened in Massachusetts. The person responsible for that detonation has to be part of a group, or he has hired people to place those packages around the world, thus providing us with an overabundance of suspects to question. As you well know, eventually, someone is going to break under torture and stress. However, my new best friend and I, also realize whoever is responsible for this mayhem is scheduling an event that supersedes any that we have been privy to. In other words, this sick person is about to set a new record for the murder of a lot of people. We believe the next event is probably going to be formidable."

The Sarge looked at the men, smiled, and said, "I feel that what you say is accurate and that the next event is going to be horrific. Our problem is simple, how do we get in front of this thing and begin an initiative taking response? I don't know the who, the where, and why of this situation. However, I do feel that their next episode will make the Springfield event look like a minor car accident. More than the notion of a coming apocalypse, we need more definitive information about who, why, and where. It's not like my cousin is involved in this matter because we neutered his ass."

Darryl interrupted Beckmire's comments and said, "Uncle, although technically considered handicapped, and unable to conduct this kind of project, there may be those who are loyal to him and want to seek justice for the kind of decree we exacted on him. You incapacitated my uncle; you didn't terminate him."

The Sarge paused to comprehend what Darryl had said. He looked at Larry and asked, "If I sent you on a one-way mission, would you be willing to select two others and try to ascertain intelligence on what has happened and what is imminent?"

Marisa stood up and announced, "Mr. Beckmire, where he goes, I go. And where I go, my children go, unless you are willing to cover us from all angles, we need to rethink that deployment."

The Sarge replied, "Marisa, I'm looking for a cohesive idea that includes risks for us all. My selection of your husband was not an assignment but a call to arms for those with a better option or plan than the one I am considering. However, let me say one thing, each of us are at risk, but if your husband is asked to assume an assignment for the good of the group, I expect him to accept or deny it on his own without input from anyone. If I go into battle, Mallory goes with me, automatically. If he goes, Jilkes goes and John Lee will follow, no matter the odds. If John Lee goes, then the group will fall into formation, and all will be present and accounted for. I appreciate your solidarity with your husband, but he knows how we work. It will not be your decision. We are a defined group, individuals have input but my people are familiar with those who have served with them, bled with them, and survived the jungle as a group. If we follow your protocol, it will lead to anarchy and that my dear, would cause our demise."

"I just re-engaged my man and if he gets hurt then I want to be there with him."

Rashida sauntered over to Marisa and whispered in her ear, "Your husband, is his son. You're making it seem as though he should get special privileges. Please see my dad later. Now, is not the time for this discourse."

Marisa sat down and broke into a crying frenzy. Larry embraced her and said, "That was really uncharacteristic of you. What's going on baby?"

"I'm fricken pregnant again!"

Larry said, "Dad, I need to speak to my wife in private. My new best friend will keep me abreast of this meeting."

CHAPTER SIX

In Denver, Colorado at the airport, a suspicious package was discovered and reported. As the news began to find its way to the hinder lands and beyond, the graphic presentations by the news stations were incredible. The Chief of Police had heard that there were four such suspicious packages found at other venues, and they were discussing a single package. He instructed his on-site personnel to gather plans of the facility and then dissect it into fours.

Once the officers retrieved drawings of the facility, they placed markers at the north, south, east, and west quadrants. The officers who searched each area, found similar devices in each quadrant. On the device in the west quadrant, a note was affixed to it. It stated, "So far, we've been consistent. Now, we will challenge your intellect."

The small details were not conveyed to the general public. It was announced that four suspicious containers were singled out and had been transported to a laboratory for analysis.

Larry asked Jilkes, "Why do they keep sending these devices and allowing people to discover them? Do you think they're trying to illustrate the size of their network? According to Victor Cherendolof, it is he who has a problem and is seeking revenge on those who killed his brother. Has he announced who is responsible for the deaths?"

"No one has said a thing to me about the suspects. However, I have to say, whoever did that work is in for a shitload of backlash."

John Lee said, "I be thinking that we be the ones responsible for his family members' deaths. Think about it, who else done kill more people than us?"

Larry exclaimed, "I certainly hope it is not us, but it makes all the sense in the world! Some of us have an unbelievable number of souls waiting for us in hell. I guess you guys have probably tripled the number waiting on you. It doesn't matter because if his family came for us, then they got what they deserved—a reckoning! The question becomes, how do we flush this person out when it is apparently an organization. I mean they plant stuff all over, and one person would have been discovered at some point in time. I mean think about it, how can a single individual place all those packages without being noticed? Come on now, in a damn airport! How the hell did he get in and who has the footage?"

John Lee said, "You're almost as smart as my African American friend. You're more forensic and he's more topical. I don't want you getting any ideas about this relationship, he's, my man."

Larry replied, "John Lee, I was petitioning you because I know I would have a problem with Jilkes. You two are a perfect match, balanced, annoying, focused, dependable, and dedicated to the premise."

John Lee exclaimed, "I just want to make sure you understand that he and I be like inseparable. I want to ask you a question? Why your woman be trying to change the way we operate?"

Larry smiled at him and said, "I could say, NYFB, but that wouldn't be very family like, now, would it? However,

I'll let you two in on a secret, my woman is pregnant again. Pregnancy is not her friend. We almost got divorced after she realized she was pregnant. When the doctor told her it was twins, she became extremely unstable. I just got her back and now she wants to protect me. I have to allow her to do that or she'll retreat into that dark abyss and I might lose her for good."

John Lee, with a curious look on his face, asked, "So what does that NFBY mean?"

Larry replied, "I don't know what NFBY means. However, I do know what NYFB stands for."

John Lee looked at Larry and asked, "Well, what does NYFB means?

Larry smiled, looked at Jilkes, and said, "Not your fucking business."

Jilkes walked over and said, "I have one simple question for you, just one. Do you trust John Lee and me?"

Larry smiled, stared at each man, and said, "With my life, my families' lives, and the group in total. I'm not that social farmer like you guys are, but I'm dependable and will do the nasty to anyone who rolls up in here with the wrong intentions."

Jilkes smiled, looked at John Lee and said, "We will make you, our cousin. You can't be our brother because we're brothers and you're Johnnie come lately. As such, and without any expectations, we will watch yours like they are ours and give a special notion of friendship. Me and the guys, well you know, are like bloodlines that can't be separated. You, my cousin, are officially being welcomed into our society without the acknowledgement or sanction of the Sarge or Mallory. We're arbitrarily making you a member."

Larry replied, "I don't know what all that means, but it sounds positive, so I'm in, and I welcome you guys to my tribe."

# # #

The Sarge saw Whitmore and asked, "How the hell are you feeling today, my friend? Any pain or other new things going on with your body that I need to consult my people about?"

Whitmore proclaimed, "Sarge, I take one day at a time! That Wajickee fella told me to drink a potion, and like a dummy, I followed his command, without asking him what the contents of the suspicious drink were. I did notice that he took the liberty of displaying a huge smile, but after I looked away, he disappeared. My only salvation is that I had a crude cup with the remnants of a drink that I will never know its nomenclature."

"My friend, if you received a drink directly from a spirit, in this land, then I would assure you minimum complications, but a long life. Enjoy all that we do and all that we will do. You can't be cured, but you sure as hell won't suffer during the interim. You, as well as I know, we all must drive to that party. However, not just yet though. May I speak frankly to you?"

"When has there ever been a need for that question?"

"Okay, I was so disheartened and despondent when I saw you at the gate and apparently crying. We have been together for a lifetime, and you pull some cheap shit like that on me and the boys. What the hell were you thinking? We're not musketeers, but you know how we roll. At some point in time, you're going to have to square with your brothers. They know and feel that something is not right. Perhaps, you can ask my wife to escort you to the hospital and have them do an analysis and see where you are in that game? In any event, we need you and we need you mentally right, most of all."

Whitmore looked at the Sarge and whispered in his ear, "Once again, you have saved me and provided me with salvation. I wanted to just sit by the water and end my adventure. You always know. You always know, and for that I am eternally indebted to you. Yes, I will address my brothers after I deal with an incredibly special woman who should be arriving in the Northern Territory in the next two hours or so."

"Does Michael know about you and his sister?"

"Sarge, he's so up into Barbara Ann, that I'm not sure he cares about us. He has often told her that as long as abuse was not in the equation, then he had no right to play matchmaker."

CHAPTER SEVEN

Twenty-five miles from Jackson Hole, Wyoming, a massive, earth-shattering explosion could be felt in towns much further away. The nucleus of the bomb, although in a desolate area, sucked up everything that utilized hydrogen, for up to five miles past the center of the detonation.

As government agencies flew to the location in desperation; a calming, seditious voice came over the news networks, and said, "Hi, this is Victor, Victor Cherendolof, and I wanted to see how far my little devices could make an impact, and it appears as though, I've reached the five-mile mark. With just a little bit of my secret formula, I can triple that reach, how amazing. Anyway, and in reference to that horrific incident in Springfield, I completely neglected to tell you people about how to contact me. So, since no one came forward with the names of the individuals that I want, I'm going to be generous and allow you forty-eight hours to comply with my original request. Now, I know you people are trying to trace, triangulate, and do a bunch of other things to find me, let me say, it will do you no good, because I am everywhere and nowhere, if such a thing is possible. In forty-eight hours, you will see that I can rule your country, scare your citizens to death, stop commerce, and close your financial institutions. Heads up people, better get all the cash you can, you're going to need it."

#

Within minutes, most of those who heard Mr. Cherendolof's remarks, made their way to their nearest branch bank only to witness lines forming outside of the institutions. Without doing anything other than making a suggestion, Cherendolof was able to create panic, a run-on financial institutions, uncertainty, chaos, and fear. The news stations televised the lines around the banks and commented about what was happening. Once word spread, there were people trying to get cash from ATMs and every other cash vending machine.

The guy running the country, called for a meeting of the Joint Chiefs, NSA, FBI, CIA, and a few other no-name agencies. He convened the meeting while traveling back from Florida, where he played golf for five days.

Everyone had a theory about what was going on, but no one had any concrete information about what groups, or individuals were responsible for the current state of affairs. The guy running the country asked, "The last time this nut demanded something, he wanted the people who killed his brother, is that correct?"

The head of the FBI stated, "That is correct, sir."

"If we know who he wants, why don't we just serve whoever killed his family, up? Look what his suggestive comments have created. The person must be Russian and has figured out how to use the Carbon Factor or whatever it's called. I need resolution of this mess immediately. This freaking person is holding us up for ransom."

"Mr. President, I think I know who he wants. I would like to turn them over to this person if they've not already figured out it's their group he's looking for."

"I'm sorry sir, what is your name and who do you represent?"

With a lot of pretense, he responded, "Mr. President, my name is Mr. Utz and I'm with one of those agencies that has a budget, but not a name."

"I'm not willing to have any further discussion of this matter until I'm back in the White House." He ended the call.

In the Northern Territory, a small luxurious plane landed. Waiting to escort the occupants to the bush were two very intense looking Aborigine men and their ladies. Prior to the plane landing, Michael called Barbara Ann and told her that locals would pick the group up and bring them to their camp. He had forewarned everyone to leave the high-heel shoes and to bring outdoor clothing.

On the ride to the camp, Barbara Ann asked the ladies if it were safe out here in what seemed like wilderness? One of the ladies told her that it was spiritual, magical, and those with hearts that are pure, would like, understand, and want to spend more time in this wonderful country.

Gerri asked, "Are there shopping malls or things like that where we're going?"

The lady responded, "You're going into the bush man; no Manhattan here, just bush, culture, magic, spirits, love, and unity."

No one asked any further questions, but the mood of the group changed. Gerri said to PJ, "I trust my friend and that's what this is all about; trust."

#

When the ladies pulled into camp, the guys waited patiently for their mates to exit the vehicle. Michael threw the macho shit out with the bath water, picked Barbara Ann up, spun her around, and said, "I am so happy you're here. I know this is different, but please, before you guys judge, get out of that New York state of mind."

She kissed him and said, "I just hope you are the person you say you are. I'm not sure if I can take anymore disappointments. On your suggestion, I left everything that I own, to be with you. I'm desperate for your love, but I will never be abused again, by anyone."

Barbara Ann started to cry. Michael said, "Barbara Ann, I love you and would never hurt you. At some point in time, you, and I are going into town to open an account in our names with an initial deposit of a million dollars. I will have access to it and you can take it and run or be that beacon in my life that I've searched for. History is just that, a sordid or magnificent list of things that happened. I'm offering you and me a new beginning. I sincerely hope you think of my workplace as somewhere that you can contribute and find happiness as well."

Gerri after enjoying a salacious kiss with Montomie said, "I was looking for the Hyatt or at least the Hilton, but I think I've found where I can be effective. My love, tell me where and what is this place? Do we all sleep outside? Do things bite you here?"

Montomie responded, "Gerri, this is the kind of place that you discover and not let it discover you. It is called the outback and is extremely unforgiving to those who wander, eat strange fruits, swim in unsanctioned waters, and sit where snakes and spiders do their traveling. Listen, I'm simply happy as hell that you're here. If you find this place too unbearable, I will understand and make it possible for you to get back home safely. I'm sorry, but as I said before, we're always on the go."

In the middle of the village the Sarge said, "Well, from some of those greetings, it looks like some of our guys could be considering a more permanent state of being. Hi, my name is Ben Beckmire. Some people call me Sarge, and others call me, well, names that I can't say in front of you ladies. I am the unelected leader of this band of misfits and the husband to Dr. Courtney, that beautiful and voluptuous lady standing next to my daughter Rashida and her husband Juan on the right, and Marisa and Larry, my son, on the left. As you can see, there are a lot of people looking curiously at you guys, but that's what they do. Each of you have been somewhat vetted, and insofar as a few minor issues, you all checked out. As you may have heard in St. Thomas when you met these blokes, you can't just waltz up in here like you own this town. Naw, this be our town, but you're welcome, but you must listen and abide by certain rules. Let me make this short and be perfectly clear. You are in the outback, and here, there be monsters, spirits, strange animals, and an amalgamation of other things that can end your life. Now, having said that, less than 100 yards directly behind where we are, is the most beautiful billabong that you will ever see. The water is inviting, the sand is pure and white, but the inhabitants of those waters will feast upon your very body. One other thing I would like to caution you about, don't go wandering off into the bush. There are so many different animals that will feast upon you. Our people here will escort you when you want to wash or use the loo. This is mother earth, respect her and she will respect you. By the way, seek advice from the locals when you need information or have a request. Please, don't go wandering in the bush. There are no return tickets available."

Alvara said, "Now, that you've scared the living crap out of us. I have a question for you. Are you purposefully, trying to get us to leave this place?"

"Alvara, that would be the last thing that I would attempt to do. What I've briefly laid out is the preliminary, precautionary notions, for newcomers. Let me say this, my guys are loyal, honest, rich, and good looking. In all my years of knowing them, I've never seen them get so excited and heated over a visit by ladies. This event is not a casual one. This event, in this place, will require you to be completely honest with each other, because in this place, only relationships of meaning can exist."

Gladstone said, "Sarge, we'll have a go at explaining things to them. Right now, I'm sure they want to eat, drink, and be merry."

"You are absolutely correct, but I would be remiss if I didn't explain boundaries, animals, and spirits."

"Well done my brother!" Gladstone announced.

# # #

PJ said to Barbara Ann, "Let's approach Dr. Beckmire and see if she appears normal."

PJ walked over to Courtney and asked, "Dr. Beckmire, are we in any kind of danger?"

Courtney exclaimed, "Oh, my goodness! Let's see. Did you fly on a strange airplane last night? Did you eat some strange concoction that was incredibly delicious? Okay, did you meet guys who are apparently in love with you? Don't bother to answer. The way I see it, you're in good hands because the people that summoned you here, are solid as a rock, respectful individuals, dedicated to family, and will do everything possible to make sure that you guys have a great and safe time. Ladies, you just hit pay dirt. If your intentions are honorable, then your world will change immediately. Keep my boys safe and happy. Thank you for coming."

CHAPTER EIGHT

In Bouarfa, on the east coast of Morocco, and less than two hours after his manifesto, Victor Cherendolof set off ordnances in the desert that had an impact range of eight miles.

Prior to Airforce One landing, the person who was in charge of the country called his Joint Chiefs and screamed, "You people had better do a better job and catch this son-of-a-bitch. He's running the fucking country, not me, damn it."

The Chairman of the Joint Chiefs was about to respond when the man in charge said, "Frankly, General, you're fired. Your assistant is now in charge."

As his plane began to approach Andrews Airforce base, the man in charge told his people that he wanted to speak one-on-one with that Mr. Utz.

# # #

Later, in the White House, the man in charge started screaming at Mr. Utz. Mr. Utz politely said, "Mr. President, I am neither your wife, child, nor servant. If you insist on screaming at me, then I will politely leave here, and you sir, can kiss my ass. Am I clear, sir? I didn't vote for you."

The man in charge said, "I guess I was getting a little ahead of myself, but Mr. Utz, you do see my frustration and anxiety, especially since he called for a run on the damn banks."

"Mr. President, I will reach out to my sources and see if they are willing to oversee this malady."

"They should, because it's them he wants, and if we engaged him and their group in a protracted fight, we might find out who the hell this mad man is."

#

Once Mr. Utz was out of the White House and in his secure vehicle, he called the Sarge who said, "Mr. Utz, this is not a part of our deal. Why are you calling me?"

"Mr. Beckmire, the person blowing up the country with a new kind of weapon is looking for you and your merry band. It is alleged that you are the people who killed his family member and he's using that justifying claim to wreak havoc on our country and the world. He has created a run on the banks, incited fear, and panic, and he keeps placing dummy devices all over the world."

"Mr. Utz, do you have any idea who is accusing us of the deaths of their family?"

"Mr. Beckmire, the person in the White House has indicted you, to me, and if he's done that, I'm sure he will throw you under any bus at the first opportunity. You know everyone thinks you people made a deal on the Carbon Factor."

"Mr. Utz, what do you think?"

#

That evening at dinner, the Sarge watched the interactions between his group, his Aborigine family, the new ladies on the scene, and the happy go lucky babies. He looked at Beatrice and LaGina and knew that the two of them would be special. He considered telling the group about what had been told to him by Mr. Utz but realized that everyone was having a marvelous time telling stories and suggesting ways to help in the camp and to move it towards the 21st Century. He knew that some things would be a long struggle for his native family. He also felt that the new female recruits could play a large part in making things grow. The Sarge followed his first inclination and that was to withhold information about the Carbon Factor.

The Sarge's phone rang again, and it was Mr. Utz, who said, "Before you growl at me and suggest other unsociable thoughts, I want you to stay put and don't think of coming this way until I can get additional information on our bomber. That's the only reason I called."

"Mr. Utz, my hesitancy in trusting you or any person working for the government is purely a function of my cousin, Walter E. Lassiter. He started out just like you're doing, giving me intel, suggesting a strategy, but ultimately, turned out to be the biggest snake I've ever met. So, please forgive my reluctance in hearing from you and heeding your suggestions, because I know you people have a higher master that you must respond to. I'll just say, I appreciate all the information and will take it under advisement."

"Mr. Beckmire, do you have time to listen to a recording I made less than an hour ago? Its short and to the point."

Mr. Utz played for the Sarge his recording of his conversation with the man in the White House. After the Sarge heard the recording he said, "You told the man you're not his wife, his child, nor his servant, and you still have a job? You told him that if he screams at you, that you would leave, and that he could kiss your ass? What's wrong with you man? You know that guy will throw you out of a flying plane."

"That is why I tape each and every conversation with him. He is not loyal, he's a bully!"

"Damn, man. You just picked up ten points with me. Oh, my goodness! How I would love to tell that guy some real stuff."

"Sarge, I'm not in anyone's pocket and my team is loyal to me because I don't ask them to do dumb shit. I used a former foe who has turned into a friend, as training material. You and I won't have to have any unethical interactions because I don't do stupid and I'm never going to do dumb. I request that you give me a few days to make sure that when and if you come back this way, you won't have the 5th Army waiting on your ass. Enjoy your family and I'll be in touch on an as needed basis. Thanks for not hanging up the phone or growling at me."

"Mr. Utz, if you have life-threatening intel, then I would request that you help us out and try to keep us safe. I appreciate what you've tried to do, but also realize, you too have a master!"

"My master will only come at me with judicious requests. He dare not request my group do something stupid. Catch you later."

The Sarge saw Mallory, Jilkes, and of course John Lee, and called them over. He said, "Mr. Utz told the guy in the White House that he was not his wife, child or servant, and if he screamed at him again, he would leave and that the guy in the big house, could kiss his ass."

John Lee exclaimed, "No, he didn't do that. Why would he do that? I guess he don't want that job no more." Jilkes looked at him and shook his head.

Mallory inquired, "Did he really say that shit to the guy in the White House?"

The Sarge said, "I heard the guy and I heard Utz. He recorded it and the guy backed down quickly, changed his tune and tone, and became extremely conciliatory. I like Utz, but as I told him, I'm suspicious of anyone that's not immediately associated with my family.

"Well, I be thinking the man in the White House is going to can his ass, so perhaps we can find a job for him too," John Lee stated.

"John Lee, you are so passionate. That's why I won't give up on your crazy ass. There's hope for you my brother," Jilkes announced.

# # #

Meanwhile, in the desert in Bakersville, California another device was detonated and this time consumed an area that approached the ten-mile mark. Hours later, satellite photos illustrated the area. Mr. Utz said to his team, "This guy is evaluating his devices. Each time the impacted area expands. In desolate places like this, perhaps the readings are false. In urban areas, where there are people, buildings, and vehicles, I'm hoping he hasn't adjusted his range for that. Just think, outside of DC, and around the beltway, an explosion of this nature would kill millions of people and completely shut the government down. Look at the spread of destruction in the damn dessert. If we calculate the range and over-lay it with DC specifications, then all would be destroyed."

There was a long pause followed by the proclamation, "The reports of suspicious packages around the country are a ploy to keep needed resources checking on every non-explosive device discovery. It keeps the specialists in the field and away from where I'm beginning to believe the next target is—Washington, DC. This guy is marking his territory with these simulated explosions. He spreads fear and panic, threatens the banking system, all while measuring the footprint he will need to potentially destroy the nation's capital and hold the country hostage for an awfully long time," Mr. Utz stated.

Mr. Utz paused his conversation again, but this time for almost two minutes and then announced, "I need to call my associates in from out of the rain and set them up as a throw-away solution just to gain intel on the perpetrator. I'm sure they'll play along reluctantly but I'm also hopeful they want to know how someone could replicate the formula for a dirty bomb that they destroyed for a second time. They'll owe me just because of the credibility gap. I mean come on now, they allegedly annihilated the formula in St. Peter's Square, in front of the Holy Father, and swore that to the best of their knowledge that these were all the materials they had on the Carbon Factor formula. I need to call my associates, but not now. I must wait until tomorrow unless you guys can find definitive information to support my suppositions or contradict them. I don't think he would go to Manhattan, giving what happened there. I'm hoping there is a speck of decency in the person. However, this guy took out the NBA Hall of Fame and thousands of neighboring people who didn't have an idea that their lives were about to be terminated because some nut had found a new tool to kill people. I'll call my associates tomorrow and try to figure out what if anything they're willing to do. In the meantime, I need you people to develop countertheories to mine or strong supporting notions. You people have until eight in the morning. Starbucks is across the street and my account # is on file. See you in the morning."

CHAPTER NINE

Mr. Utz in the solitude of his apartment, realized it was close to midnight where the Sarge was and decided to let him and his group be at peace. He thought to himself that it would be great if they could help because they looked like the United Nations—an admixture of people, races, colors, and languages. He knew this would be a hard fight to convince Beckmire and his people to engage in because of what they had been through trying to destroy a weapon that they didn't understand. He also realized the normal channels, people with suits, people dressed as if they were in the desert or some other skirmish, would not work. His equalizer would be Beckmire and his team. He needed them now more than ever, and hopefully, he could convince them to help.

#

Negative actions have a way of stimulating good people into assisting. Floating in the waters near San Quentin, four small devices were placed from afar near the once infamous prison. At exactly 0600 hours, four water-based explosions occurred and the aftermath was apocalyptic. The explosions created a tsunami that drew water and directed it violently at the prison. The artificial waves grew as high as twenty feet and pounded the prison mercilessly. Water breached the prison walls and flooded the substructures. It pounded the prison for approximately ten minutes and then miraculously, the water receded to its normal level. Everyone watching it was amazed and frightened.

Twenty minutes after the event, and in his own inimical manner, Victor Cherendolof's blurred image appeared on most broadcasting channels, and he stated, "What you've just witnessed, is my ability to target within a quarter of a mile, any structure, person, or government. If you look at the cannisters I used, you will see that it was only a small amount of my formula and I directed it at a place that I abhor. In twenty-four hours, my demands will be met or I will be forced to demonstrate my absolute power over everything and everyone in this country. The sooner you realize that the puppet in the White House, is hiding in a bunker, and by the way, it is not impervious to my reach and touch. My associates and I for now, will allow the status quo to continue. However, there is a limited time offer on that position. Until later, Obrigado!"

Twenty minutes later, west of Macau, and in China, four devices were detonated in the Ziangzhou district that resembled what occurred in Springfield, Massachusetts. The destruction covered fourteen miles in radius. Loss of life was huge, senseless, and the destruction massive.

In Russia, South of Moscow in Tula, four seemingly larger devices were detonated and the aftermath appeared as if a nuclear weapon had been detonated. Devastation was massive and loss of life was incomprehensible.

All three countries went on defensive alert, but realized, not an ounce of radiation had been detected and knew that they too had been attacked by a new dirty and cheap bomb!

# # #

It was midday when Ms. Viola announced that there had been attacks in Russia and China, all looking like what happened in Springfield. She also made the Sarge aware that whoever is doing this thing can target it. The Sarge looked at her and asked, "What do you mean by target?"

"Well, they can make that bomb focus on what they want it to. They made that prison near the bridge, ah, Sing-Sing, ah no, ah, San Quentin, the focus of the bomb and it was hit by a damn tsunami. You've got to get more people watching the news, man, before someone be done placed one of those damn things right up here in our camp."

"Thanks, Ms. Viola. Once I have additional information, I'll make a statement to the group and see what we can do to help on this one. I mean, I don't like looking for a fight, but damn they sure keep coming to us. I'll call that guy Mr. Utz and see what he has to say. Thanks again, Ms. Viola."

# # #

The Sarge made a call to Mr. Utz and when he answered, the Sarge asked, "What on earth is going on in the world?"

"Sarge, I am so happy you called me. I've been watching my clock to figure when might be a good time to reach out to you. Whoever this group is, they are pure evil. They have killed thousands of innocent individuals around the world and they can direct their detonations to attack specific targets. Now, don't ask me how they can do that, but apparently in the Bay area, instead of the results of the detonations being all over the place, it created a tsunami that hit the San Quentin prison. I'll send you a video of what we got from satellite footage and you'll see that we're dealing with a new kind of monster and weapon. To engage the Chinese, he detonated near Macau. In Russia, he detonated devices south of Moscow. This has to be a new group and their weapon of choice, I'm afraid to say, is the Carbon Factor."

"Mr. Utz, somewhere along the line, someone double dealt on this issue and I wish I knew who. Has there been any hard evidence or DNA on Helga Spengatsenburg's death? I mean after all, she's the one who jerked us around, but somehow, someone else got wind of this thing. What about the Russian scientist who went missing who had a theory that people considered ridiculous and thought that he was a moron? Has there been any chatter about him? Has there been any demands?"

"Sarge, are you serious?" Mr. Utz inquired.

"What does that mean?" The Sarge replied.

"Sarge, the initial demand was for the people who killed fifty of his friends and family. Do you know many people who could have completed that task successfully, over, and over again? If you can't, then I can."

There was a long pause on the phone and the Sarge asked, "Are you trying to be like my limbless cousin?"

"Sarge, I never want to be like him. I'm telling you the truth. The first thing demanded after the devastation in Springfield was that the government turn whoever killed his family and friends, over to the bomber. The bomber himself, acknowledged that he did not give forthright information for where and when those involved in his families demise were to be turned over to him, but instead used the time to evaluate his weapons. What's surprising is how can you be everywhere but nowhere, and there is no chatter, even deep in the sewers about him or his people. He can't be doing all of this leg work by himself."

"Mr. Utz, can you substantiate that it was my group? By the way, are you trying to rope us into some shit that you fancy suit wearing people can't manage? What's the real reason, Mr. Utz?"

"Sarge, I am no charlatan and I view you and your people as allies who I can count on. I told the leader of the free world that he could kiss my ass. I certainly will not say that to you because the free world needs you and your group, and I can't think of any better inconspicuous group, than yours to terminate the bomber. I'm just afraid that these people may be too cunning even for your people."

Again, a long silence that was eventually broken by Mr. Utz who said, "Listen, I have no clue how this is going to turn out. I just need to know if I find my head buried in a hole, that you will come and gently dig me out?"

"Mr. Utz, if you play me, I'll put a million-dollar contract on you and your family. Are we clear?"

Mr. Utz vehemently declared, "Hell, no! You're going to put a million-dollar contract on me and my family? And then have the audacity to ask me, "are we clear"? Man have you lost your fucking brain? I protect you and your family. You want to make it personal then deal with me. Never mention my family, Ben Beckmire. Never!"

The phone went blank and the Sarge sat staring blankly at the billabong. He mused to himself, "I guess everyone is not as evil as Walter." He pondered considering Walter but thought that there was no way he could amass such a force, as well as the weapon, and besides, he's tucked away in a mental hospital in Kentucky."

One hour later, the Sarge called Mr. Utz who did not answer his phone. The Sarge reasoned he was still stewing and that he would reach out sooner than later.

#

A couple of the newly attached males in the group were in various stages of relationship development. Some had managed intimacy, and a few had defined the true nature of a union between a man and a woman. Although Michael and Barbara Ann shared common space, they did not share each other. On three different occasions, Barbara Ann slyly attempted to seduce him but he resisted. Michael said to her, "The things I want from you supersede a tussle in the sack. I know it's going to be amazing, nuclear, and I know you're going to have multiple thunderous expressions, to illustrate it. I want to share my essence with you, not my need for carnal satisfaction."

"You're a strange bird Michael and one I think I love. I tried on several occasions to seduce you, and you politely and effectively demonstrated to me that what you want is much more substantial than sex. Listen, I'm a wreck. I have a husband who abuses me, and a friend who loves and cherishes me, but I don't really know him. Michael, if you'll have me, I want to stay here with you. I can help in so many ways."

Michael grabbed her hand and said, "You will never regret a minute of your time with me. I will ask the lawyers to meet with you, and you can decide the way you want to manage your affairs legally. You have just made me the happiest man in this village. You can't be accused of adultery because we didn't consummate a single thing." He kissed her and when Courtney walked up on them, she said, "I guess you're not going back to New York."

"I guess you're absolutely correct," Barbara Ann announced.

# # #

Whitmore said to Michael's sister, Azuree, "You know we have played our relationship close to the vest and I really don't know why. I mean we talked a lot, had a few drinks, but never made any move on each other. Last night I saw you in a different light and I wanted so desperately to make love to you. I watched you sleep, snore a little, then a lot, and I smiled throughout the night watching you grapple with your own snoring. You see how we pick up and leave at a moment's notice and I feel that would be terribly unfair to you if we entered into a relationship."

"Mr. Whitmore, are you asking me a question about a lasting relationship, or are you trying to seduce me and send me back home?"

"I'm certainly not trying to send you home or seduce you. I guess I'm trying to figure out what if anything you expect from me and this relationship?"

"Why don't you tell me what you want, expect, and then I'll let you know how that grabs me."

"Well, for starters, I want you in my life as a true mate, wife, or friend. I give you three choices because I'm not sure how you feel about my lifestyle and making a commitment to a man who is on the go all the time."

Azuree looked away initially and then asked, "Are there any other options?"

Whitmore fumbled with his words, and before he could say anything, Azuree stuffed his mouth with her tongue. After the kiss, she said, "Man, you'd better marry me before you leave here. There be a lot of people trying to figure me out back home. I came here to scout my first draft choice. Let's discuss our individual expectations and move on from there. I know we talked a lot about what we didn't like in people, but I felt a lot of that was posturing. Now, my friend, lets discuss the real mechanics."

# # #

Mr. Utz called the Sarge and before the Sarge allowed him to say anything, he apologized. The Sarge exclaimed, "I've experienced a lot of double-dealing bureaucrats and my trust level frankly is at zero."

"I understand how you feel, but you can't threaten my family. I would never threaten yours."

"In the future, I'll redirect my contracts to specifically target you. How's that for a quick solution?"

"That will work for me. However, I was surprised at your proclamation, because you don't seem like that kind of a person that would target a person's family. I was caught off guard and distraught about how and what you said."

After a few seconds of silence, Mr. Utz said, "Listen we're trying to pinpoint our mysterious Mr. Cherendolof and he may have given us a small lead to follow. In his last public address, he ended his transmission with the word, 'Obrigado.' It's a Portuguese saying for thank you. We know he set a device off in the southern province of China."

"Ah, Mr. Utz, last I checked, China and Portugal aren't that close to each other."

"You're absolutely correct, but Macau, the only Portuguese speaking colony is," Mr. Utz announced.

"You're right? Do you have any leads other than the use of a phrase? That's kind of thin, but we've worked on leads that were thinner than that. You need to find your way here within the next day or so. I need to have this discussion in front of all of my people so that I can get their brains to input. Is that possible and can you do it without a lot of notifications so that everyone knows where you're heading?" The Sarge inquired.

"Let me work on that one," Mr. Utz responded.

CHAPTER TEN

When it came time for the guests to leave, no one rushed or inquired about a ride to the airport. It was quite obvious that Azuree wasn't going anywhere anytime soon, and neither was Barbara Ann. Alvara moped around and PJ acted despondent. She saw Courtney and asked, "Doctor, I need to ask you a life changing question."

"Okay! What's going on with you?"

"Dr. Courtney, I don't know a thing about McArthur other than the fact that I like him a lot, he makes me smile, and if I had to say I love a man, I would definitely say I love Mac. However, he's not asked me, but I think you might know that Barbara Ann is not going back and is basically walking away from all that she has, and that asshole of a husband. I think in her case it was an easy decision and one that I support. In my case, well, I don't have a husband, or a person that is significant other than my family and girlfriends. Your group seems to attract a lot of drama, trauma, and death. I'm procrastinating about going to that airport and getting on the plane because that guy keeps me looking at a world that I never knew, like helping people. I guess I'm asking you for advice."

"PJ, I can advise you in both directions. I can tell you the disadvantages of our lifestyles and I can tell you the advantages. I love my husband and I will follow him into heaven or hell. If you're not prepared to wrap your hands around our lifestyles immediately and completely, then I suggest you head to that airport, get on that fancy jet, and enjoy your ride. McArthur is a great guy, and as a matter of fact, of all those single guys, he is a once-in-a-lifetime catch. Each one as you probably know by now, is filthy rich, loyal, caring, and is not bad on the eyesight, if you know what I mean. Listen, if you two are to be, then your leaving this compound at this time shouldn't end the idea of a perfect union. Just chose your words wisely and leave room for a parachute."

Montomie and Gerri were down by the billabong and he was about to make a move on her when there was a loud splash in the water. He jumped up and said, "OMG! I thought we were at the other billabong. Listen, we have to leave here now."

Gerri said, "I thought I saw a big alligator."

"No, dear. What you saw is a legend, a spirit, and a relative of our leader. I am not going to try to explain it to you now or here, but I will ask him to tell you about it. I can't talk about things I don't understand, but the Sarge can. Please, let's go."

Wajickee showed up and asked, "Did you make the wrong turn mate?"

Montomie winked at him and said, "I think I did, mate. I think I did."

At lunch, the Sarge thanked the ladies for sharing his family and home with positive vibes and information. He went down the line and said, "Alvara, PJ, Gerri, and Barbara Ann, it was a pleasure to meet you guys. Azuree, we know you dearly. I'm not sure if everyone is aware of this, but Barbara Ann is staying on to assist Michael, Darryl, Sue Lyn, and their guys with developing an infrastructure for the locals." Everyone cheered for her and she took a slight bow.

The Sarge said, "During our travels, Yvette, Mary Alice, Carla, Mike, Ms. Viola, Luana, and Ms. Beatrice have joined our tribe. We did an op in Hong Kong and were linked with Okema, Somara, and Yeshida. In addition, we've been joined by my nephew, Darryl, and his wife Sue Lyn, Isaiah, Michael, Desmond, Jasper, Windom, and Earther. We also have four people who are being vetted for Darryl's group, Cheapman, Harold Quick, and Nikelson. The people in the Hong Kong acquisition, well, those three ladies, along with Yvette, left everything they owned and joined our merry band and we love them for trusting in us to keep them safe and for them to keep us safe. You know, it's a hard thing to live blindly without hope. We live with our eyes open and hope that all will be well for all of us. I say all of that to say this, some of you are concerned about things, or possessions, bank accounts, or friends and family. I agree, those things are important, but what's really essential in life are the things that you treasure that your mind can engage. That feeling you get that makes your body engage. Things are just what they are, things; but love, faithfulness, and respect, will keep you healthy, happy, and horny (HHH) for a lifetime."

The Sarge took a drink and continued by saying, "By the way, Ms. Viola, we got so many babies running around here, and more on the way, I think I'm going to place numbers on their little butts until I can remember all their names. In closing, people, enjoy our meal from the earth and water and be thankful that we have each other."

From afar, the Sarge could see that Alvara, PJ, and Gerri were all in tears. Courtney said, "You're one spiteful human being Ben Beckmire. Look at how you impacted those women."

"I'll only look after they've been vetted, and if they are still here in the morning."

Montomie waltzed up to the Sarge and said, "I was about to enjoy a union with my friend, when that beast in the water made its presence known. I also saw Wajickee and he spoke to me. What's going on, my leader?"

"Listen, do you want that lady to stay or go and if she stays, is it for carnal gratification or pleasures of the heart?"

"Sarge, I'm too damn old for bullshit. I like when she's near and I like the way, she allows me to be me. Do you know how sometimes when you meet people, you put on airs? Well, I never changed me from the time I met her and she just dances around me and laughs. I was about to make love to her because I felt she was leaving. However, thanks to that brief discussion by you, I think she's staying."

"How about I assess the waters by telling another story?"

"You're in charge my brother. Do your thing."

The Sarge stood up and gently banged on his wooden table and requested, "May I have you attention for just a single moment, please. It has come to my attention that our pilots are legal and our small plane is ready to take you ladies back to the hustle and bustle. We will miss you, but in order to keep schedules, I'm afraid you're going to have to leave the compound in the next twenty minutes. Please say your goodbyes but be mindful that when flying, schedules are critical to safe air travel."

PJ was in a huddle with McArthur, Gerri was seemingly tongue lashing Montomie, and Alvara was blissfully in tears and in the arms of Gladstone. Gladstone yelled out, "Sarge, cancel one reservation. My lady has decided to stay and learn how we help people help themselves."

Not to be outdone, Gerri stood up and said, "In consultation with my new mate, my seat is available. The only way I'm leaving this bloke is if he forces me to get on that damn plane."

PJ stood up and said, "I only have stuff back east. I now have love and I want to explore that notion to the moon and back. I'm not going anywhere unless Mr. McArthur requests me to."

The Sarge said, "Well, Barbara Ann, it looks like you'll be flying by yourself. Have a wonderful trip."

Barbara Ann stood up and looked at Courtney and said, "Is he trying to bully me? I know he knew we were on the fence, ergo, his conversation about things, loyalty, and love. Michael is my man and I hope I'm his woman. Where he goes, I go and, therefore, I'm willing to assume training that allows me to be a support and not an undervalued non-assisting, questionable asset."

The Sarge bellowed out, "Well, I'll be damn, this family has just grown by leaps and bounds. Mr. Jong, do we need another new plane?"

"No need new plane, until they make more babies."

CHAPTER ELEVEN

At the airport in the Northern Territory, a sleek looking black jet landed and was ushered towards the single hangar where the group's planes were. Ben Beckmire, Mallory, Jilkes, John Lee, Jong, and Mike began to scale the steps to the plane when a voice said, "It would be nice just to sit out back in the sun and have this discussion, don't you think?" Mr. Utz came from around one of the wheel wells and held his left hand up to his ear as if he were talking on a telephone. Beckmire said, "We prefer fresh to manufactured air. How the hell are you? Nice ride, from whom did you confiscate it?"

"It belonged to that New Yorker who thought he could just deal in contraband and be left alone because someone told him he was a star, rich, and untouchable." The men shook hands and everyone else on both sides were introduced.

Once in the plane, Mr. Utz said, "I'm going to get right down to business."

Jong interrupted him and said, "We must scan you before we begin a discussion."

"That's fine with me," Mr. Utz replied.

Jong cut his unit on and two of Mr. Utz's men began to sing like fire alarms going off. Utz looked at the two men who instinctively, raised their hands in the air as if they were surrendering. John Lee and Jilkes were on them like white on rice.

Mr. Utz said, "I never would have thought that you two were the bandits. You see, Mr. Beckmire, I wondered how some of our information was in the street before we finished a complete sentence. Sarge, Mr. Jong, I thank you for helping me find additional big rats. My only question is, what shall I do with them? Shall I turn them over to you and you can escort them deep into the outback where they will never be heard from again, or just put rounds in their heads right here and now?"

The Sarge said, "I think it might be interesting to discern what they know and to understand why they're wearing wires? My guys can certainly find those answers out, but how would that look in your books? You show up with two people missing, now that would certainly cause me to investigate. Anyway, before you leave here, we'll get the information we want from them and then we'll decide if they live or die. Jilkes and John Lee, take those two out of hearing range and see if they are the cooperating types or those, we drop off deep in the outback? Oh, Mr. Utz, it is common for the spiders here to find themselves on naïve visitors. They are deadly and there is no anti-venom for their bites. My nephew knows where they are and can make it happen, that way, you don't have to account for missing personnel, just explain that they were bitten by the most venomous spiders in the outback. Think about it and we'll decide in a little bit."

# # #

Mr. Utz opened his laptop and showed the group the devastation from the detonation of the alleged Carbon Factor. He asked, "Does this look like the expected results from that product?"

The Sarge exclaimed, "Mr. Utz, we never saw, we never knew, what this damn mess could do! We had plans that were written in scientific gibberish that none of us understood."

"Sarge, how did you know where to partition the drives so that people couldn't move to the next step without the pieces that you deleted?"

"Mr. Utz, do you believe in magic?"

"Sarge, I believe in a lot of things, but I need to know who did the partitioning and why at those critical points?"

Jong stepped forward and asked, "May I speak?"

The Sarge nodded and Jong said, "I just randomly selected areas of each data disk, highlighted it, copied, and deleted that section. Now, the Sarge asked you if you believe in magic because I didn't do that by myself. It was that guy named Wajickee who somehow made all the selections and I just followed his lead."

"Who is this Wajickee fellow?"

Jong once again inquired, "I asked you if you believe in magic? Wajickee is an Aborigine spirit. It will not do you any good attempting to speak to him because you're not of our tribe and you've not eaten from the earth and the water. In other words, it ain't going to happen. More importantly, what do you want to do with those two. We can take them into the bush and guarantee you they will tell us everything we want to know."

Mr. Utz looked at Jong and then at the Sarge and said, "Sarge, our next stop is Macau but I can't have traitorous individuals forecasting my every move. I'm wondering if they informed anyone of our intent to go to Macau?"

"If I, were you, I wouldn't go marching into Macau with a skeleton crew looking for the mastermind because he used the word Obrigada. I would stay far away from there and try to figure out how he's placing these devices around the world in places that take security, seriously. Let me have those two for one hour. You and the rest of your crew can join us for a meal and some real Aborigine culture and by the way, are your pilots legal?"

"Sarge is there a hotel nearby that we can crash in?"

The Sarge proclaimed, "Dude, this ain't New York. This is the outback, the bush! Luxury left you when you stepped off that plane. Let's get through customs and we'll take you to our village and you can freshen up, eat, and enjoy my family."

"I appreciate your gesture, but we can't leave our plane."

"Mr. Utz, you see those two jets in the hangar, they're my family's. They are watched around the clock by my family. You just don't happen to see them, but they're here and as soon as we leave, twenty people will show up. Also, our pilots rotate and watch the crafts. Leave your pilots and they can join ours in monitoring the aircrafts. My family will make sure they are well fed.

#

When the group arrived in the village, Michael and his crew were returning from depositing stones in the billabong. Although not a Beckmire, Michael was allowed to board a skiff and enter the water. When they were at the billabong, Darryl yelled, "Michael, I want you to take a single stone and place it in your pocket."

"Boss, why would I do that?"

"Michael, trust me, as I trust you."

Michael picked the smallest stone in the pouch and placed it in his shirt pocket. He then threw his hands in the air as if to say, 'what's next'?

What happened next was a group of large saltwater crocs surrounded the skiff. Darryl yelled, "Michael, remove the stone from your pocket and place it in the pouch." Michael hurriedly complied, and the crocs disappeared. Michael rowed back to the beach, jumped out of the skiff, and exclaimed, "Not fair or funny boss! Not fair!"

Darryl announced, "I wanted to demonstrate what happens when one has larceny in their heart."

Darryl looked to the heavens, said a silent prayer, and announced, "Sadly, one amongst us has considered the possibility of shorting the billabong. He now knows the resolve of this mystical place and must cleanse himself of that desire to remove what is not for his benefit."

Everyone looked at each other and seconds later, Harold raised his hand and said, "I'll get my things and be gone before nightfall. The sensation that I could manage that act and feel good about myself became a burning desire to become self-sufficient at the mercy of the Aborigine people. Michael, I'm sorry, but I became weak and wanted to be in charge of my own destiny at the cost of the Aborigine people. Please forgive me." Harold turned to walk away before Darryl could say a word. A monstrous splash and image was imbedded in each man's brain.

The Great Saltie made a statement and a decision. Darryl knew what it was and agreed without mentally debating the resolution. He said, "Harold, you're a man and had you not confessed, those spiders that are dropping off you would have bitten you. Also, the apparition of the billabong, has sanctioned you and will allow you to stay. However, the next deposit must be made by you without a skiff. In other words, you must walk into the water with the pouch and present it to the billabong."

Tears fell from Harold's eyes and he said, "I'm so ashamed of myself that whatever happens to me in the water will never surpass my weakness and betrayal of you, your family, and the guys. I will throw myself into the water now if you command."

Darryl replied, "I don't want you to feed them now. Its past their lunch time. The message is clear and it is for all of us to heed."

# # #

When Mr. Utz arrived in the camp, most of the women stared at him in an acrimonious manner. They knew his arrival was the beginning of the end of their peace and relaxation.

Asiram, saw their reactions and walked over to Mr. Utz and said, "Let me be unequivocally clear, your presence here is unwanted because these women know that you might deal the card that dispenses death to their loved ones. I suggest you make your visit short, swift, relate to the facts, give us what you know, and be on your way. No need trying to act as if you're family. You are who we fear. You have the potential of making some of us and our children, sad and incomplete."

The Sarge eased over to Asiram and hugged her. He said to her, "Daughter-in-law, you know I love you and the rest of this family. We need Mr. Utz to provide us with information. He is not a flunky or a lacky, and as a matter of fact, he told the man in the White House what he could kiss. With cojones like those, I'm assured he is not self-serving, but serving in the interest of our country and not a single individual or government philosophy. Ladies, he has already told me which way I can go when I threatened his family. I implore you, please be gracious to my guests and make them feel at home. He is his own man and a family man at that."

The usual crescendo of sounds, conversations, and didgeridoos began again which meant that Mr. Utz and his crew would be treated cordially, and that would be about all. He said to the Sarge, "You know the last time I was here I became sick as a dog and then you played that spider thing on me. Please promise not to do that again. I must tell you I was unable to sleep for a couple of weeks. I was always in the search mode for things crawling on me."

"You have my word. If you'd like, I can have a family member give you a small drink that will take those negative images of spiders, out of your mind. Besides, you look as if you haven't slept in days. One way or the other, you and your people are going to get a great night's sleep and your pilots as well. You my friend, are going to learn to love the outback."

# # #

After hours of sharing intel with the Sarge and his people about the mysterious and deadly bombings, the group took time out to eat. The Sarge said, "So, in twenty-four hours, you have to turn someone in, to this person at some unknown place. Do you even have a phone number or any way of contacting the person who demands the presentation of those who allegedly killed his family and friends. Even still, I think this is a ruse. This guy has killed thousands of people in his madness and he wants a few more specific targets before he stops his tirade. I don't think so! I'm of the belief that this guy, or girl, is going to present an ultimatum to the world that will empower him as the supreme ruler or something Hitlerarian or Putintarian. I think he'll pick a couple of small countries and decimate them to illustrate his resolve. This is not going to end quickly or without a lot of dead bodies filling cemeteries. This is all a power play and the only way to win this game is to find his antennas first and bleed them, one by one. He is not personally planting these devices around the world. By the way, if you have the perfect bomb, would you allow your underlings to know how to create it? I don't think so. This whole thing seems like a government gone wild, and not an individual."

Mr. Utz flinched when he heard that last statement. He asked the Sarge if he could pause his presentation for a moment while he reflected on what was said. As a family member served another round of refreshments, Mr. Utz whispered, "Of all the things you said, that makes the most sense to me. Humor me! Suppose some third world country, or even a super-power wanted to corrupt the world order? If you blatantly, did it with aggression, then you would have the might of the entire world joining forces against you. Mr. Beckmire, I think we may be witnessing the beginning of a new world order, which is created by the single fact that I can destroy you before you know who I am!"

"Mr. Utz, I was just postulating about possible scenarios. I certainly didn't mean to take your mind to a place where it can't return. What's troubling about your premise, is that, secretly, and way back when my group was under siege, I often thought about how this could turn into a world domination playbook for the country that coveted the Carbon Factor formula, especially, if the leaders were evil."

Utz looked at him and bellowed out, "But they are evil and have proven it time, after time, after time. The man in the

White House is evil. Look at what he did to that caravan of people seeking political asylum? Or what about that terrible notion of building a wall, or drinking bleach to cure Covid-19, and I could list many other things a rationale person wouldn't consider amplifying and/or attempting to implement. Now, he could pull some sick shit off like that and so could his boyfriend over there in cold-ass Russia. Now, if you think in terms of a third world country, hey, take your pick between those new-age generals who are so beautifully decorated with medals but have never been in a battle. How about some home-grown white nationalists, or the black panthers, or even the toothless kkk? We can't minimize any group, but you just don't waltz into cold-ass Russia and plant a new dirty bomb. I'm thinking it smells like the work of a government with deep cover operatives. I'm with you, I don't think this is a one man show for revenge.

John Lee said, "All I know is that they be some sick puppies to kill all those people without declaring a police action or war. We be needing to find his ass soon before he takes down that crooked-ass government in Washington, DC."

Mr. Utz was about to respond but decided against it. He shook his head and said, "John Lee, the whole of government isn't crooked, but if you have a few, it sure makes it harder to take a positive view of the place."

Mr. Utz continued and said, "Mr. Beckmire, you're right about one thing, whatever is in that drink, just told my body it's time to say goodnight. Sarge, are me and my guys safe?"

"Yes, Mr. Utz. You'll be safe. You haven't decided what you want to do with those two infidels of yours. We can handle it, but we also can wait until the morning. Right now, they're on a skiff in the billabong. We don't have to worry about them going anywhere."

"I'm not going to ask you to tell me why, but if you can be kept until the morning then I would greatly appreciate it. I want to know who oversees them," Mr. Utz stated.

"Trust me Mr. Utz, them boys ain't going nowhere. The security guarding their asses, are big, ferocious, and hungry. No sir, them boys will be there when we come for them in the morning. My people have set up huts for you and your men. Gentlemen, sleep tight, do your business before going to sleep and for your sake, don't wander beyond the village. I beg you, don't go wandering into the night."

# # #

When the Sarge came upon his bride, he said, "You're the most beautiful and loving person that I have ever known. Would you like to sit by the water and watch the moon and shooting stars?"

"My brother, you can sit by the water, but I'll be here waiting on you to return. I'm a woman of science. What I believe that exists in that water is too much for my small brain to comprehend. I love you and you need your time to play by the water and in it. I'll bathe in the spring."

The Sarge looked at her and said, "You do know you're safe with me, right?"

"You do know that if you get bit or shot, you'll be safe with me, right?"

They both laughed and the Sarge said, "Honey, you're my beacon and thanks for giving up all that was yours to come and live a life of a vagrant and be with the man who loves you so dearly. Courtney, will you marry me again?"

Those words caught her by surprise and she began to cry. After a minute of almost hyperventilating, she uttered the words, "Why are you toying with my emotions?"

"Darling, I'm not toying with you, I'm begging you to recommit to me and marry me again, but this time in the tradition of this marvelous place."

"Ben Beckmire, if you're playing with me, I will slip you a Mickey Finn and after that, my friend, you'll never play with me again."

"Courtney, I want to marry you again, right here and right now. What say you?"

"I say I love you my husband and I always will. If you want to make me happy and marry me again in front of your old girlfriend, then I'll play the part."

Courtney smiled and Ben Beckmire said, "That was then and you see where that got me. No, my love, I want consistency like the air we breathe. You are my sunshine."

#

The next morning, Mr. Utz and his crew saw that Beckmire's group was returning from an early run. He said to his guys, "That's what we've got to start doing. We don't do anything other than eat and look at data. Once we get back, I want to make sure that we are all involved in a fitness program."

The Sarge said, "Good day mate! I trust you people slept well. Do you want to interrogate those two guys on the skiff, now or after breakfast?"

"Let's get it over with and figure out what to do with them."

As the group headed to the billabong, Mr. Utz said, "That's a strange looking dog over there."

"That's no dog mate. That's a dingo and we use them to defend us at times," the Sarge stated.

"Come now Sarge, how can you use an animal to defend you?"

"Mr. Utz, it was the dingoes that guarded us all last night long, along with the wombats and a bunch of other animals. We didn't use a single human being to protect us last night, just the animals mate."

As the group reached the billabong, Mr. Utz inquired, "Why didn't those two just swim to the shore and disappear?"

The Sarge laughed and exclaimed, "That would not have been a good idea on their part. Keep your eyes near the skiff!" The Sarge stirred the water and began to pull on a line that kept the skiff in place and watched as various over-sized, saltwater crocs, hit the water from all sides of the billabong and dead reckoned to the skiff.

"Holly shit! Mr. Utz yelled. "Will they come on land where we are?"

"No, mate! They will not come near me in an aggressive manner. I once asked you if you believed in magic. Well, this place is beyond the magical and houses the largest beast of its kind in the world; The Great Saltie." As the Sarge, Jilkes, and John Lee pulled the skiff to shore, the two men were helped off. One of the men kept saying, "I saw it. I saw it. I saw it."

Utz asked, "You saw what man?"

"I saw it!"

The Sarge said, "Let me have a go at him." If you saw it then you know it is real. It could have consumed you at any time last night but out of respect for my family, it allowed me the opportunity to ask you questions. Now, I want you to look around the shoreline and tell me if you see what I see?"

"I see them, I see all of them, but I don't see the big one."

"No, you don't, but you will see him if you lie to me. Who do you work for?"

"We are civil servants and work for the Justice Department."

The Sarge looked sternly at Utz and asked, "Do you as well work for the Justice Department?"

"No sir, I do not. When this team was put together, I was told that its members would be from different departments and they would be under my command, but I didn't do due diligence in vetting them myself. My naivety and trust in the system are both on a corrective course."

The Sarge turned to the person talking and asked, "Who do you report to and why were you wearing a wire?"

"We were told when assigned to this mission that all conversations would be recorded and that we would wear active wires at all times. We report to two guys and they go by the names of Smith and Brown. We know that's not their true names, but that's what we call them."

The interrogation lasted over an hour with no conclusive or damaging information against the men. They couldn't identify their employers and the Sarge was convinced that neither man lied. However, he did consider whether he had asked the correct questions, but realized that if larceny were present, he would have recognized it, especially in the vicinity of the billabong. Mr. Utz explicitly stated, "If either of you undermine my operation, I will have my friend gather and ship you back here as an appetizer."

#

The Sarge, after breakfast, escorted Mr. Utz, and his team back to the airport. His pilots had performed a pre-flight check list and were prepared to leave the Northern Territory for New Zealand to take on fuel for the across the pond trip.

At the airport, the Sarge pulled Mr. Utz aside and said, "If I were you, I would rid myself of those two guys and keep them out of my communications network. I understand their jobs, but you can't have them broadcasting your interactions and having discussions with a Brown and Smith. Just my advice to you. Now, on another matter, we can make the trip into Macau for you and sniff around innocently. The problem with that notion, is that we have no intel, whatsoever. That makes the inquiry suspicious, and alerts the mastermind that people are looking for him in this part of the world. Now, if you want to perhaps flush him out, we can do that and be out of there in a hurry, but then he'll know we have an idea about who he is or the strength of his group. Just a thought for you to take under advisement. Let me know and have a safe flight. You'll hear from me in a week or so and then I'll dedicate all of our resources to finding this mad person. Take care, my friend."

"Wow, you called me friend."

"Indeed, I did, but with a tremendous amount of trepidation."

CHAPTER TWELVE

The plane transporting Mr. Utz and his crew taxied on to the runway. They were placed in a holding pattern because another plane was on approach for landing. As the plane became visible, Mr. Utz realized that the plane landing was a massive jet. He thought nothing of the plane other than that it was huge. As the plane pulled off the active runway, he thought to himself, "I'd like to see who gets off that thing."

He got out of his seat, knocked on the cockpit door and told the captain that he wanted him to stall until he could see the passengers that got off the jet that just landed. The captain in turn, called the tower and informed them that he wanted to check out a light that came on in the overhead panel. The captain pulled the plane off the active runway and on to a holding lane.

Approximately, ten minutes later, the doors to the massive plane opened as the mobile stairs were put in place. Once the people started deplaning, Utz called the Sarge and said, "You had better get ready for a small war. I'm watching, who I would consider mercs, get off this huge plane. I don't think they're here for a training exercise and last I heard, the only thing of value in these parts are your gold and diamond mines."

The Sarge thanked him, wished him a safe flight, and hung up the phone. Utz tried to call him back, but concluded the man was getting his house in order.

The captain asked Mr. Utz if they could takeoff? He was told that a friend would certainly need a few extra eyes. He told him to hold in this lane until all the passengers had disembarked and to then inform the tower that there was a mechanical issue that would preclude them from taking off at this time.

Through customs a total of 257 men and women presented valid passports and expressed that they were a part of a training and conditioning team. The agents knew it was nonsense but had no real reason to deny them entry into the country. Randomly, their bags were searched and all the bags appeared to have several pieces of clothing, toiletries, pairs of running shoes, water bottles, salt tablets, and other paraphernalia indicative of what a person in training would possess.

# # #

In the village, the Sarge summoned his brain trust and informed them of what Mr. Utz had told him. He indicated that he wanted to place the village on full alert. He told the elders of the village what was reported to him and they began to fill the air with sounds of drums and the digeridoos. It was a call for distant surveillance and long-range interference.

# # #

At the airport, and once in customs, an agent asked, "Back so soon, mate?"

"I guess you can say that. I think we can give a friend a hand if you know what I mean."

"Yeah, mate, I do. You might want to bring a tool or two with you. I don't think me and my mates will be checking your bags."

"Thanks mate. I'll be sure to mention that to our friend in need."

# # #

In the village, preparations were being made for an unknown foe. Wajickee had summoned animals and critters from near and far. In essence, the village was impregnable with a defense system that was both human and animal.

Wajickee said to Ben Beckmire, "Your friend wants to come here, but needs a ride. Do you want the bus to pick him up?"

"What friend are you talking about?"

"That Mr. Utz fellow. He watched that vermin get off the plane and realized that they were here to make a play for the jewels. He's here to help. Not like your cousin with whom you went against all rules."

"In justification, I was told that I could not kill him. No one indicated that I couldn't shoot him."

"You are like your forefathers, always using the global understanding of our culture and rules. One day, I may ave to place you in a corner for trying to circumvent our laws with your 21st century interpretations."

"I will refrain from questioning the meanings of what is told to me and respond accordingly, if there is such a thing?"

"Ben Beckmire, you did it again! 'If there is such a thing.' What on earth is that other than your questioning our reasoning?"

"It won't happen again my friend. It won't happen again."

#

Mr. Utz and his guys got off the bus and the Sarge asked, "What are you going to do with those two?"

"Well, hello to you too, Sarge. Thanks for coming back to lend a hand against what appears to be, formidable odds."

The Sarge looked at him and said, "Give me a hug. I just wanted to piss you off by taking you off your game and by picking on those two guys."

"Well, if there is any consolation, they have agreed to be in front of the fire fight in order to get back in good graces with me and the team."

"How about if we put them in the billabong?"

One of the guys who wore a wire said, "I'll lead the charge before going near that water."

The Sarge said, "Welcome back to my village. Get some food, blankets, and we'll figure out our weapons situation in a few?

"Ah, Sarge, we brought our own."

"How did you smuggle them through customs?"

"We didn't smuggle anything. We told the guys that a friend of ours might need some extra help. They in essence told me to take what I wanted because they weren't going to check our bags."

"Did he really tell you that?"

"Do you think I concocted that story?"

"Okay, Utz, let's get some grit and enjoy the calm."

The Sarge looked at Mr. Utz's guys and said, "Gentlemen, do not go a wandering. The animals and critters have been summoned. Stay in camp."

Wajickee appeared next to the Sarge and said, "The focus of this assault will be the billabong. Ave the women put cotton balls in the children's ears. I found the people who smuggled their weapons and explosives into the country. Let's just say, they're out of business, permanently."

"What about the inhabitants of the billabong?"

"Not to worry about them. They're about two miles away. When those people think it's safe to go after those things in the water, another kind of critter awaits them. This will all be settled easily and all those complicit in this matter, including the damn Abos, will meet with a horrible death."

Asiram and Ava were checking their weapons when Courtney asked, "Has anyone seen Yvette and the babies?"

Ava pointed and said, "There's her husband, why don't you go and take his temperature?"

"Smart ass, maybe I will." As Courtney started towards Bernstein, Ava yelled, "You got that all wrong like you normally do. What I meant was go and see if the two of them are alright."

"We can discuss that later. Right now, I'm missing a woman and a couple of children."

As Courtney, Asiram, and Ava walked deeper into the bush Ava said, "You sometimes snap at me and I don't get it. Do you think I still want that fine husband of yours?"

"Ava now is not the time. If you'd like to discuss it in depth later, let me know. Just help me find Yvette and the children."

The group approached the billabong and saw, Yvette. Courtney said, "No sudden movements. I don't want to startle Yvette and watch her do something drastic."

Courtney eased ever so cautiously near Yvette and said, "Honey, what are you doing so close to the billabong with the children?"

"Courtney, I'm a mess. Someone from my old life is here in the camp and I just wanted to get away before he recognized me."

"Honey, is he Aborigine?"

"No, he's with Mr. Utz's group. I remember him because he was rough and did demeaning things to me."

"Before we go any further, does your husband know about this?"

Yvette proclaimed, "I'm afraid to tell him because he would probably kill that man!"

"Okay, you know we run a tight ship. Right ladies?"

Ava said to Yvette, "Courtney is mad at me because she thinks I want her fine husband. Asiram is mad at Zanthius because he's afraid to have sex with her for fear of impregnating her once again. As women, we carry a lot of shit around with us, but we're supposed to smile and be merry. I like busting on Courtney, because she will want to discuss my actions later, and then we can get intoxicated together. I love Ben Beckmire. I'm in love with my husband and I've taught him some real naughty things and he likes it. That guy out there who defiled you, if I can use that term, will probably never make it out of the Northern Territory, bad people can't exist in this sphere of harmony, love, and family. In other words, you need to get your ass up from here and get them babies back in the nursery before we're under attack again."

"Well, I'll be damned, Mrs. De Lombardo. You did that better than I could have ever imagined where to go next in my conversation. Yvette, do you want to face the accused, or would you like for the natural order of things in the outback to seek justice?" Courtney asked.

"Courtney, I want to face him and ask why he treated me like dung?"

"So be it. Ava and Asiram, are you with us?"

Asiram said, "Sometimes, it's best to let sleeping dogs sleep. You're about to embark on an unholy venture that may not end to anyone's satisfaction. Personally, I'm against it, but if you think you'll find salvation, then I'm here for you until the very end. However, I can tell you about defilement, especially when engaged by your immediate family. That was long ago and you'll get over it because you have a man who loves, respects, and cherishes you, and the children. I strongly recommend letting it go unless it comes directly to you. Only then would I engage the individual. How about you Ava?"

"I like disclosure and closure. Neither have particularly worked out in my favor. However, I stand with my daughter-in-law. If you want to confront this person and you're not satisfied with the outcome, perhaps I'll accidently shoot him in the head. How does that work for you?"

Yvette said, "You people are absolutely crazy, but the best and true friends a person could wish for. I just feel bad for Bernstein. I know he would kill that guy without any questions being asked or issues confirmed. My husband adores the earth I walk on and any slight from anyone, I feel would be terminal. I love him so very much; I call him my crusader. He found his grail and I don't want anything to come between us and our happiness."

"Wow girl, that's some tough stuff. I'll have to ask the Sarge about some notion like that and see how he responds. Anyway, your choice, but I think we have consensus, let the dog stay asleep and if he even looks your way, he will be the victim of friendly fire. Ava, that's your role, Courtney announced."

"I got that. I will kill him if he looks at her in an inquisitive manner. You know out here we have a little leverage in how we interpret the law and respond to it."

CHAPTER THIRTEEN

At 0200 hours the sounds of multiple explosions could be heard throughout the Northern Territory. It sounded as if there was a war going on in the middle of the outback. Grenade after grenade exploded in or around the billabong in an attempt to kill anything lurking in or near the water. After that barrage of ordnances were discharged, depth charges were floated into the various areas of the billabong, submerged, and then detonated. As if that wasn't enough to kill any and everything near or around the billabong, four Gatlin guns loaded the waters with their full munitions, reloaded, and fired a second and third time, under the watchful eyes of the human inhabitants of the area.

The Sarge said, "That was some display of firepower. Signal my family members to fill that area with arrows and spears."

Three minutes later, the only sound that could be heard was that of spears and arrows whistling through the air. From the north, south, east, and west, hundreds of spears and arrows fell on the mercs. Those throwing the weapons disappeared into the night over the hills and small mountains and into caves.

The two men who wore wires, decided to capture Gatlin guns. They made Utz aware of their intent by making movements of spears being thrown, and the shooting of bows.

Utz ran his hand across his throat, indicating that barrage was concluded. The two men made their way near the billabong and saw the munitions and four Gatlin guns unattended. They captured two of the guns and made their way to where the Sarge and his people had formed a strike zone. They dropped the weapons and made their way back near the billabong where they saw two men looking up and listening for whistling sounds and dispatched of them quickly and efficiently. They grabbed two reams of munitions and a Gatlin gun each. As they reached the area where the Sarge and his people were, they dropped the guns and munitions and one of the guys said, "This is not the action of a coward or a traitor. We follow orders, we don't make or give them."

The Sarge studied the two men and reflected on their actions and moved closer to Utz and said, "You might want to reconsider your viewpoints on those two, but I'd still keep them close until I could truly trust them. As a matter of fact, from what I saw, I like their style and if you like, you can leave them here with me. They captured four Gatlin guns and munitions; no small feat, and certainly a shitload of courage."

The Sarge motioned to Mallory to withdraw the team. He looked at Utz and said, "It's time to withdraw from here. Shit is about to get really messy."

"What do you mean. I think now is the time to take it to them. They've lost a significant amount of people from the arrows and spears, and now is the time to conclude this event."

"Mr. Utz, do you remember me asking if you believed in magic? Well, the animals smell blood and they are going to swell their bellies on those souls who are wounded or dead. Those who are not wounded are going to tempt their fate and try to extract the contents from the billabong and that is when the real magic begins. By morning, the animals and nature would have consumed or decimated close to three hundred men and women. Some will see the booty in the billabong and a few will touch it. However, none will live to tell the tale of riches beyond anyone's wildest imagination. This is Australia, this is the Northern Territory, Mr. Utz, and finally, this is the outback, a place that neither forgives, allows, or tolerates infidels. All that is here is for the Aborigine people, not for common bounty hunters or treasure seekers, no, Mr. Utz, only for the Aborigine people."

Mr. Utz looked at the Sarge and exclaimed, "I'm beginning to understand your strong commitment to humanity, life, family, and this place! It is truly magical and even what's more incredible is, we didn't fire a single shot. Also, you knew those guys weren't self-serving. You knew they had to express their commitment to me in a way that only I would accept—a life or death daring mission. You knew that didn't you?"

"The only thing I know, is that when I'm here, on this soil, anything is possible. Only God can make miracles, and I've seen some things happen here to my people that God had his hand in on the events."

The Sarge started to walk away, but abruptly turned to Utz and said, "You should bring your family here. Those waters might help your child with the issue."

Uncharacteristically, Utz calmly asked, "How do you know about my child, Sarge?"

"Listen, I'm a man of faith. What harm could it do? The people need her and she needs the people. Out of that combination, the possibilities are infinite. Bring her here and you might be forever disappointed or eternally grateful that you're a man of God."

#

When the night transitioned into day, 275 people or more, had been killed by Aborigine people, animals, insects, spiders, reptiles, and some as a result of dehydration. Not a single bullet was fired by Beckmire's group.

At 0800 hours at the airport, Mr. Utz acknowledged, "This place is special. All those people who came here for fortune are dead and not a single person from a gunshot. I know there is something special here. However, is the word magic synonymous to God? I'm beginning to believe it is. I'll be in touch. That Macau thing is too risky and revealing. Get your act together here and then get back to me when you're coming back my way. Thanks, Ben Beckmire. Lotsofluv for you and your family."

As they boarded the plane, the Sarge saw a slow small drip coming from the rear of the plane. He thought it was water but decided to have a closer look. The captain saw Beckmire give the time out hand signal and asked, "What the hell? The guy just gave me the time out signal."

The pilot got out of his seat, lowered the stairs, and descended them.

Once on the ground, the Sarge asked, "Is this normal?"

The captain approached the area, saw the liquid dripping, let the slow dripping fluid fall onto his hand, and exclaimed, "Mr., you probably just saved this plane and everyone on it from disaster! That's hydraulic fluid and it controls all of the main functions of the plane."

After confirming it was a simple fix, the passengers deplaned. Mr. Utz smiled at the Sarge and said, "No magic; God's work."

# # #

The plane Mr. Utz and his people flew on was repaired and inspected by several teams including Beckmire's pilots. All confirmed that the issue was minor but had the possibility of developing into a major concern. At 1500 hours Utz and his crew blasted into the sky and eventually out of eyesight.

# # #

When Darryl and Sue Lyn returned to the village, Ben Beckmire thanked him and his bride for orchestrating the whistling spears and arrows. He told Darryl that his group never fired a single shot. Sue Lyn asked, "Uncle, do you think that the bombing disrupted our bank in any manner?"

Beckmire yelled, "You, young lady called me uncle, again. Wait until I tell your Uncle Jong."

"It was he who suggested that I refer to you as my uncle. My question remains, do you think the bank has been disturbed?"

"Tomorrow, why don't we send Darryl swimming to make sure that all is in place. I doubt if any ordnances fell directly into the bank, but we'll let him confirm it after his swim."

"Uncle, there is another problem that we've uncovered. Approximately, twenty-five kilometers due west from here, there is another cave that is full of precious stones. It borders on the quadrants outlined in the court decree. We have all of the relationships in place, but the security issue is complicated, and as you know, the banking arrangements are nonexistent. I don't think that storing billions of dollars in diamonds in a billabong is 21st century thinking. We can consider building a

Fort Knox like installation here, but that would take a few years."

"Now, Darryl, that's an interesting idea. Why can't we build on stilts in the middle of the billabong, a structure that is airtight and submerges. The nearest bank that has even the slightest capability of securing what's in the water is several thousand kilometers away. As you know that road would be a great place for a modern-day Jessie James to plow his trade."

The Sarge paused for a few seconds and finally stated, "Darryl, I like the idea of building an underwater vault. Rather than taking risky roads to secure the bounty; we drive armored trucks deep into the center of the outback and have them met by helicopters that would transport the cargo to a real banking institution or to another airport, and then use our fleet to deliver the goods to a trusted bank. Think about it, but let's do something. Apparently, loose lips are sinking our ship and are putting our friends and family in jeopardy. Before you know it, the next thing that someone will try to do, is poison the waters."

"Uncle, we have a lot of things outlined, people assigned, purchase orders ready for execution, and now the idea of an underwater vault. I sincerely like that idea and I have to figure out if it is feasible and how to implement it."

# # #

Meanwhile in Yakima, Washington, four devices were found in the middle of an apple orchard. It was the first break in realizing that the ominous Carbon Factor formula had several weak points prior to detonation—it needed moisture, temperature, and range from a sending controller. More importantly, a radio control device was found abandoned near the small airport in the city. The device was purchased at a Radio Shack and had a proprietary stamp on it illustrating the manufacturer. The control device and the four packages were flown to a secret location in Quantico, Virginia.

Once the packages were thoroughly evaluated, it was determined that it was not a dud and it was a functional bomb. The analyst filmed the entire occasion and sent a copy to Mr. Utz. He in turn sent a copy to Jong who presented the package to the Sarge. The Sarge called for a meeting of the entire team including some of the women. He explained that Mr. Utz sent him a film of the evaluation of the Carbon Factor bomb that was discovered in an apple orchard in Yakima, Washington. He exclaimed, "The items you will see in the film are only aspects of the Carbon Factor! Mr. Utz believes it is temperamental and subject to moisture, temperature, and the distance from the controller device. Please pay attention because we're going to be asked how to control it, how to create the environment that it was found in and wouldn't work in, capture the person or persons behind those devastating attacks, and figure out how to prematurely detonate the devices. The assumption is pervasive that we know all of the intricacies of the Carbon Factor. No one believes that we innocently came upon this beast. Always remember, who would believe that my son, who I didn't know existed, in this world, kissed a woman, and she passed him the beginnings of a formula that could reshape the balance of power in the world? And who would consider that by chance, his father and a few ex-Vietnam era friends would show up to provide protection? What about the untold millions of dollars that accidently inured to their benefit? Also, who is going to believe that the Carbon Factor formula was partitioned into strategic parts, by this unscientific group? What person would believe that through all of this mayhem and destruction, somehow the partitioned aspects of the Carbon Factor, suddenly was up for sale by the group who blindly stumbled across it? Who would believe this mess?"

As the group reviewed the information about the apple orchard discovery, Okema said to Brown, "This discovery seems to be manufactured. Why there, why now, and why not where there are people. Do they think by destroying an apple orchard, they can bring the government to its knees?"

Brown looked at the setting and realized that it appeared to be an attempt at misdirecting the true intent of the find. He said, "Sarge, my observant wife thinks this scene is contrived. I believe it was a test situation. Now we both may be whistling Dixie, but there is a matter of fact, appearance to this discovery."

Jilkes chimed in and asked, "Why Yakima? Why an apple orchard? What value is inherent in a strike there? That's a desolate place, with a small airport. It is not a big market for anything other than the drugs coming across the Canadian border."

Zanthius looked at the video and became fixated on the entire scene. When Larry showed up, he said, "Why on earth in Yakima, Washington and why an apple orchard?"

Larry looked hard at the scene and yelled, "This is a clue. I'll bet you Zanthius's life where the next detonation will be!!"

Zanthius screamed and said, "The damn Big Apple!" He walked over to Larry and gave him a huge hug.

The Sarge said, "Why do you two geniuses think it's going to be the Big Apple?"

Zanthius said, "Dad, we're not sure of anything, but given the contrived nature of this event in Yakima, I'm betting on the fact that New York, is this guy's, next target."

The Sarge excused himself, called Mr. Utz, and gave him the intel that his two sons agreed upon. Mr. Utz indicated that he and his team would investigate thoroughly. He asked the Sarge, "Don't you think that's close to Springfield and is our guy an east coast type?"

"Utz, I've not made any determinations yet, but my boys simultaneously announced the Big Apple. I mean they could be wrong, but so far, they have been spot on when they look at the same things from different lens. Until I get a different kind of intel, then I'm making my wager on New York City. My question to you is, how can we help?"

CHAPTER FOURTEEN

As Beckmire's group plane approached a military base in New Jersey for landing, the security precautions were laid out to them explicitly. Under no circumstances should weapons of any kind be discovered on any individual. Mr. Utz was there to meet the plane and whisked the passengers away in a bus used to transport high valued targets. It was armor-plated and contained a stash of short, medium, and long-range weapons. Utz had arranged for his people along with twenty Rangers, to provide protection for his associates. They were housed in a non-descript hotel that looked like a dive from afar but was appointed with high-end furnishings and other accessories.

Mr. Utz huddled with the Sarge, Mallory, Jilkes, John Lee, Larry, and Zanthius. He emphatically stated, "If you're caught while on this mission, you're on your own. Your role is to sniff out the apparatus placement people, get a fix on who the actual manufacturer of the devices is, and get that intel to me. You are to avoid engagement at any cost."

John Lee announced, "Then buddy, you done picked the wrong sharecroppers. We don't be doing no dumb shit like you just stated. If somebody comes for my African American friend, you expect me to let him just, I mean, just take him out? If'n you be saying that there dumb shit then Sarge, we need to abdicate this meeting and get the hell out of here."

Jilkes said, "He meant to use the other big word, terminate."

"Okay people keep it real. Mr. Utz, as Mr. Lee stated, "we don't do no dumb shit like that." If this thing isn't transparent, meaning that if we don't know everything there is to know about your suspects, the organization, and everything else, then we're out of here. We are a team and we don't do well when infused with people who don't know how we work or who regulate a protocol from behind a desk. If you want our help, give us the intel, and let us decide if we can do the job. If it were that simple, you and those Rangers out there could've gotten it done, right? No, Mr. Utz, this is a bit more complicated and you don't want to get your hands dirty, but you want to tell us how much dirt we can play in."

Utz looked at the men and knew that he had lost a group that could absolve him of all impending sins. He asked, "Sarge, what do you need from me in terms of equipment?" He looked at his people in the room and suggested that they leave to avoid any complicity.

When his men were out of the room, he stated, "I still believe I have a mole in my group and, therefore, I don't trust anyone other than you guys. Let's start from the beginning."

Mr. Utz took his time and told the group everything that he knew about the new assassin and his network of followers. He explained to the group that they have two people under surveillance in Yakima for planting those devices. He indicated that they were under full surveillance—24/7. Utz provided the group with five pictures of suspects, who on the east coast, were also, under constant monitoring. As they passed the pictures around, the members of the team looked at them without any particular interest other than seeing who was under the microscope.

Jilkes exclaimed, "These guys look like your everyday businesspeople, not terrorists, who would decimate a city and its inhabitants. I mean look at these people, they just don't look the part!"

Mallory scanned the pictures in a hurry and handed them off to the Sarge who said, "Yeah, Jilkes, I see what you mean." When he arrived at the last photo, he stared at it and shuffled it back into the stack. Simultaneously, Mallory yelled, and the Sarge said, "Well, I'll be damn."

Mallory exclaimed, "I don't believe this shit! Ain't that the rodent from the Midwest who paraded around as a deputy sheriff?"

The Sarge said, "Mallory, look who he's talking with. That's the guy from the room with the two girls from the farm those carpetbaggers tried to steal from our friends." The two men studied the pictures and shared them with each other.

Utz, calmly interrupted the séance and asked, "Can you two share your epiphanies with the group?"

The Sarge explained, "Some time ago, we had a run in with these two in Wyoming. They had developed a lending scheme with several ranchers and fleeced them out of their properties. When we became aware of the problem, they had as many as four ranches in their clutches. We paid them a visit, in the middle of their celebrating another acquisition, and made them an offer that they couldn't and wouldn't refuse. They thought we were bluffing and that's when two of my team members fired large caliber rounds into their refrigerator from fifteen hundred yards away. Anyway, I don't see these two hustlers working this kind of national terror program. The deputy was just a small-time jerk and the carpetbagger, well, was just that, a thief."

The Sarge paused for a few seconds, and asked Mr. Utz, "Do you have pictures of those people under surveillance on the west coast?"

Utz opened his briefcase and pulled out a brown file folder and said, "These are the people we're watching in Yakima."

The Sarge looked at the pictures and said, "This is incredible. This is the other guy from the house that night, Mallory."

He passed the picture to Mallory who said, "Now, you talk about coincidental, these people are linked."

Mr. Utz inquired, "Are you guys absolutely sure about this?"

The Sarge looked at Utz and stated, "To the best of my recollection, I have had encounters with the two people on the east coast and the one person on the west coast."

Mallory chimed in and said, "Ditto!"

"Ditto? What does that mean?" Mr. Utz inquired.

"It means to the best of my recollection I have been up close and personal with those three people offering them their lives and some cash to do the right thing."

Mr. Utz said, "I cannot depend on my guys to manage this information, so keep it between us. I know that two of them have come clean, but I'm not sure about the other one.

#

The Sarge asked, "My sons, are you guys tired of this cloak and dagger stuff that we've been doing?"

Larry looked at Zanthius, smiled at the Sarge, and said, "Sarge, both of your sons have other responsibilities."

The Sarge then asked, "John Lee, how about you?"

John Lee replied, "I want to be with my woman and my babies, be near my African American friend, without anybody trying to shoot his black ass."

Mr. Utz asked, "Why do you call him out of his name?"

The Sarge ran interference and stated, "Mr. Utz, some things you should hear, but not react to. This relationship is very, very, sensitive, and outsiders usually don't do well inquiring about the nature of how they relate to each other. Please, let it go! Anyway, as you can see, we're a little tired of this spy game and international terrorism programs."

"Listen, I know you guys don't need money and airplanes. You already have that, plus you're in charge of diamond and gold mines, in the outback. How about I take that new plane that you picked up a year or so ago, and give you another one that will be bigger, faster, and much more luxurious than what you're riding around in?"

The Sarge was about to say something when Mr. Utz, said, "Wait, don't interrupt me until I'm finished. Okay, now that I have your attention, what if I told you that I know where there are several containers full of money that a deceased drug dealer will not need, and that I will give you legitimate numbers for bankers who will be able to account for, invest, endow your organization charities, and most of all, give all of you a lifetime get out of jail cards from the past until you're pushing up daisies?"

Larry eloquently stated, "Mr. Utz, if you would kindly leave the room, I would like to convince my dad why we shouldn't be involved in this high-level debauchery. We are people of morals, and that is what I want to speak to my dad about—morals!"

When Mr. Utz left the room, Larry pulled out a sensor that detected recording paraphernalia. The unit discovered none. Mallory asked, "Is this a coup or something?"

Zanthius replied, "No Mallory, this is an opportunity for us to shed a shitload of cash into an accountable commodity that we can help people help themselves with. Dad don't even hesitate about this one. In this event, no one is hunting us. Think about it. No one is pursuing us and looking for the formula. This thing that Utz asks, seems doable without a lot of watching our backs."

John Lee said, "I be thinking like these two boys of yours. I like the idea, that we can have clean money to leave to our children. We be done made too much money the easy way and it's time to get away from them there Jong's people because they be killing each other over our business deals."

The Sarge looked at Mallory and nodded his head. Mallory opened the door and requested that Mr. Utz join them. As Utz started his way back into the room, three of his people started behind him. Mallory said, "Sorry guys, this session is for Utz only and I'm sure he'll bring you up to date, when we're finished."

After Utz entered the room, John Lee bellowed out, "Them there guys that tried to enter the room, well, they be your weak links."

Utz looked at John Lee as if he were trying to figure him out. The Sarge announced, "Before you get lost in analysis, let's deal with the issue at hand. However, before we proceed any further, I need to have my entire team in here. I also need you to have a one-on-one with Mr. Jong about clean money, the containers, and the airplane. You will work on those get out of jail cards with Mallory and our two lawyers prior to us even considering this effort. Now, what's missing from this deal is a secure way of transporting our minerals from the outback to a secure banking establishment in Sydney. Do you think your charm can reach that far and impact our dilemma in transporting the Aborigine goods?"

"Sarge considered it done. You haven't reacted to my need for your people in Australia to handle that west coast situation for me."

The Sarge emphatically stated, "Our last handler tried to handle us for his personal gain. I'm assuming that you're much better than that Mr. Utz. If you withhold information about any assignment we may choose to consider, and one of my people are injured or killed, I will personally gut you from your small brain to your big one. No force can keep me away because I have magic on my side and you know what I can do with the animals, my friend."

"Sarge, I will divulge all details that I have about what's going on. Shit happens in a hurry, and sometimes the intel comes to me a little late. Please have mercy, at least do due diligence, and make sure that you're not over-reacting to something completely out of my control."

"Fair enough. I will wait a day before I have my associates visit your domain." The two men laughed and shook hands.

Utz said, "You still haven't given me access to your people in the outback."

"I will never give you access to my people. If you have a task, then I will assign them specific responsibilities. My people will never follow any command other than mine, Mallory's, or the succession pyramid. I can have them prepare to catch a plane from Australia tomorrow."

"Sarge, there are a lot of things that people don't know about America's capabilities, such as supersonic commercial transportation. I can have a plane there in two hours and have them in Seattle from take-off to landing in another two hours. You can't repeat this and they must never mention their experience."

"Utz, if you can get me one of those, we'll gladly be your unofficial police squad," the Sarge happily stated.

CHAPTER FIFTEEN

When Darryl and his crew arrived at the airport, a slightly modified version of the Concorde was being refueled and several men were on the ground examining the underbelly of the aircraft. Sue Lyn exclaimed, "What on earth is that? It looks like a pterodactyl."

Michael said, "It looks demonic. It seems like a plane to hell."

"Oh, Michael, stop being so Draconian in thought. You see a change in the appearance of a plane and you invoke a new rule when in fact, it's probably supersonic in nature; the plane that is."

"Boss, are you telling me that thing flies at or above the speed of sound?"

"Michael, I don't know what that thing does. My uncle instructed me to be at the airport and to be prepared to be flown to Yakima, Washington. He didn't inform me of the mode of transportation nor the speed in which the transporter could travel."

"Darryl, if you get on it, then I'll get on it and sit very close to you and Sue Lyn," Michael playfully stated.

Darryl told his crew to pack light and to leave all notions of weapons safely stored in the bush. After the plane was fueled, a lieutenant came over and introduced himself to Darryl and gave him the rules of the road.

Darryl in turn, gave those rules to his people and prior to the boarding process, all cell phones, MP3s, Apple watches, I pods, and everything else electronic, was collected. As the group entered the plane from its tail, a heavy blanket looking item hung on both sides of the plane and ran to the entrance of the cabin. Once in the cabin, everyone looked, shook their heads, and were in awe of the layout of the aircraft. It was absolutely spectacular. The seats were humongous and individual. The plane accommodated eighty-five passengers at maximum load.

After facial recognition, fingerprints were acquired from people touching the railing entering the plane. The captain engaged the intercom system and said, "Welcome aboard the most top-secret aircraft unknown to Americans. I don't make assumptions and, therefore, you people just didn't wander upon this plane looking for a ride to the Great Barrier Reef. Therefore, I suggest you sit back, relax, and enjoy the comforts of this non-existent plane. Our destination is Seattle, Washington, the birthplace of this majestic lady. Once we're airborne, I'll come back on and give you our ETA for Seattle. Enjoy the short flight."

The plane taxied down the runway without any lights on to the active runway. There were no visible starboard or port lights, and no aft white lights. There were no lights at all. Once in position, the captain informed the tower that his plane was ready for take-off and advised the tower not to monitor any aspects of the plane's flight path. A simple, "Roger that and safe travels, was the response."

All normal protocols for take-off were ignored and the black painted plane began its journey down a non-lit runway. It was less than thirty-five seconds when the aircraft lifted off the ground. To those on board, the plane seemingly was in a never-ending climbing mode. Once over the Arafura Sea, the plane began its entry into supersonic speed.

# # #

Amazingly, 1:47:56 later, the plane was on its approach into Seattle at a secret Boeing development airfield.

When the plane landed, Darryl was handed a strange looking phone, and on the other end was his uncle. His uncle asked, "How was your flight?"

Darryl said, "Uncle, I'm not sure. According to my watch, I should still be in flight for the next four hours or so, but yet, I'm allegedly in Seattle, Washington. What's going on?"

"I'm going to need you and your boys to do a job in relationship to the Carbon Factor on the west coast. Me and mine will handle the east coast where we suspect New York City might be the next target. Surprisingly, the people who planted those replica devices out there, and the people that are being followed on the east coast, are the same people we ran out of Wyoming; the carpetbaggers and the deputy."

"Uncle are you saying those guys have changed from stealing farms to destroying cities with the Carbon Factor? I find that hard to believe because it takes a helluva lot of balls to detonate a device that kills people for miles from the point of the detonation. I mean, you just don't decide to stop stealing and then choose to kill thousands of people."

"I know nephew; however, I'm looking at pictures of the people on the east and west coasts and recognized individuals that I have interacted with, negatively. Before I get distracted by giving details, there is something I must demand that you do. You traveled from Australia on a supersonic plane that many don't even know exists. You must huddle with your crew before disembarking from that plane and tell them not to say a damn word about how they got from "A to B" in record time. Any loose chatter about that event will result in your needing to fill that vacancy because that person will never be heard from or seen again."

There was a long pause on the phone and Darryl finally ended the silence by saying, "My people are solid and I place my life in their hands. It will not be a problem on our end."

Before disembarking from the plane, Darryl read the 'riot act' to his people and told them that this mission and their travel was a function of national security and any breach in protocol or small talk about supersonic travel will end with that person being thrown into the billabong or a small creature finding them wherever they may be."

# # #

In New Jersey, the staging ground for Beckmire's group, Utz received credible information about where the two suspects were having dinner. He thought to himself 'what a treat it would be if Beckmire and his group showed up in time for dessert.' He told the Sarge that the two suspects had just entered a restaurant in lower Manhattan and that they could be there in fifteen minutes from the moment they entered the secret hydrofoil that he had at his disposal. Beckmire looked at his group and told them to saddle up and be ready in ten. Asiram said, "We'll be ready in five."

"Daughter-in-law, please enjoy the accommodations and take care of those grandbabies of mine. By the way, you're one beautiful woman. Take care of yourself and I'll take care of the 'idiot spy,' aka, your husband."

She proceeded to where her husband was and said, "I know in New York City, there are more women than there are taxi cabs. Buster, you'd better stay on mission, or I'll play a Bobbitt on your ass."

Everyone in earshot of her screamed. John Lee asked, "What that there Bobbitt thing be about?"

Jilkes replied, "You remember that woman that cut her husband's prize possession off?"

"Oh, goodness! Ms. Asiram just jinxed that there boy. She can't threaten him when we don't know the threat that be waiting on us. She be done have to take that shit back or I ain't going nowhere."

Jilkes walked over to the Sarge and said, "I'm going to need your intervention in this matter that has spooked my country ass friend."

After telling the Sarge what had unsettled Big Country, the Sarge said, "Hell, I'm with him." He walked over to Asiram and said, "You have to take that statement back or half of my guys aren't going to go."

"Ben Beckmire, what on earth are you talking about?"

"I'm talking about the Bobbitt statement."

"Daddy-in-law, I tell him that every time you people go out because I want him to come back to me the way he left."

"Do me a favor. Have a word with John Lee and explain that it's something that you and Zanthius do to show how much you love each other."

After four or so minutes of discussing the issue with John Lee, he uncharacteristically, hugged Asiram, and told her how much she was needed and appreciated. She looked at him and broke into tears.

Zanthius hugged her tight and whispered in her ear, "There is no one or greater pleasure in this world for me my love. You are my dying breath. I love you so much!

# # #

Beckmire's group boarded the hydrofoil that most had never seen or heard of. It was positioned on land when the engines engaged, it meandered over to the water and once on the water, it zipped across the harbor from New Jersey to New York. It was approximately, four minutes from dock to dock.

# # #

Mr. Utz's people had staked out the restaurant and were comfortable knowing that it was not an easy escape route for those inside. He also knew that his people couldn't do the kind of interrogation that Beckmire and his group did and were proficient at.

Once the Sarge's team was spread about the area, his people were initially hesitant but felt comfortable with the coverage being given by Utz's team. The two suspects were sitting in the back of the restaurant with four men allegedly protecting them. The breach was normal, in that laser dots were shined upon each body and, therefore, their resistance was minimized if not nullified.

The two men sat and watched the door, and when the Sarge and Mallory entered it, you would have thought that they just got an early invitation to hell. Both of their heads dropped and they looked as if they had seen the ghost from Christmas past. Mallory walked back first and said, "Hey guys, haven't seen you since our late-night session in Wyoming. What's going on?"

When there was no answer, the Sarge said, "The government types can't do what we can do and get away with it. Listen, take the last bite of your food, and just peaceably come with us."

#

The four persons providing protection were placed in one vehicle and the deputy and carpetbagger were placed in the van with a part of the Sarge's team.

When the group reached the water's edge, Mallory turned to the deputy and asked, "Are you a good or great swimmer?"

The man hastily replied, "I'm neither. I can' swim."

Mallory looked at the carpetbagger and asked, "Are you a good or great swimmer?"

The carpetbagger arrogantly said, "I'm an excellent swimmer."

The Sarge asked Jilkes, "How much do you think that toolbox over there weighs?"

Jilkes attempted to lift it but immediately concluded, "It must weigh about forty pounds."

The Sarge said, "Okay, chain it to the carpetbagger's ankle and let's see how far he can swim with forty pounds of dead weight attached to his arrogant ass."

The carpetbagger attempted to push Jilkes away and that is when John Lee slapped him into an almost unconscious state. He said, "Never try to out muscle my main man. The next thing that I will do, is bleed your ass so that every swimming bacterium in the East River will have a go at your ass."

The carpetbagger said, "Take this chain off me and I will tell you everything you want to know and where to find the mastermind behind this shit."

The Sarge said, "Somehow, I don't believe you. I gave you the only warning that was available to you in Wyoming, yet, here you are again, but this time, you're a part of a crew that kills thousands and decimates entire cities. Nope, I'm not going back on my word and giving you a second chance. Apparently, someone has already made you special. No, Jilkes chain his arrogant ass to that box and push his ass into the water."

The carpetbagger yelled, "Mr. Sarge, in less than seventy-two hours, my employer is going to make 911 look like a mistake with a child's chemistry set, and in that process, he's going to rupture the entire banking system using a product that you had in your control to cover his every movement."

"Who is your employer?"

"You're not going to believe this, but we have never seen or met with him in person. He's an anomaly but he pays extremely well and up front."

The Sarge looked at the guy and inquired, "Do you have any idea what he's trying to achieve with the bombings in Springfield and everywhere else?"

"It's simple, he subscribing to world domination. Listen, in two hours, detonations will occur outside of Moscow and in North Korea. His expectations are that world leaders will come together and unite for an affront on a common enemy. That is when he will set terms. I'm just a puppet, what I am supposed to place, for discovery purposes, was just another product that causes basic systems to halt and reevaluate. He is not your normal individual so it seems, but he has no problem in instituting a scheme that will kill millions of people around the world. As a matter of fact, if that watch on your wrist is correct, he's going to detonate the product in a village near Addis Ababa, in forty minutes or so. He has announced that he hates poor people."

"How do you know so much about timetables and places?"

"I'm assuming, since my associate from the west coast did not check in with me, he is probably under your wraps. He will be able to share the same information as I have because everyone in his network is a part of a live broadcast and orientation. Check with my associate on the west coast. This is public information throughout our network. My concern is that he is without checks and balances. He has no compassion for the poor. Prior to you people storming the restaurant, the deputy and I were having a discussion on how to cancel his ass, especially in light of the fact that our contracts were for real estate development. We were locked into a situation and didn't really have many alternatives to abort it. Every member of my family is on his kill list, as well as the deputy's people. I mean this guy has pictures of nieces and nephews that I didn't know existed. You don't have to put a chain on me and drop me in the river, just tell me how we can get from under this son-of-a-bitch without our entire lineage being destroyed."

After hours of discussion about what the two men actually knew about the administrator, there was agreement and verification that a courier delivered all of the instructions. Larry said, "If we can capture the person delivering the instructions, we certainly become two steps closer to this mad man or woman. These guys are highly paid and expendable mannequins. They don't control any of the action and at the slightest screw up, there's probably someone out there with these two guys in their sights. Perhaps this is the time to consider coalitions rather than seeing how long they can swim with toolboxes attached to their asses."

"Dad, I agree with Larry, a thing that more and more, I'm inclined to do. He makes a lot of sense and is more analytical than most of us in this group. I think he should lead this operation," Zanthius stated.

Mallory shouted, "Are you people out of your fucking mind?" The Sarge threw a hand in the air and Mallory ceased the hostile approach to the discussion.

The Sarge said, "Frankly, I don't know shit about this mess and I'm inclined to agree with Zanthius. Listen, some of us are too old to understand how Microsoft Word works. These guys know this new shit, therefore, why not let them lead the charge, all while checking in with us to make sure we have their bare asses covered?"

Mallory smiled and said, "Oh, I see. I now understand what you see and mean. Please, gentlemen, pardon my outburst. What's your plan?"

Larry adamantly stated, "Mallory, we don't have a plan. We just got here like you, and we're trying to figure out relationships. I think the days of gutting, skinning, and decapitations are hopefully behind us as a team. There are other virtuous measures that can be employed to help people do the right thing and give descriptive information. Oh, and Dad, letting me lead this op is purely a function of your other son's mindset. I had no idea he was trying to pull a coup on you. I'm just kidding. I think what he should have proposed is that you let he and I attempt to think this one through before we plunge people into the east river with tools strapped to their asses."

"Larry, you, and your brother walked us through that mess in Asia successfully and without a single injury. I'm looking for more of those kind of actions as we move forward, as opposed to going in with guns blazing and people being injured in our group. Zanthius is sometimes single sighted but on point with his message but often stinging with its presentation. I suggest that you two give a call to Darryl and coordinate what methods you want to employ to corroborate the east and west coast stories by these co-conspirators. In the meantime, we have members of their team, and we'll use them or dump them if there are any inconsistencies in their stories."

# # #

On the New Jersey side of the river, Beckmire and his people began the initial interrogation of their captives without the use of a threat or torture. John Lee said, "I guess we'll have to brush their hair, massage their scalps, and make sure they're comfortable next."

McArthur replied, "Don't you get tired of abusing people? Isn't this a better and more humane way of relating to our captives?"

"Pigshit! I'd like to take his shoes off and soak his feet in vinegar or whatever people use to relax them there toes and then pull out my blade and do a foot dance with his ass until my blade goes into that foot of his and then into the floor. I'll relax his ass all right, and by the time he tells them there boys his name, I'll have addresses, next of kin, bank accounts numbers, and everything damn thing else that matters to them."

From the back of the room a voice screamed, "John Lee, calm the fuck down and stop whining like a little sheep. Brother let's try something new. Instead of pigshit, how about horseshit, but whatever we do, let's try to minimize our inflicting trauma on everyone we engage," Jilkes stated.

"Now, when he yells at me like that, I have nothing else to say because he done stated his piece and unless I totally disagree with him, then I just shut the hell up and do as his black ass tells me to do."

"John Lee, that's it. Let it go and say no more!" Jilkes mandated.

Larry walked over to John Lee and asked, "Can I have a private word with you?"

"I guess you'd better get me out of here before I have to beat his ass again."

In the hallway, John Lee appeared to be on the verge of crying and Larry noticed his eyes tearing up. Larry said, "Give me and my brother a chance to do things differently without a lot of blood and guts all over the place. Will you at least support us on this adventure and see how and if it works out?"

"Since you done pulled that job off in Asia, I know I can trust you and your brother. I just want out of this because I know one of these times, we might have to bury someone and I would be awful mad if something happen to my minority friend."

"John Lee, you do know that you have a lot of minority friends, don't you?"

"Yeah, I do, but I only have one minority friend named Jilkes."

"Listen, give me and Zanthius the opportunity to keep us all safe. If we fail, then I guess it's you and me, and that ain't going to be pretty."

"Well, hell, Larry. I ain't going up against you because you try to keep us safe. Why you want to pick a fight?"

"I was not picking a fight, John Lee. I was encouraging you to use me as the fall guy if all goes wrong."

#

The Sarge in the meantime began asking the captives questions and by and large was satisfied with their responses. Even when separated, the deputy and the carpetbagger gave identical information about their assignments and those of the people on the west coast. The deputy said, "If you ask those guys and gals on the west coast their mission, it might sound like a rehearsed speech and that is because we were given a script to remember. However, if you realize that we've stepped into a barrel of shit to earn a lot of money, then what's sadly at stake, is our families being murdered, and horrifically. There is no game being played here because we want out and can't find the door to exit without a lot of collateral damage to our families. The only thing that I know that wasn't rehearsed by us was the use of a simple name—Walter." The entire room came to attention and the Sarge slowly approached the deputy and said, "I want you to be careful and clear when you repeat what you just said. What was the name that you heard?"

"Somewhere along the way, one of the guys mentioned the name Walter, and that was the only thing that was not rehearsed."

"When and in what context was it utilized?"

"Two weeks before that carnage in Springfield, there was a truck parked outside of this desolate place where we met to discuss assignments. Printed on the truck, were the words, 'prosthetics can make it happen again for you.' I didn't pay much attention to it, and as a matter of fact, after realizing that we had stepped into some deep shit, I assumed that it was a camouflage. Anyway, I went to the men's room and entered a stall. A few minutes later, the door opened, and one of three men clearly said, "that guy is the bionic man. Walter can walk and use what's left of his arms." Anyway, into each of our accounts, $1 million was placed for the simple tasks as outlined in our interview. We were all charged with finding real estate that was suitable for development of a Silicon Valley kind of place. He and I found Springfield, Massachusetts and you see what's left of that place. We have been scared and responsive to any demands since then."

Mallory hastily interjected, "Did you ever see this person?"

"We never saw anyone other than the recruits and security. When I mentioned the name Walter, everyone froze and appeared interested in what I was saying. When I mentioned the word bionic, that really got your attention. Who is this Walter and what is he to this group?"

"Deputy, did we capture you, or did you suddenly arrest us? If I, were you, I would be hopeful of this kind of dialogue without the use of torture. Am I making myself clear?" The Sarge inquired.

The deputy said, "Crystal clear."

When Mr. Utz showed up, the Sarge asked, "Do you have some important intel that we should have?"

"Sarge, what are you talking about? Everything that I know about this matter has been shared with you. You have the two people in custody, did they tell you something that I perhaps neglected to share with you?"

"Utz, as a matter of fact they did, but I'm more interested in your notions of intel. For example, do you have any intel about Walter Lassiter?"

"Sarge, are you hallucinating or something? You butchered that guy and left him on the side of the road. What's going on?"

"Let me que up a tape of our conversation with those captives and let you hear for yourself, if in fact, this is the same person from yesteryear."

Five minutes after Utz listened to the two men discuss the only information about the person who might be the chief of terror, he said, "There is no way in hell that this could be your cousin. You cut his arms and legs off, and didn't you blind the poor bastard?"

"Utz, if this is that guy, then that would make me number one on his hit list, wouldn't it?"

Utz looked at the Sarge, internalized each statement and considered the dastardly deed the Sarge did to his cousin and decided to put out an all-points bulletin (apb) and see what came back. He said, "For all of our sakes, I truly hope your cousin died, has been buried, and his remains can be viewed by us along with his DNA certified. Perhaps he's not in control of this situation and that person Cherendolof occupies the decision-making seat."

Zanthius looked at his watch and said, "Dad, according to those guys in the other room a detonation in Africa should be happening in the next five to ten minutes. Mr. Utz, is there any way you can confirm a detonation from your sources located in and around Addis Ababa?"

Mr. Utz looked at Zanthius, went into the outer room, pulled out his cell phone, and dialed a number. Once connected, a robotic sounding voice stated, "In Addis Ababa, an explosion of epic magnitude occurred ten minutes ago."

Mr. Utz entered the room where the Sarge was and stated, "Ten minutes ago, there was a detonation of some kind of bomb in Addis Ababa. Too early to estimate casualties."

The Sarge said, "The two captives said that in a matter of hours, detonations would occur outside of Moscow and inside of North Korea. You have any back-channel connections that you can alert and gain some brownie points?"

Utz looked at him sternly and walked out of the room. He placed a series of calls and was thanked for his concern. When he walked back into the room where the Sarge was standing, two cell phones began to buzz simultaneously. It was the carpetbagger and the deputy's phones. Each were presented with graphic pictures of their families being butchered. The men screamed as they watched their children summarily executed, and their wives violated. The Sarge told Jilkes to cut the restraints off of the two men. He said, "Guys, sorry for your loss. I'll arrange transportation for you guys back to Manhattan."

"Fuck Manhattan, let us work for you until we find this deranged son-of-a-bitch," the deputy requested.

"Guys try to find your families and do right by them. Don't go down that revenge road against this group. They seem to be many and everywhere. Sorry for your loss."

# # #

On the west coast, Darryl's captives viewed their loved ones being massacred and violated as well. Mallory called him and told him to let the people go and to await further instructions because there is unsubstantiated information that

your uncle, the bad one, is somehow involved in this situation.
Darryl said, "Not funny Mallory. My other uncle butchered
him and left him blind. How can he mount this kind of
action?"

"The name Walter came up in our interrogation and these
guys saw a truck with a prosthetics sign on it. Purely
circumstantial at this point, but I can tell that the Sarge is
rattled by this information as well as you should be. Be on
guard and post guards and keep your location private. By the
way, how is Sue Lyn doing?"

"She's quite the trooper and has worked out so many
different things for the people back home. I'm really proud of
her. Mallory, please have my uncle give me a call soon.
Thanks."

CHAPTER SIXTEEN

In Addis Ababa, the explosion rattled villages near and far. The devastation was enormous with the loss of life exceeding ten thousand people who were at the epicenter of the blast and another three to five thousand who were in the reach of the enigma: the Carbon Factor. The scene was horrific, as the emaciated corpses were like fallen leaves in autumn—everywhere. The bodies of the unfortunate souls who were at the locus of the detonation, resembled what happens when lyophilization or freeze-drying is performed. It was as though a giant vacuum cleaner sucked the essence out of each victim.

In Russia, the explosion was greater than that of Addis Ababa but was in an area that was almost uninhabited. The detonation was massive, and the loss of life was great, even though the area was not a bustling metropolis. The Russian loss of life was less than five thousand people but even still, it was five thousand human beings who did nothing to antagonize or threaten the mastermind behind the bombings. Like Addis Ababa, the area in North Korea that was imploded consumed as many as six thousand individuals and mostly all were at the point of detonation.

The entire world was fearful about where the next blast would occur. Besides, everyone knows you can't just walk into North Korea or Russia, and place an ordnance, detonate it, and leave without a hitch. If nothing else would bring the world leaders together, the randomness and unpredictable detonations of the Carbon Factor was first and foremost in every nation's eyes.

# # #

In France, rioting was rocking the nation because of the implementation of a carbon tax, a tax on all fossil fuels and ultimately, a way of reducing and eliminating the use of carbon-based fuels. On huge monitors on the Champs-Élysée, near the Arc de Triumph, and on most television stations, a booming voice could be heard over the firing of tear gas cannisters and rock throwing. It was Victor Cherendolof who calmly said, "I love large gatherings like this one. It makes my work so much easier. The carbon tax, you will pay, because it will keep me from annihilating strategic parts of Paris. I suggest that you all leave now and let this silly notion of a tax be handled by me. Afterall, I believe in the use of carbon. Hang around and you will witness my resolve."

Mass hysteria set in and people began to hastily retreat from the area and head for what they thought would be a safe haven. However, the Carbon Factor could penetrate deep into the heart of a city and beyond, as illustrated in Addis Ababa, Springfield, Massachusetts, Russia, and North Korea.

Instead of the police continuing to fire teargas cannisters, they switched gears and began to direct massive numbers of people out of the city. There was a concern of another type, in the air—the Carbon Factor. Literally, millions of people began a mass exodus from Paris proper and the surrounding suburbs to places further into the interior of the country. This stimulated the thinking that the bomber was herding people like cattle and knew where they were likely to be.

As the French President watched the mass exodus, his astute wife said, "Looks as if people are being pushed towards the middle. That would make it easy for a detonation to kill millions of French men and women. I think you should order people to move from east to west and not directly south. It's a cattle game where you herd them, direct them, and slaughter them." The president looked curiously at his wife, and then ordered his people to stop directing people south and move them east and west as well.

In the confines of the bomber's quarters, Cherendolof stated to his followers, "Now this would be a monumental statement. Is there any way of placing the product in an area that would give me a maximum kill zone?" The response he received was not to his liking. He was told that there was no product left and that it would have to be manufactured. He was reminded that once the essential ingredients are assembled, detonation had to occur within twenty-four hours because of the unstableness of the formula. The master bomber announced, "Look at this missed opportunity. This would have been a magnificent and signature statement, and no doubt the response, quite conciliatory."

On the television, Larry watched the herding of the people in Paris, over, and over, and turned to the carpetbagger and asked, "How were you guys recruited and how are you contacted? I guess what I'm asking is there anything standard or is everything randomly done?"

The man was unresponsive and naturally so. He had watched his family butchered by his employer. Larry turned to one of Utz's people and asked, is there a bar in this place?" Larry was directed to the other end of the hall.

Larry asked Zanthius to accompany him and the two guys to the bar where the four men began to de-stress by drinking alcohol. The deputy ordered two Coors Lights. After several rounds of alcohol, the deputy blurted out, "I think I want another one of those pastrami sandwiches."

Larry stated, "I would love to have one of those myself with a kosher dill pickle and mustard on my sandwich."

The deputy announced, "I believe that deli had the best and biggest sandwiches that I had ever seen."

This caught Larry's attention who asked, "How many of those things have you had. You know when you eat too many of those things, the next thing you're going to have is a damn heart attack."

Everyone broke into laughter, but the carpetbagger said, "I didn't like all that meat piled mile high on the rye bread. It was as though it was someone's chance to evaluate us each time we went there."

Larry inquired, "How many times did you go there and were the same people always there?"

The deputy screamed, "That redhead was there at the counter each time when we ordered. I'd recognize his ass anywhere because I thought he was looking at me like I was into some weird shit."

The carpetbagger chimed in and said, "You know what? You're absolutely right. I thought he was kind of funny but I thought he was checking me out. I mean it didn't matter to me one way or the other, I just thought he was trying to hustle us. As I think about it, he probably got our DNA off of the utensils. After eating, I thought he worked there because he blatantly came over and started picking up trash. The owner of the place told another customer, that he was harmless and a little slow."

Zanthius asked, "Where is this place?"

"Over on 62nd and 2nd Avenue," the deputy stated.

Zanthius asked, "How did you find yourselves at the same place each time?"

"We were told that we could be seen coming, going, and noticed if we were followed."

"That doesn't make sense to me," Zanthius stated.

Larry said, "It makes sense to me because it's not that busy on that side of town. It's not like they're walking down 5th Avenue and 33rd, and if they can see them coming and going, so can the cameras in the area. Mr. Utz, can your agency commandeer the cameras in that area so that we can discreetly look at the comings and goings in that area?"

"Let me give a call. Get back to you in a minute."

# # #

Two hours later, the crew were watching video of the deli on 2nd Avenue and looking for any suspicious person or persons entering or loitering around the place. Zanthius after receiving instructions asked, "Can someone please define and describe what a suspicious person or persons look like?" Larry tapped Zanthius on the shoulder and pointed to his right. It was a mirror and Zanthius laughed.

Utz indicated that his sources revealed that the FBI had conducted surveillance on the place for over a month, looking for a member of the mob who would rendezvous with his lover. As the group watched the boring and unedited tapes, the deputy yelled, "Stop! He looked at the carpetbagger and said, "Look at the guy with the hoodie half on and off. He was in that place every time that we were." The carpetbagger looked at the still photo and said, "Look in the window, that guy was always there as well."

Larry yelled, "Hold up a minute. My name is Larry, that's my brother Zanthius, my dad Mr. Beckmire, and that's Mr. Mallory next to him are the two brothers from different mothers, John Lee and Jilkes. I can't keep referring to you guys as the carpetbagger and the deputy. What are your names?

The carpetbagger said, "My name is Sylvester, Sylvester Smoot, and the deputy's name is DeAndre, DeAndre Ridge."

"Now that we have that formality out of the way, what was so significant about the guy in the window?"

Sylvester Smoot said, "As soon as the guy in the hoodie would order, he would go to the men's room, come back, and pay, and the guy in the window would leave his seat and head to the men's room. I only noticed that because it seemed automatic, in that it was rehearsed or planned. After watching the interaction, on three occasions, it occurred to me that they must be passing love letters."

The Sarge looked at Utz and asked if they could get facial recognition on the guy in the hoodie and the one sitting in the window and he replied that it was in the works.

Smoot stated, "Oh, and that woman just walking into the place, is going to give the guy in the window a really sensuous kiss, watch."

They began to watch the tape again, and bingo, the woman kissed the guy in the window, and it was indeed intense to watch.

Zanthius screamed at the top of his lungs and declared, "I would know that fucking kisser, anywhere! That woman, my friends, is Helga Spengatsenburg. She must have nineteen lives. She's been buried, shot, cut to pieces and yet I'll bet Larry's life on it, that's Helga. I know that walk, and the odd way she touches you before she throws one of those mesmerizing kisses on you. She just passed something to that guy via that kiss and that is why the kiss is so stimulating. He's adjusting to a foreign object being placed in his mouth, while enjoying the essence of her pressing body and kiss against his, and she's reacting to eliminating something out of her mouth. Can you zoom in on her face?"

"Zanthius, why are you quick to bet my life on your suppositions?" Larry asked.

"Larry, it's a manner of speech. I wouldn't bet your life on anything other than figuring out how this shit all plays out. I know you have some theories that the group has yet to consider. Now might be a good time to expose them."

"You honor me with all that flattery. However, I'm not ready to throw out a bunch of hypotheticals now. However, I am interested in knowing whether there have been ownership changes, reconfiguration of boards of companies, that have large interests in fossil fuels. In short, this thing is not about killing us as a group, random individuals, or world domination, by having the ability of imploding devastating devices that can kill thousands. No brother, there's no profit in that and, therefore, his or her real motives will come to the forefront sooner than later. However, if you destabilize certain habits, you get the opportunity to charge a "transgression tax." I think of the carbon tax in France as more of a "transgression tax." Listen, the whole world believes in climate change except for that blonde guy in the White House. We have been corrupting the environment for ages by the use of a fuel that no one knew would come back and bite us in the ass. Climate change is real, and those who say it's not, probably have a vested interest in the status quo. It has been a staple for China, North Korea, and Russia. Until recently, it has been a main stay in America. So, with a "transgression tax" you can enjoy the harmful benefits of fossil fuels now, but however, you will pay out of your ass later. Like going to a house of sin and having the time of your life, until you forget who you're dealing with and go diving into the ocean without a tank of air. When you get home and have to perform, you'll need more than air after you pass some "bad mojo" to your partner. Carbon is plentiful and cheap but the world wants to decarbonize and build an economy that has no use for carbon but they don't want to pay for it. That "transgression tax" to me is small at this time. In twenty-five to thirty years from now, it should be at the 2,000 percent increased level. Fossil fuels are environmentally detrimental to the longevity of this planet. That's why I want to know about the change in leadership or board memberships for companies that are largely focused on fossil fuel. I think if we focus there, we might find this fiend and end his reign of terror before he harms more innocent people."

As he considered what he had stated, Larry said, "One more thought; the new technology is beginning to take carbon's place at an admittedly slow pace, but probably will increase each year. For example, the Twasla car; good to look at, probably great to drive, zero emissions on the environment, and a footprint that can be recharged and utilized over and over again without using fossils. In short, I think our bomber and/or his group, are more concerned about cornering the market on fossils in the short term by creating enough chaos and then probably doing a complete about face when he can capture the hydrogen and electrical based infrastructure. This mass murdering is all about the "Benjamins."

Everyone in earshot of Larry was amazed and astonished by his off the cuff presentation. Zanthius asked, "Are there any questions of our resident genius? One question per person, Mr. Larry has more cogitating to do in order to figure out whether his hypotheses are correct or he's just jumping for straws. I tend to think that he has something worth investigating and that's where I want to put my emphasis, Pop!"

The Sarge looked at Mallory, Jilkes, John Lee, Zanthius, and Utz, and requested that they meet for a minute in the lounge. Once in the lounge, John Lee said, "I didn't understand one damn word he said. When did he learn another language?"

"John Lee, he's just analytical and sees things different than you and I. We see the damn enemy and we just do him. He sees a human that he might be able to learn something from. I mean that's in simple terms, but the shit he just finished espousing, left me feeling like you; when did he learn that new language," the Sarge stated.

The Sarge continued and said, "I'm going to let you guys in on a little secret. If you leave him alone with an issue, he will come back with a solution. I never try to put him far out front because it can be hard to bring him back. What just happened in the other room, he leaves people trying to define one syllable words and the polysyllable ones are too big to decipher. I used to challenge him accidently, and damn, the answers were always above my pay grade or understanding capability. I asked you guys out here to inquire, did any of you get a semblance of what he was talking about?"

Utz vehemently stated, "He's your damn son. Can't you give us a heads up on what we just went through?"

"I'll simply say, Larry is onto something and Zanthius, I need you to spend every possible waking moment with him because he can get way out there. You saw how he insisted that there were more steps to getting the formula in Asia when you thought that all was understood and was waiting for you to make a grand entrance. He is different, and as such, he gets out there and someone he trusts must be close to rescue him from himself."

"Dad, I'm here for him and the team. Let's allow him to do his thing tonight and then tomorrow, we'll zoom in on his new thoughts, if in fact, his concepts or beliefs have changed. I think he's just gathering facts right now and will have to be questioned to the void. I know how to do that with him because we certainly solved the riddle of the Marco Polo Hotel."

# # #

On the west coast, Sue Lyn asked one of their captives, "How on earth do you subscribe to killing thousands of people?"

After a moment to reflect on the question, one of the guys said, "I did not know I was going to be a part of a program that is designed to kill millions of people."

"Oh, this program as you call it, is designed to kill millions?" Sue Lyn asked.

The guy looked at his partner and said, "Here's the deal as I believe it to be. This isn't about killing people; however, they are considered an inconsequential price. From what we accidently stumbled across in a lab in Yakima, the whole killing thing is just a ploy. Don't know if you people read the Economist or Barron's. In this week's editions, there was a note from the old guy who makes short statements about the market and the world, he said, 'a lump of coal in your stocking is one thing, but a coal stock or two, now you're talking.' Anyway, guys, there is a buy rating on coal. Although the mastermind is willing to sacrifice millions of people, this is about cornering the market on a product that no one wants to use. Once the switch is flipped, these people will be in power to be the dominion to run the world. To me, this isn't about revenge for a brother or friends, he could give a shit! No, this is about money and these people will use any method to leverage the outcome that they want. Think about it? The only ransom message has been about turning over some old guys from Viet Nam to the leader and even that has not been mandated again. I think once the masterminds realized the impact that the Carbon Factor could have, they began to think bigger. Apparently, this was the first successful detonation of the Carbon Factor. We are aware of what the Russians tried to do and how they continuously slaughtered their scientists and laboratories. No one knew that the detonation in Springfield would have the outcome that it did. There were no real scientists that assembled the devices and that knew where to precisely distance each unit from the others. No, it was all done by guess work. No one realized that the device would suckle everything hydrogen until it was terminated by distance."

Sue Lyn said, "Wait a minute. How do you know so much about the mechanics of how this thing worked?"

"Because I am the person who was hired to do an experiment on the use of fossil fuels and hydrogen. It was only after I received a picture of my family in bondage that I realized that I was in the midst of something terrible."

"I need you to tell my uncle on the east coast exactly what you have told me. Can you do that?"

"Listen, our families are in danger and I'm sure they realize by now that we have been compromised and are being held. We have to check-in, in less than twenty minutes and we must be in a location that is approved by them. As I see it, we're thirty minutes away from that location."

Sue Lyn yelled, "Darryl, get the vehicles ready, we have to head across town in record time."

#

The group pulled near a coffee shop where the two suspects were told to make their appearances and check-in. Darryl cautioned them about double dealing and the odds of surviving their wrath. He suggested that their first mission should be to locate their families, if in fact, this ruse was not discovered. As the two men walked towards the coffee shop, a car pulled up and two men, one who was in the front, and the other in the rear passenger's seat of a vehicle, sprayed the men and the coffee shop with bullets.

Michael, who was behind the wheel yelled, "Shall we pursue and capture?" Darryl, who watched the action was slow to respond.

Sue Lyn said, "I want those people alive. That wasn't a random hit, they targeted those two people but sprayed the place to make it look as if there was a beef with the coffee shop. I want the third car to remain and lend assistance to the wounded."

Michael and the other vehicle began to follow the shooters car from afar. On a clear stretch of open road, he told the other vehicle to incapacitate the car and that his crew would fire on it until they surrendered.

It was a textbook maneuver. Desmond performed a high-speed operation and tapped the rear of the fleeing vehicle and spun it out of control. Michael and his crew fired continuously at the front of the vehicle until the driver and two passengers got out with their hands in the air. Michael walked over to the driver and cold-cocked him. He told his people to search them, bind them, and place hoods over their heads. With the two gunmen in sight, he pulled out his weapon and shot each man in the foot, literally blowing their baby toes completely off. Each man's foot was subsequently wrapped in heavy plastic.

Approximately five miles from the scene of the abduction, he pulled near a freeway entrance but decided it was too public for what he had in mind. He continued to drive and decided to head towards the airport. Near the airport there was a stretch of road where people waited to pick up arriving passengers. He entered the rear of the van and asked, "Why the hell did you shoot those people at the coffee house?"

One of the captives, who was completely under stress as a result of being shot in the foot, managed to say, "Man, I don't know what you're talking about. Why did you shoot us? We need to go to the hospital."

Darryl inquired, "Does anyone have a knife? I need a knife."

Michael asked, "Boss, will this do?"

Darryl knowing that the captives had hoods on their heads, and couldn't see what was going on stated, "This isn't a knife. This is a machete. Why do you keep this thing? Damn, its sharp as hell! Let's bleed this guy first and then let the other two witness what a mess we made of their friend. Darryl then ran a scraper tool with a razor blade across the guy's leg and he screamed for mercy.

Darryl asked, "Did you show those people at the coffee house any mercy? I don't think so. It looked as if you sprayed the place for maximum effect. Why was this done and who paid you to do this? Now, before you give me horseshit, I'm going to cut your pants open and expose your penis and that is going to be the thing that I will summarily, cut off. Oh, and by the way, I'm going to do the same thing to your accomplice's. Make up your mind but realize, any bullshit will result in you being neutered. If that word is hard to define, then I'll make it simple; it means that I'm going to cut your dicks off and leave them in your mouths. Now, tell me everything I need to know about why you sprayed that place with bullets, who paid you to do that, and where I can find your boss?"

# # #

In the midst of the chaos, one the men asked, "Are you going to kill me?"

"I don't think so, unless you're withholding information, that would necessitate me doing some mean things to you. The local authorities are going to arrest you and we work for them. We do their dirty work if you know what I mean. Any bullshit presented by you people will be met with a grave response. In the prison that you will be sent to, we will have people awaiting our instructions. You fuck up, and mate, you will be stabbed in the eye. You're going to prison mate, not a retirement home. However, you tell us what you know and I'll make sure you keep both eyes," Darryl announced.

# # #

The United Nations Security Council held an emergency meeting in New York and it was agreed that nations should join forces in order to combat the Carbon Factor random attacks. The Secretary General felt that the best nation to coordinate a response/investigation was the United States. France, Germany, Canada, and the United Kingdom, felt that this was not a wise choice because it was alleged that the Carbon Factor was made in America. The American Ambassador to the United Nations vehemently disavowed that notion but confirmed that it had people who were close to the situation and were probably the best suited to conclude this chaos. He also hinted that the origin of the Carbon Factor was more likely Russian than anywhere else. Of course, the Russian Ambassador denied that allegation. The America Ambassador asked, "How many laboratories were destroyed while trying to perfect the formula for the Carbon Factor?" There were only stares and no verbal replies.

An aide to the Secretary General entered the room and whispered in his ear. Whatever it was, got his immediate attention. He announced to the group, "I think Mr. Cherendolof is about to make some demands. As wide screen TVs were lowered in the chamber, Mr. Cherendolof's hazy picture appeared and he stated, "So nice of all of you to be in the same room at the same time. Mr. Ambassador to France, I am trying to decide whether or not, I want to make the strongest statement to date in your country. People are being evacuated from Paris central and into parts of the country that are wide open. As you know, I'm surprisingly good at calculating distance, potential damage, and, therefore, I'm going to flip a coin that will decide whether I make history in the number of people killed from a single act of terrorism, and in record time. I have been having this soliloquy with myself and it's like watching an interception at a football game and seeing the runner make it from the five-yard line of the opposing team to his own end zone or watching that Harris guy make that Immaculate Reception. Now that's miraculous and thrilling to watch a player dodge opponents, securely enter his own territory, and then break the plane of his own goal. I say that, to say, after I flip this coin, oh, by the way, Mr. Ambassador, how many people would you guess have left Paris and are in those open areas, east and west of Paris? Don' bother guessing! I'm thinking that according to the protocols for evaluating and populating groups, I'm betting that there are at least, in that area, and fleeing from Paris, 500,000 to one million people. I'm not sure that would make me a villain or a hero. Or perhaps a madman, a terrorist, or the devil. I'm not sure which one I want to be referred to as. Anyway, let's flip the coin. Now, Mr. Ambassador, I'm going to select a side of the coin for you. I'm just thinking that you guys will always pick tails. Therefore, I'm going to select heads for me. Are we ready?"

The ambassador from the United States asked, "Before you flip the coin, what is it you expect to achieve from this activity?"

There was twenty seconds of silence when the voice on the other end said, "I'm not quite sure. I mean I have all of the money I want; I have power over the dominions, I'm in control of my existence, and I can control the fate of millions of people with the flip of a coin. As such, the coin is going airborne."

The coin was flipped high into the air and hit what one would believe was a ceiling. It landed, rolled, and settled between the side of a refrigerator and another stainless-steel looking cabinet. The mastermind yelled, "Oh hell, I can't see which side won. I'll have to flip it again."

The American Ambassador said, "When you flip a coin, all efforts must be exhausted to see the final placement of the coin. If you flip again, we will recognize that you are not a person that adheres to the rules of his game."

Again, there was silence that lasted in excess of thirty seconds. Suddenly, the voice said, "If nothing else, in these situations and negotiations, we must have protocols. Therefore, I agree, and will not flip another coin, and will allow you to watch on camera where the coin is and in real time what is moved to show the undisturbed final resting place of the flipped coin. Be mindful, if the coin is resting with heads up, then there will be an immediate detonation of my devices. No negotiations, just the sheer horror of millions of your people being annihilated before your very eyes. You have suckered me into submission on this matter but I doubt this opportunity will occur in the future."

Anyone and everyone who had access to a television, mobile devices, internet and any other medium, watched as the mastermind had his people orchestrate the movement of what looked to be, refrigeration units. After twenty-five minutes of moving objects that were not relevant to the coin flip, a before and after picture was presented to the world. The mastermind pointed to a time sequenced camera that was logged into a real time clock. He arrogantly announced, "I should be in control of this event, but I have somehow subscribed to the notion of protocols and traditional practices. The pictures you're seeing are of people clearing the way to see what position the coin made its final resting stance. It's in real time and I'm sure I don't have much credibility, but I will say that it is as sterile as a newborn baby's ass. Now, there are three cameras capturing the area and will focus on the coin. I'm not sure why I am doing this, but Mr. American pulled my chain and I saw the merits of his presentation. As you watch the final results of this hunt, so are my people who control the switches. Be there no illusion, if I win, at the moment of acknowledgement, there will be a detonation. If I do not prevail, oh well, then, I will recant and not come forward again until I'm ready to lay out how I want my world to operate under my rule."

As three independent cameras focused on the area where the coin rested, they all captured its position—it rested aside a stainless-steel cabinet and a trapped mouse. Now, if the mouse were dead, the coin could fall in any direction. If the mouse made a sudden movement to escape the trap, it would move the coin to the right or to whatever side that was dominate. The problem was that no camera could capture the prevailing side of the coin. The mastermind after viewing the cameras said, "This seems too complicated to be a protocol. I prefer to flip another coin in an area that is contained. This looks as if a mouse, a cabinet, and luck control this outcome."

"Monsieur, I am requesting that you honor the protocols that you accepted and agreed upon. I will pray that the outcome of the movement and placement of the coin is favorable to my people. Monsieur, that is all I request."

Fifteen seconds later, the silence was broken. "Monsieur, I find you a credible opponent and I will not change the game in the middle of it. As you can see, this is clearly the most important decision that you will ever make. I mean man, your head of state or no one else is allowed in this game. It is you and me! As such, I will give you one orientation modification if you like—left or right movement," Mr. Cherendoloff announced.

"Sir, I do not require any modification to the scene. Please, have the equipment moved and keep the cameras honorably placed so that the entire world will know what kind of person with whom they are dealing."

The stainless-steel unit was moved, the mouse was obviously dead, the coin began to fall towards what appeared to be the heads side, but that movement was nullified and subsequently rectified by three fleeing mice who disturbed the orientation of the coin and sent it spinning to its final resting place. The coin concluded on 'tails.' At the flip of a coin, nearly one million French men and women were spared. What a wonderful game; 'coin flipping'!

Without further ado, the mastermind screamed, "Never again will I negotiate or get sucked into one of your silly rituals. I will honor my agreement without any further hostilities in this part of the world. However, if you hear from me again, it will be with solid demands. I will conquer this world. As a matter of fact, I will flip a coin for each of the seven continents without people watching. Those who fail to win with the illustration of tails, will be my next port of operation. As a matter of goodwill, I will make this continent last, since I almost made history, accidently. Good day!"

The mastermind knew that he had corralled the French and couldn't destroy them because he didn't have the product to finish the job. He marveled at what history would say about him if he had been able to pull such a dastardly activity off. The person who gave him the same-sided coin, was summoned, and summarily executed. His reasons for terminating the person was simple; he only had a two-sided tails coin. He should have presented him with a two-sided heads coin.

The UN Security Council disseminated the tapes of the coin flip throughout its intelligence gathering divisions and the Ambassador from Canada said, "I know much that we do is classified and only sanctioned amongst members. However, I think it is time to turn this matter over to a group of people who I had the pleasure of working with from afar, in Viet Nam, and who by the way, have been accused of selling the Carbon Factor formula on the open market. We need people who don't play by the rules, who are not Blue Water, or one of those other mercenary groups that have a thirty percent profit margin included in everything they do. We should reach out to those people who have literally and quietly, provided another level of protection for this country, and the world for that matter. I'm talking about Sergeant Beckmire and his merry band of followers. We limit our exposure, liability, and involvement."

The American Ambassador said, "I appreciate you giving my people their proper due, but these guys have aged liked decomposing corpses. They survived the alleged events of the past because they somehow learned how to use an Iphone. I wouldn't put much stock in the hyperbole that precedes them or the amplified stories of their heroics. Those people are in their late sixties and early to mid-seventies."

The Canadian Ambassador asked, "Mr. Ambassador, how old are you? If I had to guess, I would say, you were approaching the ripe old age of seventy."

"Sir, I am nowhere near that age and I'm often told that I look good for a person my age."

"Mr. Ambassador, my question remains. How old are you?"

"My age has nothing to do with this conversation and what almost just happened in France."

The Canadian Ambassador stated, "You answered my question in an indirect manner. People tell you how good you look for your age. Can you imagine if you had their training and experience, what you would look like and could do? You're minimizing their talents because of the artificialness of age. Look at yourself and think about the possibilities."

The French Ambassador asked the British and Italian Ambassadors if they could freely speak about experiences their countries had with terrorist groups that the aforementioned group addressed. The British Ambassador stated that the old people were in and out before they had a chance to thank them. He plugged his MI-6 with intelligence gathering but was quickly interrupted by the Italian Ambassador who flatly rejected the admonitions.

He affirmatively stated, "If the dinosaurs had listened to your people, you would have lost half of your bourgeoisie society in a single event. No, Ambassador, your MI-6 were as wrong as the people who planned that massacre. You should give credit where credit is due. In my case, those dinosaurs, saved a significant and troubling part of my country from devastation. They acted swiftly, professionally, and disappeared immediately after they neutralized the dogs of terrorism. I for one suggest and agree with the Canadian Ambassador that we use the proven dinosaurs and minimize our exposure. They work knowing full well if they fail, the onus is completely and solely on them. Also, if I might mention the fact, they had planned to do the work in your country for free until your MI-6 types attempted to be their boss, directors, and leave all negative results on them. You do remember that little obstacle, don't you?"

The American Ambassador interjected, "I'm not familiar with them or their work but I will reach out to them via our intelligence agencies."

"The Italian Ambassador vehemently announced, "That would be a terrible mistake for all involved. They don't respect your agencies because it is your very agencies that placed fake news that they were the ones who sold this deadly bomb to the sickies of the world. If I'm not mistaken, your agencies aligned them with a head-hunter in Africa, you know the one, that cuts his people's hands and heads off if he suspects they are not loyal."

The Canadian Ambassador exclaimed, "Gentlemen, we escaped a tragedy in France because of a flip of a coin. A damn single flip of a coin! The balls of my American counterpart to demand protocol was simply the gutsiest bet that I have ever witnessed. With a fire breathing monster blowing smoke, he calmly played the game and we won."

The French Ambassador said, "Messieurs, I'm not aware of this group of people who apparently prevented terrorist activities in your countries. However, I do believe in fate and, therefore, I'm going to hedge my bet further with people who you say understand the political and personal cost of failure. Our people are fighters of a different kind, and do not understand urban politics, especially in light of the fact that we have a large immigrant population. That population brings with it, its own religion, social and political issues, unemployment, language, socialization, food, sanitation, and two hundred other problems. I need a group of innocuous looking people who can help catch a guy who is willing to create another holocaust for some damn unholy reason. Forget their age, forget their cost, if they can catch and kill this fucking guy, then we in France will build a damn statue on Champs-Élysées, honoring them."

CHAPTER SEVENTEEN

Darryl called his uncle and reported to him the essence of his interactions with the three people who shot up the coffee house. He told his uncle that the only thing that he couldn't figure out was a reference to Spain that one of the shooters had in his possession. He informed his uncle that two of the men spoke Spanish and the third was clearly a rented driver.

# # #

Darryl reported to his uncle, "Our first major deposit of precious minerals was made without a hitch with the help of Mr. Utz. The product was gathered, shipped, and accounted for in an over-the-top security process. He expressed an unusual euphoria for the success of the first transport and also gave kudos to Sue Lyn, who designed, developed, and created the first prototype of the impregnable light weight safe.

# # #

On the east coast, the Sarge asked his people if there were any written or spoken words referencing Spain that they heard or saw from any of their captives? John Lee astutely asked, "Now, why would we be looking for something written in that there language that we don't speak or understand?

Jilkes responded, "Sorry Sarge, internationally, he is still in the dark. Perhaps you should have asked him if he heard anyone speak words that he didn't understand. Listen, I love him, but he ain't the smartest gear in the engine."

John Lee replied, "I know one thing, them there fellows didn't speak African."

Jilkes was about to respond when the Sarge said, "People, please stay focused."

The Sarge said, "Darryl reported that there was a reference to Spain that one of the shooters had in his possession. I don't know what that means, but at this point, we have to look at every conceivable clue."

John Lee announced, "I don't know what they say when they speak over in that there country, but I do know that the one guy had some really strange looking socks on. I mean they were red on top, yellow in the middle with some kind of emblem and then red again at the bottom."

Larry immediately googled the Spanish flag and when it came up, he showed it to John Lee who indicated that those were the colors of the socks the fellow was wearing. John Lee looked at Jilkes and asked, "Did you happen to find a Spanish clue?" Jilkes turned away, but not before giving John Lee the 'bird.'

The Sarge seeing the exchange said, "In all these years, I have never come between you two guys. Also, never in all my years, have I seen you two continuously at each other's throats. Is there something going on that I should know about?"

John Lee looked at the Sarge in a curious way and asked, "Did you see something that I didn't see? Me and my minority friend will never involve the group in our issues if we have them. No sir! He will take me out back and try to beat the shit out of me. We don't have a problem; do you people have one?"

Jilkes looked at the Sarge and just said, "Ditto! Sarge he is weird but he is my friend and I love him. Please don't read anything into our transmissions. It's all for show. John Lee and I are as solid as a rock. He loves me and I love him but no one should try to interpret what that means and come between us."

The Sarge threw his arms in the air as if he were surrendering and calmly stated, "I know the deal, the team knows the deal, but sometimes you people seem to cross boundaries that normal, and I repeat, normal human beings, would find offensive and/or damn right demeaning. I know one thing, and that is, when it's time to deal with our issues or inherited assignments, I know you people will be at the top of your game. Please excuse me for intruding into an affair that surpasses the surreal and enters the obnoxious!"

The Sarge then looked at Jong and inquired, "Who is watching our businesses in Spain? Are we getting reports and payments or are we too busy being good guys to follow our investments?"

Jong said, "Each month I send you and the rest of the group a report. Do you people know how to read? What must I do? All of a sudden, the TV speaks in Spanish and now everyone wants an accounting immediately. What is wrong with you people? I account for everything and those people who were assigned to help me, well, they stay pregnant and unavailable for meetings."

The Sarge looked at Mallory and said, "Corporal, you and I will assist Jong with his projects, do you have a problem with that?"

Mallory was on the verge of saying something when Jong violently interrupted him and said, "You no count, he can't count, and now you want to help me? I think I'll just go and make love to my wife, who by the way is pregnant with our third child and you want me to report on numbers. Pretty soon, we will have more babies than members. All the women are pregnant again."

Zanthius smiled and said, "That's where you're wrong my friend. My wife is not pregnant."

Jong walked over to him and whispered, "You had better listen to the wind, read the tea leaves, and hear the dogs barking, my friend. Get ready for number four."

Zanthius looked at Jong and stated, "You should not wish that kind of a thing on a person."

"I don't wish for anything except our safety during each mission. I do, however listen to the gossip, chants, and prayers, a thing you my friend must learn to do. Asiram is loaded with number four and you will have another girl to balance the craziness in your world."

The Sarge yelled, "Hold up damnit it! We are entering a very narrow passageway. We never speak freely about each other's situation. What the hell is going on?"

Jong fell to his knees and yelled, "My wife tells me everything that your wives don't tell you. Please forgive me for trying to share in an uncommon manner, gossip that is supposedly between them. If you broker this information to Asiram, they will know that they have a snitch in their midst. For all that is sacred to you and me, please consider the consequences before acknowledging information that would indicate that you were informed before her amplification to you. I only ask this for the sanctity of all the men involved with women who can plot against us."

Zanthius approached Jong and bowed extremely low and said, "You my Mr. Jong, are my friend, the friend of my father, and my father's friends. I respect what you attempted to do in a backwards manner and will not explore or announce any information prior to the same being provided to me. In other words, I don't have a damn thing to say. I hope you're correct my brother."

# # #

Later in the day, Larry asked if he could see the shot of 62nd Street again. As he scanned the images, he noticed a bodega mid-way up the block near the deli. As he zoomed in on the store, he noticed in the window, a small replica of the flag of Spain. He summoned the Sarge who came along with Jilkes, Jong, John Lee, Mallory, Zanthius, and Chakes. When they walked into the room, Larry said, "I think I know where those men were being watched from."

Larry fast-forwarded the monitor to the frames of the bodega and then once again zoomed in on it. Larry said, "If you look closely in the window, you will see the Spanish flag. The bodega has the cameras and out-stretched windows that gives it an ideal view of the comings and goings, on 62nd Street. That's where we should barge in and seize the cameras. If you examine each store front, only the bodega has protruding windows and a 180 degree north to south view of that street."

Zanthius looked closely at the described scenario, looked at Larry and said, "It's eggshells, but at least I think their being boiled. That is the only place so it would seem, that has that view. I'm with my brother. I think we should get Utz to send his people in to see if the cameras are taping or storing in an off-site facility. If they're involved in this mess, then I bet you they are storing the data the old-fashioned way."

The Sarge invited Mr. Utz into the room and gave him the scenario. Mr. Utz at first acted interested at what had been deduced, but then laughed and said, "Guys, I should have told you. Those two cameras in that window belong to me. Sorry about that."

As he turned to walk away with an arrogant smile on his face, Larry quipped, "Well, Mr. Utz, if you own two cameras, then who owns the third one?"

Utz returned and closely watched the screen, and everyone watched his smug attitude disappear as he turned to his man and said, "Bring that fucking crook to me."

#

An hour later, two of Mr. Utz's men paraded two gentlemen in front of the group. Mr. Utz vehemently screamed, "Who owns that third fucking camera in your window?"

Both men became unsettled, and the older gentleman nervously stated, "My son, him not too smart, but he tried to improve our business by renting the space to another group such as yours. We did not know that there would be a problem by doing such a thing and if so, we apologize."

Mr. Utz asked, "Exactly who is this other group like mine? Do you have a contact for them and where is the captured data stored?"

"Sir, we just operate a bodega. We don't know where the information goes or who comes and collects it?"

Larry asked, "Have you seen people come and collect it in the past?"

The older gentleman said, "Yes, once, two men came and replaced the battery pack, so he told us."

Utz pulled out his cell phone, made a call and was told that the information filmed was stored on a hard drive of sorts. Utz told his people who were left there not to touch it or enter its recording path. Just keep an eye on it and make sure no one removes anything from it.

Larry asked, "Sir, do you have a large Spanish speaking population in this area?"

"Oh, no sir. Most people from Spain can't afford to live on 62nd Street and 2nd Avenue. This area is for rich people."

Larry said, "So as a bodega, do you sell the normal items but with less of an emphasis on goods that people from Spain or Mexico would buy?"

"That is correct sir. Our store is considered an upscale bodega in that we have fresh meats, fish, poultry, and we also meet the standards of certain religious groups in that we have their people doing work in those areas."

Larry then asked, "The people that rented the space for the camera, do you have pictures of them and what was their reason for wanting to place a camera in your window?"

The younger gentleman said, "I was told that they wanted to study foot and automotive traffic in the area before they committed to building a high-rise apartment on land, they own in three locations. When I asked him where the three sites were, he immediately moved on to offering me $300 per week to use our window for a minimum of eight weeks. He then peeled off twelve one hundred-dollar bills and that changed the entire nature of the conversation. I forgot why he was interested in renting space for a camera and my focus went directly to the money. It's similar to when you guys came barging into the store and offered $200 per week. Zanthius looked at Larry and then turned to Mr. Utz and asked, "Why do you happen to have cameras in a window that is potentially connected to a person who is committing heinous crimes across the globe? Why do you have cameras there?"

"That's national security. Above your pay grade!" Utz remarked.

The Sarge cocked his head to the side, and before he could begin his questioning, Jilkes asked Mr. Utz, "Have you lost your damn mind? Zanthius asked a question that needs attending to. Unless you're operating with full disclosure with us, then without a doubt, we will be out of here in the next few minutes. Is that right, Sarge?"

"That is so damn right, it's scary. Above our paygrade? Mr. Utz, you must have missed our management 101 class. People, Jilkes has lowered the flag. We're out of here unless Mr. Utz has somehow elevated us to a paygrade that allows us to hear full disclosure and not some more bureaucratic bullshit with which we are quite familiar."

Utz looked around the room and asked his people to give him a minute alone with the Sarge and his group. After the room was emptied, he said, "I have my cameras on the building where we think the largest cocaine supplier on the east coast, lives. We also think he is an illicit arms dealer, sells synthesized drugs, does money laundering, and maybe some human trafficking. My friends, 2nd Avenue is famous, it's where Nickle's Steak House used to be housed and now houses four international mob figures, three barons, and lots of house of cards swindlers. Welcome to the upper east side, where those in power try to mingle amongst the commoners. When I was told that the bomber had associations on the east side and specifically on 2nd Avenue, I tried to marshal my forces and solve this event on my own. It was clear to me after reviewing the aftermath of Springfield that I needed people who were focused, amorphous, and thorough. My people can't do what is going to be required because we have to fill out forms 101A, 120B, 221C, and part D plus forms G 26 to 65 for each bullet fired from our guns. Really! Okay, I must admit, the above your paygrade bullshit was related to the other Ops I'm running; it had nothing to do with you guys. I have complete faith, belief, and respect for what you people do to keep this country and others safe. I don't get a chance to pull a 'one-up-man-ship' on you people. As a human, I sometimes have a need to feel important. Relegating based upon the law, is not what I'm talking about. Listen, Larry went through some shit that I will never understand and he was not the person I expected to be the brains behind internal concepts that borders on the surreal and the unreal. I know the Sarge is smart, but he is surrounded by people who are smarter socially, and economically more fitted to lead into 21st century ahead of all of us. Sue Lyn, Darryl, Monica, Asiram, and Courtney; give me a break. In their own ways, they are as sharp as anyone I have ever met. Darryl is so damn smart that he's scary. And, then you add his wife into the equation, well now, that scary shit has just been multiplied. I'm not trying to sell you people a bunch of shit, I'm trying to confess that I'm the smartest person in my group and I don't match up with anyone under this roof!"

Zanthius said, "Well, I can think of a few people who might challenge you for that position but I won't go there at this time. Anyway, so you're saying this is purely coincidental. Can you substantiate that fact?"

"I have enough shit and film to lock up the drug dealer right now. I was hoping that he was one in the same, in that he was also the bomber."

From the far corner, the Sarge said, "Let's do that, I mean rouse this guy but with Jilkes, John Lee, and Jong as your backup. I would like to bring him here and shake him down and that might convince me that you're legitimate."

#

As the men agreed on the terms of engagement, suddenly, there was the sound of automatic gunfire. Clip after clip was emptied on the car of the alleged drug kingpin as he attempted to exit his vehicle. Bullet after bullet hit the bulletproof car and began to bounce all around the street. Overconfident people from a small Caribbean Island attempted to end the drug kingpins reign and take over his business—a business that was comprised of the rich, the famous, and the arrogant, as customers!

The Sarge said, "What the hell. Did you see what I just saw?" Everyone watched and heard the sounds of gunfire. Mr. Utz said, "We have to move now. In my car there are vests with agency identification on it. I'll need you guys to put those on and most of all, follow my commands."

"Do you have one additional vest? I'm coming along, as well," the Sarge announced.

Mallory stood tall and said, "Too many of our main line figures are being attached to this activity. Sarge, I suggest you send one of your boys in your place. You're needed here to command the action. Send McArthur if you don't want to send one of your boys."

"I'm going on this mission. Let's go before the locals contaminate the scene."

#

At the scene, the drug kingpin remained in his rented car because it was bullet proof. When Mr. Utz and his team arrived and flashed their badges, the drug kingpin's men backed off and gave them full access to the individual. Utz yelled, "You're not safe in the car because it's leaking gasoline. I suggest you surrender yourself to me and have your slick ass lawyers get you out on bail. If you stay in the car, I'm going to have to evacuate the area and force your men to move away from the vehicle. The kingpin hit a button on the panel and the car doors became unlocked. Before he got out of the car, Utz gave him a vest and told him to put it on. Once in the custody of Utz's team, Utz's car sped down the street with sirens wailing and made a series of left turns and headed back towards the area where the attempted assassination occurred. The kingpin asked, "Where are you taking me?" No one responded and the vehicle he was riding in made a sharp turn into the rear of a building on 62nd Street. Once in the oversized garage, the kingpin was immediately blindfolded, and his hands were placed behind his back and strapped in restraints. He offered no resistance and wondered had the shooting been a setup to allow these guys to abduct him.

In the garage, the Sarge stated, "My name is Ben Beckmire and it's unlikely you're going to survive our interrogation. That is my real name and I now request that you tell me yours. Now, before you do that, I want you to know that the federal types have left the building and you're in the midst of mercenaries. Our interest in you has nothing to do with drugs, rather we're concerned with finding out if you're the person who is responsible for the horrific bombings that have been occurring around the world. Now, this is how this is going to work. I'll ask you a question and if I'm not satisfied with your answer, one of my men will take the liberty of cutting you wherever they may choose. If you answer all questions honestly, well, we will figure out how to get you out of town and out of this business. The people from the islands are committed to ridding the area of you. They want you dead as you can see. Now, you've been in this business a long time and you probably have CDs, cash, and savings accounts somewhere. We will get you out of town, out of the business, and hopefully into one that does not have as many obstacles in operating it. You know what you do ruins a lot of lives and families. On that basis alone, we should terminate you and those boys who shoot guns in the middle of the day while children and others are trying to live their lives. Now, I've done all the talking and it's your turn. Let me start by inquiring about those who would shoot up a neighborhood. Where can we find them and the one who ordered the hit on you? Oh, before I do that, I have to make sure we have all of our cards in place. Don't go anywhere, I'll be right back."

The Sarge walked over to Utz and asked, "Are you prepared to see this thing to its limits?"

"If you mean, am I prepared to have this guy killed, then the answer is absolutely yes. Do I want those who shot up his car in the middle of the day? I want them as bad as I want to know if this guy is connected to the bomber."

"What is the status of our get out of jail cards?"

"I thought you'd never ask. I have them for every single person whose name I was given including those on the west coast and in Australia. The women and children are also included in the count."

"Okay then, two things will happen here today. One he will confess his knowledge if any about the bomber, and second, he will tell me how to find the person who put the hit on him."

#

Less than one hour later, and without a single cut or scratch, the kingpin gave the Sarge a diagram of his entire operation, including clients, suppliers, bankers, brokers, and mules. He adamantly proclaimed that he was not the bomber. He also gave the Sarge the address and telephone number of the person who ordered the assassination. He told the Sarge exactly what information he needed, in order to leave the country, and the Sarge agreed to assist. He asked the Sarge, where could he go without the notion of people looking for him. The Sarge with a smile on his face asked, "How's your Spanish?"

#

Jilkes, John Lee, and Larry were assigned to enter the drug kingpin's condo. They found, without any issues, the documents the kingpin needed and a briefcase with a ledger in it. As they were leaving, Larry noticed a note that had been slid under the door. He examined it and finally opened it. It read, 'if you want to continue doing business in this neighborhood, then you had better pay your reparation dues. I will send people for you or I might decide to pull a spring on your ass and all of your clients.'

Larry folded the document back into squares and placed it back on the floor. As the group was vacating the premises, he backtracked and gathered up the note.

When they arrived at the garage, Larry walked over to the man and asked, "What is your given name?"

"It's Calvin Jefferson. Why do you ask?"

"I found this note folded into fours on your floor under your door. Take a look at it and tell me what it means to you."

"Someone in the building has been trying to extort money from me. I typically don't let it phase me because I don't have people coming to the building, I don't work corners, and insofar as my neighbors are concerned, I receive an allowance from my parents."

Larry announced, "That's all well and good but what's bothering me is the sentence that states, 'I might pull a spring on you and your customers.' Now I'm thinking that's a reference to Springfield. You must have an idea who wrote this mess."

"Listen, there are other notes like that and a note yesterday demanding one million by Friday or I should look north for signs of what will happen to me."

Larry walked over to the Sarge and proclaimed, "Cal Jefferson has a connection with our bomber. He doesn't know it, but the guy must need some walk-around-money and has left notes under Jefferson's door. I'm thinking that he's a resident in that building. Mr. Utz, can you get the list of owners, renters, and pictures of everyone who lives in the building? I believe the person in Spain who is connected indirectly to all of this stuff is also connected somehow to this guy. We just have to figure out the connection and we might get a picture of who we're looking for."

#

Exactly one hour later, a member from the Utz team presented a flash-drive with the events of the week for the condo. Utz said to his man, "I know he didn't just hand this over to you and say have a nice day. What did you say you would do to him?"

The guy responded, "I didn't threaten him, sir. I showed him a photo of Mr. Lassiter that I came across and he was more than willing to let me into the man's condo. I told him that my friends had already entered the premises and that there was no need for me to go in."

"You sure you didn't threaten him?"

"I showed him my credentials, the picture, and he asked who that was. I gave him the short part to the story and he was much obliging."

#

Jong was summoned, and when he entered the room with his laptop, he plugged the flash-drive into his unit. As he fast-forwarded to the movements on the floor where Cal Jefferson lived, a small figure could be seen placing a neatly folded document under Jefferson's door. There was no sound recording of the event but it was clear that someone was in an alcove that was not in the view of the cameras, giving instructions to what appeared to be a child. As Larry and Zanthius watched the activity, frame by frame, they both saw what was an obvious plant. The camera caught enough of the wall where there was no camera to catch the pointed toe of a woman's shoe. Larry and Zanthius played the foot game for a few seconds and they both realized that an image of a finger appeared ever so slightly and was indistinguishable in the frame. Zanthius said, "Brother, what did you just see?"

"I saw what appeared to be a shoe, and what also appeared to be a finger grasping it. Did you see the same thing?"

"Larry, you know I like to have my own opinions but as usual, I'm sure if we were able to zoom in on that last millisecond, we would see the tip of a finger moving the object that looks like a woman's shoe. Larry, you know the two of us could strike out on our own and solve some of the mysteries of yesteryear and today and make a fortune. I don't mean no corny Sherlock shit, I mean, Zanthius and Larry, absolute detectives."

Mallory entered the fray and said, "I prefer Larry and his associate, Zanthius, 'the idiot spy'."

"Ha, ha ha! You're really a funny guy but if my dad loves you then I have to at least like you." Zanthius walked over to Mallory and gave him a man-sized hug and whispered, "All kidding aside, I respect all of you and I appreciate the way you look out for my dad. He is such a happy camper when you guys are around," Zanthius announced.

Mallory, who was taken aback by the statement, felt the sincerity of Zanthius's comments and yelled, "Oohrah! That's for you, Larry, and of course, Asiram."

Jong announced, "That's no woman and he's no ordinary child. Look how he walks and look at the size of her finger when multiplied. This picture is a fraud, there is no woman, and no child but a small person and a man."

Zanthius started to reply to what had been deduced but was quickly cut off by his father who said, "Good job Mr. Amazing. You and my boys share the same observation. From the balance of the floors, can you see where this person gets on the elevator or what stairwell they took?"

Jong proclaimed, "This flash-drive is only of floor man of interest lives. Why we no have complete data to analyze?"

The Sarge looked at Mr. Utz, who looked sternly at the guy charged with gathering the data and said, "I guess your ass has to go back and get the full video."

# # #

Precisely twenty-five minutes later, the agent reappeared with another flash-drive. He told Mr. Utz that this information was stored in the Cloud, and it's for the past six months. Mr. Utz stared at him and asked, "Why didn't you get the data for the past year?"

The man looked at Mr. Utz, headed for the door, and was asked to stand-down. Utz said, "Good job, I should have been more specific about what we needed."

# # #

Later when the man returned with more data and films, Jong, Larry, and Zanthius were oblivious to the macerations concerning the time periods. Jong yelled, "Look at that person getting on the elevator a floor below that guy's place and look at the child wandering around on the floor below him. That guy is not a man and that child is not a child. Look at how he struggles to run. I think it's a small person but clearly older age."

The trio watched the so-called child and the woman leave the building separately but enter the same vehicle. It was an Uber and it dropped the duo off thirteen blocks away from the pick-up.

A single phone began to vibrate in the room and Mr. Jefferson said, "That's one of my platinum clients in search of some euphoria."

The Sarge loudly stated, "You're either in or out of the business. If you want to say your good-byes to the people whose lives you've probably ruined, then get the hell out of here and don't look back. The people who shot up your car, won't miss the next time."

Cal Jefferson asked, "Do you know what's in the briefcase?"

The Sarge looked at him and stated, "I don't give a shit."

Cal Jefferson said, "Please, indulge me for a minute."

The Sarge opened the brief case and extracted a ledger from it. Cal Jefferson said, "Those are all of the charities I support with the illicit funds that I receive from high-end people who love to float amongst the clouds. Other than the condo and rental car, I have truly little set aside for myself because I believe that my number will be up at any moment."

Jilkes retrieved the ledger from the Sarge and began to look through it. John Lee, Larry, and Zanthius joined in and Larry announced, "Oh my, a benevolent drug dealer. Is this supposed to create a path to heaven for you or is there some other demonic reason for you serving the rich and giving to the poor?"

Cal Jefferson sat down and lowered his head into his lap. It would be at least a full minute before he spoke. Zanthius asked, "I guess, your purpose is not that holy after all, eh?"

Cal raised his third finger in the air and Zanthius dead-reckoned to him. John Lee stopped him mid-way and said, "We're not a group that be so sanctified. We got a lot of bodies waiting on us in hell. Give him a chance to let us know what the hell he be doing."

It was obvious that Cal Jefferson was crying when he raised his head. He said, "About nine years ago, my daughter and son were at school when one of their school mates showed up with a new book bag that had candy in it. The candy was heroin and both of my children and five others died from ingesting the mess. The father of the kid that brought the stuff to school was found bludgeoned to death and no one was ever convicted. It was sloppy but sympathetic police work that got those involved in his demise off the hook. In his car was a book, much like this one with clients by code and phone numbers. At first, I wanted to punish each of them but decided that I would be their new supplier, hook them, and fleece them out of their money and set up charities to help struggling families. My family was destroyed, my wife subsequently vanished into the night, never to be heard from again. I met with his suppliers and realized they were brokers on Wall Street, and after that, 2nd Avenue was mine. I gave his former clients an option, buy pure from me or take their chances from the dudes on the corner. Other than living money and I mean little at that; I don't have anything to show for the millions of dollars in drugs that I have pedaled. I have nothing because I gave damn near every penny to charities and that ledger will substantiate what I've said."

Zanthius said, "So you show us a ledger and we're supposed to believe that you don't have any funds stashed away?"

"That's exactly correct. There is $534.37 in my pocket and that is the sum total of my wealth. Now, I do have product stored but once it's sold, the proceeds go to the groups in the book."

Larry said, "I see you give funds to that preacher in Philadelphia. What's his name?"

Without hesitating, Cal Jefferson asked, "Do you mean Sullivan, Leon H. Sullivan?"

"Yeah, that's who I was thinking about. Does he know the source of your gifts?"

"Unless I missed donations 101, money coming in from an innominate source, is readily acceptable by most charities. I've not heard of many charities turning down money because the benefactor failed to reveal his name, title, and business affiliation."

"Okay Mr. Jefferson, what's next for you?" Larry asked.

"I like the idea Mr. Beckmire threw out. I have nothing and if he can get me out of this country, with the clothes on my back and the money in my pocket, then I would be absolutely free. I have nothing holding me here. Perhaps there are some small jobs that I could do for your group. I mean, I have degrees, I have common sense, I know how to hustle and I also have a heart!"

The Sarge quietly listened to the dialogue without interrupting his sons. He looked at Cal and asked, "As painful as it might be, can we google you and find any information about what happened to your children?"

Two minutes later, everyone was saddened by the information about the "wrong book bag".

The Sarge looked at Mallory and he issued his silent approval of what he suspected was going to be the Sarge's next move. The Sarge told Cal Jefferson that he would send him to a place where he could acquire a new passport, driver's license, and social security card. He then told Jefferson that he would be flown to an undetermined location to board a jet for Europe with a final destination in Spain, where their associates would meet him, house him, and give him the rules of the road. The Sarge said, "If you can follow simple directions and rules, then we can make you disappear and offer you a new life. If that's a problem, then we should just slaughter you here and right now. By the way, what degrees do you have?"

"I have a BS in accounting, MS in finance, and I'm a CPA."

Jong positioned himself behind Jefferson, looked at his fingernails, and blew on them as if he had just won something big.

Mallory looked at the Sarge and asked, "Perhaps these skills are more needed in the Northern Territory than in Spain."

"You might have a point there. Let me think about that, catch up with Darryl, and see what he thinks." He turned to Jefferson and asked, "Are you trustworthy?"

"I am very trustworthy. Of all the money I oversaw; I only have what's in my pocket. Perhaps I'm a fool but I couldn't take the very source of my children's demise and profit from it. However, I did see the virtues of making the assets available to non-profits. I know money, I don't have any money, and right now, I don't need any money. I need a way out of this thing where people in broad daylight don't shoot up the streets trying to kill you for a territory that is full of misery and regrets."

The Sarge turned to Mr. Utz and asked, "Where are you on all that you've heard and do you see any problems with where we're going with this one?"

"My people are sending his essence to the labs and we'll have him vetted within the hour."

After looking long and hard at the man, Mr Utz turned to Cal Jefferson and said, "I don't know of any person who has been supported by this group after being caught with their hands in the cookie jar. You should consider yourself special because, they like to gut people."

Jefferson's eyes opened wide and he mumbled, "What do you mean by gut people?"

"I mean they take a big old knife and start at your dick and yank it all the way to your brain and take a bite out of your heart before you cease to live."

"Yeah, right." As Jefferson looked around the room, he noticed that no one was expressing any ambivalence. He said, "You're kidding me, right?"

Utz approached his ear and whispered, "You just made a covenant with the devil, and when I say devil, buddy, I truly mean shit that is not of this world. Whatever you do, try not to get assigned to the Northern Territory."

"Where the hell is the Northern Territory?" Mr. Jefferson asked.

"Mate, that be in Australia!"

# # #

Prior to heading to the airport, Sarge assembled his team and headed over to Brooklyn. Once in Brooklyn, the team systematically, eliminated those who would shoot up the streets in broad daylight.

CHAPTER EIGHTEEN

When the group arrived in Spain, Franco was standing outside of customs with his associates. When the Sarge saw him, he assumed a defensive position as if he were expecting an assassination attempt. After the pretense, the Sarge slapped Franco's back so hard with that man-sized hug thing, it winded him. A few moments later, Franco said, "Damn mi amigo, you almost broke my back. How the hell are you and I'm glad you're here. We have made some incredible advances and the main properties are complete and we've found our way into three others. Wait, I see that look on your face. No, mi amigo, this is not a hustle we saved people from the hustlers and offered them an approach that was honest and above board."

"Franco, we just landed and you are taxing me beyond my expectations. Is there any way possible that we can have dinner in the next three hours after we settle this crew, shower, and relax for a few?"

"Boss, I've made all the arrangements. I have your new business partners separated from you because I assume you will want to vet them. I have dossiers on everyone involved and a total financial package for you to approve or disapprove. In the red ledger, there is an accounting of every penny spent on each project. In the blue book, there is the final accounting of every cent spent on the restaurant and the villa. It is much more than a hotel mi amigo; it is spectacular, grand, opulent, and full of flowers and love. When we arrive, I hope you will approve."

"Franco, since you won't let me relax, do you have an accounting of the personnel cost?"

"Mi amigo, that's a strange request, but I somehow figured that one out and got it right. You will see, if approved, me and my main crew are subject to a substantial payday. I know I had the ability to make payments to us, I just didn't feel good about doing it without a review from your people. Now, that you're here, you and your people can look deep into the books and see that all is above board."

"Franco, this is not about an audit. I'm not here to check up on you. As a matter of fact, we haven't checked up on our part of the proceeds. We've been busy and we're going to need you and the crew to do a different kind of job, perhaps."

"Mr. Sarge, me, and my people live a great life thanks to you and your benevolence. We or you could have died in a shootout from which neither of us would have benefited. I must say, I'm in a little trouble because I haven't been able to make my personal payments."

"What the shit do you mean? Is this the hustle or what?"

"Mi amigo, somewhere in the process, the money transfers weren't made and I had to mortgage my house to keep things afloat."

The Sarge yelled for Jong and when he arrived, he said, "I know where the bottle neck is but I didn't know it was a problem. Franco, I transferred all rights and privileges over to you. You have the ability to write checks up to two million dollars."

"The final documents came to me and went to my spam account," Franco indicated.

Jong said, "Sarge, he is regal and loyal. I suggest we pay all of his debts off and give him a bonus in the amount of two million dollars."

Mallory approached the three men and asked, "What's going on?"

The Sarge said, "Our friend is about to be evicted from his home because of a language issue and our failure to activate his spending ability."

"How did we mess that up?" Mallory inquired.

"It was all in the translation of events between English and Spanish. I think we got it and, therefore, we need to make Franco whole."

"Sarge, my people also put their properties in the forfeiture barrel."

"Damn, why did you people go so far without trying to contact us?"

"Because we're family. We thought that you guys had an issue and couldn't make the payments. We, as a group, were determined to live or die by our arrangements."

The Sarge looked at Franco with tears in his eyes and said, "We came here and provoked a situation that we didn't fully fund. You and your people put your homes on the line because you believed in our journey. As such, and as the president of this dysfunctional group, we will pay all of your loans off, and endow each of your people with three million dollars. That will happen after we get to the hotel, and you let me rest, and get a nap before we hopefully have a wonderful meal."

Franco looked at the Sarge, then his crew and said, "Now, I hope this isn't a hustle. Everyone in the group laughed. Jong opened his computer, completed the transaction, and said, "Funds should be in the general account by morning. Franco, I will transfer all the funds to you, and you will transfer your crew's funds to them. Just protocol, I'm not happy with people writing large checks to themselves, regardless of what the mastermind says."

Jong sent the confirmation codes to Franco's phone and told him, "In the future, you must reach out to me or anyone of us. That is too much liability to assume on behalf of a family that at any moment could be wiped off the earth."

# # #

Later at dinner everyone professed how magnificent and regal the villa was but wondered about the absence of patrons in the restaurant.

Franco thanked the ladies for their on-line contributions to the décor for the restaurant and the villa. He eloquently stated, "The restaurant is booked six days a week for lunch and dinner. As a cost of doing business, as well as good will, we closed the restaurant with the complete agreement of our partners and dedicated this night to our amigos and amigas from across the pond. Those individuals who had reservations will be treated to a free entrée and beverage at our expense. Now, Mr. Beckmire and company, we have struggled with naming both businesses and have decided to let you or your designee do the naming."

Courtney stood up, as did Asiram, followed by the entire female membership. Courtney said, "I am senior here, and I knew that my smart husband and the rest of you guys, were going to leave that task to us. Ain't that right boys?"

There was silence in the room until the Sarge said, "Unequivocally, the task of naming the resort and restaurant belongs to the ladies, if our partners are comfortable with that decision."

Courtney announced, "In our meetings, we discussed the possibility of naming the restaurant and the resort. We conferred with our partners and jointly, came up with names for both. I will leave the actual name unveiling to our member, Ava De Lombardo, since this is her backyard."

Ava rose and said, "What a strange and wonderful world we live in. For most of my son's life, I tried to hide him from the one good and meaningful person that I should have connected him with— his father. Ben Beckmire, I have always admired you. Since this journey began in Philadelphia, we have added new partners, new members, new children, new relationships, and new marriages. I myself, am waiting on the announcement by my sometimes-difficult daughter-in-law, that they are about to have baby number four. Yeah, girl, I'm letting it out, love you! Anyway, as a group, we knew we had *The Sanctuary* in the islands and, so therefore, we thought we would name the restaurant, *The Conversion* and the resort, *The View,* simple but elegant names. What say you?" All the women screamed to the top of their lungs but the men mostly clapped and could give a hoot about the naming of the two businesses.

Earlier, the Sarge received a text message from one of their pilots indicating that the package was safely aboard a flight that it should arrive in his area in less than three hours. He beckoned Franco over and said, "I have another charity program that I need you to deal with. I have a guy arriving here from the USA in a matter of three to four hours. He was seemingly, worth saving by us, and I now need you to put him to work. I saw the fees that you're paying the banks for squeaky clean records, this guy has all kinds of degrees in accounting. However, he first has to do dirty. Find some shit jobs for him and if he complains, offer him a one-way ticket back to New York. Some unbelievably bad people wanted him, so I doubt if he'll be interested in going back especially after you tell him that you have connections with a certain island group in New York. Do you follow where I'm going with this? I mean, if he works out here with you, I'll probably ship him to the Northern Territory and as a matter of fact, I want you people to meet my nephew and learn the precious mineral market and protection."

"Mi amigo, we are willing to do whatever you need. It's absolutely righteous on this side of the fence. No one is hunting us; all bad blood has been discussed, cleaned up, and we work for the common good of our collective communities. Since we're on this topic, me, my crew, and the owners of both businesses agreed and invested in three properties that are involved with people who represent what I used to be. You know with their places almost in forfeiture, we couldn't complete the relationship but now we can. My question to you is whether you and your crew want to be a part of this new business arrangement; two dilapidated restaurants in the middle of a busy tourist area, and a one-hundred room hotel by the water that is contaminated with everything unknown to man. As we see it, we can develop a safe eating and housing situation for people on a middle-income budget. As you can tell, *The Conversion* is high end and caters to that crowd. However, we have eyes on locations where we could create a moderate—less expensive version of *The Conversion*."

"Franco, I will have Mallory, Monica, Jong, and the new guy sit in on a discussion with you tomorrow. Treat the new guy like shit until he explodes and wants to leave. He comes from a shady life that destroyed individuals, families, communities, and businesses—drugs! I need to move on to another situation. Are you through with your proposals that, by the way, when you meet with my people, tell them the cost, the plan, and the timetable and who benefits?"

As the Sarge continued, he said, "Franco, I'm sure you're aware of the terrible bombings that have happened around the world. We're here because our handler thinks the mastermind of those bombings is operating out of Spain. Darryl, my nephew on the west coast, had intel that led to here. My group was on the east coast and another clue showed up that pointed to Spain. Do you know of anyone who has the ability to rally the troops and gather disciples to plant devious devices? The funny thing about all this, is the notion that his base of operation is in Madrid, Barcelona, or Valencia."

"Mi amigo, that's a lot of area to cover. If you could assemble specific conversations, then I might be able to reach across boundaries and point you in the general direction. If we go snooping in this arena, then it places us once again in the dark zone where we are looked at differently."

"Franco, I only want you to point me in the right direction. I need you to stay on this side of the road and, therefore, I know I won't have to come hunting for your ass."

"Ah, my brother, you never stop with the threats. What must one do to avoid such conversations with you?"

"You must make sure that you stay on the right side of the road. Listen, you have a shit load of money. If you want to do something different, then please consult with all of your partners. I think from that infamous meeting in the restaurant, we have come a long way, but sometimes people get greedy."

"I'm in your employ. My people are in my employ. If anyone strays, I will personally place a bullet in their head. I expect you to do the same thing to me, if you can confirm that I have screwed up. Fortunately, mi amigo, that ain't going to happen. This is a renaissance, and I'm leading the movement.

Stay focused on my friendship and stop threatening me and mine."

"Franco, I trust a lot of people that I know, but our relationship developed in a hurry. Please, if you need something, contact me. Don't get creative and call us into action. I beg of you!"

"Mi amigo, this is my last comment on this matter. I can account for every single penny that was transferred to me. I can show you how we used the community in a training scheme to develop skilled labor to build, outfit, and beautify your investments. I agree, I was a two-bit hustler when we met. I've cleaned that up, I've communicated to all of Spain that I'm in a legitimate relationship with smart businesspeople who I love, and that if you can't document the plan, the objectives, and the funding, then don't waste your time reaching out to me. That job in your nation's capital was exciting and endowing to us. You gave us an opportunity to do something for you! You asked us to do you a favor! You trusted us with a delicate project, and we delivered without the loss of life. That, my friend was as special as us retrieving that man-child from the monastery. I love you people because you have made me a respectable person as I have made my people. We didn't come back here and buy fancy cars or big houses. No, we invested every dime of our share into properties of people who were on the brink of losing their life's dreams. We saved twelve businesses on our own with the money we were gifted by you."

"Franco, you are one silver tongue rogue which is why I don't believe a thing you say. However, if you and your people took those funds and invested in people, then I will get on my knees and bow to you. Also, I will inherit that debt, invite you into our savings club where there is a monthly stipend based upon all of our investments including a fee for overseeing the diamond & gold mines in the Northern Territory."

"Mr. Sarge, your group is listed as one of our investors on those twelve properties. It was done artificially because we had no way of knowing how to list or call your group. Therefore, you're listed as a silent partner with a thirty-three percent stake in our work."

The Sarge looked at him and saw that the man he once was going to kill and who was accidently in the right place at the wrong time to direct him to his grandson, had truly transmogrified into a wonderful and amazing human being.

The Sarge stood tall, banged gently on his glass, and stated, "People, as you recall, we used to take no hostages. Last time we were here, we met a group of pirates. We were prepared to make them walk the gang plank. The reason was they were strangling people to take their homes and their businesses. The lead pirate and I had a conversation that averted a small war. He also, accidently, directed me to where my grandson was being cared for. For that information, I will always be in his debt. This pirate and his crew also came across the pond and did a job for us in DC. We endowed them for their tenacious work. Come to find out, they took their entire booty and invested it in twelve businesses that were being taken over by the kind of people they used to be. He has a silver tongue and operates according to a precise code that was crafted after he found out one of his own, was advertising their activities. What is far opposite of being Machiavellian, these pirates leveraged their homes because we didn't make the agreed upon payments to complete the projects that we entrusted them with. Listen, they took the money they made from our event in DC, invested it in people, and mortgaged their homes to complete *The View* and *The Conversion*. If the world was full of pirates like them, then it would be a magnificent place to live. I am so honored to know these rogues, and I suggest we pay them what's owed and endow them by another $5 million per man. People what do you say?"

John Lee stood up and yelled, "We should make it $8 million because they have lived up to their part of every bargain and requests that we be asking them."

The Sarge announced, "People, I give you Franco and his merry band of pirates."

Each man stood and were so overwhelmed with love and acknowledgement, they couldn't talk. They were crying their hearts out.

# # #

In the town of Segovia, northwest of Madrid, a small but meaningful event was publicly acknowledged on television when an accident occurred on an alternative route into the city that was caused by an oil spill. The importance of the accident and the reporting of it, would only be comprehended by a select few.

Larry, while taking in his daily dose of good and bad news, read the English captions on his television, and initially thought nothing of it. As he continued to scan the captions and listen to the Spanish version of the news, he decided that he would entertain the twins with a game of scrabble.

As Larry and the twins played their game, one of the twins spelled the word, "hydro" and racked up a significant amount of points. Larry and the other twin were envious of the word development and its ensuing points. However, the 'o' in hydro stretched near a triple letter score block. The other twin had in his possession, 'g- e-n,' thus forming the word hydrogen. Larry congratulated both of them. As Larry studied his letters and viewed the board, he saw no options other than adding the letter 'w' in front of the word 'ant,' thus forming the word want. His kids booed him, Larry laughed and stared at the board fixing his eyes on the word hydrogen. After nearly thirty seconds, he jumped up and screamed, "Oh shit, oh shit!"

He ran into the other room and began watching the news repeat itself. One of the twins walked in and asked, "Daddy, is everything okay?"

Larry looked at him and said, "I'm not sure, Son. I'm not sure."

As the news of the vehicle accident was broadcast, it indicated that two vans were involved in the accident. The reporter also stated that the occupants of both vehicles were injured and transported to the nearest hospital. The reporter further indicated that one vehicle was transporting liquid hydrogen in what could be considered, home grown containers and the other vehicle was carrying what appeared to be bags of burnt coal.

Larry ran out of the room and headed towards the Sarge's room gathering Jong, Jilkes, and John Lee as he ran down the hallway. On the Sarge's door, he fiercely banged until a sleepy Sarge opened it and said, "Mr., have you lost your mind?"

"Dad cut on the television. I have to show you something. As the group gathered around the television, and as the news repeated itself, the thing that struck Larry's attention appeared. He said, "Okay, here it is."

The group listened to the news and the Sarge asked, "Larry, what's so important about a vehicle accident?"

"Dad, one of the vehicles was transporting bags of burnt coal and the other was carrying a modified refrigeration unit with liquid hydrogen in it. If I'm not mistaken, those are the necessary ingredients, along with others to formulate the Carbon Factor."

Zanthius walked into the room, and Larry yelled, "Zanthius, what are the two most important ingredients, that we know of, that are needed to develop the Carbon Factor?"

Zanthius replied, "Hydrogen and carbon. Why?"

The Sarge inquired, "Where did this accident happen?"

Larry replied, "Near a town called Segovia that appears to be northwest of Madrid."

The Sarge looked around the room and asked Jong, "When is my nephew due here?"

Jong answered, "I think they should be arriving in approximately, one hour."

"Have them fly to that area and check this thing out. Larry, you make sure you give him accurate information about where this thing happened. If we can get Darryl to get his hands on one of the drivers, we can at least find out where the trucks were heading," the Sarge stated.

#

Darryl's plane began its approach into Valencia when he received a call from Jong, redirecting his plane to Madrid. Larry got on the phone and gave Darryl specifics about what had happened, where it happened, and their cause for interest. Darryl asked Larry to hold the phone. In the interim, he directed the captain to abort landing in Valencia and head directly for the airport in Madrid.

# # #

Prior to Darryl's group landing in Madrid, Franco made several calls to the Segovia area to a quasi-friend of his. He told the man that he needed some information and for it he would offer a reward. The man asked him about the nature of the information and Franco gave him sketchy details. His friend's next question was of course the reward amount. Franco told him $7 thousand US. The guy prior to getting any specific details told Franco that he would only do it for $10k. Franco bid him good day, and before he hung up, his friend said, "Okay, you cheap bastard, I'll do it but I don't do rough stuff anymore."

Less than one hour later, Franco received a call and was told the name of the hospital, where it was, and the rooms the two men were being housed. Franco told him once the information was substantiated, he would make a money-order payable to him. Franco immediately called Darryl, introduced himself, and provided him the information that he received from his friend.

# # #

Two hours later after landing in Madrid, Michael, Desmond, and Isaiah provided surveillance at the hospital. Isaiah was stationed in the lobby, Desmond was assigned to the floor where the two men allegedly were being held, and Michael stayed with the vehicle. When Darryl, Sue Lyn, Jasper, and Harold met up with Michael, he gave them a general layout of the hospital. He recommended that they extract the people during a shift change and commandeer an ambulance.

At approximately 2330 hours, everyone was in place and the two men were extracted from the hospital without a hitch. It was as though the hospital had closed down for the night and patients were on their own.

Once the ambulance was dumped, and the men were led into the van, the interrogation began immediately. At first the two men acted as though they didn't understand English, Spanish, German, or French. Michael told Jasper to pull off the road for a moment and let him have a word with the guys. When Michael entered the rear of the van, he pulled out a knife and slowly dug it deep into one of the men's leg, who screamed for mercy, in English. Michael quietly asked the man, "Where were you taking those products?"

The man did not respond. Michael looked at his bleeding leg and announced, "I think I'm going to do the same thing to the other leg and then in various places until you tell me where those two vans were heading."

The guy screamed, "We were to drive the vans to a bridge where two other drivers would meet us and pay us. That is the honest to God's truth. Our destination was an underpass, approximately, twenty kilometers from Segovia."

Michael asked, "Where did you pick up the load?"

One of the men responded, "We picked the load up from two men outside of Madrid and were given instructions and directions to the underpass outside of Segovia."

"The two men in Madrid, what did they look like? What were they wearing?" Michael asked.

"We never saw their faces and they could not see ours because the instructions for delivery included a hooded presentation and no conversation at the drop-off points and the transfer of envelopes containing our payment. Each man's face was covered when we picked up the load and we were to cover our faces once we reached Segovia."

Darryl said, "If that's all you can tell us, then I'm afraid we have no use for you guys." He made a thumbs down motion to Michael. The other captive screamed, "Wait! The man in charge, his name is Victor Cherendoloff or something like that, but he didn't seem like the boss. I had driven for those people before and each time I got that assignment, this guy seemed to be under the foot of someone else. After one conversation on the telephone, he mumbled, "one day I'm going to kill that freak." Listen, we are delivery boys, we don't have a clue about the contents of the vans. We were just told to keep them separate and to never open the back. I swear to you, this is all we know. I brought this clown along because he's my sister's husband and they have no income at the moment."

Darryl looked at Michael and walked away. The man previously talking screamed and said, "I have an address. I have an address and I know which flat he stays in, but you have to promise to set us free! Please, I don't want to die like this."

Michael said, "Do you see how bad your buddy is bleeding. You don't think I can make you tell me everything I want to know without agreeing to set you free? Listen, I'm a skilled extractionist and I know how to make a dead man talk."

"Sir, I'm just asking for a little mercy for me and him. We're just drivers, we don't make decisions and, therefore, we should be treated as such. I'm begging for our lives because we really thought we were just making a delivery. It was only when our written instructions demanded that we wear masks at the transfer points, that's when I really became scared."

Darryl looked at the men and whispered, "This address, how credible is it and how did you happen upon it?"

The man doing the pleading said, "I think it's very credible. I drove this guy to an area, he got out of the car and started walking. I drove about a quarter of a mile away and stopped for a beer because I had made some extra money and wanted to celebrate. I saw him walk into a restaurant and five minutes later, he came out with a woman. They walked, within eyesight, right up the street and went into a flat. I sat there and had three beers, and eventually fell asleep in my car. I slept all night and received a call to pick up my passenger where I dropped him off. I saw him leave the building and I waited before I went to our rendezvous point to pick him up. He never said a word, got into the car and was on the phone speaking in what appeared to be a combination of Russian, French, and Spanish. I know where he stayed and the restaurant where the woman came from. Will you let us go, is my concern?"

Michael in the meantime had linked wire ties together and placed them on the bleeding man's leg. He said, "Your skin is barely broken, the blood that's flowing is a function of your fear, heartbeat, and knowing that at any moment, we could kill you. We are not going to kill you and I need you to relax and breathe slowly."

Michael asked, "Would you recognize the woman if you saw her again?"

"It was dark, but she had long flowing hair and was tall," the man said.

"I want you to show me the restaurant first and then the flat. I want you to go into the restaurant and see if you see the woman," Michael stated.

#

Two hours later, Darryl and his crew had identified the woman, released their hostages at the hospital and broke into the flat where the woman lived. Sue Lyn methodically took pictures of the flat, and of a man, a woman, and a child in a frame on the wall. In the bedroom, and under the bed, was a small arms cache including assault rifles, pistols, knives, and what appeared to be smoke grenades. Pictures were taken of the cache and she noticed that an extra clip was visible but the matching weapon was not there indicating that the subject was armed.

The guys reconvened and ate at the restaurant across the street from where the woman worked, so that they could watch all movements. Darryl called the Sarge, reported their findings, and told him they were camping out until the woman got off from work and hopefully the man showed up.

CHAPTER NINETEEN

Victor Cherendoloff was aware that his drivers did not receive the merchandise. He was aware of the accident and suspicious of the whereabouts of the drivers. He felt that somewhere along the way, the plan had been compromised and, therefore, vacated all known residences and modified all points of contacts.

As Sue Lyn studied the pictures she took, she noticed that the child in the picture seemed happy and loved. As she zoomed in on the picture, another framed pictured featured the child only with a look of fear on her face. Under the picture were the words, 'remember me in all that you do.'

Sue Lyn showed the picture to Darryl, Michael, and Isaiah. She asked them if they saw anything unusual in the picture. No one had zoomed in on the picture in the background. She then zoomed in on the picture and they all agreed, the child was being held against her wishes and the guy they thought was Victor Cherendoloff, was probably a fake.

Darryl called his uncle and explained the situation to him. He said, "I wouldn't be surprised if there are a number of people running around with that name. I bet you the guy we're waiting for is a pawn in this event." The Sarge suggested they stay the course and at least try to follow the woman.

No sooner had the Sarge recommended that course of action, the woman hurriedly left the restaurant and headed in the direction of her flat. Darryl asked Sue Lyn to follow her from a distance.

The woman reached her flat and looked around to see if she was being followed. She scaled the steps and entered the building. Sue Lyn continued on her journey and passed the building and never looked in its direction.

Ten minutes later, the woman came out of the building with two backpacks. She looked around then proceeded down the steps. At the base of the steps, she turned left and that's when a car sped near her and fired several shots at her but missed her terribly. Darryl told Michael to drive to where the woman had fallen down. In the meantime, Sue Lyn fired two rounds at the car, disabling the vehicle and hitting the driver in the head. The passenger in the rear, tried to exit the car and that's when Sue Lyn fired a shot hitting him in the shoulder. The rest of the team were on him before he could retrieve his weapon.

With the intended victim of the shooting in one vehicle and the shooter in the other, Beckmire's crew took off towards the airport. Darryl and Sue Lyn went through the backpacks of the individual in their vehicle and searched her from head to toe. In the woman's bag was a small caliber weapon and a small pocketknife. Sue Lyn unloaded the weapon and placed it in her bag.

The injured shooter had a knife but no identification on him and Michael realized that his wound was serious. He immediately started asking questions and the guy made the unfortunate mistake of spitting in his face.

Michael reached in his pocket and removed two paper napkins that he took from the restaurant. He saw a rag on the floor, picked it up and tied it tight around the mouth of the guy. He wiped the spit off his face, pulled out his knife and without any hint of what he was going to do, dug his knife deep into the man's shoulder. The injured man screamed in pain. Michael withdrew his knife and plunged it into the man's other shoulder and began to yank and move it from side to side. He then screamed, "You spit again, and I will cut your fucking tongue out of your mouth. Michael removed the rag and said, "I'm going to ask you just once, why did you try to shoot that woman?"

The man between gasps of air stated, "I was paid to kill her. She and her man are targets."

"Where is the little girl?"

"I didn't have that assignment but I'm sure by now she's dead."

Michael feeling disgusted, took his knife and drove it deep into the man's leg and yelled, "Where are they holding her? Don't you fucking lie to me. Where are they holding her hostage?"

The man in a weakened voice said, "If she's alive, they are holding her three kilometers from here."

"You show me how to get there and I won't take your eyes out." The man told Michael to drive down the street until he told him to make a right turn.

Michael called Darryl and said, "They're holding the child three kilometers from here. We have to try to extract her."

Darryl said, "That might be costly because we don't know what we're up against."

"Darryl, we can't stand by and not try to save the child."

Sue Lyn announced, "And we're not going to standby. We'll follow you and make shit up as we go along and hope for the best."

Darryl said, "Listen, we don't have time to do reconnaissance or anything else, you make that son-of-a-bitch give you good intel and then you whack his ass."

After obtaining information from the injured man, Michael called Darryl and said, "We'll be there in less than ten minutes. We're going to drive by and you can find out if there is an exit in the rear and that's where you'll give me and my crew cover."

Darryl said, "I need you to be careful and deliberate. Leave your emotions in the vehicle and remind yourself that you work for me and I need you in one piece. In other words, don't do stupid and watch your back. Do you feel you retrieved believable information from that shooter?"

"I can only hope so."

In the vehicle Darryl was in, the intended target of the assassination was distraught and incomprehensible. She kept saying, 'pobrecita; mi bambina,' over and over. Sue Lyn asked the woman if she spoke English and was told that she did. Sue Lyn asked the woman if she were hurt and the woman responded that she was not but her child would be murdered. Sue Lyn then asked the woman, "Why would people try to shoot you in broad daylight? Who are you and what is it they want from you?"

The woman began to cry harder and announced, "They have my daughter, they corrupted my husband, and now he has to do exactly what they say or they will kill our child."

"Is your husband Victor Cherendoloff?"

The woman jerked her head, looked at Sue Lyn, and asked, "How do you know that name?"

"I know that name because that person is responsible for killing thousands of people in America and other places around the world."

"My husband's name is Marketo Valdez. He was forced to assume the name Victor Cherendoloff to make sure that the real person in charge of these hideous crimes could go undetected. My husband and many others around the world have assumed that name."

Darryl's phone rang and it was the Sarge who inquired about what was happening. Darryl told his uncle that they were in the process of breaching a facility to save a child and that he would get back to him. Before hanging up the phone, Darryl told his uncle that there were many people named Victor Cherendoloff.

The captive pointed out to Michael the building and the flat where the child was being held captive by a man and a woman. He cautioned Michael that they may have a suicide vest on the child. Michael said, "If the child lives, you live and I get you out of the country. If the child is dead, then my friend, I will spread parts of your body all over Spain."

Approximately two minutes after making that statement, his captive saw a man hurriedly walking down the street with what appeared to be goods from a local grocery. The captive frantically motioned to Michael that the guy approaching the van was one of the people in charge of the child. Michael told Isaiah to pull his weapon on the man and hold him while he and Desmond breached the front door.

Like clockwork, Desmond's size sixteen foot kicked open the door to the flat and Michael ran into it with his weapon ready. In the corner of the dining room, a woman frantically tried to strap a suicide vest on a child. Michael fired a round into her head. He initially didn't see the remote control for the vest and signaled Desmond to get the kid. As he backed out of the flat, he saw sitting on the windowsill, what appeared to be a remote-control unit.

Back at the van, Isaiah said to the assassin, "Looks like you live my friend. Desmond took the child to the van where her mother was. Michael told the assassin to get the hell out of the van but stated, the money you were going to make is sitting on the table in that flat.

The bloodied man limped up the steps and into the flat. After a few seconds, Michael hit the remote and there was a small explosion.

The mother of the child, after a quick evaluation of her complicity in the murders of people by the Carbon Factor, was subsequently disavowed of any involvement and was released near the airport. The mother was given $10k.

#

Darryl and Michael reported to the Sarge what had happened and was told to head to the airport and meet the group in Valencia. Darryl stridently commanded, "Everyone out of the vehicle, except Sue Lyn and Michael. After everyone had exited the van, Darryl said, "The next time you pull some cowboy shit like that, it will be the last time you enjoy working for me or this family."

Michael began to craft his response when Sue Lyn came to his defense and prosecution by saying, "I agreed with you Michael. We couldn't leave that child to fend for herself. I disagree with you when you doubt Darryl's wisdom and experience in these matters. You didn't let him finish his statement before you essentially told him that you couldn't standby and not try to help that child. Michael, you crossed the border on that one. I suggest you find a way to get back into Darryl's good graces and never doubt or challenge his decisions. He was gracious; his uncle would have injured you."

Michael broke into tears and began to beg for understanding without saying anything other than, "I'm sorry, boss. It will never happen again."

Darryl said, "You're not my dog. You're my right-hand man and as such, if I'm wrong, then I want to hear from you. I don't want a lackey hanging around, who is afraid to counter my decisions when they have absolute information to the contrary of my decisions. Mister, you had better figure this shit out or you're out of here."

###

In Valencia, some of the group met at *The Conversion*, the restaurant they were partners in. The Sarge looked about the room and asked Darryl, "Where's your crew?"

"They're probably doing penitence with their leader. Michael and I had operational differences when he pulled morality on me before I could finish my thoughts."

"And he's still standing or working for you?" The Sarge inquired.

Sue Lyn proclaimed, "I told Michael that he would have been injured had he confronted you. Darryl on the other hand, took a different approach and verbally crucified him and gave him a single option. Uncle, he made Michael cry."

The Sarge said, "It takes a big man to cry and a bigger man to admit his issue. Did he cry because he was wrong or since you hurt his feelings?"

Sue Lyn said, "Uncle, Michael cried because of both. He wasn't insubordinate, he just didn't let Darryl finish his statement. I jumped in and saved them both from each other by agreeing with Michael and knowing that later, I would have the opportunity to speak to my husband about the issue. I also, and I must admit this, prosecuted Michael as well."

"Honorable wife, do you mind if I answer my uncle?" Darryl inquired.

"No, my wonderful husband. I'll let you tell your side of the story." She kissed him on the cheek and said, "Others are waiting to speak to your uncle."

The Sarge said, "Nephew, I know how you feel, but there is a fine line between making a decision and having all of the information before making a decision."

"Uncle, that's exactly what I told Michael. I vociferously told him that I didn't want a lackey and that it was up to him to figure out the best approach to being my right-hand man and not a 'yes man.' Anyway, if you have no further questions on that matter, I would like to talk about the notion that there are several Victor Cherendoloffs operating under duress. We were able to save a woman and her child in Segovia but the man in the equation, got away. We took the woman and the child to the airport and gave them funds to get out of the country. However, she adamantly stated, that there were many Victor Cherendoloffs."

"If you wanted to cover your tracks, that's not a bad strategy. Did you find out where the materials were heading?"

"The crash site was toxic in the sense that it had too many on lookers trying to see what had happened. The men we abducted, were the second in a trilogy of drivers to handle the products. They confessed that each group's identity was secret, their faces were covered, and there was no communications. Their expectation when arriving at the designated drop-off point was an envelope with their fee in it."

"That seems like a lot of steps to protect someone who is not in the area. It makes me think that the real Victor Cherendoloff is somewhere in Spain and I'm betting he's more likely to be found in Madrid than in Segovia. Now nephew, if you really want to admonish Michael, send him and his crew on the plane to Madrid and let them snoop around. You never know, they may find another Victor Cherendoloff hanging around."

# # #

In a far corner, Jong and Franco were having a discussion and the Sarge asked Darryl to go and see what was going on. When Darryl arrived, Jong said, "I'm trying to tell him how to invest the funds within our group and he wants us to invest our funds in his group. He doesn't understand that we have more than him and he gets a better bang for the buck if he joins us. He thinks we can get more if we join him."

Darryl introduced himself again, and said, "My uncle asked me to see if you two needed arbitration?"

Franco said, "Mr. Jong's numbers don't add up to mine and, therefore, I want him to explain why pooling our funds with you is better for us."

Darryl said, "Perhaps, the dissimilarity in language and money makes all the difference. Franco, you do things with the euro, is that right?"

Before he could answer, Jong yelled, "I'll be damn. You're talking in euros and I'm speaking in dollars and there is a significant difference. Okay, Franco, let's play your game. Thanks Darryl."

#

Darryl interrupted his uncle and Mallory and said, "Uncle, I want to send Michael and his crew back to Madrid and see if they can stumble onto some credible intelligence. Perhaps, they might be able to find the husband of the woman we took to the airport. Do you see a need for them here?"

The Sarge replied, "Are you sending Earther and Windom?"

"Uncle, they're a part of the team."

"Okay nephew, you manage it but limit our exposure."

Darryl summoned Earther and Windom and told them they were heading back to Madrid along with the rest of the group. Earther said, "Boss, what's up with Michael? He acts as though he lost his best friend."

Darryl's head dropped and he said, "Keep an eye on him. I had some strong words with him when we were in Segovia. Help him make good decisions."

#

As the group gathered in front of *The Conversion,* Darryl said, "Sue Lyn and I are not making this trip. I know we just came from Madrid but now you're going back. If anyone has a pressing matter or problem that conflicts with that, please let me know. Michael is aware of the general information we're seeking about a certain Victor Cheveldayoff, the alleged bomber. If you're lucky, you might find the woman and child we saved hanging out at the airport waiting on her husband. They are key, and if necessary, bring the entire family back here even if you have to kidnap them."

Darryl looked at Michael, and said, "There's cash on the plane and the pilots are legal. People, Michael is in charge and I expect you to follow his orders as if they were mine, because they are mine. I have full and unwavering faith in him and his leadership. Rally on Michael! That's it and I'll see you guys in a few days. If I can clear it with my uncle, Michael, perhaps you guys can do a bit of sightseeing and things like that. Oh, and by the way, everyone has at least $4k on them, right? Okay, if not, Michael, deal with that matter. Have a safe trip and stay in touch."

# # #

In Madrid, Michael split his forces into two groups. He sent Windom, Earther, Giuseppe, Quick, and Jasper to Segovia while he, Isaiah, Desmond, Cheapman, Nikleson and Harold checked out Madrid. Their first stop was the commercial airline gates.

At one of the Iberia waiting gates, there she and her daughter sat, obvious, exposed, and frightened; the woman and child that Michael rescued. The woman saw Michael and he motioned with his finger for her to exercise silence and discretion. Michael told Isaiah to hang out near the terminal and for Harold and Desmond to provide cover for the woman and her child. As everyone held their positions, from afar, a man could be seen walking towards the terminal along with a host of other people. He stood out because of his photograph, that was taken by Sue Lyn in the man's flat. Michael recognized him, and as the man approached the terminal, Michael walked towards him and said, "If you go into that terminal, your family will be murdered. Take a deep breath and just hang out here with me. I know you're not the Victor Cherendoloff that the world is looking for. But you have information that will help us narrow our search for the real person. Your choices are simple, agree to help me find the real Victor Cherendoloff or watch your family, from afar, be shot and killed. What's it going to be, Marketo? I saved your wife and daughter once today and I'm prepared to do it again, but you have to tell me everything you know about the real Victor Cherendoloff."

Mr. Valdez cried, "Please, don't hurt my family, I will cooperate!"

"Okay, Mr. Valdez, this is how we're going to play this thing. You're going to walk past your wife and child and two minutes later, they will follow you to another terminal where all of you will board a private plane that is headed for Valencia. You have my word; nothing will happen to you or your family as long as you play by the rules that I have laid out for you. Is that clear?"

"Please, mi amigo, don't hurt my family and I will tell you everything that I know."

# # #

In the terminal for private planes, Michael called Darryl and told him that he found the woman, and child, as well as the husband. Michael said, "Boss, if I can be so bold, I would like to put those people on our plane and send them to you. I want to join my guys in Segovia. I split my forces and sent Windom, Earther, Giuseppe, Quick, and Jasper to Segovia to check out a few things but this whole scenario smells volatile to me. I just want to get these people out of here and catch up with my guys. I do not want to leave them in Segovia and I can't afford to wait on them to get here because I fear this cargo is mucho importante!"

"Michael, I trust you and your judgement. Do what you think is right by you, your men, and the people we need to obtain information from. Once you've made that decision, tell the pilot to call me with his ETA and I'll be there with backup. I will switch pilots and have you extracted once you gather your people and get you back to Madrid."

"Darryl, I'm of the opinion that a solid lead is in a safehouse in Segovia, that Marketo kept referencing. I just want to get these people to safety, check out a few other possibilities, gather my men, and get out of here."

"Put them on the plane, have the pilots do due diligence in terms of searching them and secure the cabin while in flight. We don't know these people and I'm hoping everything checks out. Good luck in Segovia and keep me informed."

# # #

Two hours later, Michael caught up with most of his crew and listened to gathered chatter from people who drank too much vino. He asked about the whereabouts of Windom and Earther, and Isaiah pointed to a restaurant across the street. Isaiah asked Michael about the safe house and was told that it had been recently trashed as if someone was in a hurry to cover their tracks.

#

In the meantime, Windom and Earther met a native American who worked in Segovia driving tractor trailers. He happened to be on a three-day suspension for driving beyond the prescribed number of hours in a twenty-four-hour period. His load, according to him, was non-perishable and could sit for months without spoilage. Windom asked him how he came to be so far away from Minnesota, and he replied, "Falling in love with the wrong woman can lead a man to strange and faraway places."

Windom announced, "I am called Windom and he is named Earther, and we too are from Minnesota. What is your name?"

"I happen to have two names. My given name is Nashata." After he gulped down a large amount of vino and burped, he said, "My assumed name is Victor Cherendoloff."

Both men kicked each other and skipped any reference to his assumed name and Windom asked, "Is the food good here, and if so, what do you recommend?"

Nashata said, "The vino is better, the food is okay, big portions and cheap."

Earther beckoned the server over to the table and ordered two bottles of red wine, two hamburgers and fries and asked Windom what he would like."

Windom said, "I'll have two burgers and fries. Nashata, have a drink and some food on us fellow 'Minnesota Nice' people."

Nashata said, "Ah, 'Minnesota Nice'." I was going to ask you about that to make sure you people are authentic."

"Hell, we be more than authentic. The entire government is trying to run us off our land so that they can run a damn pipeline through our homes. When it comes to them folks, we ain't 'Minnesota Nice'."

It was apparent that Nashata was beyond the legal drink limit, if in fact, there was such a thing in Segovia. His words were slurring, his eyes were blurry, and his stories became more believable. Windom asked him, "How did you get a name like Vincent Cherendal or whatever you said?"

Nashata, looked around the room and said, "My assumed name is Victor, not Vincent, Cherendoloff."

Earther replied, "That almost sounds Russian."

"It is Russian. I'm also a spy for the CIA and that name gets me into places where all kinds of things go on."

Windom said, "Nashata, we don't want to get in your business. We just want to have a drink with a brother from Minnesota."

Nashata looked at him and then around the room and whispered, "You remember that bombing in Springfield? Do you remember the name of the guy in charge of that massacre? Anyway, his name was Victor Cherendoloff—one in the same!"

Windom pulled his chair closer to the man and asked, "Did you kill all of those people?"

"One in the same, my brother. One in the same! As a matter of fact, I believe my load is half grain and the other half cooked coal!"

Earther asked, "Nashata, what does one in the same mean? Does it mean you're the man who killed all those people?"

"One in the same, my brother. One in the same!"

Earther said to Windom, "We should pay the bill and get out of here. This guy is either telling the truth or making shit up, but either way, we don't want to have any knowledge of this shit." He motioned for the waiter and gave him a hundred-dollar bill and told him that they had to go.

Nashata said, "Guys, I need a ride to my place. It's just one and a half kilometers away."

Earther said, "Okay, but no more stories."

Windom said, "I have to hit the restroom, I'll be right back."

Once in the restroom, Windom called Michael and told him about their encounter. Michael told him that they were near and to keep the person close.

#

Once in the van Nashata passed out. Michael called Darryl and told him about their discovery and wanted to know if they should take the subject to the airport and transport him to Valencia. Darryl thought about it and decided to do just that.

#

In Valencia and at *The View*, Nashata when he woke up, was offered coffee and food. He asked Windom where was he, and was told by Earther, that he was in Valencia. Earther further told him how he passed out and wanted to travel to Valencia with them and how he got his wish.

Darryl and Sue Lyn were introduced to Nashata by Michael and was given a briefing about the conversation that Earther and Windom had with the man. Sue Lyn asked, "Is your name really Victor Cherendoloff?"

The man studied her and asked, "Is your name really Pocahontas?" He laughed and said, "Of course not. My given name is Nashata and I'm from Minnesota."

Darryl realized the apparent dislike for women, decided to intervene, and take over the inquiry. He said, "Listen, my name is Darryl, and she is my wife and we're sort of the leaders of this rag-tag-group. Can I get you something to drink or eat?"

"Right now, I'm good. Who are you people and how did I get to Valencia?"

Windom smiled, looked at Darryl for any hesitancy and said, "We flew you here on our plane. Your story in the restaurant was interesting and we sort of decided to be 'Minnesota Nice' and kidnap your ass."

Everyone broke into laughter except Nashata who said, "That's against the law."

Windom said, "So is confessing to be 'one in the same.' You know, the guy Victor Cherendoloff who massacred those people in Springfield as well as in Africa."

The mood changed and Nashata said, "I was just jesting with you guys."

Earther said, "We're not jesting with you. You know what's even more hilarious, is that you said, half your load on your truck was grain and the other half was burnt coal. Few people know about the significance of burnt coal my friend."

Nashata stood up and announced, "I'm out of here." Four different weapons were cocked and pointed at him. Earther said, "Boss, may I continue, or do you want to handle this from here?" Darryl nodded for him to proceed.

"Nashata, let me continue by saying, there is no record of us being in this country. No picture of our plane, no passports, no nothing. Now, let me give you a little history. Another

Victor Cherendoloff was smuggled out of Segovia along with his wife, after two men attempted to assassinate her and their daughter who we saved from a suicide vest. I say all of that to say this, you can't take your ass back to Segovia. You won't last a minute. Once your people figure out you've been missing for a few hours, they'll issue a hit order on you. Now, I'm trying to be 'Minnesota Nice' and save your ass. You have to work with us."

# # #

In the meantime, Marketo Valdez was summoned by Michael to see if he recognized Nashata. Looking through a crack in the door, Marketo said, "He is the man that came into my house, handed me a grenade with the pin out and took my daughter. Once my daughter was in the car and driven away, he replaced the pin in the grenade and gave me a list of things to do."

Michael asked him to hold that thought and stepped out into the hallway where Sue Lyn and Darryl were. Michael repeated what Marketo had said to him about Nashata. Sue Lyn said, "Let's introduce them to each other and see the reaction."

"Honey, I want to talk a little more to that guy. You people just hold tight until I call you into the room, if I decide on that course of action."

# # #

The Sarge was summoned to the room and was briefed about the conversations and knowledge of certain consistent products necessary to enhance the Carbon Factor. The Sarge entered the room with Jilkes, John Lee, Jong, and Mallory. He introduced each man and indicated that it would probably be Jilkes and John Lee who would conclude this interview. Nashata asked, "Just how do they conclude interviews?"

The Sarge said, "Oh, when they're done, there is usually no one alive but them two, a lot of blood, and body parts. Now, I just have a few questions before I turn this event over to them. Where is your truck with grain and burnt coal?"

"That's an easy one. It's in Segovia."

"Okay! Did you load your own truck?"

"Naw, I don't do that, you know, union shit."

"How did you know there was burnt coal in the trailer?"

"I was told what my configuration would be by the man who hired me and made me assume the name, Victor Cherendoloff."

"Can you describe him and where were you to deliver the grain and the burnt coal?"

"Listen, once I missed the timetable, all bets were off. The delivery points were changed, the person receiving it was changed, and I was on a hit list unless I could explain to their satisfaction, what happened."

"I have another person outside saying that he too is Victor Cherendoloff. Is it possible that there are more than one of you?"

"Friend, there are a least ten that I personally know of," Nashata replied.

"How is it you're privy to who, what, where, the contents of your vehicle, names, and a lot of other things? Are you getting sleepy time information from your woman who is not afraid of him?"

"Friend, I guess because I was one of his confidants. Now, I'm just a dead man walking, and so is that woman I love, except she might survive because she wasn't afraid of him or his maladies!"

At that moment, the faint sound of broken glass could be heard and the instantaneous splattering of Nashata's head could be seen. Everyone hit the floor, Jilkes extinguished the lights and the Sarge realized that this was not coincidental. This assassination was targeted, and he knew they were in the right place.

After everyone was extracted from the room, Michael yelled, "You people saw the window, set up a perimeter and see where that shot came from. With the flashlight app on his cellphone, Michael crawled back into the room and pulled the lifeless body of Nashata out of the room and into the hallway. To his surprise, Nashata, still had a pulse. As Michael yelled for help, he saw that the man had no entry or exit wounds, just a large gulf in his scalp. The reflected shot, through the window, creased Nashata's head rather than penetrated his skull.

Later from the rear of *The View*, Nashata was removed and quietly taken to the hospital. In the interim, the police had been summoned and a body bag with pillows in it had been taken from the front of the villa and in plain sight of prying eyes.

# # #

In the hospital where Nashata was taken, Michael stated, "I'm glad you're going to be okay but I fear as soon as they hear you're still alive, those people will be back to finish the job."

Nashata, with tubes running down his throat, motioned for a piece of paper and a pencil. He wrote, 'don't leave me here.

I can give you strategic information about the group, their backers, and finances.'

Michael looked at him and said, "I'll bring it up to my boss and will get back to you. What you have to offer is thin and we did you a favor by bringing you to the hospital. We need more before we can commit to helping you escape the demon that you're protecting."

Nashata stated, "I can't believe they tried to kill me. I've been a loyal servant and protected them. I am no longer that gullible person, especially since my woman finds comfort in helping that fucking freak. Listen, I think this guy knows your leader."

Suddenly, the lights flickered and instead of a slow titration effect, a liquid was gushed into both arms of Nashata. He became comatose immediately and his heart stopped as if it were on a timer and the bell rung indicating time was up. Michael attempted to provide CPR while screaming for assistance, that never showed up. Nashata, a clue to who the bomber is, was dead before he could complete his comments.

In Valencia and with the entire group in attendance, Michael recalled the exact words that Nashata had said to him. Darryl requested, "Michael, please tell my uncle what the man said before he was murdered."

Michael turned to the Sarge and said, "Nashata thought that his leader was familiar with you. He said to me, "listen, I think this guy knows your leader." Those were his last words before the lights flickered and he began to convulse, and the next thing I knew, I was trying to provide CPR on him. He frequently mentioned that his woman helped the guy a lot, and that she wasn't afraid of something and I never got a definition of what that something was or is."

The Sarge mumbled, "How can so many be aware of me and I'm not knowledgeable of them? Something is going on, and I need access to the underground. As he started to walk away, Michael announced, "I know two people down there, but I would have to confirm and reconfirm any information that I received from them."

"I thought you got most of your buddies out of there."

"I did! Those two never recovered from what we did and used that reason, perhaps excuse, to get bogged down in drugs. They get the word and they pass it on sometimes to others. If you want to subsidize them with money for drugs then I'll try to reach out to them. However, Sarge, I've never been high on synthetics, and I don't have a clue as to how far and how long they go on those drug-induced trips. My current team is clean, those two just loved to party."

The Sarge looked at Michael and said, "You did me a favor once, twice, or perhaps more. I'm not sure about how many times, but I am sure that I need you to follow every lead possible. Think about it. Why would the very essence of the Carbon Factor be discovered as a result of a vehicle accident in Segovia, Spain? Whoever that son-of-a-bitch is, he was going to wreak havoc somewhere in Spain. Do me a favor and ask your bosses if they would take a moment out of their busy schedules to meet with me in the next hour or so?"

# # #

Less than an hour later, Sue Lyn, Darryl, Michael, and Mallory met the Sarge in the lounge of the restaurant. He welcomed each person and said, "Darryl, I want to borrow

Michael for a special detail while we're here in Spain. Is that going to create a problem for you?"

Sue Lyn replied, "Uncle, please do not use the idea of eminent domain in annexing our staff?"

"Sue Lyn, what on earth are you talking about? Eminent domain is about the land and finding reasons for the government to take property for the good of the community. When you sequester someone, you literally lock them up until a certain act is completed. Remember, I discovered Michael and his crew first. They're on, what I consider, consignment to you. However, I will respect your wishes and at least state that my need is specific and related to Spain."

The Sarge continued, "As you know, Michael was with Nashata, before he died. He mentioned some key information about our bomber including he thought the person knew me. He also indicated that his woman was not afraid of the person which led me to think that something physical is out of whack or he's a bully. Nashata, also acknowledged, something that I thought was somewhat braggadocious about the events in Springfield. Now, for a truck driver, he seemingly knew a lot about what was going on including the contents of his load; burnt coal and grain or fertilizer. Windom or Earther acknowledged that the guy spoke in a cavalier manner about the Springfield situation and when questioned, he responded, "one in the same." Are these things coincidental or did we just lose an especially important connection to the person creating this mayhem? I frankly don't believe in coincidences. I need Michael and his crew to sniff this thing out while we're here and try to avert another catastrophe."

The group agreed that the burnt coal and grain or fertilizer were not coincidental, and at some point, in time, a union would be consolidated and the results would be a more destructive example of the Carbon Factor's capabilities than was illustrated in Springfield. The Sarge vehemently stated, "I want every living soul on this one including the children. We need a comprehensive approach to this one and that means telling the women everything that we don't know about the Carbon Factor, the bomber, Springfield, and what we read about Addis Ababa. We need to begin to act like one of those big corporations that have Research & Development departments that can spend resources trying to figure out the best way to solve problems, create solutions, and enhance shareholders value." He looked at Sue Lyn and asked, "How's motherhood coming along?"

She smiled and whispered in his ear, "Uncle you should try it one time. Then you can tell me what it's like."

The Sarge smiled and replied, "Sue Lyn, if I could do that then there would be no need for the weaker sex, assuming that man is the weaker of the two. However, if the converse is true, then I'm afraid what this world would be like; men having babies and women having to work."

"My favorite uncle, I think we should end this conversation before I have to repeat some of your thoughts to your favorite and only wife."

The Sarge looked at her and bowed with respect but iterated, "You my lovely niece started this discussion with your suggestion that I should attempt certain activities."

"Uncle, once again, I want to move forward without embracing my favorite aunt, your wife, into the philosophical discussion."

"Thank you, my niece, I think we can conclude this topic and move on to that which matters to the existence of many people in this country."

## CHAPTER TWENTY

Zanthius entered the dining area and walked directly over to Larry, and in front of his kids and wife, asked, "Larry, if you received a magnificent kiss from a woman, would you forget it, even if you witnessed someone else receiving it?"

Marisa said, "Hello Zanthius. We're having dinner right now with the kids, would you like to join us and further embarrass my husband in front of his children?"

He looked at Marisa and then the kids and stated, "Well, kids, uncle Zanthius has done it again. He has gotten so involved in a puzzle and he needs your dad's input. Your daddy kisses your mommy and nobody else. My question was not about a kiss, it was about an idea if you know what I mean."

Larry, calmly took a bite of his fish, smiled at the kids, looked at Zanthius, and asked, "How much deeper are you going to excavate that hole? Tell you what, I'll catch up with you later once I've cleared my children's brains of kissing. You know, they think it's taboo!"

Zanthius walked away, realizing that he was so focused, he neglected to evaluate Larry's surroundings. He saw the Sarge and said, "I just made a mess out of things with Larry. Dad, can you just go over and make sure there's no friction at their table?"

"Son, they don't do friction. He'll get back to you after he secures his family."

#

Larry showed up and said, "Brother, sometimes, you are greater than special. What is it you wanted to ask me?"

"Larry and Dad, would you forget someone who was a spectacular kisser and/ or lover? Of course not. I'm telling you, there are two things that are bothering me. The first one is the aftermath of watching the video Mr. Utz showed us, with the woman kissing that man in the most luscious manner possible. I know everyone discounted my announcement that I knew that walk and that positioning of the hand prior to the kiss. Since that time, I have replayed my moments with Helga, over and over again. Guys, I swear on my own life that even though the woman's whose face is not clear, but I know it's Helga. If I'm correct, I think she used Nashata to move more than coal and grain or fertilizer. You guys remember when Michael stated that Nashata said that his woman was not afraid of the person who was in charge, on more than one occasion? Dad, I know this next idea is farfetched, but I need you to do me a favor and make a call to that sanitarium your cousin is in residence and make sure that he is still there. I know, this is crazy, but it's been bothering me and the only thing that I come up with is what I laid out," Zanthius stated.

Larry said, "I'll be damn!" He pulled out a piece of paper from his back pocket and unfolded it. It was a crude drawing of boxes with connecting lines and question marks. He gave it to the Sarge and said, "Dad, I have had the same thoughts. Suppose the little box is Helga, and the big box is the bomber, your cousin. It's possible, after all, she's been reported dead on several occasions, but always seems to resurface with a new battery ready to start! Here's a question for you Dad, have you reached out to inquire about your cousin's health lately?"

Zanthius looked at Larry and sternly asked, "Are you fucking with me?"

The Sarge said, "Watch your mouth. Why would he play with you on a thing that impacts us all? Look at this, it doesn't have names, but it sure as hell sends the lines back to the beginning and that is where my cousin comes in."

Zanthius replied, "Down by the billabong, it was clear that we would provide clarity to situations when there was none."

Larry exclaimed, "Marco Polo and Japan."

The Sarge pulled out his cell phone and called the sanitarium. When there was no answer, he became concerned. He then called Mr. Utz and asked him about his cousin. Mr. Utz informed him that his cousin was murdered by the parent of one of the men he sent needlessly up against you guys. The Sarge asked Mr. Utz when this had occurred and why wasn't he informed? Utz told him that he had just found out about it a day ago. The Sarge thanked him, turned to his boys, and said, "Walter, was murdered by the parent of a person he sent into battle against us. His demise happened two weeks ago."

"Dad, I didn't hear you ask for confirmation, DNA, and/or pictures of the corpse. Sorry to say this, but this entire adventure has been about some unbelievable shit happening, and I am now of the belief, if I don't see it, I don't believe it. I'll bet Zanthius's ass that your cousin is alive, well, and living in a bionic suit like one of those Marvel characters."

The Sarge never said a word, but instead, dialed Mr. Utz back. When he answered the phone, the Sarge requested, "Can you perform a complete DNA test on the corpse and obtain pictures of the event? My boys are of the belief that our bomber is my cousin."

"Sarge, tell your boys to stop smoking that legal stuff. We did DNA testing and it came back, 99.99999% Walter Lassiter. Catch you later."

Hearing the information, Larry asked, "Did they dispose of his limbs after the amputations, and if so, did they burn them or store them in some sort of cryopreservation state? Dad, things are more than they seem today. Shit looks green until you put on a different pair of glasses and then its pink."

The Sarge paused for a few moments, and held a finger in the air, and said, "That fucker told me that he wasn't dead yet, and I wondered what he meant. This is all too weird to be true. The man is dead, Helga is dead, and the Carbon Factor is alive. Let's focus on what we know that is real. Even if my cousin is alive, he can't walk, he should be blind, he has no arms and legs, and he's hideous. I want to keep my focus on what I know and I can see."

Zanthius looked at his dad and said, "Perhaps, you will allow my brother and I to proceed down this street as long as it doesn't interfere with anything that you need us to do. I have one request, and that is to be able to speak with Mr. Utz, once we've figured out other ways to confirm DNA; if at all possible."

The Sarge looked at his boys and said, "I'm not discounting anything you're saying or doing, please keep it to yourselves unless my guys beat it out of you."

Larry proclaimed, "We're family! I don't see that event coming into play."

The Sarge gave Zanthius Mr. Utz's number. He texted Mr. Utz in the interim advising him to expect some radical questioning from his two sons and for him to be open and honest with them.

#

Beckmire's group along with Darryl's, made their way to Madrid and Segovia. In Segovia, Earther, Windom, and Michael spent time in local pubs hoping to stumble upon another loquacious conspirator who may be connected to the worldwide panic and fear of the Carbon Factor. They unfortunately were unable to elicit information and didn't notice anyone that looked or acted suspicious.

On the third day of their individual stakeouts, Michael switched places with Windom. After ordering a pint, he watched a well-dressed woman enter the pub and sit at a table with a reserved sign on it. He inconspicuously texted Earther. The text said, 'may need assistance.' Five minutes later, two huge human specimens walked into the place and sat at the table with the woman. The woman said something to them in Spanish and they got up from her table and walked over to where Michael was sitting. One of the men indicated that the lady in the corner wanted to have a word with him. Michael flashed his make-believe wedding ring and continued to read the English printed newspaper. One of the guys sat down next to Michael and showed him his weapon. Michael said, "Listen, I only have $100. I don't want any trouble and hopefully my wife will join me soon. Please, let me be!"

Earther aggressively fell through the door and Windom grabbed him and said, "We only have time for one more and then we must head to the hotel and then to the airport."

The two men looked at them and then at the woman. The woman threw her hands in the air as if she were surrendering.

The guy with the weapon said, "Give me your money Yankee or I'll blow your head off."

Michael looked intently at the man and cautiously put his left hand in his pocket and pulled out a $100 bill and crumbled it up. He said to the man with the gun, "It's a good thing you're carrying. Where I'm from, people would make you eat that thing."

The man smiled, pulled the weapon out of the holster, and proceeded to hand it to his friend. Surprisingly to the men, Earther focused his weapon on the men and Windom targeted the woman in the corner. The barkeep reached for the telephone and Windom flashed the weapon at him. Michael told the guy that was holding his $100 bill, that he would be back in a moment. He walked over to the woman, turned a chair around backwards, and announced, "If you reach into that bag, I will blow your head off." He then sat down near her table. He took out his cell phone, called Darryl, and explained the situation to him. Darryl told him restrain them and to escort the three people outside.

Outside waiting was Desmond, Quick, Giuseppe, and Isaiah in two separate vehicles. Once everyone was restrained, Michael walked over to the barkeep and peeled off five $100 bills and said, "Sometimes, you need to ignore what goes on in your place. Am I clear?" The man stared at the bills and nodded frequently.

In the vehicle that the woman was in, she quickly acknowledged, "This is all a mistake and apparently a game that men play when they have guns. If you'll let me and my associates go, we will call this a no harm, no foul, situation."

Michael replied, "You seem to speak English extremely well and even know some of the cliches. Where are you from?"

"That's unimportant. What matters is this situation has the capability of being blown out of context and then we must advise the local magistrate that Americans are parading around town with automatic weapons, a crime punishable by life imprisonment if found guilty. As I stated, so far, this is all a misunderstanding, but if you proceed down this road, things could become extremely agitated."

Michael looked the woman up and down and fumbled through her purse where he found a small Beretta pistol and packs of euros and dollars. Michael took his cell phone and took an unexpected photo of the woman he was detaining. He also noticed the initials "HS" emblazoned on the medallion inside of the expensive looking purse that the woman had. What really fascinated Michael was the three different passports that were tucked neatly in three different compartments. After viewing each passport, Michael said, "I half ass expected to find one of these with the South African emblem on it."

Michael then instructed the woman to kick her shoes off. The woman hesitantly complied. Michael retrieved each shoe and noticed the housing in the right shoe that hid triple bonded razor blades. In the left shoe, and not surprisingly, was a double-sided knife. He smiled at her and stated, "You certainly are equipped for perhaps any trouble that might find you. Tell me something, are you a spy?"

The question caught the woman off guard and she clumsily stated, "A girl can never be too careful these days."

Michael shot back, "Yeah, razor blades in one shoe and a double-sided blade built into the other stiletto, and professionally mounted I must mention. I'm not even going to talk about the awfully expensive Beretta that's in your purse. Come now, make it easy on yourself, tell me who you are, what you do, and perhaps we can cut this trip short."

# # #

After placing the subjects in different vehicles, in front of the car Isaiah and Desmond were in, two concussion grenades exploded that distracted everyone in the nearby vicinity. The two men in the car with Isaiah and Desmond were sprayed with machine gun fire. Isaiah received two superficial wounds to his left shoulder and lower arm. Desmond miraculously escaped injury. The woman in the car with Michael, received a direct hit to the head from a sniper perched 200 or so yards away. Michael used her body to shield himself from the next round that entered the woman's torso and grazed his arm. Desmond shifted the gear into 1st and slammed his foot on the accelerator in time to miss the third shot which tore through the trunk of the car. Earther and Windom returned fire on the people in the car who had sprayed Isaiah's vehicle with gunfire.

Michael called Darryl in Madrid and reported what had happened and the extent of their injuries. He was directed, by Darryl, to head to the nearest hospital and leave all weapons with Earther and Windom. He told Michael that he and others were on their way and to be mindful of what information they told the police.

Darryl talked to his uncle and told him what had happened. His uncle said, "We must be getting awful damn close to something. How can they methodically eliminate their people who are captured? I guess it means that they have someone watching everyone at all times. Okay, you, Sue Lyn, and Mallory head over to Segovia to the hospital where the guys are heading and Darryl, Mallory is senior on this detail. Is that a problem?"

"Uncle, we all work for his majesty!" He smiled and walked away.

Mallory followed Darryl and said, "Darryl and Sue Lyn, these are your guys, your op, and, therefore, we're coming along as backup. Your op, young man, and young lady, I am a guest."

Darryl started to say something when Sue Lyn nudged him and whispered, "Don't you know how they operate. Haven't you seen enough of them to know that he didn't want to make Mallory junior to you and knew that Mallory would yield to you? Your uncle is a sly fox, always watching the protocol lamp."

# # #

The Sarge summoned Jong and announced, "I want to relocate our group from Madrid to Segovia, how long will it take us to get there and can you find us secure housing?"

"Sarge, I am from Asia. I think we are in Spain. Can you ask Ava?"

"Mr. Amazing, eh! Okay, get those cars and vans ready, we're heading to Segovia, because every time we get close to catching a player, they're assassinated. Fortunately, our people only sustained minor injuries. Why didn't they attempt to kill us as well? I'm hoping the shooters are just poor shots and that our people should have been in the equation as well. Think about it, two concussion grenades, a car sprayed with machine pistol fire and two direct hits to the subject of the investigation. Do me a favor, call my nephew and request that he gather as many personal effects as possible of the people who were killed. Tell him to check their shoes, pouches, lining of their jackets and everything else. How can we get so close and, on every occasion, have those we catch, assassinated within our midst? I think we're in the right place, but we're playing the wrong game. I think the perpetrator knows we're here and in force. We need to develop a new strategy."

As the Sarge considered his options, he yelled, "Delay that request to get the group to Segovia. I'm assuming that Okema, Yeshida, and Somara have been made because of their international issues. I want Larry, Marisa, Mary Alice, and you Jong, to be the lead on this one. I don't want anyone else around or even near. You have twenty minutes to think about it and another ten to convince Larry, Marisa, and Mary Alice. I will position Jilkes, John Lee, and Brown as your back up and attempt to smuggle their wives into the area without them being discovered. I know they're a hot commodity because their government is trying to embarrass them for leaving without the normal concluding conventions. Please, just think about it and let me know."

# # #

In Segovia at an outdoor restaurant, Larry and Marisa sat and ordered Mahou, a local beer that is brewed in Madrid. They also had jamon iberico (prosciutto) with cheese sandwiches. On the other side of the street, sitting at an outdoor fountain and having a burger and a coke was, Jong and Mary Alice. Watching both couples from windows and other secure points were, Brown, John Lee, Jilkes, Somara, Okema, and Yeshida.

Darryl had recommended that Larry and Jong not be armed and to trust their mates with any shooting scenarios. As

Larry and Marisa enjoyed their sandwiches, which were cut in half, two alleged beggars walked over to their table and grabbed the other halves of their sandwiches. Larry being extremely annoyed, stood up and asked, "Have you lost your damn mind? Those are our sandwiches!" One of the homeless looking men, showed off his knife and took a swig of Marisa's beer and asked, "You sure you want to be with him honey? He can't even protect you."

The Sarge prayed that Larry would let the two men bully them and not beat the shit out of them. Zanthius said, "Pops, they crossed the ass whipping stage when they touched their food."

"I know son, but Larry will take all kinds of shit before he goes off the reservation and kills those two."

Larry said, "Come dear, let's leave this place. As Marisa started to get up from her seat, the guy near her said, "Honey, I like you. I think I'm going to keep you here with me."

Larry yelled, "Enough, if you're going to rob us, then get on with it!" The two men made haste escaping, but not before yelling, "We'll see you again Black man; we'll see you again."

A few minutes later, the police arrived and asked what happened. Larry told him that two locals attempted to bully them but everything was okay. The police person asked Larry if he wanted to file a complaint and Larry told him that they were just street punks looking to harass visitors.

Jong saw what happened but never made a move to intervene. He knew Larry could manage the situation and, therefore, he didn't blow his cover by coming to Larry's rescue or assistance.

#

Meanwhile, as the group had coverage from the east and west, Michael remembered that they abandoned the cars with bodies in them, but he left the dead woman's handbag in the car. He asked Earther and Windom to escort him to the garage to obtain the purse. Upon entering the garage, two men were randomly ransacking vehicles in search of a prize. Earther and Windom started to chase them when Michael said, "They didn't hit our car. Let them go."

After retrieving the purse, and other items from the car, Michael asked Windom to siphon enough fuel to ignite the vehicle.

#

Once in the room, Michael emptied the contents of the bag onto the bed. It confirmed what he first discovered about the woman; three passports, a pistol, and other sundry items. As he viewed the passports, each picture of the woman had a different hair style and color as well as different color eyes. In her wallet was a fair amount of euros and dollars, several debit cards, and a miniaturized phone book. Her cell phone was on but locked and he immediately turned it off in case it was being tracked. As he looked closely at the handbag, he realized it was heavy, and the construction of it didn't match the weight. Michael looked at the emblem with the initials, "HS" and attempted to move it. On the first and second try, nothing happened. However, on the third attempt, the inside façade gave way to a hidden compartment with a list of names, payments, and scheduled deployments. The biggest discovery was a list of sites where the Carbon Factor was assembled. He asked Earther to get Darryl and Sue Lyn and to bring his uncle and Zanthius. Tell them it's urgent.

# # #

After analyzing the contents of the handbag, Zanthius said, "Michael, this is an incredible piece of undercover work. You know, the woman who started this adventure, had the same initials, "HS"."

Michael replied, "I asked her if she was a spy and she became a little flustered. I had her remove her shoes and imbedded in one shoe was a double-sided knife and the other had triple razor blades bonded inside, for maximum effect."

Zanthius said, "I wish somehow, we could have gotten her here and interrogated her. What did she look like?"

Michael pulled out his cell phone and pulled up a photo of the woman who had been shot in the head. When he saw the picture, Zanthius fell to the floor and screamed, "Dad, it's her. It's Helga Spengatsenburg."

The Sarge replied, "Are you sure?"

"Dad, this is the woman who slipped that guy a capsule in New York, and this is the woman that caused me, and the rest of you, all of this mayhem. My friends, please meet the one and only, Helga Spengatsenburg!"

"I'm afraid she won't be causing you any additional issues. Her head was literally split in half. The bullet tore everything in her head up. The second round that hit her knocked her from one side of the car to the other. I used her body as a human shield to escape the assassin's bullets. She, my friend is dead, dead, and dead!" Michael stated.

Zanthius said, "She has been the bane of my existence ever since I encountered her in Switzerland. She is the mother of one of my children, but now we all can rest in peace. Where is her body?"

Michael looked at Darryl and then at Zanthius, and emphatically stated, "I personally burned the car we were in. Our DNA and fingerprints were all over the place. Not sure if it was the smartest thing to do, but I made the decision and only her body and DNA remained in that car."

Meanwhile, Jong reviewed the information from Helga's purse and tried to figure out the meaning of the symbols, colors, and numbers that were written on a piece of paper. The list of numbers and letters created a challenge for Jong because there was no reference point. He enlisted the assistance of Larry and Zanthius. All three men were stuck in thought until the Sarge walked by, looked at the list and asked, "What is located at 42 degrees north and 73 degrees east?"

Jong replied, "How would we know?"

The Sarge said, "I'm just guessing that's latitude and longitude indicators and perhaps the single letter "s" is significant to a place."

Larry asked Siri and her response created a panic in the room.   Siri responded, "Those coordinates reference Springfield, Massachusetts."

Zanthius said, "Oh my God!"

Larry, asked Siri where is 76 degrees north and 66 degrees east? Her response was Caracas, Venezuela. He subsequently asked Siri about 40 degrees north and 4 degrees west and her response was Barcelona. Finally, he asked Siri, where is 17 degrees north and 4 degrees west and her response was, Mali in Africa. Everyone in the room was shocked at the discovery.

Larry said, "Dad, I'm afraid the next bombing may take place in Venezuela and they aren't that friendly to Americans at this point in time. The government is in turmoil and I doubt if we could get in and out of the country safely."

"Son, why would we even attempt to go into the country. It's all being apparently orchestrated from here. If we can find out who the mastermind is and put an end to his or her reign, then we might save people here in Spain, Venezuela, and Mali. Going to those countries won't solve anything other than people might think we're complicit in killing thousands of people. No, son, our best bet is to try to find more clues and close in on the person wreaking this havoc. They're making a point and will eventually try to take over the world. I used to think that was humanly impossible, but I'm now of the belief that if you control the Carbon Factor, you can control the world."

Zanthius said, "Pops, I think you're grossly over-valuing the capability of the Carbon Factor. The military might of the countries of the world wouldn't yield to such defeat. Perhaps, it might make the world realize that their insular way of existing requires rethinking and a call for unification. We can't exist in our own little world and not share the pain and in our case, the blame for the utilization of the Carbon Factor."

"Son, seemingly, you got the kiss, you had the thrill, you made the baby, and we were called up to protect your ass, you know, like the delayed application of a condom. Don't blame us for the Carbon Factor, it was all your doing, with a little bit of the bill going to your wife. However, we will get past this as well."

Jilkes and John Lee walked in and saw Jong looking at the piece of paper with the numbers on it. John Lee asked, "Where them there coordinates be to?"

Jong looked at him and asked, "How the hell do you know they're coordinates?"

"Hell, Jong, any half-wit would know that. That there be the first thing you learn in school. How to get to, how to get from, and where the two is and where the from was."

"What did you just say? Who else knows this language that only you speak?" Jong asked.

"This here African American speaks it better than me. They used to give us them maps and we'd make them simple so that he could understand them. That there extra little zero to the right of them numbers always caused him a problem, so I just put the numbers down, the directions, and we were on our way. How you think we saved your dumb ass?"

The Sarge said, "Okay, enough with the bullshit! People are going to die while we stand here and jerk each other off. We need to disrupt this process and try to find something that the Carbon Factor needs that we're not aware of. It just can't be burnt coal residue, and liquid hydrogen, if those are the ingredients. There has to be something else that's needed in order to make it detonate and gather energy until it consumes everything in its path that requires hydrogen. We need to find a chemist or a scientist and attempt to figure it out."

Mallory said, "If we do that, then we either have to employ them or kill them after we've figured out this mess."

# # #

Windom and Earther knocked on the open door. When Michael came out of the room, he asked, "What's going on guys?"

Windom said, "Boss, we're tired and are in need of rest and some family time. Will you be needing us in the next twenty-four hours?"

Michael smiled and replied, "You know after those people in the oil business settle with you guys, I hope I can auction my services between you and these people."

Earther said, "We don't plan on leaving this pack. Once we sign on the dotted line, we're moving on that land that John Lee has."

"You're full of shit," Michael stated.

Windom said, "I kid you not. We're going to set our people in motion, build a gambling free environment, and make those people train and employ sixty-five percent Native Americans on any pipeline breaking the state lines of Minnesota."

"Guys, I think we're in a discovery mode at the moment, but as you know, shit changes in a hurry. Do your thing! Bullshit! Oh, my God! Come in here, guys."

As the three men entered the room, Michael yelled, "Fertilizer! People spread it, over their crops, and lawns for growth. We need to find out if the Carbon Factor requires fertilizer because given its propensity to be destructive on its own, and by adding carbon residue and liquid hydrogen, perhaps that's the beginning stages of the bomb. Sarge, is there any way of tracking fertilizer shipments or purchases? Think about it. How can the two ingredients create such a catastrophe? I'm of the belief that there is another necessary starter ingredient; fertilizer of some sort!"

The room became quiet. Zanthius asked, "Pops, can you get film from Mr. Utz depicting the before and after scenes in Springfield?"

"I suppose I can son. Why do you ask?"

"I would like to see the days leading up to that catastrophe, if anyone left bags, or sprayed the mess in the area. We've been consumed with what happened and not what occurred leading up to the detonation. I think we need to get basic and that requires Larry and I to go into our 'what if' mode."

# # #

On the local news, five days after a body was discovered in a charred vehicle, the identity of the person was confirmed by the coroner's report. The DNA analysis confirmed that the body in the vehicle was that of Helen Weber, a person who went through great lengths to look like someone else, including body, facial, hair, eyes, ears, and nose reconfigurations. It was also reported that DNA from another individual was collected and is being investigated before any further announcements are made.

Asiram saw it first and announced to herself, "Great bitch, I know you're waiting on a final confrontation between you and me. You're not going to come back into our lives and reclaim the child you created with my husband. I will gut you, cut you, and decapitate your head, burn your essence, and make sure you're no more. I promise to be more thorough than those who have announced your death in the past. On this I promise you."

Zanthius entered the room and saw that Asiram was upset. He asked, "Okay, honey what did I do now?"

Asiram looked at him, smiled, and stated, "I just heard the news that the body found in that car was not Helga Spengatsenburg."

"Honey, the picture Michael had of the woman prior to her head being blown off was Helga."

"Zanthius, listen. The news stated that it was someone else and named the person. They also stated that someone else's DNA was found but they're not releasing information on that until they can confirm the identity."

"Oh, I didn't know that. Damn, I did feel that her demise happened too easily, and Helga so far has never done anything easy. Baby, I'm sorry, but eventually, we'll catch her if she is among the living. I'm hoping we don't have to encounter her and that she somehow, falls upon death at the hands of another. I would hate for our child to know that we murdered his mother!"

Asiram looked at Zanthius and started to cry. She said, "That woman is going to try to take our baby from us one way or the other, Zanthius. She is one cunning bruja and probably has a plan in place to deliver us to hell and take the child we love and that she mothered. I'm not going to let him out of my sight from now on. I feel this evil and manipulative bitch has her sights fixed on our child."

Zanthius attempted to calm Asiram down but she was hell bent on calculating how to get to Helga first. He said, "Asiram, I know you're trying to figure this thing out and get to her, but please let it go. This is like my father wanting to kill his cousin but, in the end, he strategically fired four shots into him requiring amputations. An act, I consider, stretches an edict to its maximum without violating the principal rule. We will get Helga or someone else will. However, you and I cannot be involved in the actual termination of our son's birth mother. Please, let it go!"

#

The Sarge received a call from Franco and decided that the group was going to have a family dinner in Valencia. He summoned Mr. Amazing and asked him to make it happen.

## CHAPTER TWENTY-ONE

The flight from Segovia to Valencia was less than an hour. Franco and his crew met the group at the airport, assigned men to guard the plane, and to provide overall security for the ever-growing group.

Once in '*The Conversion,*' the owners cornered Franco and it appeared as though there was a problem. He threw his hands in the air and spoke to the group in Spanish. Giuseppe Giovanni walked over and calmed the situation down and acted as though he were in control. As Beckmire and his group began to find seating in the new and massive restaurant, champagne corks could be heard popping in the room. Franco walked away with a pissed off look on his face.

Giuseppe Giovanni commandeered the public address system and boldly announced, "From mistrust, aggression, chaos, threats, discovery, and destruction, this wonderful place was born and seeded by foreigners. It was a matter of seconds that determined the fate of this concept that was on the brink of being destroyed. My friend, my boss, Franco, is one smart businessman. Don Carlo hated him and the owners of '*The Conversion*' loathed him as well. Everyone now loves Franco because Franco loves everyone. The little distraction in the corner was the owners of both places demanding that he remain and receive accolades for his vision, his honesty, energy, and most of all, his love for all of us. When we didn't receive funding for certain activities from our partners, it was Franco, who put all of his funds into the projects and subsequently leveraged his house to make payroll. Of course, that encouraged me and the rest of us to do the same. However, it is a second, that separates that moment, from chaos. He is not going to say anything nor is he going to ask for anything. I found out what a great humanitarian this guy is and tonight, I'm glad that all of you are here to pay tribute to the man of the hour—Franco!" There were loud acknowledgment sounds and hand clapping that lasted over 4 minutes.

Franco eventually, said, "They made me say something and I didn't want to be a part of this ceremony, honoring little old me. I get my strength from working with honest and good people. I must admit, my past is not so good but my today and tomorrows are filled with ideas of how to help people help themselves. That is all I have to say. Enjoy your dinner and thanks for coming from Segovia to honor me, my friends. Everyone in this room owes a debt of gratitude to you people who could have just ignored a problem. Thanks, my friends!"

There was a hiatus in the room and Courtney elbowed the Sarge so hard, he winced. He rose from his table and asked if he could say a few words.

The Sarge announced, "Life is a funny thing that one must grasp or it will slip between your fingers—seconds! I will confess that I did not like Franco because he kissed my wife's hand, a thing that I had never done, and demanded that she have dinner at his table."

With a sarcastic look on his face, the Sarge said, "Imagine the nerve of that dude." There was a lot of laughter.

"However, I did not know that my wonderful wife, had a pistol and shoved it in his side." The place erupted with louder and longer laughter.

"The thing I want to stress is simple. Those who appear to be your enemies, often become those who you can trust the most. I must say, when I entered the room, I saw conflict and I didn't like it. I thought that we as a group or me as one of the leaders, had made a terrible mistake. Giuseppe Giovanni, I like the way you staged that. It was a ruse, but you can imagine my dismay when I see those who I thought had overcome obstacles and issues of trust, were in the midst of another disagreement. Listen, we consider all of you family and as such, we don't ask what happened to the last thirty cents that we provided you. If a person steals from us, they steal from their family. *The Conversion* and *The View* are shining examples of people who trust each other. We turned a significant amount of control and funds over to Franco and by golly, he delivered. When Mr. Amazing forgot to make payments, Franco and his people put the very money they earned from us, into the operation. However, that wasn't enough, they mortgaged their homes to make *The Conversion* and *The View* possible. People, that's commitment. Let me say one more thing in closing, none of you in this room will ever want for anything as long as you help people help themselves. Both of these businesses are a gold mine. In the future, my people here won't have to secure money with their homes. With the support of my group, we're going to keep a fund open in the name of *The Conversion* and *The View* in the amount of $10 million dollars. This, fund, will be managed by Franco with input from you, our partners. Mr. Amazing, Jong that is, will have secondary signatory responsibility for funds. The idea people is simple; I want you to find other depressed family-owned businesses and offer our assistance. You know not to do stupid and you know how to manage your businesses. We're family and Franco is a smart uncle that we trust. He is a good human being and not that rogue we thought he was, when we first met him. I trust Franco with my life. Please, raise a glass to Franco, a person who we expect to seek out those with bad and/or failing businesses and offer them a hand-up and not a hand-out!" There was thunderous applause and everyone had teary eyes.

Prior to leaving for Segovia, McArthur had asked Gladstone and Montomie if they had heard from their lady friends, and they both confirmed they had. He looked a little sad but stated, "I guess I need to make a direct commitment to her or I'm going to lose her if I haven't already. You know this constant companion thing is hard for me to envision, therefore, I tend to want to stay aloof and operate according to my game plan. I guess, everyone doesn't agree with the nature of my plan."

Montomie replied, "Brother, you have got to get over that shit. We're not spring chickens and it feels great, the warmth of a woman's body near you, if only to secure you during the night. I don't know about Gladstone but I can assure you, if I have to get her here on a commercial flight, then that's what's going to happen in the morning if she wants to come."

"I was thinking the same thing. I spend a lot of time on the phone with her so I might as well be with her," Gladstone stated.

McArthur looked at both men and smiled. As the men got off the elevator, they went to their respective rooms. When

Whitmore opened his door, he saw Azure leaning on a chair, in a floor length mink coat, and was *au naturel* underneath. Whitmore didn't ask how, when, how are you, or anything else. That first kiss would last the balance of the night and his mind would be fully convinced that he needed this woman in his life on a permanent basis. They shared romance and passion, decadent adventures, and heavenly sighs, and acknowledged that they would create a sense of desire, safety, nurturing, and love, forever. The only words uttered between the two were, "I love you so much."

Gladstone and Montomie knew that Alvara and Gerri were coming for a short visit. In their respective rooms, the sounds of love, passion, and satisfaction were abundant and clearly stated. Each man and their mate created an atmosphere of sheer bliss.

# # #

In Segovia, the person with the Carbon Factor formula recognized, for security's sake, that he had to terminate several of his trusted, cloned, and essential personnel. He was aware of the nature of his quest and realized that the entire world was looking for him or what he controlled, the Carbon Factor.

Zanthius and Asiram remained concerned that the never dying Helga Spengatsenburg, continued as a threat in their life. Asiram was convinced and believed that she personally should terminate Helga if she were alive but felt it would be fitting if Rashida, Luana, or one of the other women removed her burden of killing her son's birth mother.

Meanwhile, the Sarge received a call from Mr. Utz who confirmed that there was DNA of Helga in the car but it appeared to have been strategically injected into the

nomenclature of the victim's bone structure. Mr. Utz
indicated that the majority of the DNA was that of a Helen
Weber. He concluded that Ms. Weber had been injected with
Helga's DNA in the form of blood and skin grafts and that
Helga went through an elaborate scheme to attempt to throw
people off her trail. Mr. Utz wondered if the Sarge's cousin
had the same biochemist to create illusions for himself as well.

The Sarge said, "At this point, I'm betting that my cousin
is not dead and that he and Helga are planning a horrific act
that will make Springfield and the other detonations look like
small fireworks. I knew I should have killed his ass but Darryl
kept reminding me that I could not execute him because he
was family.

# # #

Outside of Barcelona, Spain, two tractor trailers were
stopped at a truck stop. The stop was routine and random. The
officers conducting the stops were only interested in catching
drivers who were illegal in terms of their time, and over-
weight vehicles.

The drivers of two trucks appeared to be confused about
their manifests and couldn't give an acceptable explanation
about the origin of the odor of burnt smelling objects. After
further investigation, it was discovered that the trucks were
carrying fertilizer and burnt coal in an obvious structured and
separated, combination. The police weren't sure what they
had but knew they needed a supervisor to come and provide
oversight, especially with the strong smell coming out of one
of the trucks.

An hour later, chemists, police, and military personnel
showed up and began a thorough evaluation of the contents of

the trucks. From the top of one of the trucks three vented compartments were emitting a significant amount of a smoke like substance. The other truck's load was locally made fertilizer. The authorities became highly suspicious because everyone assumed that fertilizer was the core ingredient in homemade explosives. As the police began to check the contents of the truck, in the forward part of one of the trailers, were four large refrigeration looking units. Initially no one considered the units a threat until a junior officer mumbled to another officer, "This is all too suspicious. This resembles what the Yanks say caused the destruction in Massachusetts; burnt coal, and some other product. We should clear this area of people in case I'm correct."

Approximately two hours later, as the news stations converged on the area, everyone was speculating about the contents of the trucks. The news stations could only state that there was police activity at a truck stop and that people were being evacuated from the immediate vicinity.

Ms. Viola, forever watching television yelled to Luana, "Get that scoundrel of yours in here so that he can hear this story."

When Chakes arrived, he asked, "Why you be bothering me, Sister?"

"I think you need to hear what them people on television be saying about some stopped trucks near Barcelona."

Chakes knew not to discount Ms. Viola's concerns because she had been correct so many times in the past. As he watched with interest, the words fertilizer and burnt coal appeared on the screen in the subtitles. He yelled, "Oh shit!

Those are some of the suspected ingredients that make up the Carbon Factor." He ran out of the room and headed towards the Sarge's room picking up people on his way. First, he gathered John Lee and Jilkes who heard him, and were followed by Montomie, Gladstone, and McArthur. At the Sarge's door, John Lee said, "You best not be banging on that door. You might want to consider knocking lightly because if they be busy, he's going to be mad as can be and she might find a way to poison your ass."

Chakes knocked on the door and when Courtney answered it, she said, "John Lee and Jilkes put you up to this. Didn't they?"

"Courtney, they did not. I need the big guy. Is he available?"

From around the corner, a voice could be heard saying, "I'm on my way. I was taking a nap, what's going on?"

"Sarge, Ms. Viola called me in to her room to show me something on the television. It was two trucks that were stopped and were loaded with fertilizer, burnt coal in one, and what appeared to be refrigeration units in the other. Now I'm not sure what that means, but damn, aren't those key ingredients of the Carbon Factor formula?"

The Sarge said, "They damn sure are. Where did this happen and who stopped them?"

Chakes replied, "Sarge, I'm not sure exactly where this happened, but it was north of Barcelona at truck stop. However, after seeing the two trucks and the evacuations taking place, someone must have suspected something and more importantly, they must know about the Carbon Factor."

The Sarge looked at Jilkes and asked, "Can you locate Mr. Amazing for me?"

#

Approximately, ten minutes later, Jong waltzed into the room and the Sarge said, "I'm glad my life wasn't depending upon your visit."

"Me having bathroom issues. I was under exposed when your hit man threatened my wife," Jong replied.

"I didn't threaten you or your wonderful wife. I just simply told her that our lord and master needed you in his room. How does that come across to you as a threat and when did I earn the title of hitman?"

"You too sensitive? My wife sensitive, all the women sensitive, and now you sensitive," Jong announced.

"Anyway ladies, we need to get to Barcelona and check out this matter."

Jong inquired, "Why we go there? Why do we send everyone? Your nephew has plane and men. Why not send them, no one knows who they are but everyone knows who we are because when we land, we have babies, women, angry looking men, and more new faces from the other guys who now seem to be in love."

Mallory walked in and asked what was going on. The Sarge gave him the skinny on the matter and posed the question that was on the floor that was asked by Jong. Mallory looked at Jong and decided his point was well taken. He stated, "I agree with Jong, let's entrust the young guys and lady to do the dirty work. We're always out front and if there is ever going to be a transition of this group, then we have to keep baptizing them by fire."

The Sarge thought for a minute, called Darryl and Sue Lyn on their phone. Minutes later when they showed up, the

Sarge said to them, "I want you guys in front on a situation that just happened in Barcelona."

Sue Lyn asked, "Are you referring to those trucks that were stopped carrying the core components of the Carbon Factor?"

"You people must be mind readers."

"No, Uncle, we occasionally watch the news. We were in the process of calling you when you called us. We were going to ask if you wanted our team to head to Barcelona and check things out."

"As a matter of fact, that is exactly what I would like to happen. Are your people rested?"

"Yes Uncle, and they all are abreast of the situation. They too watch the news when available," Sue Lyn stated.

# # #

In Barcelona, the team got as close as possible to the truck stop without drawing any suspicion. Earther, Michael, and Windom, watched people in hazmat suits from afar, enter the trailer and exit with items, and place them in what appeared to be a bomb disposal unit. It immediately became apparent that the person in charge of this action was aware of the Carbon Factor and its components. Every detail of the extraction process of the materials was managed meticulously. From what appeared to be a command center, several men in suits huddled and looked at documents that were removed from the trailer.

Sue Lyn noticed that the underbellies of the trailers were glowing as she viewed them through her infrared lenses. She informed Darryl of what she saw and he took a look. He called

Michael and informed him of what he saw and asked him to cautiously investigate.

Michael approached the area and was told to leave. He yelled, "You guys had better check the underbellies of those vehicles. From afar, we saw flashing lights."

The response from a police person was, "Sir, we know exactly what we're doing. Please leave the area."

Sue Lyn and Darryl heard the conversation and instructed Michael to rendezvous with them. Twenty minutes later, and approximately a quarter mile away, Sue Lyn said, "There is a group with a monocular watching the action like we are. Some of them appear to be armed."

Darryl and Michael watched and studied the faces of the three men as one of them appeared to be counting with one hand and looking at the trucks with a monocular device in the other hand. When the motion of his hand hit what appeared to be a final number, both trucks exploded but not with the intended impact that it would have had if the contents of the trucks were strategically placed.

Darryl screamed, "Oh shit! Those guys just blew those trucks up. I'll be damn. Those working the scene are dead or severely injured. Look at them crawling on the ground for help."

We should go and help them," Sue Lyn remarked.

Darryl said, "Honey, there is nothing we can do and plus, Michael has been exposed and we can't take a chance on him being recognized. Listen, we tried to give them a heads up and they didn't investigate the information they received. No, we can't expose ourselves."

#

All the news stations carried sporadic and inaccurate details of the explosions at a truck stop. Further complicating their story was the indication that no bystanders were injured. There was no mention of the nature of the items removed from the trucks or the planned detonations. The news spin on the event was that there was a fuel leak and one truck ignited the other and, therefore, a dual explosion occurred.

#

At the shattered command center, people were in shock and concerned about the nature of the explosion. Most of their chatter was incoherent because they all seemed to have suffered from concussions. While Darryl, Michael, Isaiah, and Desmond, watched the events, Sue Lyn captured pictures of the alleged perpetrators on her camera.

As Sue Lyn recorded the events that were unfolding at the ad hoc command center, two remarkably familiar faces appeared in her lenses. It was Earther and Windom gathering up pieces of paper and making off with them. Sue Lyn said, "Well I'll be damned. Earther and Windom are down there picking up evidence. Oh, my goodness!"

#

Later, when Earther and Windom returned, Michael laid into them about operational procedures and being accounted for at all times. Earther said, "Chief, we had an advantage and decided to take it when we saw one of those men, seemingly, giving a count and then there was the detonation. We saw what they touched and where they were. Unfortunately, they all wore gloves. However, we saw the vehicle they left in but it was probably stolen. Anyhow, we were in the right spot and decided not to risk communicating with you because we didn't know what system they were using. It's all my fault, Earther wanted to get the hell out of there, but I saw the opportunity to get us closer to our target. You're in command, we violated protocol, but it won't happen again unless we just happen to get lucky."

Michael smiled, looked at Sue Lyn and Darryl and asked Earther, "How did you guys let so many assholes into your country?"

Earther said, "We had open borders, non-aligning tribes, and a foe who used bullets against arrows. Not a fair fight but nevertheless, one that we should have seen coming from the beginning. It's like in the hood; if you see one cockroach, you can damn sure bet the rent money that there are a million others in hiding."

"Okay, enough of this profiling stuff. Were you able to capture anything of value?" Darryl asked.

Windom replied, "I'm not sure but one of those guys left his wallet on a rock, and not surprising, unless it is staged, it's your worldwide Federal Bureau of Investigation."

# # #

When the group was together again, Darryl put gloves on, looked at the wallet, flipped it open a couple of times and said, "If this isn't real, then it's a helluva copy. How can they operate here with impunity, in a foreign land? This is not a province of the United States of America. Gather the troops, we're out of here. My uncle needs to make some calls to figure this mess out. We're out of our league on this one. Michael, gather the troops and get us out of here!"

## CHAPTER TWENTY-TWO

In Valencia, the group met Darryl and his crew. Darryl gave the Sarge information and the credentials of people who were allegedly involved in the discovery process at the scene of the explosion. Darryl gave Michael the nod, who said, "Sarge, my people, Windom, and Earther, recovered the badge. When I saw the individuals through the glasses, I realized that they were armed, and from the looks of their clothes, they appeared to be Americans. When I flipped the wallet open, it exposed a badge that appeared to be legitimate, I knew we were in over our heads on this one. Sarge, I know you guys know what's best, but the fact that the fricken FBI is running an open op in Spain required me to inform my bosses asap!"

"You know Michael, it's the little things and information that matter. I thank you for not being cocky and dismissing the relevance of your findings. I'm going to make a call and, in the meantime, Jong, make sure the plane is ready to depart within the next hour and nephew, I recommend you guys do the same. Speaking of planes, I think you guys need a larger plane. What say you?" All of Darryl's people who were near, confirmed the idea.

#

The Sarge called Mr. Utz, who conveniently avoided answering the call. Mr. Utz was waiting on another call that would clarify why American spy types were running ops in Spain. Mr. Utz had received a courtesy call indicating that agency individuals were assisting on foreign land where he had people doing a "look see op."

Mr. Utz returned the Sarge's call and emphatically stated, "I need you people out of there, pronto. The FBI is overseeing those trucks and are planting information and DNA from you people at the scene. Somewhere along the line, you pissed off the wrong people and they want you and your family behind bars or terminated."

There was a long pause and silence on the line. The Sarge broke the hiatus and said, "What the fuck else is new? People have been blaming us for global warming, the development of synthetic heroin, the floods along the Mississippi River, as well as that volcano eruption in Italy. Mr. Utz, if people with badges come for us, we will deal with them on a terminal basis. We haven't done a fucking thing other than try to track down the son-of-a-bitch that has the formula and has killed thousands of people. We're off the grid. Don't try to track us and if you do and show up, you will be handled violently. Good day and goodbye!"

Mr. Utz interpreted the message that the Sarge gave him as his farewell salutation. Utz also realized that his group was compromised and that the FBI had their fingers up everyone's ass. He sent a text to John Lee from a throw away telephone that read, "this is a mess—at home it can be secured—help your families."

When John Lee got the message, he said to Jilkes, "Who be sending me some dumb shit like this?"

Jilkes casually looked at the message and after reading it several times said to John Lee, "You were used as a decoy. That message is for the Sarge."

The two men met up with the Sarge and saw Jong as well. Jilkes said, "Make ready the planes and we have only a few minutes to execute an evacuation. This is a message that was sent to John Lee, and I'm thinking it's from Mr. Utz."

The Sarge read the message and yelled, "We are out of here in twenty minutes! Gather all the children and forget about the other things. I need a head count by groups and I want that plane on the runway with the engine running if I have to kill everyone in the damn tower." The Sarge looked around the resort and saw Franco. He yelled, "Franco, I need you to go to jail for me because I have to get my family out of here in a hurry. I need you to corrupt or capture those in the tower to let my caravan on the runway to catch a moving plane."

"Mi amigo, calm down! Everyone in the tower is on our night payroll to build the other investment properties that we have agreed upon. I unfortunately have a recalcitrant family member in the tower who I will kill or corrupt if he doesn't get with the program. He is my half nephew, and he thinks that I am still a crook. For you, I will threaten to neuter or kill him. I'm not sure if he's really my blood because his mother, allegedly my cousin, is somewhat of a crossdresser who forgot what part she was supposed to play one night and got pregnant in the interim. We could never decide who the potential father was because she had a record-breaking night, if you know what I mean. Gather your people. We will manage those people at the truck site and more importantly at the airport. I do not suggest that you board your plane on an active runway, mi amigo. That would have a lot of eyes watching the abnormality of what would be considered an irregular boarding process. I'll oversee your transportation and the airport. You handle the rest of your family, mi amigo."

#

The entire extraction process created a new sense of leadership within the group. Two of the younger children were stressed out because they wanted to continue to watch TV and play games. Ms. Beatrice became the calming factor and explained to them in terms that they understood, what was happening. Zanthius and Asiram noticed her actions and admired the way she helped organize the retreat.

Asiram said, "Now that child is the real deal! She calmed both of those children down and presented another focus to them; flying to where the animals are strange, beautiful, and where they can play and have lots of fun."

Zanthius said, "Honey, she is the future Queen. I don't know why I'm saying it like that but deep in the bowels of my soul, every time I see Beatrice, I feel like I should bow down to her."

#

At the airport in Valencia, Franco's people, staff from *The View* and *The Conversion* were all over the place and looking more like mobsters than entrepreneurs. Carla, the captain, had every aspect of the plane quickly inspected by airport personnel but decided that they needed to do their own screening once Beckmire's team passed through customs.

Everyone was on high alert and when she broached the subject with Jong, he plainly said, "Go for it!"

Take off was delayed by twenty minutes. Franco had put into play, individuals who would alert him of movement by the local federales and who would institute disruptive activities. Carla had the alternative pilots as well as the copilot examining every inch of the aircraft, even though cameras and personnel watched it around the clock. When Beckmire approached her, she expected him to ask her if this was necessary. To her amazement, he loudly stated, "Captain, this is your domain and I will never question your judgement. Continue the good work to keep us safe."

The Sarge could see her eyes swelling. She said, "You will never know how much that means to me—your confidence in my decisions relative to your plane."

"Captain, this is what you do, and I will never countermand your actions. You are my pilot in command, and I trust you with my family, your family, and everyone else who joins this crazy ride."

# # #

After a thorough inspection of the aircraft was conducted, Carla allowed everyone to board. There was a lot of moans and groans but the Sarge quickly silenced the noise. He yelled, "If there is anyone who would like to end this adventure and get off this plane, please exit quickly!" There was a stillness that was uncommon on that typically happy plane. The seat belt sign was engaged and Captain Carla indicated that the plane would head for the active runway at faster than normal speeds. We will immediately get this lady in the air. Just so you know, our smaller plane is directly in front of us and is 1st in line for takeoff. It is being vectored to the north and we will be vectored to the east. Mr. Jong, I need a destination.

Courtney looked at the Sarge and said, "I need salt water, love, fruity drinks, and laughter. Can you do that for me?"

The Sarge looked at Jong and said, "Tell Captain Carla, we're going to St. Thomas." The roaring sound of approval was acknowledged. Gladstone looked towards the front of the plane and got the attention of McArthur. He made the sign of a telephone, and the rest was obvious. McArthur broke protocol and placed a SAT phone call to his friend and asked if she and the other ladies would like to rendezvous in St. Thomas. He was told that she didn't know about the others, but she would be there waiting. He told her that he would try to get the plane in Maryland sent to New York for an immediate extraction.

The Sarge said, "People, we can only stay there for three days. After that, unscrupulous people will be tracking us. I will keep this promise to you, but when I say it's time to pull up, then we pull up and head all the way west—Australia. We can't play in familiar backyards for long periods of time. Just so you know, our FBI was running an op in Barcelona, and I think they wanted to involve us surreptitiously in it. Thanks to Michael and his crew, we captured a set of credentials that were true and pure. Somebody wants to make us the bomber. Anyway, I want to find peace, love my wife, and play with all the babies in this group. Three days people and then we're off on another adventure."

# # #

As the plane was descending into St. Thomas, Jong passed a note to Courtney that read, 'do you think we should name the plane'?

Courtney passed it across the aisle to Monica who also smiled and ran her hand across her throat. She said, "Talk about telegraphing your passes! Not a good idea for this group. Anonymity is the best cover this group will ever have."

Courtney looked back at Jong and ran her hand across her throat.

# # #

On final approach, Jong made a call to Mr. Carter letting him know that they would be landing in the next hour or so and if possible, they would like a ride to the resort. Mr. Carter went into a frenzy because the resort was booked solid. He said to his ex-wife, "My partners are landing and want to come to the resort. What should I do?"

She said, "Have your staff call the other high-end places and see if they have space. Honey, you can't just put people out of their rooms to accommodate your partners. Meet them and explain the situation to them. Their true colors will come out but from what I've seen, they won't make a fuss. Them people be natural and understanding, not pretentious and demanding."

"Beyond all of that, you called me, honey! Did you mean it and are things that good between us that we can stop pretending?"

"Man, I no pretend. I'm just looking for a retirement package." They both laughed, hugged, and kissed tenderly.

Mr. Carter said, "I'll meet them at the airport and explain the situation to them. Can you, personally, check with our primary competition and see if they want to make a deal and seal our futures on a positive path?"

"Man, you go, I got this. Is our son coming as well?"

"Mrs. Carter, they didn't provide me with the manifest. I'm praying that he is coming home and he's safe. That's all I can do."

#

At the airport, an obviously, visibly shaken man was meeting his partners. Courtney saw him first and pulled the Sarge's arm and said, "No matter what he says, relax him honey. Mr. Carter is under a lot of stress for some reason or another."

Ben Beckmire said, "Hey, Chris! What's going on? Do you have room for our crew?"

"Ben, the resort and all the other properties in *The Sanctuary* are completely full."

Beckmire said, "Oh, my! Any idea where we can secure this group?"

"I have my ex-wife working on it as we speak."

Monica overhearing the conversation inquired, "Mr. Carter, the space between the main resort and our partner to the left, do you think we could cordon off that area, pitch tents, and install portable facilities. I mean, we could run hoses from the main properties and set up showers and loos. The kids are used to sleeping in nature and so are we. I'm just throwing that out Mr. Carter, it's totally your decision."

Mr. Carter looked frantically at Ben and then at Monica and said, "That's a wonderful idea from my perspective, but I'm not sure your people can adjust to sleeping in makeshift accommodations."

Courtney said, "We should kidnap you and take you to the outback with us, Mr. Carter. We do fine wherever we are. We don't require a lot of catering."

#

After Darryl's plane landed and after clearing customs, Michael saw his dad and ran to him. He said, "Man, I've missed you. You look troubled. What's going on?"

Mr. Carter hugged his son and told him how things were going and that all the properties in *The Sanctuary* were fully booked. Michael smiled and said, "Dad, these blokes sleep outside in the outback all the time. You really need to see how things happen there."

#

In the meantime, Mrs. Carter created a new relationship with competitors and had procured accommodations for the group, although in separate facilities. She called her ex-husband and told him the news and anxiously asked if their son was on island. Mr. Carter told her that he was hugging him as they spoke and that he would be there shortly. He also told her to get in touch with the group that owns the tent business because, their partners were going to spend the nights on the beach in tents.

Mrs. Carter said, "I told you these people were not hollow. Is Michael okay, does he look healthy and strong?"

Mr. Carter said, "Honey, we're all coming home to make do with what we have. There is no stress and I'm fine. I'll need you to triple the security and make sure that we have 24/7 eyes from the water, hills, beach, and everywhere else. I need people in place in the next two hours, darling."

"Man, you be trying to seduce me by calling me darling. Anyway, I like the sound of that, baby!"

"Mrs. Carter, I'm in the midst of people at this moment, but later, I'm going to have to take you for a walk and speak to you about all these hot words you keep throwing my way."

"I can't wait man. I'll fix us some special punch to watch the sun set."

# # #

Another strange text message appeared on John Lee's phone. He summoned Jilkes and together they sought out the Sarge. The message was simple; 'expect company in thirty-six to forty-eight, depending upon weather.'

The decision to camp outside was a home run. Everyone loved the idea. The kids swam until they couldn't walk and slept late into the next morning. The ladies from New York when they arrived were told of the living conditions, and they honestly loved, and embraced the idea. As a matter of fact, on the second day of inhabiting tent city, three independently strong, educated, smart, and sexy women, agreed, unbeknownst to each other, that they would marry and forever be a part of this adventure. They independently agreed and announced that they would travel with the group, learn its ethos, and become members of a clan that helps people help themselves. Gladstone, McArthur, and Montomie, proposed individually and secretly to Alvara, PJ and Gerri, respectively.

In a tent near the hill and away from the rest, Michael and Barbara Ann wrestled with her status, abuse, and a suggested intervention. Barbara Ann gave Michael a list of reasons why she felt that it would be immoral for her to continue the relationship that she thought about and desired with him.

Michael said, "I will never create stress—this way or the highway, situation with you. I will say that my nights and days are always full of memories of you and that will probably last for a long time. I'm not asking you to decide, but it's time for us to do the math and decide if 1+1, truly equals, 2. If it truly is a proven formula, then I say, there is no reason for you to go back to that abusive situation. Insofar as I am concerned, your attraction is about things, pictures, and memories. The love that I have for you, is present, accounted for, and concerned about your well-being. The choice is purely and clearly yours. My choice and choices are clearly about you."

Barbara Ann, balling her eyes out yelled, "How do you know you really like me. Is your fantasy about sex?"

Michael reached for her hand, kissed it gently and proclaimed, "Oh, my dear! I have surpassed the notion of seeking just pleasure. I am focused on trying to find the mental stimulation that I seek and need, as I continue on this journey called life. We have not consummated our desire, nor have we stimulated each other to enter that zone of craziness and thank God we've had the time to question our involvement. I am convinced that what I feel, is spiritual, and not carnal.

However, just so that you'll know, my spirituality will stimulate my carnal, and the results will be nuclear. Just saying!"

Barbara Ann began to laugh and that's when Michael took the opportunity to focus on her wonderfully shaped lips. He placed a soft kiss on the side of her left cheek and then another on the right side. He patted her eyes with a tissue. While her eyes were closed, he sneaked a soft kiss to her lips that turned into a monumental expression of desire on both sides. Barbara Ann searched his mouth deep with her tongue as she felt the passion that had been missing in her life for a long time. Michael accepted her inquisitory tongue and began to express his desire by searching deep in her throat with his tongue. The two tongues met, the expressions exploded, and the love making proceeded. Each were confused at first because they had not experienced the other's particular and/or peculiar proclivities. It was a short minute before they synchronized their intent, movements, and desire. Minutes later, a newly well-oiled machine was mutually providing ecstasy, harmonization, and explosive episodes of passion beyond their combined expectations. It was astounding, and although against certain vows and ecclesiastical doctrines, their acknowledgement of pure love and respect, exceeded any doctrines written by man or interpreted by clergy. Although they would not announce an engagement, they would illustrate the power of pure and unadulterated love.

# # #

On day three of the group's sun and sand adventure, at breakfast, everyone was gabbing about their wonderful experiences. Beatrice walked to the middle of the created compound and whispered something into Chake's ear. He looked at her in amazement and asked her to go and tell the Sarge exactly what she had told him.

Beatrice walked over to where the Sarge was sitting and asked if she could tell him something. He hugged her and told her of course. Luana and Ms. Viola watched as she expressed herself to him. After whispering in the Sarge's ear, he looked at her with a look of surprise and curiosity. He started to blurt out a command but decided to ease into a new conversation. As Beatrice walked back to her seat, the Sarge announced, "As I indicated before we arrived here, three days is our maximum visit. Now, I have it from a wonderful source, that the children are interested in leaving here and heading for their educational experience in the outback. With that in mind, here are the choices, or rather, here is the decision, those planning to continue on this journey will be ready to depart this place within the next hour. I suggest that you eat up and prepare for a blast into the sky because in addition to the children's request, I have been informed that others are on their way here to bother us. People, enjoy your breakfast but please be prepared to leave paradise in the next hour or so."

Courtney asked, "What the hell was that all about?"

"Baby get your shit together and let's get the hell out of here. The little one told me that bad men were on their way here to capture us."

"Oh, shit! I knew she was special. Honey, reverse the order and tell people to forget breakfast, have Jong call the pilots and let's get the hell out of here. Last night, I must admit, I had a dream that you were being carted off in handcuffs. Baby, please, get us out of here now."

The Sarge looked at her intently and smiled. He kissed Courtney and said, "You are such an asset. You make me whole." She smiled and kissed him back.

The big man fumbled with his telephone and a few seconds later said, "Transportation to the airport leaves in thirty-four minutes. Forget breakfast, retrieve your get out of here bags and let's go. People, this is not a drill. Some very nasty people are on their way to put us in cuffs."

Michael looked at Barbara Ann and said, "Take this debit card, it has about $15k on it. Get to the airport and call me or text me soon."

"I'm going with you Michael, if you will have me!"

Michael hugged her and said, "Not only will I have you, but I will keep you for the balance of our days on earth. That decision makes we whole and I love you so very much. I have to clear this decision with the Sarge and Darryl." He turned to walk away and skipped back to Barbara Ann and said, "If you don't go, I don't go! It's as simple as that. No more separation and wondering about your safety and my mental health from missing you."

Sue Lyn had already stated to Darryl that Michael was in love with the lovely lady and that more than likely, he's going to want to bring her with him. The last time they separated, the husband beat her badly. Just letting you know what I think is going on with your main man."

Three minutes later, Michael saw Darryl and asked for a few moments of his time. He explained in detail his feelings, expressed his knowledge of the vetting process but was adamant about being with Barbara Ann. Darryl told him that he would check with his uncle and get back to him.

Five minutes later, three additional seats for Azuree, Gerri, PJ, and Alvara, had been reserved on the large jet and one seat reserved for Barbara Ann on the smaller plane. Yes, those friendly skies were about to get a lot friendlier because love, family, the mission, and the future, were the only thoughts running through people's minds. All were safe and all were happy.

Darryl's plane blew down the runway first followed by Captain Carla with an intermediate stop in Mexico to refuel. The children watched movies, read books, and were visited by Mr. Sleepy. The adults held hands, kissed on occasion, and wondered how this magnificent, awe-inspiring, and dangerous adventure, would end.

CHAPTER TWENTY-THREE

In the outback, the Sarge huddled with Mallory, John Lee, Larry, and Jilkes. He was looking for ideas that would require the women and children to stay put until they could provide full attention to the matter at hand—The Carbon Factor!

Jilkes said, "Sarge, we have been on this road trip before and it didn't end well for the male species. Do you recall when certain activities were withheld until the correct, in their mind, decisions were made. I'm not sure I want to go back down that road again. Oh, and by the way, we've added four more of their kind to the group."

"Yeah, I know. Did we fully vet them on the island?" The Sarge asked.

"I'm not sure," Jilkes stated.

"Larry, you're junior in this meeting, can you find Mr. Amazing and tell him we need him in a meeting. Oh, and if you see your brother, quietly mention it to him. You know if that fire breathing and gasoline consuming daughter-in-law of mine gets involved, this ship is sunk."

# # #

The newcomers, especially those who had visited the outback before, reinforced the rules to each other. Essentially, no wandering off, no swimming in the billabong without clearance from Wajickee or other members of the village and most of all, respect the animals because they're friends, not pets to play with, but animals to respect and leave alone.

Courtney realized that the new members of the group needed indoctrination as well as expected roles that each person would play. She announced that there would be a meeting of the women to go over expectations, as well as, what one can do, and what one shouldn't do, while in the outback.

Hearing about this meeting gave Beckmire the perfect opportunity to meet with all of the men to plan on how to leave the women and try to conclude the Carbon Factor saga. Just prior to Zanthius and Jong arriving, the SAT phone was brought to him, and on the other end of it was Mr. Utz. He said, 'Ben, I have a rat in my group and I had to communicate through John Lee because he still has that flip phone. The FBI has attempted to link your group to the ownership of the two tractor trailers that contained the contraband. The smartest thing done in all of this was the actions of your man that absconded with the lead agent's credentials. His fingerprints authenticated his credentials and, therefore, that stratagem had to be abandoned. If I, were you, at some point in the near future, I would send a picture of the official credential, outside and inside to that exceedingly popular newspaper organization in Washington, DC. I would also say that this identifying material was found near the site of an investigation into objects deemed suspicious and related to key ingredients of the Carbon Factor formula."

Beckmire paused for a minute and asked, "Does Spain continue to look like a place where the person in charge of this mess, will continue to operate?"

"Ben Beckmire, I'm not sure of anything anymore, except you guys pissed someone off and they are going through extraordinary expenses to frame and have you people destroyed. I need you to really think about all of the people you have gone up against that could come close to masterminding this expensive, international, and deadly endeavor. Anyway, for some odd reason, I believe I'm being watched and followed. I am cognizant of the time difference. If I hear of anything or if you can figure out who the hell you people pissed off that wants to kill you, others, and frame you for their work, please let me know. Take care and watch your back!"

"One more thing before you go. I appreciate you getting that information to my man and giving us an opportunity to get out of dodge. I owe you one!"

"Buddy, you owe me more than one! Catch you later."

Michael saw the new ladies heading for Courtney's meeting. He said, "Ladies, it's nice to have you all here. There are certain gentlemen, including myself, who are more than ecstatic that you're here in the outback. Now, Mrs. Beckmire is going to give you the skinny of this place but I want to say, don't wander, pick-up nice-looking bugs, attempt to pet the koala bears, touch, or kill spiders, and for sure, stay away from all snakes. Now the billabong is another matter. If a local is in the water, then it's safe. Ladies, enjoy your meeting." He slid next to Barbara Ann and kissed her on the cheek.

# # #

The Sarge, at his meeting, was asking for solid reasons to leave the women folk in the outback and head back across the water to handle and conclude the problem at hand.

Mallory stated, "I am having the best sex that any man my age could have, and with my wife. I'm not going to give her the opportunity to join your son's fire and petrol breathing wife in another one of her crusades. Listen, God forbid that one of them or one of us catches that fatal bullet, they know what they're in for and what we're up against."

Mallory looked at McArthur and asked, "Are you peoples' ladies aware of what we do and that people die, and so could we?"

Gladstone replied, "They were here before when we had to bail in a hurry and I guess they got the message."

"Gladstone, there will be no guessing on this matter. You newly in love people had better take this opportunity to explain to your mates what we did in the Nam, against the mob, and how we got drawn into this never-ending saga. It's important that they know all of the details people, not the flowery ones, but the dirty and disdainful acts that we have had to commit in order to protect and support members of our group and our country," the Sarge stated.

# # #

Near one of the caves in the village, Courtney welcomed the newcomers and emphatically announced, "My husband thinks that I'm going to stay here and dig for gold or something else, while he and his crew, go across the water and attempt to conclude this bomb mess. I don't know about you guys, but

I'm about to button up a certain privilege area until common sense is restored in that man of mine."

Asiram said, "You have got to be kidding! There ain't no way in hell my husband is meeting with his father, your husband, about making a journey and doing work without me. Why that little shit!"

In the back of the group, Ms. Viola's hand went into the air and she said, "Sometimes, you got to let the man be the man. They be doing what they think is best for you ladies but they be dumb as tree trunks when it comes time to trying to express issues with you people. Now, if I were you, I wouldn't wait until they be coming to you with some sorry ass story. I would put a sign up saying, "that door to the happy face is closed until further notice." Don't wait on them to throw it at you, give them a view and tell them, I hope this works for you!"

#

On the other side of the village, Darryl, Sue Lyn, and Michael were relating to a problem at one of the mines. The unusual security service inflicted immediate pain on two workers. Two miners were bit by snakes and spiders. Deep within their bowels, they attempted to smuggle stones from the mines for their personal enrichment, it was first thought.

Darryl said, "There must be some extenuating circumstances surrounding this situation. Those snakes and spiders are considered extremely venomous and deadly, yet these two men are only in shock. Darryl said, to Michael, "You and I are going to take a hike to the village where these blokes are from. Sue Lyn, I need you to go to the hospital and keep me abreast of what's happening with these blokes. I have a strange feeling that they did this under duress and, therefore, the animals are alerting us that something else is in play. I mean, what would make you, an Aboriginal person, who is aware of the curse, the animals, the snakes, and spiders, take such a risk? Someone else is involved in this matter. Sue Lyn, you know strangers can't really handle those stones."

At that moment in time, Wajickee appeared and suggested that he would accompany her. He stated to Darryl, I am happy you considered other alternatives in this matter. Yes, they attempted to steal from their own people, but your mindset realized that something else might be at play here. I'm so proud of the work I've done with you."

Darryl looked at him and said, "Well, I thank you for all the wisdom you've bestowed on me, my friends, and my bride."

"Michael is truly a friend and will never deceive you for a bauble, a woman, or a scheme. He, my young liege, is truly blood that is not yours but is of blood that is sacred in another part of the world."

Michael hearing this asked, "Then can I petition you for a raise?" Everyone broke into laughter.

# # #

Wajickee escorted Sue Lyn to the hospital. Darryl and Michael walked several miles towards the village, followed on the periphery by other members of his crew. Darryl knew that they were not alone.

During the walk to the village, Darryl asked, "Do you really love Barbara Ann?"

Michael looked at him in a curious manner and replied, "Do you truly love Sue Lyn?"

"I guess I should have prefaced my question with a statement. I asked you this question because she has a tracking device hidden in her bag. In the morning, a man will come to claim his wife and will be prepared to engage in violence. If your relationship is sexual, then you my friend will lose the battle, and poorly. If you love Barbara Ann, he will be exposed and will not be let in the country. You and she will meet his plane in the morning and your decisions will determine the future of your relationship. Michael, you know there are a lot of strange things that go on here. This my friend is fact. You will inform Barbara Ann of the impending arrival of her husband and the two of you will meet his plane at eleven in the morning."

"When I asked if you loved Sue Lyn, I was truly being obnoxious. But, how do you know this information?"

"You're in the land of mystics, my friend. Actually, my friend at the airport associated her name and address with a passenger who is on a flight from New York. I just added the magical shit to it to mess with you."

Michael looked at him and said, "I don't care how you color it or present it. I don't doubt anything that occurs in this place. Are you serious about the husband?"

"Dah! Yes Michael! He's coming here to kick your ass and claim his wife so that he can beat the shit out of her some more. In both instances, neither of these will occur because I can send him back with the smallest of creatures and then you'll be free to marry Barbara Ann without any strings attached."

"Damn, Darryl! I don't want to start a relationship after conspiring to kill the woman's current husband. We shall confront him and give him the opportunity to realize that beating her is not the answer to solving marital issues. I guess she will have to confront him as well. Until now, we had never kissed. She was as pure as the sand around the billabong."

"This I know Michael. This I know! I will make sure he returns to New York without incident. Let me speak with Wajickee about this."

# # #

Once the two men approached the boundaries of the village, Darryl said, "Let's take a sand bath. We both smell of sweat and we don't know who is who in this village."

As the men watched the comings and goings of the villagers, Michael said, "There is something amiss in this place. There are no men or male children around."

"That too I noticed my friend. Look at the hut to the far right, if he's an Aborigine person, then I am in trouble. Oh, look closely at the item on his left and the bulge in his shirt. He has weapons. The question is how many more are fused into the place?"

Less than two minutes later, two men with similar coloring, came out of another hut with two young girls. One of the men slapped one of the girls on the butt and she ran off into outback towards a billabong.

Darryl said, "Windom, and Earther should be appearing over the horizon along with Desmond, Isaiah, and Harold. They will be armed as well. Did you happen to bring a weapon?"

"Darryl, I know you didn't bring one so, I brought one for you. It's a girly gun but I believe you can manage it. Will Earther and Windom know where we are?"

Darryl looked at Michael and said, "Next to my uncle and his crew, those two guys, it is alleged, were the real deal in the

Nam. They allegedly, could track a snake across the country, but my uncle and his people could track a damn ant. Of course, they know where we are, and when to engage if we engage. So far, I count four suspicious non-Aborigine looking people. How many do you count?"

"Well, my liege, I happen to count six; hahaha!"

"Oh, I see, you're counting those two women who look blonde right?"

"That is correct my friend."

"Sorry to disappoint you, but they are Aborigines. We come in all sizes, colors, and shapes my friend," Darryl responded.

How shall we engage them?"

"Michael, you and I are going to waltz into that village as if we belong there."

"Darryl, respectfully, I disagree with you. There is an absence of men folk. You and I are not dressed like the indigenous people, my friend. I suggest since we can't see what's going on in that one hut, and I haven't heard any screams, we just wait and watch their nighttime routine. No sense in putting us or any villagers in danger by going in with blazing guns."

"I wasn't prepared to go in shooting, Michael. I suggested, obviously a bad idea, that we walk in like we belong. That shooting thing is your idea."

# # #

The plan to wait and see became annihilated when one of the men slapped a little child. Darryl signaled to Earther and moments later, both groups began their slow, methodical, and deadly capture of the village. Michael and Darryl miscalculated the number of people who seized the village, but a total of six were terminated and one was held with a gunshot wound to the leg. Darryl instructed Michael to get the injured man out of the village and bleed him for information about those who structured this deal.

Desmond and Isaiah dragged the injured man away from the village and Isaiah said, "Desmond, this is where we leave this poor bloke. This is the place where the animals can have anything that they find beyond this point."

The two men dragged the fella ten paces or so beyond their artificial boundary and Isaiah said, "I hope you kissed your children goodbye, before you left. The damn dingoes are going to be here shortly after smelling all that blood flowing from your body."

They started to walk away and the man yelled, "Wait, don't you want to try to make a deal based upon what I know about who is in charge?"

Desmond replied, "You have got to be kidding. We're like the cleaners, we just process dumb asses and leave them for the animals."

"I'll tell you who is in charge if you get me to the hospital."

"Dude, you ain't got a prayer. The damn wombats are going to bite through your bones and leave the scraps for the dingoes, all while your ass is still alive and watching them eat at your extremities."

"I know where the next detonation of the Carbon Factor will occur in the next week or so!"

Isaiah and Desmond stopped in their tracks, but neither turned around to look at the man. Both men's hearts began to race as they realized the importance of those simple words, Carbon Factor. There was a ruffling in the bushes and

Desmond yelled, "The animals done smelled your blood. Isaiah, help me pull him back over the animal free zone."

The intent of the guys was to leave him for the animals unless he had powerful information to exchange. This guy's problem was that he slapped a child, and there was no volume of information that he could share that would save his life. His chances of surviving were slim to none, since he hit a child.

Desmond began to plug the wound and Isaiah rushed to summon Darryl and Michael. When they arrived at the scene, Desmond said to his captive, "Okay, don't waste time, tell them what you told us."

"I want guarantees before I give you any information."

Michael whispered something in Darryl's ear, and he said to the man, "My friend, you're in the outback. You can't call Uber or Lyft and wait for a ride. We have a doctor in our camp who can help you but your information about the Carbon Factor was also known by another survivor in the village. So, we have the place of the next detonation. Your problem is that your information has to be better than your associate's."

"You think I don't know what you're doing? You guys don't know shit. I know this game and I've played it before. Okay, Mr. Smarty pants, give me the state and I'll give you the city and the date!" The captive stated.

Michael was about to say something but was aggressively, waved off by Darryl. Darryl said, "If I give you that information, and if you lie to me, the animals will feast upon your body and I will have your entire family decimated."

Darryl, as if in slow motion, asked Desmond to free the captive and give him a piece of paper. Darryl then said, "I'm going to write the name of the state down and give it to Desmond. I will write it first. As a matter of fact, I will include the city as well. I know that I will be correct, but you my friend must confirm the city indicated and the timing of the event. You will hand it to Isaiah."

Other than Darryl, no one realized that Wajickee was there in spirit form. He guided Darryl's hand and it wrote, 'Miami, Florida'. Darryl then handed the folded piece of paper to Desmond.

When the captive was provided the response, his eyes opened as big as bowling balls and he exclaimed, "I'll be damned! How on earth did you know?"

Isaiah handed Darryl the note from the guy that said, "Go fuck yourself, chump! You can't play me!"

Darryl said, "You violated the agreement, I'm sure the dingoes are hungry by now."

The guy screamed, "You don't know the fucking date!

Darryl spit on the ground, looked at the man and said, The 'Ides of March'! Which is approximately, two weeks from today!" He signaled to Desmond and Isaiah to take him beyond the no animal zone and leave him. As the two men gathered the injured man, he screamed, "Miami is a big fucking place. Let me try to survive and I'll tell you exactly where."

Darryl looked at the man and said, "You have nothing to bargain with. Just so that you know that I know—South Beach!"

#

Walking back to the village, Wajickee appeared next to Darryl and said, "We make an incredible team. That was amazing my young friend. You have credible information that could save millions of lives. Give it gently to your uncle and his incredible associates. For the next few days, I'll manage that diamond issue and frankly, I manufactured the importance of it because I wanted to see you and your uncle. There is a move afoot to replace me with an updated version of a spirit. Sadly, I was told that I've been doing this too long and, it's time for me to move on. Darryl, you know, none of us, well, I guess I'm clearly a picture of immortality but the fact is, all of you will one day die and I'll be a figment of your imagination.

"Wajickee, why are we talking about such things? Is there an impending death within the group?"

"Darryl, death is as relevant to life, as food is for nutrition. It's all a part of the universe we live in. You may live longer than Sue Lyn, but it's important that your time in this reality is spent in harmony."

"Is Sue Lyn ill?"

"Of course not. That was like a metaphor. Sometimes you take me too literally. You must act like your uncle as if nothing bothers you and there is no task that is too big for you to oversee. However, I do need you and your uncle to petition for my continued services."

# # #

In the village, Darryl saw his uncle and told him that he had gathered some disturbing intelligence relative to the next detonation of the Carbon Factor. His uncle looked at him and said, "Good work nephew, let me get the guys together."

"I'm sure you mean guys and ladies, don't you?"

"Wow, thanks! Don't know if you know it, there is a conspiracy going around amongst the women and they're threatening to hold back certain privileges from the men."

"Uncle, I'm sure you're aware that Sue Lyn runs ops, and directs my crew on occasion. Unless she's straddling the fence, then I won't have that issue to deal with."

Ms. Viola was walking towards the billabong with a couple of locals when the Sarge said, "Hello, Ms. Viola. How are you doing?"

"Oh, Mr. Sarge, I be doing a lot better than you be doing. Boy oh boy; that woman of yours has nitro glycerin in her veins and I want to cool my heels and be away from what I think has turned into a revolt by the proletariat. Them dress wearing kind, are on strike and are after blood. Don't you tree swinging people ever learn? Didn't you have this problem not that long ago? I be fine and I hope you are to, after this incursion. Come find me if you be needing some counseling when this is over."

"How can I get in front of it?"

"How long you been running this group? Damn man, just say someone raised the idea and was banished from the village. All be well then, but don't let them fire breathing witches, I say that with all the reverence in the world, come to you first. Put that fire out quick man, or you be like that scoundrel my daughter married, always buying flowers, and begging for forgiveness. You know this place better than most, I think they done drank some kind of potion and it done turned them into damn brujas. That's why I'm going down to watch the crocs. I don't want to see a whole bunch of grown men on their knees begging at the same time."

Darryl said, "Oh, my! I really want to see you work your magic on this one uncle. This looks like it's going to be quite the show!"

The Sarge asked Darryl, "Do me a favor, find one or two of my guys and tell them they need to find me down by the water. Oh, and please, tell them it is urgent!"

Twenty minutes later, the men assembled by the water where the Great Saltie was known to be and the Sarge yelled, "Damnit! One of you horny sons-a-bitches, told your woman about us leaving them here and going to do our thing. Now, I know we're a group of honest men who value loyalty and integrity. I need the man who made a significant reference to our plan to step forward."

Everyone looked around at each other and expected the guilty person to step forward to be tarred and feathered. No one moved a single muscle to step forward. Larry raised his hand and everyone gave him the jaundiced eye. He yelled, "Hold on a moment before you people attack me. I raised my hand because I have a question. Dad, how many times have you unsuccessfully tried to eliminate them from your battle planning and/or direct confrontations? How many times?"

The Sarge acted as if he was in deep cogitation and Larry said, "Dad, when you meet without one of them in participation, you open the gates to speculation, by the time one of them tells the other, and the other tells two others, then what has been communicated is that we've found an island full of thirty-two-year-old virgins and we're leaving them here. They don't communicate specifics; everything is embellished."

McArthur said, "My lady just got here and I tried to cozy up to her and she said that she had to attend an election for officers of their newly formulated 'Fair Treatment

Organization.' She just got off the damn plane and those women have corrupted her in less than six hours. Sarge, Montomie, Whitmore, Gladstone, and I, watched the last time you tried to do what you're planning and how you guys slept on the floor in some cases. You said we would never fall into that trap again but yet, here we are."

The Sarge said, "I have been in charge of this group for a long time. I'm not going to snitch on the person who raised that issue and tried to march it forward. I'm going to boldly go where the women are and tell them that their lack of participation in our initial meeting was an oversight and one that will never happen again and that the perpetrator of that vile thought has been summarily banished from the group. Now if that don't get it, then nothing else will. Mac, what's this 'Fair Treatment Organization'?"

# # #

That evening at dinner, the Sarge made his elongated speech touching on everything from the earth to the moon. He welcomed the new members of the group and admitted to them that they would be vetted, and until then, some activities such as working in the diamond mines or gold mines would be restricted. Everyone laughed. The Sarge then amplified his position on security. He said, everyone here has a responsibility for our joint security. I say that in hopes that our new members are aware of the kind of existence we live. He searched the eyes of his associates and then said to the group, "You know it never gets too old to express how we came together to perform in such an unorganized manner and play symphony after symphony with harmony." He told the group, tonight he would not take the time to explain the nature of the group because he wanted to spend quality time with his bride.

#

Standing high on a hill as the sun portrayed his shadow, a lone Aborigine man stood on one leg, with his spear in his hand, the other leg resting on his standing leg, and watching from far, far away. Darryl said to the group, "If you look to the east or to my right, you will see a sight that is as reverent in Australia as any you will ever see. Behold, he represents goodwill, peace, prosperity, and vengeance upon anyone who would harm the Aborigine people." It was a somber moment!

## CHAPTER TWENTY-FOUR

The group was in Australia for two solid weeks and for many, the wonder and nature of things was fascinating. The new ladies took complete control of the educational processes and infused new techniques and demanded that technology become a part of the process ASAP! ASAP means "as soon as possible," everywhere else. In the outback and with this group, it meant, "all satisfied after performing," meaning you make their wishes happen, they will keep you with the happy face!

#

The two men who were bit by a snakes and spiders, recovered almost immediately after it was discerned that they were coerced into stealing from the village. The ringleader of the concept, tragically met with his demise by a single spider bite.

Mr. Utz found the mole in his group and dispatched him back to the FBI. He called the Sarge and said, "My brother, it's time to come home. I need you and your people in South Beach. I don't need to tell you why but I need you, and the country needs you as well."

"Would this be the same country that is interested in seeing us in jail? Or the same one that hired Mercs to terminate everyone connected to my group? You see Mr. Utz, I have little respect for certain authoritative agencies that can place DNA and other artifacts, to make it look as though we are the bombers. Now, if you want to get us new get out of jail cards, let's say, in two days, then we'll consider coming back. I'm sure you can understand our reluctance to make a commitment and wind up in jail for a crime that we tried to prevent," the Sarge stated.

"Mr. Beckmire, have someone send me the names of all your people including the children and I will have all of the paperwork in your hands in 24 hours and that's a promise. Listen, you know I follow orders, but I want you to know that I would never knowingly walk you to the gallows," Mr. Utz stated.

The Sarge exclaimed, "That's so comforting! You see Mr. Utz, that's exactly what I'm talking about; your knowingly sending me to the gallows. Get me the papers and I will speak to my people."

"How about you speak to your people before I get you the papers?"

"Mr. Utz, then your cause is lost and you're on your own in South Beach. We had a faint and unsubstantiated idea about what we were up against until your people tried to make us the fall guys. Now, you can get the papers or forget this number. Catch you later, my brother!"

The Sarge saw Jong and asked, "How are you doing and how is the baby?"

"Mr. Sarge, I know this game. What is it you need me to do?"

"Jong, I want to first of all know how you are doing, how the wife is doing, and how the baby is doing. After you answer those questions, I will ask you something else."

"Sarge, everyone is good, happy, healthy, and enjoying being in one place longer than four days. Do you realize we've been here for over two weeks? That is an amazing feat for this group and guess what? No one has tried to kill us!"

"You're right buddy. I need a list of every person involved in our group, including the children. I told Mr. Utz, that we won't help in that South Beach mess until we all have get out of jail cards."

"I agree with you. I think Darryl, and his crew are so strange, that they should be in the front on this one. I mean look at them, Earther, Windom, Michael, Isaiah, Desmond, that scary one Harold, and the rest of them plus you throw in Sue Lyn and your nephew. I mean they all look strange in a way but no one would track them like they can track us. They know who we are and what we look like. They don't know anything about the young upstarts."

The Sarge paused for a minute and from left field asked, "Do you think they need a bigger plane?"

Jong said, "Why you no listen to me when I bring you strategy? You listen to John country ass Lee, and Jilkes, Mac, Mallory, and everyone else. I bring you my opinion and you ask me about fucking airplane. I am going to resign my position!"

"Mr. Jong, are we about to have a problem? When you were talking about your strategy, didn't you see me shaking my head in agreement? I thought we had moved on from that one, and that your idea was a solid one, and the one that we would use. Why are you always looking to hurt my feelings?"

"Now I hurt your feelings. What is wrong with you. Do I need to slap you again?"

"Naw, buddy! I'm just messing with you. When we get together at dinner tonight, I'll ask the group for input.

Anyway, back to the airplane business. Don't you think they need a slightly larger aircraft to do the kind of work we do and be comfortable getting out of town?"

"I will look into it. Will we have four planes or three?"

"We will never need more than three, I don't think. What say you?"

"I say we propose the sale of the current plane and pick up at least a twenty-person configuration with longer range capabilities."

"I'll see you later, I want to spend some time with the babies by the water. Catch you later."

#

Mike, holding Carla's hand walked towards the bush and the Sarge yelled, "I hope you people know the rules."

Carla turned around and said, "We were looking for you, boss. My husband has some intel he wants to share with you."

"Hi, Sarge! I got a few messages from the sewers, and they were very unsettling to me. One of my sources stated that Walter is alive, your cousin had a son who has sworn vengeance for all of those involved in his father's decapitations. I initially discounted the intel because I thought he was a poofter or in plain terms, effeminate. The idea about his son was not disarming but the rumor that Walter is alive, scared the shit out of me."

The Sarge looked at him and said, "Walter is getting a lot of play lately. I think he's planning to come out and make a statement. His statement is going to be in South Beach. I need you to call on the SAT phone and tell them intel is critical and rewarding. By the way, we did fund those two pilot projects, right?"

"Ah, Sarge, we did and they're working well.   The problem with the one in DC is that malfeasance is suspected of those in control."

"We can deal with that. I need to find out if my dreams have relevance. I need information about my cousin. Mr. Utz professed that he was dead and that there was DNA to confirm it. You're telling me he's alive, has a son who has joined the hunt for our demise. What a family I have. Thanks guys and enjoy your walk but remember the boundaries."

# # #

Rashida and Juan set up the virtual shooting gallery and Asiram and Courtney strongly suggested to Barbara Ann, Alvara, Gerri, and PJ, that they spend a significant amount of time getting use to firing weapons through virtual reality. Gerri asked if it was reality based with blood and wounds spewing blood? Courtney responded, "As real as it gets without actually taking a human life."

Rashida explained the nature of the virtual experience, that would seem real, and suggested that they approach it as if it was a life-or-death situation.   Alvara sarcastically exclaimed, "Oh come now, it can't be that bad!"

Rashida smiled and muttered to herself, "Bitch, you'd better not miss."

Rashida knew exactly what she was doing when she told them it would occur during the hottest part of the day and in a cave that had no breeze whatsoever. She wanted them to realize that in nature, extremes are hard to manage. As expected, Rashida knew there would be resistance to the setting as well as the huge and awkward googles. Juan assisted the ladies with the gear and each began to sweat and complain.

Juan yelled, "This is not a New York fashion show; this is our reality and what we contend with on a daily basis. Now, let me say this, if you fail in this mission, you will not be able to travel with the group. This activity is designed to show you how you can protect yourself, your mate, each other, and the entire group. Ladies, we kill people! We help people! If you can't subscribe to the idea that someone is out there trying to hurt you, your mate, or other members of the group, then you should get the hell out of here in a hurry!"

Barbara Ann raised her hand and said, "Listen, this is sudden, and we've been drinking. I would like to hold this activity in abeyance until the same time tomorrow when the temperatures are at their peak. We know what security, support, and pulling the trigger, means. It's been a discussion and now it's closer to a reality. Rashida, I would hugely appreciate it if you gave us the opportunity to speak amongst ourselves and if there are any incapable of supporting the mission of the group, then they won't be at tomorrow's activity."

Rashida looked at her and said, "I like you guys and this shit is as real as it gets until you're standing over a body. I've killed in a single day, over one hundred people. The reason is because members of their group put suicide vests on my daughter, the other children, and told them that it was to protect them. Now, ladies, if that don't piss you off, then you're truly not cut out for the mission that this group has in front of it. There is nothing wrong with loving a man from afar, except that shit gets old! Tomorrow it is ladies, and may I suggest that you guys cut back on that sweet-smelling stuff you use. Although we're in a no-fly insect zone, and please don't ask me how my dad and his family controls that, but sometimes a nutty bug gets through and that can be painful.

Listen, it's all natural here and there is no need for pretense. I'll see you ladies tomorrow."

# # #

Asiram and Courtney saw the group exit the cave early and Courtney said, "You owe me 100 bucks. I told you that Rashida would put the fear of God in them and that they would ask for another timetable. Listen young thing, I didn't get to this age by being stupid and I know my daughter don't take no shit from nobody."

Asiram said, "Mom, you set me up. You knew Rashida was going to kick their asses, but you gladly took the bet."

"Yeah, like the first $100 bet you made with my husband, hussy!"

"Mom, how many years ago was that?"

"Oh, I don't know, but it's my job to minimize my husband's gambling losses." The two women laughed and hugged. Asiram's eyes watered up and Courtney asked, "What the hell is going on?"

"Mom, I am worried about my other mother. She seems to be in a lot of pain and I'm not sure you're aware of the fact that she had some form of cancer when we first got this rag tag army together."

"Baby, we're in the land of magic. Have her talk to Ms. Viola, because I think she's the real witch, and then let her talk to the spirit that loves her, Wajickee!"

"Mom, what the heck are you talking about?"

"Wajickee is not human as we know it. He assumes bodies to conduct conferences with Ben. He also remembers the human concept of love and he keeps Ms. Viola as healthy as a fruit tree. Ava has many reservations but has gotten over a lot of them regarding the unnatural order of how things work and happen here in the outback. Obviously, she didn't want me to know, so I can't suggest that I go with you. I don't know her pain, but if she asks Ms. Viola to help her, she will ask Wajickee, and spirit or not, he's in love with that bruja."

"You're an amazing woman and friend. You stabilize this entire group and you don't even show or use the powers you possess. I admire that and I've learned a lot from you and Ava and more importantly, I love you both so very, very much."

# # #

Courtney saw Barbara Ann and called her over. She asked, "So, how did it go?"

Barbara Ann said, "It didn't go at all, Mrs. Beckmire. We took the wrong attitude in there and Rashida, cut us into small sections and threw us away. I asked for a follow-up session tomorrow, under the same conditions and without a lot of drama and attitude. You know that little punch is rather addictive. I like how it gives me courage when there is none."

"Honey, it affects each person differently. Barbara Ann, this is the outback! Here the impossible happens and you never really get over the fact about what you saw or think you saw. One day if you ladies survive the orientations, my husband will take you to another billabong and there your faith will be assessed, and hopefully, acknowledged."

"Your daughter is the real deal. Is it true about the suicide vests?"

A scowl came across Courtney's face and she replied, "Not a memory I or any of us normally will speak about. You guys blend in and keep volunteering for things and soon you'll be a voice to be heard. I love that new "ASAP" expression you quickly placed on your men. Now, that gets my vote and Asiram's as well. Ain't that right baby?"

"Mom, I'm happy everyone here has a partner and peace is amongst us all. Barbara Ann, if you like, I'll go into the fire pit tomorrow with you guys and work you through it."

Barbara Ann looked intently at Asiram and replied, "Naw girl! This is something that we must conquer or get on a slow boat back to New York. I appreciate the offer and if you need me to help you with those wonderful babies, I would be honored."

Rashida walked out of the cave, and Barbara Ann looked at her and made a screeching noise with her teeth. She walked away and avoided conversation with Rashida. Rashida said to her mother and Asiram, "That one has some bones buried in a closet or two. I get the feeling that she knows how to use a weapon but feigns as though it's her first time. There is something about her that I don't trust."

#

At dinner, the Sarge gave his usual state of the group address and wandered into far away scenarios about the world, politics, the environment, and the president. Just prior to his conclusion as people began to yawn, he said, "I want you people to enjoy this meal and each other, but I also want you to think about the possibility that my cousin, Walter, is alive and is the architect behind the Carbon Factor bombings!"

A stillness engulfed the entire camp. As he turned to walk away, Courtney said to him, "Honey, if you share your grief then we are all a part of it. If you hold it in, then it's yours and we move about freely without a sense of urgency or concern. Please address your notions and concerns to the group."

The Sarge turned around and recognized that he had everyone's attention. The new members of the group were asking, who is Walter?

The Sarge said, "I have information from someone I truly trust, that there is the strong possibility that my cousin is alive, well, and bionic. On the other hand, I have it that his DNA was totally matched with a victim killed in a fire at an institution for the mentally insane. I also heard that he has a son who has sworn to kill everyone connected to the group that tortured his father. Now that group would be us and I don't know what to believe. The one thing that we've all learned, is that my cousin is as resourceful as the cockroach. I did to Walter what my great, great, great, grandfather did to Mr. Cheeks in his time. I wasn't allowed to kill my cousin, and it was strongly reinforced by my nephew, Darryl. He continuously told me that I couldn't kill a family member. Okay, so, when we captured him and he begged me to put a bullet in his head, I thought about my loving nephew. I shot him in both shoulders and both knees. I knew where to approximately, place the bullets to achieve my intended outcomes—amputations! I had asked Dr. Beckmire years ago about amputations and began to secretly study them online whenever I had a private moment which with this group, was practically, almost never. Anyway, I perfected what I thought was the perfect placement of a bullet. It wouldn't kill him, but each would have to be dealt with separately, and they were. Unlike my ancestors who slapped hot iron on the points of severing, I relied heavily on my research and the information that I could steal from my amazing and brilliant wife. So, to summarize all this, here is what we may be up against. I was told that my cousin is dead, and the proof is by way of DNA at a fire scene. I'm also told that he has a son who is now interested in terminating all of us. I'm also told that Walter, my cousin, is alive, and is bionic. Who the hell knows what to believe, I want every living soul to make sure they're proficient and efficient on all the weapons in our cache including the bow and arrow."

The Sarge took a drink, paused, and said, "On another point, I'm happy that our holdouts and unmarried people, have succumbed to that box that bewitches men and that they have selected mates. To the new mates, I say love, honor, protect, and get with our program. It's full of love, respect, but it's aggressive and terminal. If you fail to act, one of us might suffer as a result. We will help you in any way possible to understand that this is not a game and when we pull a trigger, someone does not get to play the game again!"

Boldly, and without any notion of impunity, Barbara Ann stood up and inquired, "Mr. Beckmire, I personally feel as though some of the other women hold us newcomers in contempt and I'm wondering why?"

Asiram stood up, but was overshadowed by Courtney who emphatically stated, "Our commune is drama free."

Courtney paused for a few seconds and blurted out, "My husband was once involved with Ava De Lombardo, they share a son, my son and her son, Zanthius Beckmire De Lombardo. Put yourself in our place. We don't know you, but you show up on our beach and find some very fragile and, oh well, horny ass half naked men on the beach."

The entire place broke into laughter. "Now, I'm a doctor, sworn to protect life and yet, I've had to conclude many lives in the interest of the group. Once we get to know you and after a few cocktails, trust me, we'll bond or, oh well, let me be frank again; you'll be shipped out of here in a hurry!"

Barbara Ann said, "Now, I think I'm speaking for the rest of us that just joined this caravan; this we can do. But please, don't judge us before we read the playbook and understand what sport we're involved in. You guys have been together for a while, give us a chance to do the grunt work and earn your respect and trust. That's all we ask! Teach us and help us. We're east coast kind of ladies, we don't know much about this outback stuff, but we're learning and loving it."

Courtney, stared at Barbara Ann for a moment without responding, left her vantage point, walked directly to Barbara Ann, and gave her a massive hug. She was followed by Monica, Ava, Rashida, Asiram, and the other women. The newcomers were welcomed officially in the group and the drinking commenced. PJ eased up to Rashida and Juan and asked, "Do you think I can get some additional time tomorrow on the simulator to understand the use of the weapon I've chosen as my sidekick?"

Rashida responded, "Let me know when and I'll be there for you. As a matter of fact, I think you all should come and play in the dungeon with me and get the feel of so many different emotions you'll experience if we're ever under attack and you have to defend an aspect of our environment. See if you can make that happen and I'll make it easy at first and then I'll put you guys under pressure."

Barbara Ann asked Monica if she could have a conversation with her about her marital status. It appeared to be a stressful request because the Barbara Ann's head and eyes dropped towards the ground. Monica said, "Give me a coin or something of value and I can act momentarily as your lawyer."

Barbara Ann unclasped her necklace and handed it to Monica. Monica replied, "Now, I can act in an official capacity because you have engaged my services. Now, what is it you want to accomplish, beyond the divorce aspect of marriage?"

"My husband has sworn to me that if I left him, no corner of the earth is off limits and that he would find me and beat the shit out of me."

Monica mused, "Oh, I see! He's going to waltz into our encampment and lay a hand on you. My question is simple; is he suicidal? Anyone of these guys could probably best him and a few of the women as well. I'm not advocating violence, but it's highly unlikely that you'll ever be under attack or the threat of an attack by your husband while you're a member of this group. Darryl and Sue Lyn highly regard Michael, as well as the Sarge. What is it you want legally? Do you want payments, furniture, money or what?"

"Monica, I just want peace and not have to look over my shoulder for a man who will hurt me."

"You don't want none of those earthly things you've accumulated? How about joint bank accounts, do you have any of those?"

"We have a few joint accounts, but again, I just don't want him showing up and creating a problem and I want him to sign divorce papers as soon as possible. I'm convinced that he's already corrupted my current lawyer and, therefore, I don't believe a damn thing she says."

"Okay, let me sort it out, but I'll need your address, his name and a picture if you have one of him."

"He's easy to find, he's all over Facebook."

The two women continued to talk about other things including the dynamics of the group. Monica gave her the lay of the land and suggested that the group avoid starting and/or being involved in a clique. She told Barbara Ann to stay friends but create new ones without sacrificing old ones. This thing is for the long haul and as soon as you're vetted, you people will start to earn credits toward health care, retirement, housing, and monthly stipends that amount to hundreds of thousands of dollars.

# # #

Michael and Darryl returned from the mines with Isaiah and Desmond and went directly to his uncle and told him what created the breach in security and what was implemented to avoid it in the future. He whispered to his uncle, "So far, we probably have picked off the floor of the caves, close to one million dollars in stones.

The Sarge looked at him and said, "You're joking, right?"

Darryl motioned Michael closer and asked him to give his uncle an estimate of what has been picked off the ground. Michael said, "Sarge, your nephew thinks it's a million, I'm of the opinion that it's more like 1.5 to 2 million and I'm not exaggerating. However, he's the boss, so I allow him to be right on occasion."

The three men laughed and the Sarge asked, "When I give you guys special assignments like I did in Segovia, what happens to the security at both the gold and diamond mines?"

Darryl looked at the Sarge and replied, "Uncle, no matter where we are, the name Beckmire stands for all things right and mighty, Wajickee is never far away. Although he is unable to physically intervene with an issue, he for sure can send the animals to do his or our bidding. We have discussed other security measures, but I must admit, your calls do come at inconvenient times, on occasion."

Michael asked if he could make a comment and the Sarge nodded yes. He said, "You know where I'm from, and since coming here, I have learned a lot, made a lot, and have helped a lot of people. This place is magical and if you have larceny in your heart, then you will attempt to do stupid. These people are concerned about the building of schools, hospitals, roads, and infrastructure for their future. You miss a few baubles, then so what, the animals will have the culprit before he or she gets a chance to enjoy the by-products of our mission."

# # #

The SAT phone rang. It was Mr. Utz who stated, "I have those credentials for everyone in your group, including your new inductees."

"Mr. Utz now therein lies the problem. You have them! I don't have them in my hand to look at and make sure legally, you don't try to screw us in the end."

"I'll have them in your hands in two days. According to the timetable, something is scheduled to happen in South Beach in the next two weeks or so."

"You could have had us on the ground, but your people in the FBI, tried to paint us as terrorists."

Michael in the meantime is in the background motioning to the Sarge to pause the call. The Sarge asked Mr. Utz to hold on for a second. Michael emotionally said, "Have him set up a television interview where you or someone in the group gets a chance to tell our side and what we stand for. The world thinks we're mercs and traitors. This is an opportunity for us to return to nature and not worry about random attacks or accusations!"

The Sarge studied Michael's enthusiasm and said, "Mr. Utz, a new development has occurred. Can I get back to you in the next hour?"

"Of course, you can, but each moment we waste, we endanger the lives of thousands of people."

"I understand that. Give me an hour. Thanks, and goodbye!"

The Sarge studied Michael's expressions and without saying a word, reached over and gave him a man-sized hug. He turned to Darryl and asked, "Nephew, can you get the entire camp together for a special meeting in the next ten minutes?"

"I'm on it, uncle. However, I saw that look of approval you gave Michael. Please do not remove him from my group."

"Nephew, you will never have to worry about that. He is committed to you and Sue Lyn but honors my position and secretly calls us the old heads!"

Darryl looked at Michael and smiled an awareness of the fact.

# # #

As the entire group gathered in the center of the village, an exuberant Sarge announced, "We have a new head of communications and he works for my nephew, Darryl, and his wife Sue Lyn. This new person is Michael Carter, my friends. Now, while I was on the phone with Mr. Utz, speaking about our get out of jail cards, midway through my phone conversation, Michael is jumping up and down and trying to get my attention. He profoundly reminded me that we're always on the run because people do not know our story, and as such, he, being Michael, has volunteered to tell our story to a major network subject to or without Mr. Utz's approval. The impetus for this is the FBI's attempt to frame us for the events in Segovia. Everyone that has knowledge of us either wants to manipulate us or accuse us of doing dastardly things against the government we love. Michael's plan allows us to be handler free and volunteer to manage complex issues that ordinary agencies fail to achieve because of the bureaucracy that engulfs them."

The Sarge paused for a few seconds and then continued by stating, "Insofar as Michael being the new head of communications, I was just kidding. I would like to ask someone who has been involved in this matter since the very beginning, who has credibility and respect, to handle this effort for us. I can't ask my daughter-in-law or my sons because they remain three of the most wanted people on the planet. No, I was thinking of asking my wife or Ava who were there when the first shots were fired. I'm trying to find ways out of this mess that we've inherited. My guys are getting older, slower, and I'm forgetting where I assigned them—not a good thing for them or me. We need closure on the Carbon Factor and make it a thing of the past. Everyone saw the pictures of devastation and death that occurred in Springfield and the other places around the world."

The Sarge continued after consuming a large amount of water, and said, "If we can get those credentials from Mr. Utz, as well as give a meaningful presentation about what we have done and why, then I think the world will let us live out our lives in peace. The way we're going, we leave one handler for the next and they all have their own interest at hand, and not that of our entire group. I'm scheduled to call Mr. Utz back shortly, but I want to know what the group thinks about our going public to express how we got here, and what we've had to do to survive. I need to see hands of those who do not like this idea or plan."

No hands were immediately raised, but Courtney and Ava's hands went into the air at the same time. The Sarge said, "Well, one of you should yield to the other."

Courtney said, "I yield to Ava."

Ava looked at the group and said, "First of all, for all that we've done, I thank God for minimizing our injuries and shielding us from death. To truly tell this story, only Zanthius and Asiram can tell it from the beginning until the end. Then of course there is information that only the Sarge and you Courtney can tell, and then there is the machinations of the entire group. My vote is for the two of them to write the beginning chronicles of 'the idiot spy,' a fascinating story of people, come to Jesus moments, betrayals, watching children in suicide vests, love, wealth, helping people help themselves, and salvation. I yield to my friend, Mrs. Beckmire."

"I really don't know why I like that woman, but I must say, I've come to love her. I wholeheartedly endorse her suggestions of those who could best present our story, Asiram and Zanthius with intermediate inputs from the Sarge and I, as well as, Ava, Rashida, Mallory, and the Fab 10, Larry, and later, Michael. I love Michael's idea and I thank God that we didn't feed him to the fish on the night that a prematurely converted person met with his demise. We have a lot to tell and we need it done professionally. Perhaps, we should do our own filming and editing until we are certain that we do not admit to massacring thousands of humans who had one thing on their mind and that was to eliminate us entirely. As I consider this idea, I think we should create the manner and format in which it is presented. We hand a news station a completed file and tell them that it cannot be edited under any circumstances, that becomes a joke."

The Sarge looked at Michael and said, "You remember that first thing I asked you to do?"

"Yes sir, I do!"

"Your next idea is to be whispered to me and not in front of a lot of people. Am I making myself clear?"

"Yes sir, Mr. Sarge. I just thought it was a way for us to get from being perceived as bad guys, juxtaposed to the world understanding how we've been manipulated by people in power, for their personal benefit."

"My nephew Michael, wants to make sure that I don't try no eminent domain kind of actions on you and I promised him that you, as long as you want, will work for Darryl and Sue Lyn, and besides, I have enough smart people working for me as it is."

# # #

The Sarge called Mr. Utz back at the appointed time, and said, "My group is tired of being overseen by handlers. They want the public to know what has happened to them and how they entered this world of *conjured and distorted truths, marco, marco polo, helping friends and chasing diablo, mechanized mayhem,* having to create a *Sanctuary,* elicit *deific intermediation,* all while witnessing *treachery,* and *destruction.* One of the preeminent benefits to happen during all of this, so far, is, *hell, the gang's all here.*"

The Sarge paused for a few seconds and finally confirmed, "We have been managed by senators, their vassal's, their emissaries, their friends, family, and countrymen. We want to tell our own story, and as such, in addition to those get out of jail credentials that we're securing, we want to air a documentary about how we ended up on the terrorist watch list, were branded as traitors, charged with the murder of thousands of mercs, accused of holding the government hostage, suspected of conspiring to sell the Carbon Factor formula to the highest bidder, and a thousand other crimes and charges that are all befitting of a beheading for all of us, if they were true. No outsider can do this, only members of this group can let the world know how we have been manipulated by our government, held hostage by other governments and threatened both internally and externally by governments, terrorist groups, drug lords, triads, and independent senators for their own personal benefit."

Mr. Utz tried to interrupt the Sarge, but the Sarge vehemently stated, "Mr. Utz, when you talk, I listen. Now, I expect the same consideration in return. As I was saying, you either make this happen or we forget about trying to help you and those millions of people in South Beach that you people have not told that a terrorist attack is imminent. That last FBI thing has us wondering, what the hell are we doing and who are we doing it for when the very people or government that we thought we were trying to help is trying to frame us for being the bombers!

No sir, moving forward, we call the shots, or we stay the hell in Australia and here my friend, if you're not invited, you pay a penalty if you come—death!"

"Sarge, your request is a little extreme. I suggest that you people remain an anomaly and that way, no one knows who you are or what you do for this great country of ours."

"Mr. Utz, it's dinner time here. Unless you have some suggestions as to how we can enhance our pronouncements, then I would like to eat. If you can't find an independent news outlet that will handle our manifest, of what we've done for governments around the world, then I strongly suggest you find someone else to knowingly go to Florida with the mindset of being killed by a nut who controls the Carbon Factor formula!"

"Wait, Sarge. Suppose the notion of South Beach is a ruse?"

"Suppose it's not! Catch you later," the Sarge said.

CHAPTER TWENTY-FIVE

Asiram and Zanthius spent the most time with the cameramen and reporters from a US supported news station in Sydney, being filmed in the dark and with their voices modified. They gave precise information about the meetings in St. Moritz and the discovery and acknowledgment of a new dirty bomb called the Carbon Factor.

Zanthius explained how a spy kissed him, passed a capsule into his mouth containing information about the Carbon Factor formula, and from that point until now, they have been on the run hiding where possible and being asked to accept assignments in London, various parts of the United States, Spain, Hong Kong, Japan, Australia, and Italy. They spared no details relative to the influence peddling by corrupt politicians, off book mercs, people with unlimited access to the US Treasury and billions of dollars unaccounted for and managed by a single individual without a reporting/audit function. Asiram cried on que, when it came time to discuss how her home in Pennsylvania was shot up and her home in Virginia was blown-up as well as her ranch in the mid-west. She indicated that the senator from Virginia, who died from an overdose of Cialis and Viagra, who was once her neighbor, and the senator who dared to become President, used the military to conduct express and illicit maneuvers to obtain the formula of the Carbon Factor.

Ben Beckmire, Courtney, and Ava described the scene in Philadelphia when there was an assassination attempt on their lives. Ava described how the meeting took place and that her intent was to inform Ben Beckmire of his son, Zanthius, that he did not know existed.

All the filming and interviews were held in the outback and, therefore, was controlled by Beckmire's group. Satellite phones were useless because Rashida set into motion several devices that would interrupt any transmission of data. The idea was to control every aspect of the interview, take the materials and place them in a safe place for the group's security.

After a week of interviews, questions, filming, and a desire to want to get this story out to the public, Beckmire enlisted the assistance of Wajickee, who drugged the film crew, and exposed their camera and recording equipment to the hot outback mid-day sun. It was a roast! Rashida in turn coded the materials and had Darryl place the materials in the cave covered with jewels, snakes, and spiders. Unknowingly, Mr. Utz's group would transport the pouch with the recording devices to a bank in Sydney and place the contents in the vault with the diamonds and gold extracted from the various mines.

The Sarge said to the film group, "Listen, we gave you a free for all anecdotal depiction of who, what, where, and why, we were used by our government, as well as others. We can't allow you to use this information at this time, but your names are on a receipt at a large bank in Sydney if something happens to us on this next adventure. You my friends are in the outback where things are never what they seem, and dangers are abound. In order to protect you guys, we have taken your materials and sent them to a bank. The ruse about overheating equipment was just that, a distraction. At some point in time, we will allow you to produce and show the materials. I'm thinking the work you've done will earn you many awards and acclamations, however, just not at this time. If you were to try to produce the information that you gathered from us, your lives would be in great danger. The information we shared with you might seem like a fictional novel, but it is real and active. Therefore, we have decided to protect you from the people who don't look at you but who shoot you in the head and keep walking. Again, we thank you for the comprehensive work you accomplished but it is our learned opinion that you wouldn't last a day if you tried to show or tell the things we told you. Listen, I know, some of you think you have some of the materials saved on your phones and other portable devices but I assure you, it's probably gone. As a matter of fact, your being here is going to be a blur tomorrow because of the wonderful farewell punch you guys drank. Sleep well and we will keep our word, one way or the other, you will have full reign over the materials you recorded."

#

As the group prepared to board their plane to Florida, Wajickee said to Ben Beckmire, "The wrong decisions will leave you with long-term misery. Don't do what is obvious, do what makes sense to you and only you. As the leader, many things in Florida will be about distractions and glitz. Stay focused and committed. Your people are loyal and will fight the best fight. You've sent Darryl ahead because he and his group are innocuous. You are a Beckmire, and here your name creates thunder. In those other places, your name is synonymous with chaos. Use it to your advantage my friend. Announce your victories and the number of men roaming around in hell awaiting your arrival. Scare them, and the best way to do that is to let John Lee and Jilkes have their way with someone you might recognize."

Before Beckmire could ask a question, Wajickee was off to Dreamtime; a place where from afar, he could watch and hopefully direct the final episode of this adventure!

# # #

On the plane ride to Miami, Jong recognized that a group this large would certainly be noticed and, therefore, decided to make individual reservations for each member of the team. He sent group links to an available hotel that was dated but was directly on the beach.

Darryl, on the other hand rented space away from South Beach and got a large bus to transport his people. Mr. Utz came in handy in that he delivered a footlocker to Darryl's location that included handguns, suppression devices, and ammunition to accommodate the entire team.

Michael said to Darryl, "If there's one thing that I've learned from your uncle and his crew, is don't trust gifts." He randomly selected a 9mm pistol, and three bullets from the batch of ammunition. He attached the suppression device and loaded the weapon with three rounds. He stepped outside of their lodgings and fired the weapon at a trash bin. Three shots, three hits.

Darryl asked, "Are you becoming my uncle in disguise? I mean, you have a lot of his antics, paranoia, determination, and traits that have proven successful and life saving for this group."

"Your uncle said that he is tired of being managed, passed around, and, therefore, I'm just protecting his nephew and giving input into things that come to my mind as it relates to our collective security. Can't hurt shit with a blank unless you fire it directly in their eyes."

Darryl looked at his group and inquired, "How would you guys like to go and start a fight in a bar full of rednecks?"

Every hand in the room was in the air and Earther broadcasted, "I'm in, if I can hit the biggest person in the bar that reacts to our presence."

# # #

Deep off A1A South, Windom yelled, "What better place to make a statement and find out information than at a joint called, '*Selective*'."

Michael replied, "That looks like a place that's advertising for people with open minds about their sexuality. I think it's a bar where all proclivities are considered. From all of my experiences on the island, if you want information, there is no better place than where people who are connected in one way but are disconnected in others, if you know what I mean."

Sue Lyn said, "I think you might have a point, but hey guys, look to your right about fifty yards down the road. Do you see the sign that says, '*Not Selective*'?"

Darryl said, "They're both making a statement. Okay, Jasper, Quick, Harold, Isaiah, and Desmond will escort Michael and Barbara Ann if you think she's ready to see how we roll, Michael it's your call. Earther, Giuseppe Giovanni, and Windom will escort me and Sue Lyn to the other place. If the temperature is not right, get out and call us or we'll call you. For goodness sake, try not to use weapons unless the other side reveals them."

Michael said, "I prefer to switch up talent because I have a rookie with me. Give me Earther, Windom, and Isaiah, and you take Jasper, Giuseppe Giovanni, Harold, and Desmond. You know boss, if we found two more guys who are hard pressed that we could unpack and make them a part of our team, I think we would have achieved parity—ten plus two like your uncle and then we expand from there but we keep and make sure that we are the ten that you and we can trust with each other's lives. Just speaking out of turn, but also sharing your latent vision."

Darryl looked at him and realized that Michael had a visit from Wajickee and was given information and suggestions. He turned to Michael and asked, "In the outback, did you have a strange dream that revolved around an interaction with a spirit?"

"Darryl, in the outback, everything around you is strange and spiritual. My dreams scare me, my responses leave me curious, my interactions and reactions leave me confident. I don't know what's going on but if I have stepped across any lines of authority, I apologize and yield to your wisdom unless I have empirical information, sorry boss!"

"Michael, no need to apologize because I recognize that my family plays in the minds of others to make sure that my decisions are reasonable. I respect your input and your value to this team. Your manner of approaching me and Sue Lyn is with profound respect, honor, and we appreciate that. Sue Lyn is my Courtney as you are my Mallory. Everyone has a role. On our next visit to my home everyone will be anointed and prevailed upon to make the same kind of commitment that my uncle's guys have made to him. Listen, each of us are mortals. There are no guarantees that any of us will survive this adventure. However, we can to the best of our ability, protect each other's backs. Michael, you take Windom, Earther, and Isaiah and head to the *Not Selective* joint and we'll take the *Selective* place. The rest of you guys just hang out close but not too close to each place."

# # #

Thirty-four minutes after being in the *Not Selective* joint, Earther was denied his second drink. Michael joined him at the bar and asked if there was a problem and the barkeep replied, "He keeps looking at that man's woman at the next table and we don't want any trouble."

Michael turned to look at the positioning of the table and the couple, and said, "Sir, that's impossible. He does not have eyes in the back of his head and has not turned around once since we've been at the table."

"Well, this is my place and I can serve whoever the hell I want to."

Isaiah came up to the bar with five one-hundred-dollar bills in his hand and asked the barkeep, "Can I have a private word with you?" He then slid the bills toward the barkeeps hand and showed another stack of bills in his other hand.

Isaiah said to Michael, "Boss, let me deal with this one. I think I've gotten his attention and, therefore, I believe he's a gentleman and will realize that there is a mistake that can be corrected without any problems."

The two men stepped towards the men's room and when they entered it, Isaiah quickly displayed his weapon and badge. He asked, "That guy with that young woman, are you covering for his ass?"

The barkeep said, "Sir, the whole idea of denying your friend a drink is because I saw the bulges in your outfits. That guy and his two friends with that young woman, well, there is clearly some kind of devious plot with that group. They freeze every time that door opens. I'm hoping you are police of sorts and can rescue that lady. They have literally told me not to answer my damn phone because they're expecting a call on it. The guy sitting to the left of the girl, broke a guy's nose for staring at him. That was my excuse for getting your attention."

"Okay, listen, we're on another mission, but I assure you we'll handle this one, first."

"Oh, and that guy masquerading as that lady's man, was overheard by the waiter who got his nose broke, that they had to get out of town before it disappeared."

Isaiah asked, "What did you just say?"

"I said the guy with the woman told his people that they had to get out of town before it disappeared."

There was a loud bang as if someone kicked a door. Isaiah said to the barkeep, "You'd better kiss me like you mean it or we're both dead."

One of the men from the table walked in on them and said, "You, fucking freaks, get a room. Hey, you, barkeep, wash your fucking hands before you go back out there."

Both men spat on the floor and agreed that the kiss was disgusting but thanked each other for the quick thinking. Isaiah said, "If you mention to my people that we kissed, I'll put a bullet in your ass.

The guy from the table walked out and said, "Can we get out of this freak ass place. I mean damn, two guys are back there, swapping spit. Can we leave?"

The man sitting next to the girl whispered, "We have less than twenty-four hours to vacate this area starting at midnight. Don't fuck this up and create another scene. The barkeep bailed you out of the last fiasco, don't mess this up. Your choices are yours, but if the man finds out you jeopardized his placement of the product, you're a dead man!"

Isaiah walked in from the rear and the guy looked at him and spat on the floor. Isaiah smiled and said, "Sometimes, this job requires me to do some really vile shit, like shooting your ass—pow, pow!"

Isaiah carefully placed a round into each of the man's leg. Before the rest of the table with the young woman could react, Michael, Windom, and Earther were on the group with weapons pointing. Michael yelled, "What the hell did you just do?"

Isaiah yelled, "I think I found some kidnappers who may have some critical information about what we're here for. Boss, get this shit out of here and the girl."

The guy who was shot in each leg, yelled, "If she crosses that damn threshold, we're all dead!"

Michael, after gaining permission from the young lady, gently, and respectfully, opened her coat and saw that she was encased in a plastic vest that contained a liquid formula that had three chambers that connected in the middle of her body. The materials didn't look formidable, but no one really knew what they were. Michael called Darryl and told him that he and his team needed to get there and not to dally. In the interim, Windom removed the weapons from the people and placed them on a table in the rear.

Meanwhile, Barbara Ann was stunned by the sudden act of violence and vision of a man bleeding profusely from leg wounds. The man sitting next to the young woman vociferously commanded, "Do not touch that device! It is motion sensitive and radio controlled. If she crosses that threshold this whole damn place will evaporate."

Michael instructed Earther to duct tape the wounded man's legs. Michael then inquired, "What the hell do you mean evaporate?"

"Just that! This is that new bomb that killed all those people in Springfield, Massachusetts."

That statement got everyone's attention. Michael called Darryl and suggested to him to get in touch with his uncle because they may have walked in on the real deal and it has an alleged twenty-four-hour detonation timetable beginning at midnight.

## CHAPTER TWENTY-SIX

On his way to the 'Not Selective' joint, Beckmire gave a call to Mr. Utz and informed him of what his people had told him. He urged Mr. Utz to get to the 'Not Selective' bar off A1A, and that he was on his way to the place. He also told Mr. Utz that his people feel that this is the real thing.

# # #

When the Sarge arrived near the place, he decided not to go in like gangbusters but instead, trickled in two at a time until he had six of his people in there with him. Once in the place, he informed Mr. Utz to leave the neckties in the car and come in two or three at a time. He told the rest of his people to assume defensive positions and keep an eye out for a triggerman.

Darryl and Michael gave the Sarge a quick and dirty briefing of the events. The Sarge asked who shot the guy in the legs and was told that it was Isaiah. The Sarge smiled and said, "Get him over here."

When Isaiah entered the huddle that the three men were having, the Sarge asked, "Why did you shoot him?"

Isaiah thought for a moment and said, "For one, he's a real jerk, and two, they were carrying. His wounds are superficial.

If I wanted to hurt him, I would have placed each round towards the center by an eighth of an inch."

"My question remains, why did you shoot him. Did you get clearance from Michael?"

"Mr. Beckmire, I did not. When I heard the words disappear and twenty-four hours, I went above my pay grade and executed what I considered, a relevant reaction."

"Did you consider the fact that you could have placed your team in harm's way with an independent action?"

"Mr. Beckmire, I had them all covered, and I placed my body between them and the team's. I just reacted because I knew discussion and dialogue wasn't going to get us to where we wanted to be in the alleged timeframe."

"Okay, Isaiah. I'm not going to try and call this one, but apparently you got us closer to the bomb but not the bomb maker. Suppose this is the consequence he expected from us? Well, he has us all in the same damn place now, doesn't he?"

"Mr. Beckmire, may I say one more thing?"

"Go ahead."

"If the information is correct, he has millions of people in the same damn place."

# # #

Mr. Utz showed up at 2345 hours and waltzed into the place as if he were intoxicated. He meandered over to the Sarge and asked, "What's going on?"

The Sarge pointed to the table where everyone had their hands on it. He said, "Take a respectable look under the young lady's coat."

Mr. Utz asked the young lady, "May I have a look under your coat? As a matter of fact, can you remove it?"

One of the men yelled, "It's like a fucking magnet. You move it and you detonate whatever the hell that mess is."

Michael informed the Sarge that it was alleged that the device was motion sensitive and radio controlled. The Sarge stepped away and called Rashida, gave her the address, and told her that he needed signal jamming equipment where he was, and in a hurry.

The Sarge saw Barbara Ann sitting in a corner by herself and eased over to her and asked, "May I get you a cocktail?"

Barbara Ann smiled and said, "I would love to have a rum and coke if possible."

"Any preference of rum?"

"Yes, Cruzan."

When he returned with two rum and cokes, Beckmire asked, "So, Barbara Ann, I guess you were here when the guy was shot?"

"Yes, I was, and it happened so fast, I didn't know what to do. Michael and the others ran to that table and everyone was pointing a gun at someone."

"I know you weren't comfortable with what you saw, but do you realize that we often do this sort of thing?"

"Mr. Beckmire, perhaps I should restate my experience. I have never been around live gunfire, the sound scared me, the guy bleeding shocked me, and I said to myself, everyone has a gun but me."

The Sarge laughed and said, "Cheers!" They bumped glasses and he walked back to the bar where the barkeep was babbling about the disappearance of everything in the area. Mr. Utz asked, "Did you hear of any other places where someone was strapped in a vest like that one? The barkeep told him that the only thing he heard that was consistent, was not to fuck this up and we have exactly twenty-four hours to get out of dodge. Mr. Utz asked him, "What were they going to do with the girl?"

"Sir, I don't know!" the barkeep exclaimed.

He looked at Mr. Utz and said, "They didn't seem too anxious to have her tag along. The one who is supposed to be her man, offered to let the others have a go at her, if you know what I mean but they declined. I don't even know if the lady can talk. She's been sitting there like that for a couple of hours and has never uttered a single word. Occasionally, they appeared to inject her with something."

Mr. Utz said to the Sarge, "I have to call the bomb squad."

"If I, were you, I would wait until my daughter gets here and jams the signals in the area. They say the vest is radio controlled, not sure you want that exposure until we can at least kill the signal."

"When will she be here?"

"Mr. Utz, if that's the real thing, we're all dead and you should have a drink. You're obviously scared."

Utz looked at the Sarge but said nothing. He ordered a vodka and tonic and the two men clinked glasses and took a swig of their drinks.

Ten minutes later, the door opened and it was Rashida, Juan, Asiram, Zanthius, Courtney, Larry, and Mike.

Rashida said, "Dad, Juan and I tried to sneak out, but you know these people, they spy on us all the time."

"Baby girl, I need you to jam all signals in the immediate area; say, half a mile radius? Can you do that?"

"Dad, we can create a log jam up to three miles and each time they fix it, another jam is invoked. Why don't we do the maximum, just to be safe. Why are we jamming in a bar?" The Sarge pointed to the young girl at the table and suggested that caution be exercised. Rashida and Juan walked over to the table and immediately saw the vest and its contents. Rashida said, "Oh shit! Is this what I think it is?"

Zanthius bellowed out and said, "If I were to guess, this is the product of the Carbon Factor formula. Dad, am I right?"

"Son, I don't have a clue what it is, but those people were talking about the area disappearing in twenty-four hours which is now down to twenty-two and counting."

Asiram asked, "Who is the lady wearing the vest?"

"Asiram, I don't have a clue and she doesn't talk very much. Try your luck and see if you can get a response or determine if she's damaged in some way," Michael asked.

Courtney kissed her husband and said, "You know what dude? "I'm going to revoke your freedom pass. I don't want to bury you or go to your funeral! I want to die with you and, therefore, when you go out on these one-way missions, I want to have the right of first refusal. Is that understood? I'm never going to say this again, get with the program or I'm out of here buster!"

Ben Beckmire watched as his bride walked away with tears in her eyes. He knew that her words were not to be trifled with. He sucked in his manhood and walked over to where Courtney was sitting with Barbara Ann and got on his knees and said, "I love you more than life. Some of our missions are dirty, violent, and deadly. I don't feel right taking my wife to a place where my men might gut someone from their midsection to their brain. If you ever leave me, I will conclude all that is me! I love you and I can't operate effectively when I have to consider that when I return or if I return, my wife may or may not be there. Is there someone else you're interested in?"

"Slap! You humiliate me again and I'm out of here. I will shoot myself in the head before I let another touch or enjoy those pleasures that are yours for life. Don't ever come at me with that bullshit!"

The Sarge behaved like a dog in training. He eased up to Courtney and kissed her neck. He whispered, "My definition of life is you, my love. I'm a man, and not a real smart one, please ignore my innuendoes. I was trying to be macho, but my life is you and if something happened to you, I would never find peace on this earth."

The Sarge finally reached Courtney's cheek and then her lips. It was like a movie scene, until Mallory and Monica walked through the door and Mallory profoundly asked, "Sargent Dum Dum, what the hell did you do this time?" The Sarge and Courtney looked at each other, laughed for a moment and sealed their love with a kiss in front of all, including the captives.

# # #

Asiram asked the young lady if she was okay and if she needed to go to the ladies room? There was no response verbally or otherwise. Asiram looked at the chair the young girl was in and saw that it had a transmitter underneath. Asiram slowly got up and walked over to the Sarge and Larry, and said, "Under the seat the young lady is sitting in, there is a transmitter. I'm not sure if it receives or sends a signal."

The Sarge beckoned Michael, Darryl, and Sue Lyn over and he said, "Did you people know that there is a transmitter under the chair the female is sitting in?"

Michael threw his head backwards and said, "I fucked this op up from the beginning to the end. Shit, shit, shit."
He looked at Isaiah and asked, "What did you do after you shot that guy in the legs?"

"Boss, I placed a transmitter under her chair that would give me intel on their conversations. Did I screw up again?"

Michael, Sue Lyn, and Darryl hugged him, and Beckmire said, "You may have exonerated your earlier actions of firing without permission. Has anything of significance been said?"

"No, sir, Mr. Beckmire. The only thing uttered is that our families are dead!"

The Sarge looked at him and said, "Damn, that's a bargaining chip if we can figure out the dynamics of why they're sitting with this comatose young girl."

The Sarge walked over to the table and said, "Looks like we're all subject to a rude conclusion. Now, some of you have loved ones in bondage. Who is this young woman? Oh, and dude, those flesh wounds will probably start getting infected in the next fifteen to twenty minutes."

He paused and looked around the room and asked, "Isaiah, which solution are your rounds from?"

"Ah, sir, I drew them from the lung group."

"Oh, I see. Okay, sir, you have less than fifteen minutes to live. In the next two to three minutes, you're going to start struggling to breathe. Now, Dr. Beckmire over there has an antidote for each virus that we dip our bullets in. The Sarge looked at his watch and hoped that by suggesting an issue, it might take control of the person's mind and deliver the intended results.

The guy with the flesh wounds internalized the issue and began to breathe heavy and consistently faster. The Sarge said, "Okay, it's happening keep breathing faster. You tell me what I want to know, and I'll get the doctor to give you a shot and get you to the hospital. Who is that young woman?"

"I don't know her. The guy sitting next to her showed up with her last night and she has been drugged ever since."

The Sarge asked the guy, "Where did you find her, what did you people do to her, and who put that vest on her? Don't fucking lie to me, asshole?"

"Most passed on the opportunity to enjoy her except the guy next to her," the guy stated.

Asiram walked over to the guy and said, "I hope you enjoyed your last orgasm!" She fired a round towards his head that only grazed the man. She then looked at the alleged husband and pointed the weapon at his penis and asked, "How old is that child?"

The Sarge yelled, "People, stop shooting our only leads. I need coherent responses, not messes." He then looked at the alleged companion of the lady and said, "Answer the damn question."

"I don't know. That's who they gave me to oversee this part of the operation."

"Who gave you?"

"Dude, what do you want me to say? They have our families and if we don't do as they say, then they'll execute our people."

"Did they tell you to have your way with this woman, while they held your families in bondage? Did they tell you to do that?"

Barbara Ann, unsuspectingly, walked over to the table where the confiscated weapons were placed, picked up a .45 automatic, walked unimpeded to the captive's alleged companion, and fired a single round into his head. The entire place was shocked! Michael couldn't believe what he had witnessed, nor could anyone else. After firing the round into the man's head, Barbara Ann dropped the weapon and screamed, "That's what they did to me. They drugged me, raped me, and left me for dead!" She screamed and cried her heart out. Michael grabbed her and hugged her tightly and said, "You'll never have to worry about that, ever again, my love."

The Sarge yelled, "What the hell is going on here? Why are you women shooting our only leads?"

Suddenly, the comatose young lady screamed, "My anchor is 100 yards away! She's 100 yards away. Everyone is a 100-yards away!"

# # #

With approximately fourteen hours remaining before detonation, the Sarge asked Michael, "How is Barbara Ann?"

"Sarge, I'm not sure. Since she shot that guy in the head, she's been off the reservation. I tried to talk to her, but she responds with strange comments. I think she tried to fit into our way of life too rapidly, and, therefore, is beginning to slip into an abyss. I touched her hand and she literally tried to hit me. Something during that encounter with those guys resurfaced a serious negative scenario. Sarge, I don't know who this woman is. It's as though she's been possessed and I'm in need of a Wajickee to unfold this mystery."

"Son, I am going to need you front and center during the next fourteen hours or so. If that's a problem, let me know so that I can take your place personally. You, my friend, have a Beckmire kind of third sense and I need it. However, I realize that your woman has to be first in your life, and you need to be with her. Don't over promise and under deliver. If you can't give me your all, then stay with Barbara Ann, and try to help her surface whatever demons exist within her mind. She is a great catch son, do what's right."

"Mr. Beckmire, you do realize that you called me son on two occasions, don't you?"

"Michael, your dad is in St. Thomas, but here, I feel like you're one of my boys, just like Isaiah, Harold, Giuseppe Giovanni, Desmond, and everyone else. John Lee, Jilkes, Bernstein, Chakes, Gladstone, Whitmore, Jong, Brown, Montomie, and McArthur, are all my sons. You just joined an exclusive, members only organization, my friend."

# # #

In the pocket of the man that Barbara Ann shot in the head, was a piece of paper with an address and a series of numbers that resembled a combination lock for a safe. Sue Lyn looked the paper over and became fixated on the placement of the number seven in each series. As she studied the presentation of the numbers, her analytical brain began to sequence the numbers and formations. Fifteen minutes later, she announced to Darryl, that the South Beach apocalypse would happen on the 7th day, which is today, at the 7th hour which according to my calculations, is one hour and forty-nine minutes away. She then said to Darryl, exactly seven seconds after that, those chemicals on that child and three others would begin to brew for seven tenths of a second and then detonate.

Darryl asked, "How can you be so precise in the timetable?"

"Honey, we don't have time to analyze my findings. You must believe or not believe in me."

Darryl studied his wife's expressions for a few seconds and decided that she was the brains in their household. He saw Michael and yelled, "Have you seen my uncle?"

Michael turned around and pointed in a direction. Darryl saw his uncle and once he caught up with him, said, "According to my wife, we have less than one hour and a half to incapacitate at least one other carrier. If we can find three, then I assume the damage would be localized and controllable. I'm assuming, uncle, that it requires a certain fixed distance for the four parts to gravitate towards the center, thus creating a shit storm to the epicenter. Can you get Mr. Utz to get an aerial of Springfield and perhaps one of the other places devastated by the detonations?"

# # #

The Sarge gave Mr. Utz the conclusions Sue Lyn stated clearly and said, "Either you get me this information in the next ten minutes, or me and my people are out of here. Don't fucking dawdle around on this one. We have less than ninety minutes to find the second and perhaps the third carrier or we're all history."

Mr. Utz walked away from the Sarge, pulled out another cell phone that was rather large, dated, and dialed a number. He said to the person answering the phone, "We have less than an hour before South Beach becomes no beach. What's your decision?"

"Is my place safe and out of range of this testament as to why people need me to run this country?"

"Sir, it's like a strategical strike; precise, on point, and with the collateral damage that we want."

"Mr. Utz, I suggest that you and your team disassociate yourselves from your current location. I have no way of stopping this terror. God Bless me and God bless America. Oh, by the way, do I have any weak links there?"

"Your special friend concluded the only link to you, and this terrorist attack will unfortunately, conclude her existence. Sir, knowing that the country is going to beg you to run again after this event, it might be good if you moved your colors from red to black to indicate to your followers that it's time to turn the proletariat into the masters, and annihilate those who are not true Americans, in a surreptitiously quiet but brutal manner, of course. It is time for the new revolution!"

"What about those people who have been a pain in my ass since the capsule was obtained, will they be around to create an issue for me later?"

"I assure you, they followed the ploy, deciphered the information, and concluded when things would happen. They will all be dealt with in the next hour. I will personally deal with their demise."

"You know children grow up to become a pain in the ass. Will that be a concern for me?"

"Sir, every child, woman, and man will be terminated along with thousands of others. This I guarantee!"

"Mr. Utz, you are a patriot and an exceptionally good friend. You know what must be done and I trust you with the future of this great country. I want you out of there in the prescribed timetable. Remember, no clues!"

# # #

Later at the hotel, Courtney escorted Barbara Ann to her room and gave her a mild sedative, a thing that she requested, that would put her to sleep. In a matter of seconds, Barbara Ann was out like a light.

Asiram and Rashida entered the room. Asiram asked Courtney, "How is she doing?"

Courtney replied, "The poor thing is probably in need of sleep, much like the rest of us. Rashida, in the meantime, began to look around her room and noticed a bag pushed half-way under the bed. She reached down and pulled it from under the bed and said, "Girlfriend, has a lot of people to call. She also has some pretty heavy drugs to consume, as well. Look at this stuff, I think the lady has cancer."

Asiram, after viewing the contents of the bag asked, "Why so many phones, and why does a person who works from nine to five need so many different cell phones and, oh shit, this is a communication device used by spies. Who the hell is Barbara Ann?"

Rashida took pictures, installed a bug in her room and cloned the cell phones. When they left the room, they went directly to Asiram's room, and began to review what they found. Rashida said, "I need Monica and Sue Lyn. Sue Lyn has an eye for things that are out of sync."

Twenty minutes later, Sue Lyn knocked on Asiram's door and when she opened it, she gave her a hug and then immediately walked over and hugged Rashida.

Rashida said, "I have a transmission that was made from our general area to a number that was shipped around the country and landed in Washington, DC. Now, wait, before you give me your Sherlock Holmes version of my paranoia, Asiram has a simple looking device that can do a lot of spy type shit. Now, we trespassed into Barbara Ann's room and found multiple cell phones and a list of numbers that we're sure, that only you can make sense of them. In addition, from this location, another call was made to a number in Washington, DC that we could not decipher because it was encrypted."

"Rashida, you like Darryl, you give me stuff, but don't tell me what you want. Do you want me to look at numbers, cell phone calls leaving the area, calls coming into areas, and translate what was said?"

Sue Lyn smiled and asked, "Where is Monica. We need a lawyer to fine tune where we go with information that was not volunteered to us?"

Asiram laughed, hugged her, and said, "Once you drop that load, we're going to go somewhere and get drunk!"

"No, my sister. We will go somewhere where people won't know who we are and have a good time without killing, maiming, or threatening anyone."

Asiram, yelled, "Deal!"

# # #

Back at the '*Not Selective*' Rashida continued to jam the signals coming into the area. In addition, all communications made from the area, as well as those attempting to connect with someone in the quadrant, were recorded. As Sue Lyn and Asiram tried to make sense of the list with scrambled numbers on it, Rashida continued to listen to random conversations that included things about drugs, sex, wife beating, cheating, and everything else that people do, and concentrated on key words, country, patriot, loyalty, our people, our kind, and future of our great country. Rashida placed those words in a data base of the most frequently used phrases by hate groups and to her amazement, the White House showed up. She entered the key for recent conversations, and bingo; Mr. Utz's conversation with the White House was revealed. Rashida was the only one who knew the capabilities of Asiram's phone that she carried around like a baby. It was the most prolific unit the government had ever developed that could access complete conversations using key words. Rashida played the conversation back several times before she asked Asiram to get her dad in here.

Asiram said, "Rashida, you seem upset. Is everything alright?"

Rashida looked at her and said, "Get my father, and everyone else in here, now!"

# # #

Eleven minutes later, the Sarge and most of his team showed up at Asiram's door. Rashida waited patiently to disclose her findings and was not going to reveal them until everyone was crowded into the room or the hallway. When she realized that the room was not going to accommodate everyone, she yelled, "Hey people, I'm going to have a private conversation with my father, Asiram, Sue Lyn, Darryl, Courtney, Monica, and Mallory. It will be their responsibility to share my information with you if they so choose."

As the room emptied out, Rashida said, "I'm not sure if we will live until tomorrow. It appears that this entire thing, was orchestrated by insiders and people, that I think, we trust. Dad, Mr. Utz, is a puppet for someone in the White House. I suspect, Barbara Ann is in cahoots with Mr. Utz and is a plant. I also think she shot that guy before he gave her up. In addition, Sue Lyn thought that we had eighty or so minutes or something close to that, we don't. Mr. Utz guaranteed someone in the White House that all of us, including the children, would be dead. Dad, he is a snake and has a plan to escape within the hour."

"Baby girl, those are some strong accusations. Do you have proof of what you say?"

"Dad, we need to concentrate on the second, and hopefully the third person wearing the vests. We have less than an hour, and according to our drug induced young lady, the connectors are 100 yards away. Mom, I know they say that the vest is rigged, but you and Jong must look closely at it, and figure out a way to disengage it. Without calling names or naming individuals, this seemingly leads to the highest part of our government. No wonder, the revealing of taxes was a problem, it shows too many of his associates on his payroll."

Rashida looked at her father and said, "Dad, you have to tell Michael, and he must decide what to do with his lady friend. We don't have a lot of time to have seances, we need to move expediently on all fronts. We have enough people to search a one-hundred-square yard area. We need to start now."

Courtney chimed in and said, "The 'mickey' I gave Barbara Ann will keep her out for the next two hours. That will give us enough time to let Asiram or John Lee attend to her ass. What about the others? You know they all come from the same fabric."

Rashida said, "I can't vouch for anyone, but I can say that Barbara Ann had all the signs of being on a mission, other than Michael. You know in the outback, strange things happen, and my attention was always on Barbara Ann, even to the point I had her in several of my discomforting dreams."

The Sarge said, "Damn, I liked that lady for my son. It's going to be hard to tell him about her."

Courtney responded, "Ben, he's not your son."

"Baby, all the boys here, are my sons. Anyway, Rashida, I suppose you and your friends have a plan."

"Thanks dad, we do!"

## CHAPTER TWENTY-SEVEN

Later back at the 'Not Selective' bar, Sue Lyn calculated the approximate distance and placement each person wearing the device should be. She pinpointed the most likely places the individuals would be for maximum impact from the detonations. She realized that being inside of a building might limit the impact because of the various materials utilized to build structures. The two things that stuck in her mind were, carbon and water. She assumed that the devices were the catalyst for the combustible process, but that it still needed to engulf all hydrogen-based products in the area. She hoped her basic assumptions about the Carbon Factor were correct as she considered the assignments for members of the team to head out in an aggressive search for other people wearing the devices.

The Sarge said, "I know this is all new to you and to all of us, even though, we've been living this nightmare for a long time, we never took time to figure out what triggers it. I say that, to say this, give it your best shot. If we do not capture at least one device in the next hour or so, then I want my entire team out of here, but not before we give a general warning to the officials. Perhaps, we should give them a heads up. What's your take?"

Sue Lyn said, "Uncle, based upon what happened in Springfield and those other places, it won't matter. From what

I saw, the Carbon Factor sucked up everything hydrogen-based in its designated area. Oh, shit! Oh, shit! Don't you see it? Designated area is the operative phrase. This thing can only work with all four components activated in their designated area. Let's get that vest off that woman and drive it as far away as possible. If we capture another, then we do the same thing, thus limiting the ability of the components to interact, react, and create the hell storm that happened in Massachusetts and those other places. Uncle, I think that is the key to avoid thousands and perhaps millions of innocent lives being lost."

The Sarge assembled, met with the teams, and gave them explicit orders. He commanded John Lee and Jilkes to drive the package as far away as possible and was conflicted by their joint responses. Jilkes said, "Me and my mate are not running away from this. We designate your two boys to fill that gap."

The Sarge yelled, "That's called insubordination!"

John Lee said, "No sir! That be called love for our brothers and if this thing goes south, then me and my friend be going south with our other brothers."

The Sarge started to debate the issue when Mallory jumped in and said, "We don't have a lot of time to discuss this mess. If we don't find another vest in the quadrant in the next hour or so, I think every living soul should head as far and as fast out of town as possible, preferably, towards the airport where we can regroup."

#

The women and children were dispatched to the airport and placed on the two other planes belonging to the group. Prior to their leaving, Asiram said to Ava and Courtney, "You two ladies may become the surrogate parents to a lot of children. Courtney and Ava, I love you and you two have been the only people who have been a mother to a stubborn child. Take care of the boys and my princess as well as, the rest of the tribe and don't look back!"

Courtney walked over to Ben and said, "I'm not leaving without you and that's that! I told you I will die with you, not away from you."

Ben Beckmire's eyes filled with tears and he said, "Courtney, this time you will do exactly as I say without any retort. I want you to get on one of those planes with all my grandbabies and remember this roller coaster ride. Honey, it was the best time of our lives, and you know that we did a lot of bad things to people and it was bound to catch up with us. You and the children will never have to worry about a thing but I want you to kiss me, tell me you love me, and that I was a good man and a good husband. Those are the only words I want to hear from you, my love!"

#

After a lot of goodbyes, the group was scuttled about to the projected coordinates that were conceived by Sue Lyn. With less than fifty-five minutes to go, no one had found anyone, or materials located in their areas. The Sarge said over their communication devices, "People, I think we need to give it another twenty minutes, and if not by then, we vacate."

Asiram came on the line and said, "Daddy-in-law, let's make it a full thirty minutes. My soul would rest easy knowing that I didn't run to save my own ass!"

There was quiet on the airwaves and the Sarge bellowed, "You heard the lady, dig deep, aggressively, and by God, try to save these unknowing souls!"

Gladstone and Whitmore were assigned Isaiah and Desmond. Desmond asked, "Without looking like crazy people, how do we begin the search?"

Whitmore asked, "How old are you son?"

"What the hell does age have to do with a mission that is sure as hell about dying?"

Whitmore looked at him and said, "If we live through this, me and my brother are going to work with you people to make you as smart as we are." There was a lot of laughter until Isaiah stated, "That is an uncommon presentation. Look at the coat, look at the guy, look at them handcuffing that female to that metal bench."

Gladstone pointed and said, "Rookies, take an easterly and westerly approach so as not to shoot each other. Me and my man are going straight forward. This is not an inquisition; this is an execution. Shoot first, and we'll figure out if we were right or wrong, later. This mission is about taking chances and damn, I don't want to be sucked into a giant vacuum cleaner."

Isaiah and Desmond approached from the east and west in a hard and determined fashion. They ran towards the subjects with their weapons drawn and caught the people off guard. Gladstone and Whitmore calmly walked towards the scene and Whitmore said, "Look at those fucking cowboys! They just shot the information! Oh, well!"

There was panic all around the area and Gladstone yelled, "She's wearing a bomb! Leave the area! Call the police!"

Whitmore said to Isaiah and Desmond, "Get the van and don't stop for shit. We're going to race out of town with this thing, hopefully beyond the detonation zone."

# # #

In another part of the designated detonation area, Asiram said to Zanthius, "Our children will probably never see us again, and I just hope I was enough woman to satisfy you."

"Are you crazy?" You're more woman than any woman I have ever met. Also, you're the best mother, lover, friend, hater, and ass whipper, that I know. I know my two mothers will cover all the bases for our children. However, I need you to focus. I'm not committing suicide yet, so until I blow that whistle and tell you we're out of here, we stay focused."

# # #

Two planes took off, with quiet and concerned passengers. The children realized that they were on different planes, that their parents were missing and that a sense of sadness was rampant throughout the planes. Ms. Beatrice said, once the seat belt sign was turned off, "I want to play an adult game with my friends."

Ms. Viola asked, "What game might that be, my love?"

"I'm betting that my dad, and everyone else we left there, will find us soon!" She began to cry uncontrollably. Ms. Viola asked, "Baby, do you love your dad and brother?"

"Grannie, that is why I want to make a bet that he finds me and tells me how much he loves me, my brother, mom, and maybe you. He is my hero!" Beatrice continued to cry hard. Courtney got out of her seat to calm her down. Ms. Viola said, "That child knows what is happening and I'm confident that it's all good. We have such a village here. We have spirits, love, family, and friendship. I'm taking my grandbaby's bet and saying that all will join us soon, safe, and unharmed."

# # #

Sue Lyn continued to focus on her projections and realized that two of the four might have to comingle. She reduced the probability of spacing to half the size of the prescribed detonation zone. As she looked at the distinct factors that could affect detonation of the devices, she realized that her assumptions could be correct. She calmly called Asiram and said, "My friend, please reduce your focus by fifty percent and I mean now."

Asiram said to Zanthius, we have to move in by fifty percent."

"Why?"

"Damn it, because I said so!"

As Zanthius, Asiram, Bernstein, and Brown reached the prescribed coordinates, Zanthius said, "OMG! Honey, look at that child trying to get free from those handcuffs."

Bernstein yelled, "You and Zanthius provide cover for us. I'm sure the people who locked her there are long gone but give us cover. Call Chakes and Montomie and tell them to bring the van. We're down to thirty-two minutes by my watch."

# # #

Whitmore said, "Sometimes you have to shoot to wound and not to kill."

Isaiah, replied, "You said this was an execution and that's exactly what we did. We executed the plan that you prescribed.

When Desmond retrieved the van, they cut the handcuffs off the young lady and drove her due west. Whitmore called the Sarge and told him that they were driving the person they found with the vest, due west."

The Sarge called Zanthius and said, "When you people free that woman, drive due east with that vest."

Sue Lyn and Darryl removed the vest from the young lady in '*Not Selective*' and realized that there were no additional triggers on the vest. Darryl gave it to Michael and Harold and told them to drive the vest south and towards, what they thought, was a vacant baseball field.

When they arrived at the field, kids were in the midst of a game and Michael drove onto the field blasting four short blasts of his horn. He continued to do so, and two very astute parents knew that was a warning sign. The parents started screaming for people to leave. Pandemonium broke out and people started fetching their children and running for their vehicles. Michael said to Harold, "We have exactly fifteen minutes to place this thing and get the hell out of here."

At second base, Harold removed the vest from the car and sat it gingerly on the base pad. He backed away from the bomb and eased into the car and Michael took off. As Michael was spinning wheels to get distance, Harold saw a child approaching from right field. He didn't see a parent and told Michael to slowly drive up to the child. When in position,

Harold said, "Son, where are you parents? Everyone is leaving or have left because there is a bomb threat."

The boy looked at Harold and then continued to walk towards home plate. Michael started slowly backing the car up as Harold tried to convince him of the inherent dangers of proceeding towards in field. Michael slammed on the accelerator, propelling the car backwards and then slammed on the breaks. Both men jumped out of the vehicle and Michael yelled, "You're putting us all in danger. Look, there is no one here but the three of us. Look at that item sitting on second base, that's a bomb!"

The child began to sign indicating that he was deaf, and Michael fell to his knees and signed with the child. Michael asked where he lived and suggested that he go back home. Meanwhile, Harold was close enough to the child to grab him. After securing the child, Michael looked at him and signed "We are trying to help; we are not bad people."

The child began to cry, and Michael signed, "Where do you live?"

The child pointed to a series of row houses and indicated number two. They sped to the place, the two men stopped, and got out of the car with the child. When they approached the door, it was obvious that it was a home for the hearing impaired. Michael said, "Oh shit! He pushed a button that was in a bell slot that flashed lights around the premises so that people could respond. A remarkably beautiful woman, around thirty-two or so, opened the door. Michaels's heart fell to his feet and he signed, "We have someone who lives here and there is going to be an explosion in ten or so minutes. It is too late to try to evacuate all of you here. Do you have a basement?"

The woman signed yes, and Michael signed for her to get everyone in the basement with blankets. The woman didn't panic, she hit another button that flashed red lights, and methodically orchestrated an evacuation to the basement for the fourteen residents of the house. When they were all in the basement, Michael said to Harold, "Take the car and tell my parents that I died trying to help others. I can't leave these people here."

Harold pulled out his cell phone and called Isaiah and informed him of their status. Isaiah told Darryl, and he called Michael and asked him if there was any way possible to abandon their position and be out of the range of the bomb in the next eight minutes? Michael told Darryl that they were in a home for the hearing impaired and he felt that this was his destiny. He looked at the woman, smiled and signed, "We are not going to leave you guys. If this thing hurts one of you, it will hurt all of us. We're not going anywhere."

The kids didn't believe what was going on and watched the interaction between Michael and the woman in charge of their home. She smiled at Michael and signed, "The kids think that you like me, and that you staged this event to, well, you know, to try to seduce me."

Michael smiled and signed, "I am a gentleman. I will express my feelings if we live through this event." The members of the house saw how serious he became and began to think that this was not contrived, but a real and serious event.

Michael signed if there was chewing gum in the house and everybody laughed. Behind Michael, was a cabinet that was full of gum. After being informed of its location, Michael signed that he wanted everyone to chew as much gum as possible in case the concussion from the detonation caused them to bite down on their tongues. He told them he wanted the chewed gum placed on their upper and lower teeth.

Harold told him that he was going to have a look to make sure no one else was hanging around the area.

As he viewed the field from the front window, he saw two children approaching second base. He screamed, "Michael, we have two children approaching second base!"

Michael signed to the lady what was going on, and they rushed upstairs.

He and Harold entered the vehicle and raced towards second base. The car was in neutral when they arrived near second base and both men jumped out and scooped up both children and ran to the vehicle.

Michael hit the accelerator shooting grass everywhere and raced towards the house. As the little girl tried to fight him while he was driving, he looked at his watch and realized that he had two minutes. When they arrived at the house, the house mom and an aide were there to assist with the two children. The entire group rushed into the house and as Michael was about to slam the door shut, he realized that he didn't cut the vehicle off. As such, it was a conductor. He ran to the car, and to everyone's amazement, they thought he was abandoning them. He cut the car off, ran towards the house and signed, "Everyone in the basement!"

As he attempted to catch his breath, the woman looked at him, smiled, and touched her heart. He lowered his head, touched his heart, and made the sign for embracing.

# # #

In four separate locations on South Beach, simultaneous and massive explosions rocked each area that the bombs were placed. Unfortunately, there was loss of life, but not to the magnitude it would have been if the Carbon Factor placements had been actuated. Hundreds were killed, versus, hundreds of thousands.

The house Michael and Harold took refuge in, along with several others, sustained severe damage to their structures. The house mom began to cry when she saw the damage because she knew that she didn't have the funds or insurance to repair the place. The property was in a prime location and was being sought by real estate speculating types. Michael signed, "What's more important than being alive? Nothing, he retorted."

She signed, "This is my house, those kids were abandoned, and I don't have the funds to repair it."

Michael stared at her for at least a minute. He smiled, and assertively signed, "My friends and I do! Let me clean up this bomb mess first, and I promise you, we will be back to help you. In the meantime, I'll call management and have them move you and the kids into a hotel on South Beach, until this place is fixed."

She signed, "Why would you do that?"

"Because I can, and we help people help themselves. I would like to make your place a project of mine. In doing so, I would have to see all aspects of your operation and then we'll rebuild in a matter of months by using three crews around the clock. There is a lot I can do and want to do. You should consider trusting me and not look at me like you did when you thought I was running to the car to save myself. I must try to reach my people and make sure they're okay. There are a lot of explanations that I owe you, but they will come in time. Give me contact information and I will have people evaluate the damage and correct it. You guys will stay in a hotel, on the same floor, with all the privileges. I can also speak to my boss and see if you guys can stay at our resort in St. Thomas, your choice, but I must check on our people and make sure everyone is okay. Besides, I have some unfinished emotional business, that I must deal with!"

## CHAPTER TWENTY-EIGHT

Slowly but surely, members of the group began to show up at the hotel. The Sarge stood at the threshold stoically, taking a head count of his people. He gave each person a man-sized hug and told them that he loved them. After an hour, Asiram, Zanthius, and their crew were still missing. In addition, Michael and his crew hadn't shown up as well.

Standing in the same spot at attention, the Sarge patiently waited for the missing members of the group to arrive. Darryl and Sue Lyn joined their uncle because Michael and his crew were still out of contact. The entire phone system in the State of Florida was disrupted by the destruction, and the heavy call volume. He saw a van flying down the road and hoped it was members of his group. When the vehicle came to a stop, it was Michael and Harold. The two men got out of the car and Michael said, "Mr. Beckmire, Darryl, Sue Lyn, Harold, and I have just committed funds to rebuild a place that saved our lives that is a home for abandoned and hearing-impaired children. We want to make it a project for the group. The blast destroyed most of the structure, but it was that basement and chewing gum that saved them and us."

Darryl said, "Michael, I'm glad that you and Harold are okay. As you know, there is a situation that you need to manage. Insofar as the hearing-impaired group is concerned, we'll take care of that. Your immediate issue is probably more problematic in that a serious breach in our security was committed, by your mate."

The Sarge asked, "Would you like someone else to address that for you?"

"Sarge, if it were Courtney, would you want someone else to oversee it for you?"

The Sarge said, "Manage your business, Son!"

"That's the third time, Sarge."

"Manage your business, Son!"

Late to the party was Asiram, Zanthius, Bernstein, Brown, Chakes, and Montomie. Zanthius said, "Dad, these people saw a sign that read, 'the best damn martini on earth,' and we stopped."

"I was worried about you guys. I don't think what you did was smart, but I didn't see that sign, now did I?" He hugged each person and told them that they have a lot of unfinished business to take care of. I'm waiting on Whitmore, Gladstone, Desmond, and Isaiah, and I think I see another van heading this way."

Two hours later, Michael gently woke Barbara Ann up and asked, "Are you okay? You left the planet for a while. Meantime, we saved South Beach, killed a bunch of bad guys, saved a lot of children, and we're about to get out of dodge before the heat finds out it was us who stopped the potential carnage. Although there was loss of life, it pales in comparison to the hundreds of thousands or millions that might have been impacted."

"What are you saying? I mean, how could there be loss of life and yet you saved millions, as you say?"

"Barbara Ann, do you remember that night on the beach when we first met? Anyway, I'm sure you do, as well as our other rendezvouses. You know I never once, attempted to have sex with you, because the feelings I had for you superseded any carnal notions that engulfed me. My mind and body were focused on an amazing human being that I wanted to share, well, everything with. I finally had a significant amount of money that could support us for an exceedingly long time and keep us involved with a group, or better still, a family that cherishes life, love, honesty, commitment, and loyalty. Barbara Ann, you fail at each of those characteristics. We know who you are, who you work for, and your suicidal mission. That's why you had Courtney provide you with a drug that would let you sleep through the mayhem and ease you into hell knowing that you had betrayed every person that loved you, including your friends, and me. You were going to meet us all in hell, but not betray the mastermind of these mass murders, the President of the United States of America, and his associates; a power-hungry individual who will do anything to turn this democracy into a ruse."

"So, now what? I really don't care what happens to me because I've been betrayed by everyone that I ever cared about. Are you going to beat me? That won't matter to me because I've been there and done that. Listen, I like you a lot, but you have no ambition. You're happy with your strata, you like going from place to place killing people, stealing money, and living in your glass house. So, what's the deal? How do we conclude this mess?"

Michael smiled and replied, "Seems to me your handler's have posted your picture all over the world for terrorism with an extreme warning that you're armed and dangerous. You didn't die from the blast, but you will have a helluva lot of explaining to do. I love you so much and as such, I must turn my back on you. Where I'm from, that means, you're a part of the living dead."

Michael turned to walk away, and the sound of a small caliber weapon being cocked, could be heard. He said, "If you fire that shooter, John Lee and Jilkes will gut you like a pig."

Michael reached for the doorknob, paused, and said, "Fuck it!" He systematically pulled his weapon, proceeded to assume the kneeling position, and said, "Rashida and Asiram found that shooter and put blanks in it."

Barbara Ann pulled the trigger and nothing happened. Michael said, "Perhaps I was wrong, maybe they didn't put blanks in your weapon." Michael aimed and fired a round into Barbara Ann's head and walked out of the room!

Everyone in the hotel heard the sound of gunfire. The Sarge and his group knew exactly what had happened. He sent Jilkes and John Lee up to Barbara Ann's room to figure out how to extract the corpse. As Michael headed for the bar, the Sarge and Mallory walked over to him and said, "That shot was heard around the world. Was there another way to conclude that act?"

Michael smiled and replied, "Mr. Beckmire, do you remember when you met me and what you asked me to do? I'm sure you do, but anyway, I gave her the option of leaving without conflict from me. She pulled a weapon that Asiram and Rashida discovered and switched rounds. I genuinely believed the woman loved me, but her addictions and handlers had her under their fingernails. If that weapon were loaded, she would have shot me in the back. Can you imagine that? The person you love, shooting you in the fucking back!"

The Sarge said, "Son, this too will pass, and you will find another."

"Sarge, you guys want to hear something funny?"

Mallory said, "Amuse us, if you can."

"The woman in charge of that home for abandoned kids that was destroyed where Harold and I hid out, well, you guys have got to see this lady. Although she is hearing impaired, I remembered enough of my training as a Boy Scout, and in the military, my alternative communication strategy was signing, and I was able to communicate effectively with her. Oh, shit! I need to book rooms for them on the beach and give them full access to the hotel's amenities. I made this decision on my own and I will pay for their expenses. I will need help from the foundations to restore their core home."

Mallory said, "This sounds like a job for Franco and the group. What say you?"

The Sarge smiled and said, "Give him a call and see if they're busy and if they can spend a few days in South Beach."

The men laughed and Mallory said, "If the ladies are headed to the island, then we can send one of those planes for them. I assume that we're leaving here within the next two to three hours."

"Find that damn Jong and have him get us out of here as soon as possible."

"What about the body?" Mallory asked.

The Sarge said, "Having saved South Beach, perhaps we should take the body with us and have Michael deep six it. What say you, Michael?"

"Guys, I wouldn't want to leave here until I make sure those kids and that lady are secure, and I can't do it by phone.

I need to head back there and take them to a hotel. Can you ask Jong to assist me?"

"You're really committed to this project, eh?"

"Sarge, I just killed the woman, I love. I sure as hell hope this does not become a habit." He looked at the two men and Mallory cracked an uncontrollable smile that led to the beginning of a huge sigh and loud laughter.

The Sarge said, "I'm going to send Jilkes, John Lee, and Jong, to make sure they find them space on the beach. Mallory, call Franco and tell him that in a day or so, we'll send a jet for him and his crew because we have a construction project for him and his people to oversee. How is that for an immediate plan, Son?"

"Sarge, you've called me son a total of six times. Let me say it warms my heart, thanks!"

"This is lucky number seven. Son, are you okay, about what you did to the woman you loved?"

"If it were up to her, she would have shot me in the back. That's the most hurtful thing about the situation. Anyway, I need to make arrangements for those hearing-impaired people."

"This is number eight. Son, you have two hours to make all this happen. Get three stacks from Jong and give it to the woman and tell her it's for incidentals.

# # #

Michael took Jilkes, John Lee, Isaiah, and Harold with him. When they showed up with three vans, he cautioned everyone to be respectful because the people were hearing impaired. They witnessed the group scrounging around trying to recover clothing and other artifacts. Michael's eyes watered and he said, "This is so unfair."

When he got out of the vehicle, the woman turned around, smiled, fell to her knees, and began to cry. Michael eased up beside her and touched her ever so lightly on the shoulder. He didn't know how to sign handkerchief, so he signed, inadvertently, the description for a dish cloth. She laughed, stood up and faced Michael. She paused, wiped her eyes, and signed, "Are you an angel?"

"I'm just a man who survived a horrific event, in your house that was destroyed. Me and my people want to fix it and thank you for your hospitality at such a critical time."

"Why did you come back?"

Michael began to cry, and John Lee walked towards him, but was stopped by Jilkes who said, "He just shot his woman. Let him get through this on his own."

Michael really bawled his eyes out. He looked at the woman, threw his hands in the air and turned to walk away. She touched him lightly and signed, "You seem troubled. This is not your fault what happened here today. I am happy you returned. We will be okay."

After a few minutes of heavy breathing, Michael signed, "I know you will be okay, because we're going to rebuild your place, escort you to a hotel, give you cash for incidentals and a credit card that will cover your stay, no matter how long. I just lost a loved one and I'm sad, but I'm also committed to keeping my word. I have to get to the airport in two hours. Therefore, me and my friends are going to take you to a hotel on the beach where you will stay as our guests. We will send a plane for our friends in Spain to come over and oversee the rebuilding and expansion of your place. We will collaborate with your neighbors and see if they're interested in selling their places and if so, we will build you a home, staff it, secure it, and endow it with funds."

With tears flowing down her face, the woman asked again, "Are you an angel?"

"No! I'm a man who lost his love and has found someone who appeals to all of his moral fibers."

"Why are you telling me about another?"

Michael exclaimed, "I'm telling you, about you!" He signed, give me a minute. He turned to Jilkes and John Lee and asked, "Can we send a plane for those kids and the lady and bring them to *The Sanctuary*?"

John Lee said, "I'll call the Sarge and propose it. There be lots of room on our plane because our women folk and children took the other two planes."

# # #

In St. Thomas, Ms. Beatrice sat by the water quietly with several of the other children. An hour later, all the children were sitting by the water as if they were expecting a boat to arrive with Santa Claus or someone on it.

The Sarge called Courtney on the SAT phone and told her that all their people were good and that they would be on the ground in an hour. Courtney screamed to the group, "All of our men are coming home to roost!"

Little Ms. Beatrice yelled, "That's what I'm talking about. My daddy is coming home and everybody else's daddies too."

The Sarge said, "We had to eliminate Barbara Ann, but we picked up another thirteen or fifteen children who are abandoned and who are hearing impaired. This is Michael's quest, and we support him, and it. Baby, I did not mean to sound so adamant when I told you that you will listen to me and do as I say. We've never operated like that, but I needed you there with those women and children in case things went south. Please forgive me, but I had to know that you were safe and, therefore, I could focus entirely on the mission. I love you so much, Mrs. Beckmire, and I will see you soon."

"No, Ben Beckmire, I love you. Those words only reinforced the notion that you love me and everyone else in this group. Tonight, Mr. Bear, we're going to rock the foundation of *The Sanctuary*. See you soon!"

#

An hour later, their main jet landed. There was no fanfare, and Mr. Carter was there to provide them with transportation. He was made aware of the new special guests and had called ahead to the university to engage people who could sign.

When the van pulled into *The Sanctuary*, the Sarge said to Mallory, "My God! Look what we've been a part of my friend. Look at this place, it's amazing."

Mallory stated, "You know Sarge, we've done some horrific things to people who would have reciprocated if they had gotten the upper hand on us. In the process, we've amassed bundles of money that allows us to live well, help people help themselves, mount missions like getting our friends out of the sewers, and now, helping a bunch of hearing-impaired children. God is on our side!"

At *The Sanctuary*, everyone awaited the arrival of the group. The women and children welcomed their family and friends. Ms. Beatrice was the showstopper, she cried her eyes out, and after she hugged, kissed, and told her dad that she loved him so very much, she announced, "I made an adult bet, and everyone owes me. My daddy came back for me, my brother, my mom, Sister, and the rest of you. Your daddies came back as well. I was not sure about this trip, but I am so happy that all of our families are back together again, Mr. Sarge."

Ms. Beatrice turned to Chakes, with her eyes full of tears, said, "I love you so much and I pray that you love me as well. You keep my mom happy, me smiling and you tolerate Sister."

Chakes laughed, smiled, and hugged her tightly and whispered, "Your mom, you, and your brother are my definition of love. By the way, I don't tolerate Sister, I love her. We just speak differently to each other at times. Does that concern you?"

Ms. Beatrice announced, "I know you love her."

When it was the Sarge's turn, he hugged and kissed Beatrice on the cheek. He said to her, "I have another adult task for you to accomplish. Do you see all those children who appear to be afraid? Well, they're special in the sense that they are hearing impaired. Do you know what that means?"

"Mr. Sarge, of course I know what that means. That means they can't hear, and they talk by hand language. Is that right?"

"You're absolutely correct. After we get them settled, I'm going to need you and the rest of the kids, to show them around and learn how to get along and talk to them. Can you make that happen?"

"Mr. Sarge, we will make them feel like friends and at home. Maybe someone can show us how to talk to them. That would be good so that we all understand each other. It would be nice if we could have sort of a school."

Chakes after hearing the dialogue, said to Beatrice, "You make me so proud. You are always willing to help. You have a birthday coming up soon. Is there anything special that you would like to do?"

"Daddy, I want to go the African American Museum in Washington, DC. Can I do that for my birthday?"

"Honey, you know we're always on the move. However, I promise you this, if not on your birthday, then no more than thirty days later, we'll do it. Would you like the other children to come as well?"

"Oh, dad, that would be a great treat for all of us."

# # #

Michael was signing with the woman and finally realized that he did not know her name. He signed, "I'm embarrassed! I have to introduce you and I don't even know your name."

She signed, "It's not the name you called me on the plane, Barbara Ann. I read lips, my friend! My, name is not Barbara Ann. My name is Ayesha."

Michael signed, "Oh, so sorry." As he was about to continue signing with Ayesha, PJ interrupted him and inquired, "Where is Barbara Ann?"

Before Michael could respond, Darryl appeared, as though magically, and said "I need to debrief you and your friends, and I need to do it now. Can you assemble them?"

# # #

Fifteen minutes later, the ladies assembled in Barbara Ann's room with Michael, Sue Lyn, Darryl, as well as Gladstone, McArthur, and Montomie. Darryl wasted no time, pulled no punches, and bluntly and unapologetically stated, "Your friend, Barbara Ann is dead. She tried to shoot Michael in the back, she was in cahoots with the bomber, his minions, and other bad people. She acted as if she was distraught and shot a man in the head who was about to give us details about who he reported to. Your friend, and Michael's former lady, was a double-crossing, money hungry, manipulative person. Those so-called beatings by the husband, well, they too were contrived. The so-called husband was her partner, part-time lover, and source of information about our very move. Her reach was far, as far as the failed diamond mine heist. I don't think you believe what I'm saying, but the facts are clear, and you can question your current mates about what happened and who was high on the order-giving list; it was your friend, Barbara Ann. Her resolve was to have all of us in the locus of the detonations. She was going to kill us all. Are there any questions?"

PJ shouted out, "Where's her body?"

McArthur embraced her and replied so that everyone could hear, "You know our business and that question is not relevant. The query you want to ask, is simple, and that is, do you trust me and love me?"

PJ continued to cry and whispered to McArthur, "Will you terminate me when you get tired of me?"

"PJ, Asiram and Rashida placed blanks in Barbara Ann's weapon once they discovered it. She aimed her weapon and tried to fire it twice at Michael's back. She used everyone involved in our group. Mainly, she violated Michael's trust, love, and respect, for a few dollars, the amount of which was miniscule compared to what Michael's potential pay and benefits from all that he does for the group. Listen, I would never hurt you, under any circumstances. Unfortunately, everyone is being vetted again to make sure that no one else is conspiring with our sworn enemies. PJ, would you ever try to kill me?"

"My love for you, is stronger than any feelings, I have ever had. I trust you Mac, with my life and I will never betray you. If I ever have the feeling that this is not going well for me, then I will leave, without any drama."

Darryl stated, "The materials on the bed were found in this room, Barbara Ann's room, by Asiram and Rashida. I would like to inspect each of your rooms to see if any bugs were installed by your deceased friend. I know I was direct and profound in my statements, but I needed you guys to understand that we don't kill our own. She tried to kill my right-hand man, and that's a no-no! By the way, you all were eventually going to be targets. She thought that all of us would be in the same place, South Beach, when the Carbon Factor was detonated. What a friend!"

## CHAPTER TWENTY-NINE

The university sent several individuals over to *The Sanctuary* to assist with the individuals who signed as their only manner of communicating. Ms. Beatrice was very accommodating to the other children and after the first day, had learned twenty-five signing expressions. She was the unofficial tour guide and showed the children around all the properties that made up *The Sanctuary*.

On the beach, Michael sat only staring at the water and running his hand through the sand. The Sarge said to Courtney, "Michael will need us all to get over that thing he did. If it were me, I would be concerned about my poor choice but be thankful that I was first to act conclusively. I mean, if there were real bullets in that weapon, she would have shot him and probably concocted some weird story that would have us believing that he tried to hurt her or something to that effect."

"Ben, I'll be waiting for you. Take your time and try to console him, but damn man, you'd better be quick about it. I need to have my man!"

The Sarge headed towards Michael and saw John Lee and Jilkes on their way with a bottle of rum. He hesitated for a moment but moved quickly to join the brotherhood on the beach. Jilkes said, "Brother, and I mean exactly that, you did what you had to do. You saved a lot of people, including these people who are asking you to join with them in a drink in the celebration of life and friendship."

Michael looked to his right and said, "Oh, my, here come Chakes, Mallory, Gladstone, McArthur, Jong, Brown, Bernstein, Whitmore, and Montomie."

Jilkes said, "If you look to your left, Darryl, Sue Lyn, and your crew are on their way. Brother, it looks like you have a lot of love showing up to support you in your actions."

The Sarge announced, "Those are my sentiments as well. You saved any number of us and maybe all of us. I'm glad we decided to get the women and children out of there, because the plan was to kill us all and you helped squash that notion."

Sue Lyn announced, "Too much talk. Not enough drink. I want to drink and then I talk!" Everyone laughed and received a shot of Cruzan rum.

Darryl said, "To my right-hand man who I trust to protect, honor, and love each and every member of our group; to Michael!"

John Lee said, "So Michael, that there woman who talks with her hands is walking around *The Sanctuary* as if she was looking for someone or something. You might want to go and give her a hand and direct her to a dinner or something. She be one good-looking lady."

The Sarge said, "I have strict orders to report for duty. Corporal, I leave this rowdy bunch under your command and good luck with that one."

#

After doing several shots of Cruzan rum with the team, Michael walked over to where Ayesha was and signed, "What a beautiful evening. The sunset should be spectacular."

"How do you know so much about this place?" Ayesha asked.

Michael pointed to Mr. Carter and signed, "That's my dad. This is his place. The bank was about to take it from him until those guys came down, envisioned what a picture of paradise could look like, and became his partners. They paid off his loans, put several millions of dollars in an account for him to have the place demolished and rebuilt. At first, he used to be on the lookout for some unnatural demand, but it will never happen because these people don't operate like that?"

"Where did they get their money?"

"Ayesha, sometimes, by doing the right thing, things and opportunities prevail themselves upon you. The mission of this group is to help people help themselves. We are not involved in any illicit or immoral events that earn people money. No, we're about trying to save humanity from itself with its new destructive weapons like the one set off in the baseball field across from you. That detonation along with three others was supposed to form the basis of a cataclysmic explosion, mirroring the event that took place in Springfield, Massachusetts."

Ayesha signed, "How did you get involved in this matter? Are you with the government or something?"

"On occasion, we work for the government and other governments as free lancers."

"I know I sound apprehensive and unappreciative, but I am not accustomed to people offering to help me and my kids out. Usually, they are courteous, but more often than not, they don't really want us near."

"Are you describing your neighbors?"

Ayesha's head dropped, and her eyes became watery. She signed, "They think that I'm retarded and that the kids were abandoned because no one wants a moron as a child and definitely, not living near them. They think the kids are going to go crazy and burn the house down and that theirs will go up in smoke with ours."

Michael signed, "Then we buy the whole damn block! We make them an offer they can't refuse and then develop a school for the hearing impaired as well as a home for those who are homeless. I need you to stay right here, while I put this matter in motion. I see our lawyer and I want to get her involved."

Ten minutes later, Michael showed up with Monica and Ava, and once again they were all properly introduced. Michael explained that the neighbors thought that Ayesha was retarded, and that the children were abandoned because they're morons and they are concerned that one of the mentally imbalanced children will burn them all out one day. Michael said, "I want to pursue taking over the entire block and developing a home for the hearing impaired and those who are homeless. I'm bringing this to you guys first, because, you know, you control certain things that make my counterparts think and act irrationally."

Ava smiled and asked, "Are you talking about sex?"

"I'm not at liberty to have a conversation about sex with another man's wife, without him being present."

Monica replied, "Cut the bullshit or I'm walking away."

She paused for a few seconds, looked around, and said to Ava, "Walk with me, please."

The two women huddled, and at one point fiercely functioned as though they were going to come to blows.

They returned to where Michael and Ayesha were and told Michael to sign exactly what they say: "Ayesha, Michael lost a woman he loved who betrayed him and us. Do you have a romantic interest in Michael, and/or are you trying to advantage him in any way, shape, or form?"

Michael signed those exact words cautiously and looked at the two women and asked, "What the hell does this have to do with what I'm trying to do?"

"Listen young boy, we are trying to help you get over the mountain. You had to perform an arduous task, and we supported you. We just want to make sure this person is on the up-and-up."

Ayesha began to sign, and Michael looked away. She hit his arm forcefully, and vehemently signed, "Why are you ignoring my input? I want to answer for myself and not speak to the back of your head."

Michael smiled and said, "I killed the woman I loved because...."

He was abruptly cut off by Ayesha who signed, "I guessed that, and I hope you get over it. I asked you twice, are you an Angel? No one has ever considered me and my abandoned kids. The social worker, when she visits, acts as if they are lepers or something contagious and refuses to increase their allowances for books and other reading materials. I want you to tell these ladies exactly what I say, I am not trying to take advantage of Michael in any way, shape, or form. I asked Michael twice if he were an angel. I just met Michael and I went walking on this beach with hopes of finding him alone, but now, all of you people are here embarrassing him and I about feelings and emotions. I just met him; do I like him; hell yeah!"

Ava said, "Damn that reminds me of when I met that damn Ben Beckmire." She looked at Monica and said, "Hussy, I will slit your throat if you mention this small indiscretion to our friend. Are we clear about the rules?"

"Damn girl, one day I'll tell you a few secrets about that hunk of a man. Anyway, finish your comment to these guys."

Michael interjected, "Ah, Ayesha reads lips—you might want to hold some of your commentary until you two are alone. Actually, it appears, you might have given us a new bargaining chip, just kidding."

Ava said to Michael and Ayesha, "Monica, believe it or not, did the same kind of thing with an adoption agency. The kids were being abused and she went in with the help of our group, demolished the place, rebuilt it, and hired a friend of the family to run it. Also, her two brilliant kids are from that institution. If all the people on that block sustained damage from the blast, when Franco gets here, we will send him down there to make a deal with them and then devise a plan to build a bigger and better residence for the homeless/hearing impaired youth. Michael, we like your plan, and we give it our full endorsement."

Although Michael was signing, Ayesha was reading lips and crying her eyes out. Michael signed to her, that they are not the final vote. Ayesha signed to him, "You had better learn your supporters from your adversaries. Those two women are large in the equation of your organization."

The two women bid them farewell and walked away. Unsuspectingly, Ayesha, jumped into Michaels arms and he caught her. She was full of tears from the kindness generated by the group, and he was full of tears from killing the woman that he thought was his everything.

#

Courtney after a marathon session with her husband said to him, "You need to get back in shape young fella—I don't like leading this parade."

The Sarge replied, "Darling, you don't have to lead. Sometimes, just the thought of holding and being in you is more amazing than trying to achieve some acrobatic position that is designed for the noticeably young, that concludes in the same ecstasy."

"Ben, I'm talking about your heavy breathing. It might be time for all of you people to undergo physicals again. I know this Carbon Factor mess has you tied in knots, but your breathing reminded me of someone who is laboring to breathe. I just want you and your team to attain physicals again. You know it's been almost eighteen-months."

"Honey, now that we know who the real enemy is, it becomes easier for us to focus on a particular individual rather than trying to figure out who's on first base. Did I sound that bad?"

"Baby, I bring it to your attention because I've never heard you labor so hard to breathe. I mean, you could have allergies, bronchitis, or any number of things, but you'll only find out if you submit to an evaluation. Why don't we gather the entire team and tell them we have business in town and go straight to the hospital that we invested in?"

"Okay, I'll leave the ruse to you. We'll get blood drawn from everyone and figure out what's next after that. I guess prevention is so important."

#

The next day, after a lot of moaning and complaining, people began to realize the importance of monitoring their health on a consistent basis. Four of Beckmire's team were cautioned about their sugar intake and three were cautioned about their blood pressure. Darryl's team, well, they were all in good shape and relatively young. The pilots and Mike were given clean bills of health also. Courtney said to the pilot-in-command, "I want you guys evaluated every four months, is that a problem?"

Carla responded, "It makes sense. It's more than the industry standards but we don't get paid by industry standards and/or rate and, therefore, if you want us to do it every four months, then it will be done."

"You're such a character, how is the baby doing?"

"He is as active as the rest of this group. Doesn't cry a lot and Mike is my angel, he's like a midwife."

#

At dinner, Beckmire began the evening by announcing that he thought the federal, state, and local governments were comprised of crooked people. He said, "First there was my cousin, Walter, such a smooth horseshit talking dude that could charm the fur off a bear. He turned out to be a freak, murderer, thief, and molester. The Sarge also stated that Walter stole tons of money from the government, a lot of which, has fattened their coffers. We owe him a lot, we owe him nothing, and we gave him what he deserved."

The Sarge then told the group about the coming of Mr. Utz, and how he showed up and looked like a true "G" man;

honest, full of integrity, and loyal. The Sarge informed the group that he was a puppet for someone in the White House along with someone who they thought was their friend, someone's lover, who joined their party late, along with many of you.

The Sarge then said, "How on earth can anything be so damn important that you would kill your lover, your friends, and perhaps yourself? We're not sure if there was an escape plan in progress, but it seems doubtful. Her, handler, wanted her dead. Mr. Utz has become the new Walter, to me, and I want to put a timetable on him and that damn Carbon Factor. My wife has informed me that I'm getting older and that this gallivanting is for younger men. Personally, I don't feel old but the results of the blood test and other screenings, concluded that some of us need to deal with our health before it attends to us."

John Lee raised his hand and was acknowledged. He said, "I won't feel satisfied until we find and destroy that there Carbon Factor and Mr. Utz. I'm not looking for any new adventures, I just want to go to my new house with my wife and babies and yell across the street to my minority neighbor."

Jilkes responded, "Sarge, he's been that way since day one, and nothing is going to change him. However, I agree with his country ass. It feels like we're quitting, half-way through the process. No one knows more about the Carbon Factor than this motley crew. We now know that it must be strategically placed to achieve its intended results, and that is devastation! We also know that it needs to have four parts of its materials spread equally. I mean we could tell people about the signs but I'm not feeling fulfilled on this one because I feel that this thing is on us to conclude, especially since Mr. Utz feels as though we're all expendable, including all these children."

Whitmore stood up and yelled, "Why do we always have these sessions. Is this another pep talk? Sarge, you know damn well, we don't leave anything unfinished. Furthermore, we now have the brawn to do the heavy lifting. As we mature, we use these young boys to do the grunt work. It's time we became advisers."

Everyone laughed except John Lee who asked, "How can brawn do heavy lifting?"

The Sarge replied, "Ask Jilkes when the two of you have a private moment. Every time I have a need to have a serious discussion, one of you knuckleheads interrupts me with that gung-ho mess. Now, I'm going to finish my thoughts. I know you people are tired, jet lagged, and desirous of having a permanent roof over your heads. Well, so am I. I understand what you mean Whit when you say, 'we don't do unfinished.' I also understand what you mean John Lee when you utter, 'you won't feel satisfied until we destroy Utz and the Carbon Factor, and Jilkes, I completely agree with you when you say, 'that it feels as though we're quitting half-way through the process.' Listen ladies and gentlemen, we've been blessed and are extremely lucky. We've had plenty of wounds, but no deaths other than the pretend to be friends and family member. We've come into tons of money, we're helping the Aborigine people establish their mines, their local services, their educational institutions, we're helping our friends here, and in Spain as well as the local farmers in Middle-America. We've put in play a process to get our vets out of the sewers, back into schools, with no interest loans and to provide them with funds to live on and to pay child support. We have endowed schools in Philly, Chicago, New York, Yakima, Portland, Los

Angeles, Minneapolis, Denver, and the list goes on and on. People, we have committed $300 million to those projects alone. We have diligently tried to address all things that are Vet related. We've endowed hospitals, and as a result of Darryl's sidekick, we are apparently going to rebuild a neighborhood and expand it for the hearing impaired and those who are homeless."

The Sarge took a drink of water and continued by saying, "The young lady, Ayesha, I believe that's her name, signed Michael, and asked, 'if he were an angel'? I don't know sign language, but I do know what it means when people make gestures, look to the heavens, and touch their hearts. To her I say, you're looking at a confluence of angels."

Chakes stood up to say something and the Sarge yelled, "Didn't I say I was going to finish my thoughts. Ms. Viola, I thought you taught that scoundrel a thing or two."

The Sarge sustained, "Now, as I was saying, before I was rudely interrupted by one of my own, here is what I would like to do. I want to shut this operation completely down for seven weeks and in that time, I would like to have thorough physical exams conducted on every living soul in this community. That will take our friends in town probably a full week. I then want to see my house in John Lee's backyard and stay in it for at least a week. Oh, and those of you who haven't purchased land, I suggest that you get to it before the two slum-landlords increase the prices. After that, I want to spend eight days in the outback, and two days in Sydney proper. I, my friends, also want to head to Middle-America for a week, and then a week in Virginia, and I want to spend a week in Valencia and Barcelona. Finally, I want to come back to St. Thomas for a week and get a briefing from my nephew about the work his team has been able to do on the matter of the Carbon Factor and Mr. Utz. Oh, and, since you guys are new, you get two weeks off, one of which must coincide with my team in the outback."

Darryl stood up and the Sarge looked at him sternly. He sat back down and indicated that he was stretching. The Sarge reiterated his initial premise and that was, he was going to finish his thoughts.

After a water pause, the Sarge stated, "Since I was once again, unapologetically, interrupted, I will continue with my thoughts. Now, I realize that two weeks may not be enough for the highly active young people that we work with, so I'm modifying my edict to add in another week for a total of three. I know by that time period, my nephew, Sue Lyn, and their right-hand man, will provide us with details as to when, where, and how to conclude those who control the Carbon Factor. I pray to God, that they can deliver this matter to us for conclusion! Now, finally, are there any questions or requests for leave from duties? If so, I will entertain them, in the order received."

Bernstein raised his hand and Yvette attempted to pull him back into his seat, and he looked at her and said, "Baby girl, I have a legitimate question to ask Julius Caesar."

He turned around and said, "Sarge, I think you need to clarify what you mean by that seven-week scenario. Are you saying that you and Courtney are going to take a break from the rest of us for seven weeks? Now, the thought of that would be challenging. The more likely scenario is that we all are going to be together, therefore, my question can be considered as non-relevant and probably obtuse, since I know how we roll."

The Sarge replied, "Next dumb ass question?"

John Lee stood up and said, "Now, I'm really confused, and if I'm confused, my minority friend ain't got a clue. How we going to do seven weeks away from each other. That Bernstein has a problem. I told you how he tried to date me. That's right Yvette, he asked me out to dinner or something strange like that, without my minority friend being present. I don't want to forget my point; wait, what was my point?"

Jilkes stood up and said, "Sarge, that's the first sign of the effects of Agent Orange, but in his case, he was exposed to it before he was born. Sarge, personally, and speaking for my rabid country-ass-friend, we would prefer to do our bidding at Ms. Asiram's ranch. That way, they'll have to drop bombs on us and the entire world will witness that event. We're not going to live forever and many of my dreams in the outback were about fallen comrades."

The room became extremely quiet. Courtney rose from her chair and proclaimed, "We are not immortals! We have an expiration date stamped on our butts, not like the high-tech stuff written on my son's intestines. Listen, the love of my life is going to die. Jilkes, John Lee, Brown, McArthur, Whitmore, Jong, Ava, Asiram, Mary Alice, Mallory, Monica, Bernstein, Chakes, Luana, Ms. Beatrice, Ms. Viola, Montomie, Gladstone, Rashida, Larry, and everybody else— are going to die. We're all going to die! Perhaps, and hopefully, not together but we're all going to leave this place called earth." With tears in her eyes, Courtney said, "When and if my husband predeceases me, and in his name, and memory, I'm going to scour the world looking for his replacement unit, a thing that I know is impossible, but not improbable!" The solemn mood turned into loud and boisterous laughter.

Once the atmosphere calmed down, the Sarge started a retort to his wife's acknowledgements but decided to say, "Good luck with finding someone like me. You know, and a few of my friends who inadvertently broke into our room while we were playing house, (he looked at John Lee and Jilkes, and frowned) realize that there are no replacement units for the two of us. You're my universe, as I know, I'm yours. My wife has put the map of reality on our situation. However, right now, I want to eat, drink, and enjoy all of the people who make up our community. In conclusion, the unfortunate notion of our group is that if one is collected and bartered, all of us are at risk. Therefore, we stay together, play together, and fight together! I'm sure Mr. Utz believes there's discord as a result of a key member's associate, being extracted from the equation. No, Messrs. Bernstein, Jilkes, and Lee, we stay together and that way, we live to fight another day. Separately, we're a bartering chip."

Chakes abruptly stood up, Luana looked at him, and Ms. Viola asked, "What you be doing man?"

"I'm still the man of this house, Sister! Sarge, I saw my daughter, the twins, Monica's children, and Rashida's daughter, helping those children who have speaking or hearing challenges. I think that it might be a good thing if we all learned some basic sign language that is focused on an emergency. In addition, since my all-knowing, and all-powerful mother-in-law tries to dictate my very thoughts, I would like to freely state that I knew one of the new members to our community was a snake and I prayed hard that it was not the love of my life. My dreams in the outback were tainted by a vision of someone who seemingly acted in the best interest of the group, but secretly plotted to annihilate us all. I just want to say, this is a long journey, and we do not eliminate our own. I direct this to the new members of our community and say, your choice in mates, represents the pick of the litter. You will never be challenged, you will never be abused or treated without respect, and you will always be loved by every member of this tribe. On those words, I suggest that some of you, let your departed friend and her memory, find its place in that community designed for her type. Sister is the best! I suggest you make some rum punch with her, try to discern the nomenclature of the punch formula, and attempt to understand how close this group is. It is an amazing amalgamation of good people who work only to help people help themselves! That is all that we do—it's not about us, but it's about the people we can help!

the end

also in the 'idiot spy' series

Available at Amazon and BarnesandNoble.com

www.ingramcontent.com/pod-product-compliance
Lightning Source LLC
Chambersburg PA
CBHW030249270626
47156CB00021B/258